EMPIRE
OF HATE

EMPIRE

RINA KENT

To the heartbreakingly obsessive souls

AUTHOR NOTE

Hello reader friend,

This book isn't as dark as the rest of my books, but it contains themes of sexual assault and eating disorder. I trust you know your triggers before you proceed.

Empire of Hate is a complete STANDALONE, but it may spoil events from *Cruel King*.

Sign up to Rina Kent's Newsletter for news about future releases and an exclusive gift.

My boss. My enemy.

I escaped my life.

Leaving everything behind wasn't easy, but I did it.

I turned the page and flew over the ocean.

This is my new beginning.

My new chapter.

My new book.

Or so I hoped before I met my new boss.

Daniel Sterling.

Rich as sin, illegally attractive, and the face of every magazine cover.

Oh, and the reason why I escaped in the first place.

I made his high school life hell.

He won't stop until he gives me a taste of my own medicine.

PLAYLIST

"Creep" – Radiohead

"Another Life" – Motionless in White & Kerli

"7 Billion" – Marina Kaye

"Wrecked" – Imagine Dragons

"Faking Love" – Tommee Profitt, Jung Youth & NAWAS

"Try Again" – Walking on Cars

"The End" – Alessio & Charlotte Lawrence

"Sweat" – The All-American Rejects

"Disillusioned" – A Perfect Circle

"The Gold" – Manchester Orchestra

"You Broke Me First" – Conor Maynard

You can find the complete playlist on Spotify.

EMPIRE
OF HATE

PROLOGUE

Nicole

Age eight

I HAVE AN UNHEALTHY OBSESSION.

Or maybe a few.

Not sure what that expression means. Unhealthy obsession. But I heard Mum's therapist friend tell her that once.

She said Mum needed to control herself and not let her obsessions take hold of her or else it'll start to affect me.

I think it's too late and Mum has already passed that gene down to me.

When she was sleeping, I tiptoed to the living area, took the tablet and hid under the blanket, and typed the term on Google.

It was dark except for the tablet's light that I brought down to its lowest level so Mum wouldn't catch me. She doesn't like me staying up past my bedtime.

She doesn't like me to do many things, actually.

Like being too friendly, talking to people, or playing.

I should always be studying to become something important and make her proud.

I should always remember that ever since Papa drowned last year while saving me, we're on our own.

Papa might have been a knight and part of the aristocracy, but he accumulated enough debt that cost us our house and everything we owned.

Mum managed to marry a lord soon after. Uncle Henry is nice. He paid all our debts and treats me better than my mum sometimes. He doesn't tell me to always eat my vegetables or study or not make friends because they'll use me.

He tells me I'm smart, too, which Mum has never said, even when the teachers tell her that.

But I'm not smart enough to understand what "unhealthy obsession" means on my own, which is why I searched it last night while I was holding my breath and typing with sweaty fingers.

The results that showed up made my mouth fall open.

An unhealthy obsession is to have an extreme interest in something or someone.

It's to constantly think about them.

It's to do something repetitively, even against your will.

It's to have a compulsive preoccupation with them and being unable to chase them away, no matter how much you try.

I stared at the words written on the tablet in disbelief. How is it possible that they found exactly how I feel about things?

Are they psychic?

The thought made me shiver and I had trouble getting to sleep. So I kept reading on and on about obsessions, especially the unhealthy type. And the more I read, the harder I was struck.

It was as if someone had peeled my skull open and poured hot liquid inside it.

That liquid has been burning my brain ever since. Maybe this is one of the times where I have to put on a smile and pretend everything is fine as Mum taught me to.

Never show people how you feel, Nicole. Always wear a smile and be on your best behavior like a lady should.

Her words flow through my veins instead of blood. Everything she told and taught me is always the first thing I think about before I do anything.

She saved us, my mum. She got a rich, influential husband who's also nice and lets us live a luxurious lifestyle.

I think she had to make him divorce his previous wife and leave his biological daughter behind, but that's okay, right?

If Uncle Henry wanted them, he wouldn't have left them.

They're lower class, Mum said. *They don't fit with him like you and I do, Nicole. You're lucky I made this life happen for us, so don't screw it up.*

I won't.

I can't.

I'm *lucky.*

So I don't even talk about Papa. I miss him, but if I tell Mum that, she'll be angry.

I don't want her to be angry, which is why I can't be a disappointment.

She's done everything for us, so I have to lower my head and follow the rules.

That's why I'm smiling at one of her friends now. Mum is hosting a tea party in Uncle Henry's mansion and invited other powerful men's wives and their children.

I took them on a tour earlier and showed them my toys. Uncle Henry bought me many of them—after Mum made me donate the ones Papa gave me.

She told me they're cheap and not suitable for our current standing.

I hid one small doll that has peach-colored hair and a snow globe that Papa brought me for my fifth birthday. I don't care if they're cheap. I like them better than the expensive ones. It's weird, but I can still smell Papa on them and it makes me calmer.

I hid them so the children won't touch them. They can play with all the other toys, but not those two.

The whole time, I kept smiling and laughing and being the perfect child that Mum has brought me up to be.

"Nicole is so well-mannered."

"She's like an adult in a little body."

"Mark my words, Nicole will grow up into a fine young lady."

"Like mother, like daughter. You raised her so well, Victoria."

That's what all the women tell Mum, fawning over me as if I'm a miracle child.

A conservative, elegant smile pulls at her lips.

Everything about my mother is. Conservative and elegant, I mean. She's beautiful—the most beautiful woman I know. Her blonde hair seems to be in competition with the sun on which can shine brighter. She always wears it in a neat French twist, which highlights the soft lines of her face and her full lips that she usually paints a light color.

I take after her in almost everything except for the eyes. Hers are a cobalt blue that appear as deep as the ocean and just as mysterious. Mine are green, muddy, like my papa's.

Mum is like a goddess and I don't think I'll ever grow up to be as beautiful as her. Despite her appearance, she's completely compliant with the aristocratic way of doing things. Which means she never enhances her beauty, wears red lipstick, or dresses provocatively.

Even now, she has on a soft green dress and a simple matching sweater. But she's still the prettiest of all the women present.

And they hate that, so they talk behind her back. Once, we were at a charity event and when I went to the bathroom, I heard them call her a gold-digger and a whore who sells herself to the richest man available. Mum caught me listening and told me to go back to where the kids were.

Her expression didn't even change, as if she didn't hear them talk badly about her behind closed doors after praising her in front of everyone.

I think that's how the world works. As Mum said, it's best to never show your emotions in public.

It's how she got this far after surviving an abusive household when she was young.

It's how I became lucky.

So I shouldn't be thinking about leaving the children that she explicitly told me to keep company.

The girls and I are sitting in the garden across from our mothers and having a tea party like them with my extravagant tea set.

The boys are playing football far enough away that they won't interfere with our peaceful time.

It's a rare sunny day in London, although the clouds sometimes decide to play peek-a-boo with the sun.

I pour more tea for one of the girls, but my attention is unfocused. Or more like, it's stolen by something I shouldn't be giving weight to.

The boys.

One of them, to be more specific.

His face has turned red from all the running after the ball, and his lips are parted with each pant.

He has weird hair that's neither dark nor light, as if it couldn't make up its mind on which color to be, so it settled on a mixture of both. Like the color of the earth under the sun and the tone of premium wood.

But his eyes are what I noticed first. They're blue and light, but not as muted as Mum's. They're glinting in the sun as if they're reflecting its warmth. As if they're mimicking the sky and trapping the stars.

Yes, stars are visible during the day, but only through his shiny eyes. Not only can they be seen there, but they also have that magical pull.

Like Disney films and the wildest fairy tales.

His name is Daniel.

It's a normal name on everyone else but him.

We've been studying in the same class ever since I changed schools after Mum married Uncle Henry.

Everyone in school loves me. The teachers, because I'm a good girl and smart. The kids, because I'm popular.

Not Daniel, though.

He's never spoken to me. Never even looked my way.

As if I were invisible.

His mother recently became friends with Mum and this is the first time she's invited her to our house.

I've been over the moon ever since I learned that he'd be coming over with his mum. I didn't know why at first, until I learned what "unhealthy obsession" meant last night.

I think I have one for him.

Which should be stupid, considering he doesn't even know I exist, but I always find myself watching him.

Like now.

I don't even know what Chloe, the girl I poured tea for, just said. But I continue to nod anyway, so she'll keep talking and I can watch him.

So I can see how he runs and tackles the ball, then scores. His teammates gang up on him and he grins.

I stop breathing.

Something happens when he grins or smiles or laughs.

His cheeks crease and one set of dimples appear. If he were an angel, those would be his wings. If he were a prince, that would be his crown.

Daniel is simply so…beautiful.

My cheeks catch fire and I focus back on Chloe for a second and laugh at something she said before I lift my head again.

This time, Daniel's bright eyes that resemble a combination of the sky, sun, and stars are staring at me.

No, glaring.

His lips are pursed, the dimples gone, before he shakes his head and goes back to his game.

What…?

What happened just now?

Ghostly hands squeeze my chest, and my heart starts to thump loudly. I did something wrong and I don't know what.

Why did he look at me for the first time and glare?

My fingers shake on the teacup and Mum gives me a side-long stare. I carefully put it down, trying to breathe deeply as she taught me.

I'm going to screw up something. I can feel myself losing control and if I do, Mum will be mad.

So I stand up, smooth my white dress with lace and smile. "I'll be right back, girls."

I don't wait for their replies as I walk in a brisk pace toward the house, staring at my golden flat shoes with lace ribbons that match the ones in my hair.

Today, I wore my best clothes so I'd look pretty. I even asked Mum to leave my hair loose because it makes me feel like a princess.

I wanted to be a princess because that's what princes want.

But he glared at me.

Overwhelmed, I go to the kitchen, make sure none of the staff is looking, and then I steal two peaches. I hide them behind my back and sneak to the pool house.

The drawn-out curtains hide the light except for sneaky rays that spill through onto the wooden floor.

I sit on the carpet and kick my shoes away. I've always loved to sit on the ground with my feet outstretched, but Mum hates that, so I come to the pool house to do it.

This is the only place where I'm out of her sight and can do what I want.

Like eating peaches.

I'm allergic to them, but they're my favorite food. I like the calm they bring me after every bite. So what if I have red, swollen lips? It'll go away after a while.

Loving something that hurts you is also an unhealthy obsession, I think.

I shouldn't be doing this when we have guests, but I'm freaking out, and peaches erase that feeling.

They're on my side.

I take the first bite and close my eyes to enjoy the sickeningly sweet taste. My tongue tingles, but I continue chewing and sucking the positive energy. The first peach is almost finished, and I tell myself I'll take my time with the second one.

"Peaches."

I startle, my eyes snapping open, and that causes one of my preciously stolen fruits to roll down on the ground and bump into someone's shoes.

Before I can be relieved that Mum didn't catch me, I rake my gaze over the person who did.

Daniel.

He stares down at me with mild annoyance as if I'm a beggar at the side of his house who keeps blocking his way whenever he goes out.

The blue of his eyes that's usually bright and sparkling is a little muted now, but the rays of the sun streak his hair to give it lighter strands.

Even though he was running for more than half an hour, his shirt is tucked neatly in his trousers and his face isn't all red and sweaty like mine whenever I do any physical activity. Only a slight flush dusts his cheeks and nose.

He bends over and catches the fruit that unapologetically bumped into him, then rolls it between his fingers as if it's the first time he's seen one. "Do you always hide to eat peaches after being mean?"

I swallow the contents of my mouth and my lips burn as if I've kissed fire.

But that doesn't matter.

Because I think Daniel just spoke to me.

For the first time in weeks, he sees me.

Just to make sure, I search around me in case someone else came into the pool house.

Maybe it's a ghost?

Or his imaginary friend?

No. He was actually talking to me. I'm the only one hiding to eat peaches.

My brow furrows when I focus on the last bit he said. "Who's mean?"

"You."

"M-me?"

"You're mean and stuck-up. I don't care if you do it to anyone else, but if you laugh at me again, I won't let you."

Wait. What is he saying?

"I didn't laugh at you."

"You did with Chloe just now."

"No, that's not…" My tongue gets stuck and my words won't come out.

Usually, eating peaches only makes my lips swollen, so why does my tongue feel numb?

"Do you enjoy acting superior when you invite people to your house?" he continues. "I can play your game, too. I'll tell your mum that you've stolen peaches and are eating them. If you're hiding to do it, then it must be a bad thing."

"No… Don't do that…"

My tongue barely moves and my words are drawn out. My hand involuntarily opens and the half-eaten peach falls to the ground.

"I can be mean, too." He starts to move and I stand up abruptly.

The world spins around me and the room pulls me down. A buzz fills my ears before a thud echoes around us.

It's me, I realize, when my blurry vision focuses on the ground.

I fell down. My limbs feel like they're in an awkward position, but I don't even care about that as I strain, "D-don't…"

My eyes are half-closed but I make out his silhouette facing me again. "If this is some tactic to stop me, it won't work."

"Peaches…" I mumble. "I-I'm allergic to t-them…"

A body crouches by my side and then my head is placed on

a warm surface. It's Daniel's thighs, I think, because he's staring down at me, his eyes wide.

"Your lips are red and weird." He reaches for me, then retracts his hand. "I'm going to tell your mum."

I grab his wrist with my sweaty hand and dig my nails in. "N-no…she'll punish me… I'll be fine…"

"You don't look fine."

"It…will go away…"

"Are you sure?"

No. Because this is the first time I've gotten this dizzy, but that's okay. If it means he'll just continue to hold me.

"It'll go away if you keep me in this position," I lie.

Daniel carefully removes my hair from my face. "If you're allergic to peaches, why would you eat them?"

"B-because I like them."

"You're weird, Nicole."

I've been called pretty and smart and a good girl, but never weird. I think I like that better.

I like not being so perfect.

"I…I have toys… My favorite doll and snow globe are behind you in the secret…d-drawer…"

"I don't think you should be talking about toys right now." His brow is furrowed again and I don't like that. I want to see his dimples instead.

"G-get them…my toys…"

"For what?"

"J-just do it."

"I think I should go find your mum."

"N-no…please… I told you, sh-she'll punish me."

"Then you shouldn't have done something you'd be punished for."

"You do that all the time a-at school." It's why I noticed him in the first place. He often gets sent to the headmaster's office for pulling pranks and generally having fun.

I liked that. The way he laughed and didn't care what the grown-ups said about him.

I wished I could be like him.

I wished I wasn't lucky and didn't have to talk a certain way, walk a certain way, and breathe a certain way.

"That's because I don't like rules," he says. "But I don't go hurting myself."

"I-it doesn't hurt."

"You look and sound like you're in pain."

"It'll get better if…" I swallow, but my tongue feels too big for my mouth, like it'll roll out onto the ground.

Daniel stares at me as if that's exactly what's happened, then he wipes the side of my mouth, where some peach-flavored drool escaped.

If my cheeks could get any hotter, they would. This is so messy and wrong, and Daniel shouldn't witness me like this.

"If what?" he asks.

"I-if you get my toys."

He releases a breath that sounds a bit exasperated, then keeps a hand on my head to stop me from moving as he rummages behind him in the drawer.

Soon after, he produces my doll and snow globe and puts them on my stomach. "Happy now?"

"Y-you can have it…"

"Thanks, but I don't play with dolls."

"N-no, you can have t-the snow globe."

Maybe if I share my favorite toys with him, he'll like me.

Maybe he'll also see the beautiful girl trapped in the snow and think about how he can get her out without breaking her world apart.

"It's nothing serious," I blurt when he remains silent, examining the snow globe between his fingers. "It's…it's…because y-you're letting me use your lap."

He stares at the side. "Whatever."

My heart falls and something stings in my eyes.

Ah.

Even sharing one of the last things I have of Papa didn't work.

He might have talked to me and held me, but I'm still invisible to Daniel.

"It's still girly," he says.

"It's...it's a beautiful bride."

"You like that? Brides?"

"I-I do..." I lick my swollen lips and try not to think of the bitterness that's stuck at the back of my throat or how it hurts to breathe. "When we grow up, will you marry me?"

His eyes widen, but he looks away.

My heart shrivels and breaks in my chest.

Once again, it was all for nothing.

"Nicole?"

My lids slowly close and a tear slides down my cheek.

Is it the pain of the peaches or the pain of being invisible?

Maybe it's the pain of having an unhealthy obsession.

"Nicole, open your eyes!"

For what?

My head lolls to the side and bumps against his knee. He smells like peaches.

Or maybe I do.

"I'm going to call your mum."

The scent of peaches disappears and so does he.

And I'm left on the ground with my half-eaten peach and the doll.

Abandoned.

Lifeless.

Invisible.

ONE

Nicole

Twenty-one years later

IF LIFE THROWS YOU A LEMON, YOU SHOULD PROBABLY EAT IT or else you'll remain hungry.

At least, that's true in my case.

The fact that I got fired from my last job should say something. Apparently, I'm not supposed to call a customer a "creepy old man" if he "accidentally" touches my butt.

And okay, maybe pouring water all over his head was a bit of an extreme reaction, but I don't have a filter when it comes to these types of things.

Not after everything that's happened in the past.

So now, I'm hoping one of the companies that I interviewed with will call me back. Otherwise, Jayden and I are screwed.

I might not have finished university, but I did study at Cambridge for two years, and I have some experience.

But oh well. It's brutal out here in New York, so my small amount of experience may mean nothing.

"Are you okay, Nikki?"

I lift my head from my task of chopping vegetables and stare at the adorable face of my little Jayden.

He looks so much like me, it's a little freaky. But his blond hair is shinier, like my mum's, and his eyes are a light brown, like a warm forest during a sunny day.

Despite being only nine years old, he's the definition of a blessing. I don't know what my life would be like if he weren't around.

"I'm fine, baby."

A delicate frown appears between his brows as he trudges toward me. "Stop calling me that. I'm not a baby anymore."

"As if." I ruffle his blond strands and he whines wordlessly. "Have you taken your medication?"

"Yeah, I did. I told you I'm not a kid."

"If you say so."

"Uh-huh." He strains to see what's on the stove. "What are you making for dinner?"

"Fish. Your favorite."

A slow grin spreads across his beautiful little face and every hardship I've ever gone through seems to vanish into thin air.

As long as Jay is happy and safe, I can fight through every battle and win any war.

He hops onto the stool and faces me. "I love the food you make."

"You mean you love fish."

"That, too, but anything is great. You're the best cook I know."

"I'm the only cook you know."

He grins again. "You're still the best."

I reach over and ruffle his hair to which he whines again. "Where did you get that sugarcoated mouth from?"

"Myself. And stop messing up my hair!"

"No."

I put the fish in the middle of a plate and take extra time to display the sauce and the salad in an aesthetic way, then I slide it in front of him. "There you go."

He digs in, not bothering to hide his glee, and I just stand there, watching him with a satisfied smile.

I search for the asthma control medication on the living area table to see if he really took them. Due to troubled housing as an infant, he developed severe symptoms, and he has to take medication for it.

Sometimes, a quick-relief inhaler is enough, but most of the time, medication is needed to control it. Which is why I need to find work soon if I want to keep him healthy, well fed, and with a roof over his head.

Though this small studio flat is humid as hell. The landlord told me he can do nothing about it and that if I hate this place, I can beat it.

He knows full well that I couldn't afford a hut on the streets with my finances.

"This is so good," Jay speaks through a mouthful of fish.

"I'm glad you like it."

Lolli, our black cat with white paws, who somehow jumped onto our balcony about a year ago, meows. Jay gives her some of his fish that she gets engrossed in.

"By the way," he says without looking up. "The landlord came by earlier today and was yelling about rent."

I wince. "Sorry you had to deal with that, sweetie. I'll talk to him."

He lifts a shoulder. "I told him he'll regret treating us like shit when we become rich, because we'll buy this whole-ass building and kick him out."

"Jayden! You're not supposed to talk to the landlord that way."

"That's the only way to talk to jerks like him." He pauses chewing and stares at me. "Where's your plate?"

"I'm not hungry."

"You're never hungry, Nikki." He narrows his eyes. "Are you skipping meals again?"

"Of course not, and how dare you look at me as if you're the adult?"

"Well, maybe I should be so you won't skip meals."

"Just eat your fish, Jay."

I spent all my food budget so he could eat fish today after months of craving it. So what if I skip a few meals? When you're poor, you don't have the luxury of complaining.

"You eat it." Jay pushes his half-finished plate toward me.

I slide it back. "No, you eat it."

He starts to glide it across the counter again, but I grab it, too, and we start a war of glares.

He's a stubborn little shit. I wonder who he takes that after.

My phone rings in my back pocket and I grab it without releasing the plate.

I don't recognize the number flashing on the screen so I answer cautiously, "Hello?"

"Is this Nicole Adler?" a woman asks.

My heart picks up speed and I unconsciously release the plate and wipe my palm on my apron. "Yes, this is she."

"This is Diana from the Human Resources department of Weaver & Shaw's law firm. Congratulations, you got the assistant position."

"Oh, thank you. Thank you."

"I wasn't done, Ms. Adler. You'll start on Monday and will be assigned to a junior partner and he requires a three-week trial period. If you fail, you'll be paid for that period and won't be permanently employed. If you succeed, we'll sign a long-term contract."

I gulp. "I understand. I'll try my best."

"Perfect. I'll email you the requirements for your job as well as a virtual tour of the firm. It's imperative you arrive early on Monday."

"I will. Thank you."

The moment I hang up, a tiny squeal bubbles in my throat and Lolli judges me with her little black eyes as if I've lost my mind.

"What happened?" Jay stares at me with expectation. "Good news?"

"I got a job at a huge law firm." I round the counter and squeeze the hell out of him in a hug.

"I knew you could do it, Nikki." He strains, but he squeezes me back.

I pull back, my smile vanishing. "You might have to spend more time with Mrs. Potter next door when I'm not around."

She's a kind elder woman and the only neighbor who welcomed us when we first moved in here. She loves Jayden and even Lolli and often watches them whenever I'm working.

"I don't mind. She makes delicious pancakes."

And then my little gift in life insists that I share the rest of his meal with him.

To celebrate.

From now on, I won't have to live on the run from his father.

From now on, I'll have the means to fight back.

On Monday, I wake up early.

After I prepare a lunch box for Jay, I place it on the counter with a Post-it Note that says "Don't forget your lunch" and then bang on the bathroom door so he'll hurry up.

He woke up groggy from sleeping in an uncomfortable position with me. This studio flat is the only thing I could afford with my various low-paying jobs. One sofa bed. A kitchen. And a very small bathroom.

But that'll change.

I'll make sure I'm fully employed and we'll move out of this shithole in this bloody loud neighborhood.

My new boss can't be as demanding as the many others I've worked for. He's an attorney, after all.

I step out of the flat with a smile on my face. I don't even pay attention to the screaming neighbors, the stench of alcohol, or the passed-out drunk by the side of the road.

I don't even mind the crowded streets. Okay, maybe a little. Even though I've been living in the States since Jay was born and moved to New York last year, I still can't get used to how fast-paced everything is here.

It's like everyone is chasing something and won't stop unless they reach it or drop dead.

Sometimes, I miss London with its peaceful afternoons and even its strained relationship with the sun.

But London and I are no longer on speaking terms. Not since I ran away from it faster than a speeding train.

By the time I reach Weaver & Shaw, I take a pause.

It's massive and intimidating as well as elegant. I remember feeling like a mouse when I first came here for the interview. I applied to much smaller companies, too, because I thought it'd be virtually impossible to be accepted at this one.

I'm pretty sure I don't have enough experience. But maybe they took the two years I spent at Cambridge into consideration? After all, it's one of the most prestigious universities in the world and I did study business.

Though not American or anything specific to New York City.

Whatever the reason, I'm the one who was called into this famous law firm that has a few of the best attorneys not only domestically, but also worldwide.

They have branches all over the States and Europe. Even one in London, from what I learned from the other applicants for the assistant job.

Security lets me in once I give him my name.

My head is held high as I walk past the vast creamy white

walls. Everyone here looks prim and proper—elegant, too—and I think I did a decent job of dressing the part.

I'm wearing a white button-down that's tucked into a black pencil skirt. I also wore my only good heels that I save for professional settings, such as this one.

My hair is gathered in a ponytail and I put on natural-looking makeup and peach-colored lipstick.

My phone case is the same color. My key chain, too.

I kind of never got over my obsession with that fruit. Even though it nearly killed me when I was a child.

After a trip to the Human Resources department, I sign the trial contract and get my temporary access card. Diana, a kind middle-aged woman, tells me to head to the seventh floor, then gives me an 'I hope you make it' look.

But I don't understand why she shakes her head as I leave her office.

The occurrence keeps puzzling me as I take the lift to the seventh floor.

I try to breathe deeply since it calms my nerves. Then I touch my pendant that shares the color of my eyes. The one I've worn for the past sixteen years.

You can do this, Nicole.

You have to. For your own and Jay's sakes.

When the lift stops, I get out with a small smile on my face.

There's an open area for interns where many of them are busy typing at their computers or reading documents.

But that's not what I'm here for. Diana told me to head to the second office on the left.

All the junior partners and associate attorneys have glass walls, but the one I'm walking to has the blinds drawn.

I straighten my back, walk through what I suppose will be my office until I reach another door, then knock on it.

"Come in."

The deep voice with a British accent causes a foreign feeling to constrict my chest and I pause.

No. It's only my stupid imagination that I can never manage to control. There's no way in hell it's him.

That would be just tragic.

And cruel.

And every negative word in the dictionary.

Chasing that ominous thought away, I push the door open and freeze.

My heart drops to the base of my stomach and I cease breathing when my gaze meets those blue eyes that stole from the sun, sky, and the stars.

It is him.

The man who ruined my life as much as I ruined his.

Daniel Sterling.

TWO

Nicole

THIS IS A TRICK OF MY MIND.

A cruel twist of my imagination.

A nightmare.

Yes. That's all this could be about. A nightmare. If I wake up now, it'll all be over.

If I wake up now, I'll be drenched in sweat and have tears in my eyes, but it'll be an illusion.

I'm not actually facing Daniel after eleven years of running away and trying to erase everything about him from my memory.

So I blink once, twice, but he's still crystal clear in front of me. Like a hurricane that's growing in intensity with the mere purpose of hitting me.

Breaking me to pieces.

Tearing me apart.

His presence is no different than being crushed over and left to perish. Not only is it imposing, but it also tugs on strings I thought I cut off a long time ago.

Strings that are currently vibrating inside me for the mere fact that I'm right in front of him again.

The last time I saw him, we were only eighteen, but he's older now, more masculine. All man.

His jaw has squared and his hair that used to fall haphazardly all over his forehead is styled with subtle elegance. It's become darker, too, as if he made it his mission to kill any light strands that streaked it.

The way he sits behind his desk is laced with nonchalance, but it's not lazy—more like commanding. It's like he's a powerful king who expects everyone in the court to bend to his royal decree.

He leans over, places his elbows on the table, and interlinks his fingers at his chin. It's a habit he used to do whenever he was deep in thought or angry. I'm not sure which feeling is more prominent right now, because his face is a blank slate.

His eyes, that I used to predict his mood through, are expressionless, muted, almost as if someone stole the stars from within them and blocked the sun. The only thing that remains is a bottomless blue, like a starless, moonless night.

And they're zeroed in on me with a cool that chills me to my bones. Maybe cool isn't the right word. There's a coldness in there, an icy quality that's meant to freeze me to death.

He used to have the type of beauty that brought me peace and calm. Now, it's savage, unrestrained, and with every intention to hurt.

I'm not fooled by the way he looks. By how he wears his tailored gray suit like a supermodel or how he sits majestically like some lord. I'm not fooled by his unperturbed expression or seemingly calm façade. Because it's just that.

A façade.

A way to pull me forward like prey, then pounce on me, devour my flesh, and crunch my bones.

"Are you going to stand there all day?"

I flinch, partly because my illusion that this is a dream is long gone. He's right there, in person, and waiting. And partly because of his voice. It's so deep but laced with a velvet-like quality. Which makes him sound approachable when he's anything but. He also sounded disapproving just now, as if I'm a worthless rock in his shoe.

"Either come inside and close the door or get out. Leave your access card at HR while you're at it."

I force myself out of my haze and close the door with clammy, trembling fingers.

This job is important, not only for me but also for Jayden.

So what if I feel like dissociating from my own skin or digging my own grave? What if I feel like turning back, running, and never seeing those blue eyes again?

It doesn't matter.

Jay's survival and health do.

If I have to work for Daniel in order to provide for him, then so be it. Besides, there's no flash of recognition on his features, so maybe he forgot about me.

Maybe he erased everything that happened between us and he's now a new man who couldn't give a damn about the past.

The thought tugs on those stupid heartstrings and I inhale deeply to put a halt to my reaction. But it's all involuntary, pulled out from deep inside me by an invisible force I can't control.

"Good morning, I'm the new assistant. My name is Nicole Adler." I'm thankful my voice doesn't waver and remains calm, almost as neutral as his indifference.

"I don't care about your name. I'll forget it once you fail the trial period." He stares at his luxurious Swiss watch before he slides his icy stare back at me. "And it's half past eight, which means you're late, so there's nothing specifically good about this morning."

My stomach contracts and it has to do with his harsh words as much as his voice. I need to get used to it right away if I want to stay professional and keep this job.

"I'm sorry about that, but I had to finish up some paperwork with HR and—"

"All I hear are meaningless excuses," he cuts me off. "Don't repeat such behavior or your trial period will end before it even starts. Are we clear?"

"Yes," I say, even though I want to scream, and not about this situation, but about all the chaotic thoughts and lines broken up inside me like distorted music playing underwater.

I want to scream and ask him if he'll really pretend he doesn't know me. He must've seen my résumé. He knows it's me. I doubt he's known many Nicole Adlers in his life.

But why does it matter?

In fact, I should be happy that it's impersonal. That way, I can pretend this is only work that I'm using to keep a roof over my and Jay's heads.

"Good." He stands up and I suck in a harsh breath, hoping to hell he doesn't hear it.

He was magnetic while sitting, but when he's at his full height, it's almost too blinding and unbearable to look at.

Not only is he tall, but he also has a mystic, attractive way of carrying himself. His shoulders are straight, his wide chest in perfect proportion with his jacket, and his trousers outline his long legs and thighs. I wonder if they're still muscular from when he played football back in junior and secondary school.

The thought is chased away from my head when he rounds his desk, then leans against it, his legs crossed at the ankles as he faces me.

He seems to be waiting for something, but I'm not sure what, so I ask, "Do you need anything?"

"Your brain, Ms. Adler, or did you leave that at home this morning?"

I grind the back of my teeth, then I breathe in copious intakes of air. "If you tell me what you need, I'll get right to it."

"What else would I need from you other than taking notes of what I want to be done?"

"Oh, sure." I retrieve the tablet HR gave me from my bag and have barely opened the notes app when he starts speaking in rapid-fire.

"I need my coffee from Dolcezza at eight a.m. sharp. Black with exactly one gram of sugar. Then, you'll go through my schedule and recheck with clients about their availability. You'll remind me of my domestic court dates and book the phone calls with international clients. If there's a flight, you'll book it beforehand and send me constant reminders about it. My lunch should be picked up from Katerina's at twelve thirty. My dry cleaning should be put in my flat at three p.m. Then you'll manage the schedule of when I'm playing golf with the mayor and other influential figures. Always keep your phone with you in case I text you for something urgent—that includes nighttime."

I'm breathing heavily from the onslaught of information. My fingers ache from typing all his instructions and I hope to hell I didn't miss anything.

The last bit he says throws me off and I look up. I wish I hadn't because he's staring at me like a hawk who's zeroing in on his prey. It's almost like he enjoyed seeing me sweat and scramble to write it all down.

Clearing my throat, I ask, "Nighttime?"

"We work on international clients' schedules, who, if you brought your brain with you, you'll realize are in different time zones than us. If that will pose a problem, you know where the door is."

Damn this jerk. He's been trying to get me fired since the moment I walked into his office. But he doesn't know how desperate I am or how much I need this.

He can show me his worst and I still won't back down.

"I was only asking for clarification. I'm fine with it."

I just need to make sure I keep my phone on vibration mode so as not to disturb Jay.

"Not that it matters." He lifts his haughty, straight nose in the air as if I'm beneath looking at. "Needless to say, I don't tolerate mistakes. Miss a chore and you're out. Mess up and you're also out. Are we clear?"

"Yes."

"It's yes, sir."

I bite the inside of my cheek so hard, I'm surprised no blood explodes in my mouth.

"Are you daft or bad at following instructions, Ms. Adler?"

"No."

"No, sir. Now, say it." There's a challenge in his tone, coupled with a strange gleam in his eyes. It's nothing bright or shiny like the Daniel I know.

This one is sadistic, glinting with only one intention.

Humiliating me.

But screw him.

If he thinks my pride will stop me from stooping low, then he doesn't know how much of a thick skin I've grown over the years.

"No, sir," I say with a coolness I don't feel.

"That's how you'll address me from now on. Are we clear?"

I nod.

"You have a voice, use it."

"Yes, sir." The last word gets stuck in my throat, no matter how much I try to swallow past it.

The jerk must find pleasure in making me feel as small as a dead fly stuck to the sole of his shoe.

But it doesn't matter. I went through worse for Jay, and I can do this, too, if I put my mind to it.

Daniel can be the worst boss to ever exist, but I won't break.

Not after I've come this far.

"Now get out and do your job." He doesn't even spare me a glance as he turns around and walks to the window of his office that overlooks New York City.

For a second, only a second, I stand there and watch the hard ridges of his back. I watch how his jacket creases at the contours of his wide shoulders as he places a hand in his pocket.

I'm not even looking at his face, but the mere image of him turned away from me fills me with a sense of trepidation.

It's the invisible line again. The knowledge that he'd never see me.

"Are your legs nonfunctioning, too? Or is it your ears?" he says without facing me.

"No," I say, then quickly blurt, "sir."

"Then why the fuck aren't you leaving? You should've been out of here thirty seconds ago."

I give an awkward nod that he doesn't see, then I walk to the door. Every step is like dragging a mountain with each leg.

My fingers are sweaty on the tablet and a slight tremor takes refuge in my limbs.

It's as if it takes superhuman power to step out of his office without somehow melting in the process.

When I reach my desk in the space that's in front of his door, I throw my weight on the chair and hold my head between my hands.

Bloody hell.

I lost a few years of my lifespan in there, and the worst part is that it's only the beginning.

The worst part is that what's coming will probably be worse than what's gone.

The phone of the desk rings and I jerk, my leg hitting against the wood.

"Ouch," I mutter, massaging the hurt spot before I pick it up with a calm tone to my voice. "Hello."

"It's not hello, it's Weaver & Shaw, Daniel Sterling's office, how may I help you?" His strong voice filters through the phone like doom. "If you lack competence, how the hell did you even get the job, Ms. Adler?"

"I'm sorry."

"You're sorry what?"

"*Sir*," I grind out, my fingers turning sweaty on the phone.

"Repeat that, but without attitude this time."

My nails dig into my skirt and I wish I could rip it and reach the flesh. Instead, I suck in a deep breath and say as calmly as possible, "Sir."

"You still didn't get me my coffee, in case you haven't noticed. It's about an hour late."

I grab the phone with both hands to hold on to my patience. "I only learned about your requirements today."

"So it's my fault the coffee is late?"

Yes. Why the heck can't he just get his own freaking coffee himself?

Because he's a jerk, that's why. But I can't say that, or I'll definitely get fired.

"No, it's not," I say with a fake smile. "I'll get your coffee right away, sir."

Beep. Beep. Beep.

I stare at the phone with incredulousness. Did the bastard just hang up in my face? Yes, he did, and I need to stay calm because murder will cost me Jayden.

Breathing in deeply, I grab the company card, then head to the coffee shop outside the building, assuming that's where Daniel gets his coffee.

Then I stop when I catch that the name is different from the one in my notes. I put it in the maps app and have to do a whole fifteen-minute tour on foot—while wearing freaking heels—to finally find the place.

Why can't he use the normal coffee shop near the firm? Better yet, there's a perfectly equipped cafeteria at Weaver & Shaw from which all the employees get premium coffee, but how can he be a bastard if he doesn't get his coffee from some obscure place away from the main street?

Once I get inside, I'm surprised by how small and cozy the coffee shop is, almost like it has the traditional setting of a pub. The name is Italian, though—*Dolcezza.*

The strong smell of fresh coffee makes me crave one myself, but one glance at the prices and I completely change my mind.

Yeah, I'll just make a regular one in the office.

After I get Daniel's coffee, I place half a teaspoon of sugar, assuming that's relatively close to the one gram he spoke of.

When I get to his office, I'm sweating like a pig and my feet are screaming in pain from the marathon I just went through.

Straightening my shoulders, I knock on the door, then go inside at his gruff "Come in."

I find him staring at his watch. "Not only do you not bring coffee on time, but you're also another thirty minutes late."

"The coffee shop is fifteen minutes away."

"Not my problem. Walk faster." He snaps his fingers, which is my cue to give it to him.

I hand him the coffee and rein in an exasperated sigh.

He takes a sip, then his lips twist. "Did I not say one gram of sugar?"

"That's what I put approximately."

"That's more than one gram, Ms. Adler, and don't do "approximately" again." Then he throws the cup of coffee in the rubbish bin.

The cup I went to hell and back for is now in the rubbish.

"Go get me a new one and make it right this time. I want you here in twenty minutes and you'll make up for the extra hour you wasted."

He's got to be kidding me.

I stare at him, but no, he's not kidding. He's staring at me with expectation.

He lifts his chin in that haughty, jerk way. "Do you have a problem with what I just asked, Ms. Adler?"

Oh, I get it now.

He's trying to make me quit, isn't he?

Well, he doesn't know who the heck he's dealing with.

"No, sir," I say, another fake smile plastered on my face. "I'll get a replacement right away."

I can play your game, jerk.

If this is his form of revenge, then I'm playing, too.

We'll see who will hold on until the end.

THREE

Daniel

LEARNED EARLY ON TO BECOME A CAT WHO'S FULL.

The type of cat who plays with his prey, tormenting it just for fun. And because he's not hungry, the process can go on forever, until either the prey continues floundering in pain or dies of shock.

It's a principle I've applied in my life ever since I found out about it.

I made sure to never be a hungry cat who offers their prey mercy and to make sure I play with them until I'm satisfied.

The reason I chose to become a solicitor is also because of that. I steered clear of criminal law and its needless hassle and chose international law instead.

That way, I get to feed the cat and never let it go hungry. With time, I became known as the player of the law circuit.

Not because I'm actually a player, although I am, but because I play games. Whether it's psychological or manipulative, I'm not beneath playing games to win cases for my clients.

I'm not beneath being the ultimate player everyone wishes they could beat in court.

It's how I obtained the type of reputation where people think twice before going against me.

I'm all fun and laughs until I flip the switch and turn everything into a game.

I'm playing one right now. One that's different from all the other games I've played.

Usually, I only play a game when I'm ninety percent sure that I'll win. The ten percent is the fun risk factor. This time, however, I'm not sure if that's the same percentage or if it's slightly lower.

Perhaps it's higher because I won't stop until I crush this game.

Until the prey decides to perish on its own.

Sitting behind my desk, I smooth my tie and watch through the space separating my office from Nicole's.

She's been reading through a contract draft that I asked her to proofread while simultaneously answering incoming calls, which obviously distracts her, because she shakes her head and flips to the previous page.

I lean back in my chair and watch the flutter of her thick lashes over her cheeks as she stares down at the paper.

Like yesterday, her hair is gathered in a ponytail, which highlights the soft contours of her face and her plump lips that are the color of peaches.

It doesn't matter how many years pass or how old she gets, Nicole was and always will be beautiful. The provocative type.

The type I want to snuff out and shove down her slender throat.

Today, she's wearing a dark green shirt that brings out the color of her eyes. They're like a forest in the middle of winter. Mysterious. Manipulative.

Deadly.

That's what she's always been like—a lethal poison waiting for the next victim to attack.

A venom that's designed to make people lose their minds.

Which is why I started this game.

She fucked with me first, and it's time she has a taste of her own medicine.

When I saw her in one of Weaver & Shaw's halls, I couldn't believe my eyes.

It's been eleven years. Eleven fucking years since I last saw her, but that one glimpse was enough to provoke the raging monster inside me.

One glimpse and it all came crashing down on me without mercy.

So I gave HR her name and asked what she was doing here when she's supposed to be in fucking London where I bloody left her.

Turns out, Nicole was applying for an assistant position in the firm. As the bitch karma would have it, I recently let go of my one hundredth assistant, so Nicole was the perfect fit to fill in the role.

She'll be my target for these couple of weeks and then she'll beg me to let her go.

Little Miss Bitch will wish she'd turned around and ran the moment she saw me in my office.

I impatiently wait until she's engrossed in the file again, then I lift my phone and press the button that connects me to her.

A slight jump lifts her shoulders and she purses her lips before picking up. To give her credit, she sounds welcoming. Soft, too. "Weaver & Shaw, Daniel Sterling's office, how may I help you?"

"Are you finished with the contract?"

She stiffens visibly, steals a glance at me through the shutters, then stares back at her desk. "I'll be done with it in a few."

"A few isn't a time frame. You should've been done with that ten minutes ago. Just like you should've brought me coffee three minutes earlier this morning. If my lunch is also late, don't bother coming back. Are we clear, Ms. Adler?"

She pauses for a few seconds, probably to get her bearings. She's clenching one of her fists on the pile of papers and grabbing the phone so tight, her knuckles look white.

It must be so humiliating to go from being the queen bee of

the school to becoming an assistant. To go from wearing name brands and putting on premium perfume to buying cheap clothing from the store.

She was the type of bitch who walked all over those weaker than her with her designer heels while carrying her Dior bag. The type who smiled but never meant it because she excelled at being a fake, ugly monster who looked sweet like peaches but was rotten on the inside.

Considering what I know about her, I'd have sworn she would've cracked by now. She would've called me a "bloody idiot" like she did back then and walked out.

Her pride comes before everything. Even when she fell from grace and her mother was no longer in the picture, she never lowered her head or acted like a victim.

Never.

So the fact that she's been keeping up with my ludicrous commands and harsh treatment is strange, to say the least.

It's almost as if it's not the same Nicole from back then.

"Yes, sir," she says after a while.

My chest expands, then constricts in equal measure. I shouldn't be feeling this fucking conflicted about the way she calls me "sir" when I intended to break her down with it, but fuck me, I'm not used to it.

Not one bit.

And I'm not sure whether that's a good or a bad thing.

"I need that file in five minutes. If there are any mistakes, you're fired."

I hang up and pretend to focus on the screen of my computer. I can see her from my peripheral vision snapping the phone in place and glaring at me.

When I lift my head, she tactfully slides her attention back to the files.

I retrieve my phone, then I send her a series of tasks via text, separately.

Go to the IT department and get me a tech.

I need the draft for the Miles contract in thirty minutes.

Lunch in sixty minutes.

Another coffee in eighty minutes.

Book a meeting with Judge Harrison today.

Cancel golf this Sunday and come up with a good excuse.

Prepare a birthday gift for the mayor's son.

Another coffee in two hundred minutes.

Any failure to perform these tasks and you're fired.

She clenches her fist every time her phone dings or vibrates. I continue doing it on purpose to distract her.

What? I said I would play, not that I would play fair.

I toy with her, scattering her attention every few seconds. She has to check the phone, then go back to the document, flip back a page, look at the phone again, and so on.

Her cheeks turn red and I swear she's about to stand up and storm in here—or storm out.

Before she can do so, the door to her office opens and my friend, Knox, appears in the threshold.

We both came from London after secondary school, even though I'm one year older than him.

Knox and I studied law together at Harvard, passed the bar together, and got into Weaver & Shaw at the same time. He specializes in criminal law, though, because he loves dealing with criminals.

He's a freak like that.

Recently, he was the counsel of one of the parties in a public trial that got the media's full attention. It had his own personal drama involved as well, but he came out of it even stronger than before. The fucker.

Anyway, Knox never knocks, but he also rarely pays attention to my assistants.

Today, he does.

My friend pauses at the threshold and gives Nicole a once-over. Since he came to our secondary school right after she left, she doesn't recognize him.

But he recognizes her.

Perfectly so.

In fact, a sly grin paints his lips as he stalks toward her.

I stand up, letting my phone fall to the desk before I march toward the door. The moment I open it, I hear the sadism in Knox's tone. "My, my, who do we have here?"

"Excuse me?" Nicole asks incredulously.

"Knox," I call his name with a coolness I don't feel.

He gives me a mischievous grin. "Aren't you going to introduce me to your new…*blonde* assistant?"

I don't miss the way the fucker emphasizes the word "blonde" and I'm about to use his tactics about "how to get away with murder" against him.

Nicole, however, seems confused more than anything else. All her earlier irritation has disappeared, too.

I grab Knox by the shoulder. "You, come with me."

He reaches into his jacket, retrieves his card, and puts it in front of Nicole. "My name is Knox Van Doren. Call me if you need anything, Ms.…"

"Adler," she says. "Nicole Adler."

"And the mystery woman finally has a name." Knox smiles wide like a bloody twat and I resist smacking him upside the head and revealing my reaction to the whole situation. "Call me."

Before she can grab the card, I swiftly lift it and bark at her, "You have five minutes for that report."

Then I pull Knox with me into the office and lower the shutters, blocking her and her slightly bemused, slightly frustrated expression out of view.

After clenching and unclenching my fist, I face Knox, who's made himself at home and is sitting on the sofa.

His legs are spread wide and he has his arm thrown nonchalantly over the back of the sofa. That fucking grin is still plastered on his face that's begging to be punched with a professional boxer's strength.

"What the fuck is wrong with you?"

"Me?" He feigns innocence, searching behind him for someone else. "I haven't done anything except for introducing myself ever so casually."

"Stay out of this, Knox."

"Afraid your mystery girl will choose me? Oh, wait. She's not a mystery anymore. Her name is Nicole and she's a bombshell."

"First of all, fuck you. Second of all, this has nothing to do with you, so go wank the nearest pole."

"Thanks for the image, but I'm going to have to decline. I'm happily engaged and don't need your disgusting methods."

"Congratulations for being a twat. Now, can you screw off, please? Some of us have to work."

"Didn't seem like it when you were watching her like Radiohead's "Creep.""

"You're one to talk about the creepy factor, considering your Viagra-on-steroids sexcapades during working hours."

Knox taps a finger on his lips, not bothering to hide his sly smile that resembles a fox in heat. Not that I've seen one, but I imagine this is the expression they would have. "Oh, that. Good times."

"At least one of us thinks so."

"Your opinion on the location of my sexual encounters ranks with the importance of the Queen of England's involvement in national affairs, Danny. Superficial, reserved, and holds no value. Now, back to the subject at hand. I assume you're still holding a grudge? It's been, what?" His hazel eyes twinkle with amusement as he starts counting with his fingers. "Eleven fucking years, no? Normal people would've moved on by now."

"I'm not normal people."

"You sure as fuck are not. Normal people don't hire their nemesis as an assistant."

"That's because they lack imagination. This is the perfect way to torment her."

His expression is deadly serious as he asks, "And then what?"

"What do you mean, then what?"

"You're doing this for a result, no?"

"No. The endgame isn't necessary, the process is."

He chuckles. "Crazy cunt."

"I should be calling you that for your recent involvement with the mafia."

"We're cool." He smooths his tie. "Besides, the tables have turned now, and you're the main entertainment."

"I'm no one's bloody entertainment."

"We'll leave that to the court of the group chat. I'm sure everyone will agree that you brought this shitshow upon yourself."

"It's not a shitshow. It's called cold-blooded revenge."

"You're still holding that much of a grudge, huh?"

I stare at the closed shutters and I can perfectly imagine her on the other side. Only, she's not the desperate Nicole who stooped low to work as an assistant.

All I see is the girl who made my and my best friend's lives in school hell.

The girl who was on a mission to destroy everything pretty I held of her. Everything…innocent.

It's smudged in dark red blood now. Dry blood that's been there for over a fucking decade and refuses to come off.

But now, I'll use her to scrub that blood clean.

"It's not a grudge, Knox. It's a fucking game."

Like the one she used to play back in the day.

This time, I'll win.

FOUR

Nicole

Age eighteen

I'M DOING THIS.

Yes, it's wrong. Yes, I'll probably regret it and curse all my unlucky stars come morning.

But to hell with that.

To hell with being a good girl and counting every step before I take it.

To hell with being lucky.

I don't want that. I never wanted that.

All I've ever wanted are peaches and him.

But I lost them both.

At eight, my allergic reaction to peaches nearly got me killed. So I can't eat the fruit anymore—if I want to remain alive, that is.

I can't even wear perfume with a peach smell if it has the natural fruit as an ingredient. So I wear cherry perfume instead and pretend it's my favorite scent.

My wardrobe is filled with pink, peachy-colored outfits. My bags. My shoes. Everything.

Just because I can't consume it, doesn't mean I can't stare at it from afar.

The same applies to Daniel.

We've had the rockiest relationship ever since that day. Although calling it a relationship is an overstatement. We're mainly acquaintances who attend the same schools and classes and are shoved together at the same social events.

That day, I couldn't tell Mum that I ate peaches on my own or else she would've been the one who killed me instead of the allergic reaction. So she assumed Daniel gave them to me, went to his mother about it, and he was grounded.

He thought I was the one who incriminated him. After that, I tried telling Mum that I did it on my own, but she wouldn't believe that a "good girl" like me would do something so nasty. She preferred to believe the saying that it's always the boy's fault.

Whenever I tried to speak to Daniel at school, he'd glare at me and ignore me.

I keep missing him. Every chance. Every encounter. Every damn day.

I end up biting my lip and choking on the unsaid words he refuses to hear. He told Chloe, my close friend, that I should rot in hell.

I waited until I was alone in the bathroom and cried.

That's what I do when it gets to be too much. I hide and cry where no one can see me tarnish my good-girl image.

Good girls don't cry.

Good girls don't let people see them weak.

But it's been too much over the years.

When we were eleven, we went to one of our mothers' gatherings and I might have followed Daniel from afar.

Sometimes, I just want to watch. It's okay if he doesn't want to talk to me. I'm not going to make him, I just want to see him.

I saw him steal the cake and take it to the other boys. Our eyes met and he paused, his blue eyes twinkling.

"Don't you dare say anything, Peaches."

That's what he's called me since we were eight, but only when he's not mad at me. Only when he actually talks to me instead of ignoring me.

And I think I've fallen in love with the fruit even more since that day.

"I won't," I whispered, smiling.

It was one of the times I felt so goddamn proud. Because Daniel was entrusting me with a secret. We had something in common and I intended to keep it.

However, soon after, someone tattled on him and he thought it was me. I shook my head and went to him, but he pushed me until my back hit a tree.

"Stay the hell away from me, Nicole, or I'm going to hurt you next time."

"It...wasn't me."

"Sure it wasn't. Is that why you smiled after saying you won't. You like making people trust you just so you can hurt them, don't you?"

My eyes stung, but I couldn't allow the tears to escape. I didn't let Daniel see me cry when he hurt me before and that won't change. "You're a bloody idiot."

"And you're a bitch."

That's what he started to call me after that. A bitch.

It got worse when my stepsister, Astrid, came to live with us after her mother died when we were fifteen.

Uncle Henry told me to take her with me to Chloe's birthday party so she'd make new friends.

And guess who the only friend she made was?

Daniel.

They fell in the pool together and then got out laughing and disappeared to where I couldn't find them.

Since then, they've been inseparable.

Since then, I've been forced to see him come to our house, make me feel invisible, and only care about Astrid.

Sometimes, it's like he doesn't see me. And the only time he does is when I'm mean to Astrid.

Mum dislikes her because she's middle class and not from our social standing. I didn't really care about her at the beginning, but she just had to get close to Daniel.

She had to be friends with him in one freaking day while I've been hopelessly trying for seven years.

One day, I hid her sketchbook, just because I wanted her to fret. But it was Daniel who got mad at me, got in my face and told me, "Is your life that boring that you find pleasure in making other people's lives hell? Why do you have to be a bitch?"

Because he only sees me when I'm being one.

It's not like I'm physically hurting anyone. I'm just tired of being a good girl, tired of feeling lucky and privileged.

Daniel has never seen me during all the years I've been a good girl. Hell, he hated me for it, so maybe that's not the answer.

Maybe all I need is to become so bad that he'll only look at me.

Even if it's with disapproval and glares. That way, he's at least looking at me.

So I've kept being mean to Astrid, especially when he's around. I've kept being a thorn in her side and making her life as miserable as mine.

I hated her and was jealous of her. I envied her lighthearted energy and how she couldn't care less about the luxurious life she was thrust in.

I was jealous of her for making Daniel smile and show his dimples.

He's never directed that smile at me.

Never.

I could only watch it from afar.

Until now.

I have to end this ill-fated relationship. I have to stop Daniel from misunderstanding me.

From looking everywhere except at me.

From making me invisible.

Today, we're at a party to celebrate the football team's win.

The captain of the football team, Levi King, is hosting the party at his mega-rich uncle's holiday mansion.

Everyone from school had to drive for hours to get here. The car park is filled with all types of luxurious German cars that parents buy for their kids.

After all, everyone who studies at Royal Elite School is the elite of the elite. It's the school from which prime ministers and parliament members graduate.

Papa and Uncle Henry studied there as well.

And so did Daniel's father, Benedict Sterling. He comes from old money and is the CEO of a computer engineering company. Daniel and his older brother, Zach, are the sole heirs of a multibillion-dollar fortune and a multitude of real estate that extends beyond borders.

Zach is already studying to take over after his father retires, and Daniel is expected to follow in their footsteps. Or that's what I gathered—I mean, spied—while Mum was talking to Aunt Nora, Daniel's mother.

I do that a lot, spying, staying around just to hear crumbs about his life.

That's how I learned that he's a picky eater and only has specific places he eats from. But I don't think Aunt Nora knows the actual reason why her son is that way about food.

I do.

Because I followed him the day his taste in food changed forever.

I was around the corner when he threw up his guts and leaned against the wall to catch his breath.

He didn't see me, though, not even when I constantly left him my precious peach lollipops so he could chase away the bitter taste of vomit.

But that won't be the same after today. I'll make sure I'm out of the invisibility shadow that I've been living under for the past ten years.

I scarcely pay attention to what Chloe and the other girls are talking about. Which is mostly boys and fashion shows and the latest gossip.

Vain, vain, and more vain.

But I'm lucky and privileged to be part of this life, so I don't have the right to complain. Besides, what's the point?

Isn't this type of luxury what other people strive for?

"Your dress is so pretty, Nicole. Is that Dior?" Hannah, one of the girls, asks.

I pause my obsessive watching session of the entrance and focus back on the conversation.

My dress is light peach-colored with subtle streaks of gold. It's short enough to graze my upper thigh, but it's not tight enough to make me look cheap. Its straps are an elegant gold and it's low-cut enough to show a hint of my cleavage.

It's a "You can look, but you can't touch" dress at its finest.

My hair is loose and falls straight to the hollow of my back. I'm wearing my lucky peach-colored heels that allow me to stand taller than all the girls here.

The whole look makes me feel elegant and powerful, but most of all, beautiful. Like I can win battles and conquer mountains.

Or more like, a particular mountain that I haven't even been able to scratch the surface of for years.

That's how obsession works.

At first, you just want a glance, a touch, a word, but then greed takes over and you can't get enough.

I can't get enough.

"It's Dior," I tell Hannah with a smile. "Uncle Henry got it for me."

"You're so lucky your dad is a willing sponsor of your lifestyle."

Chloe, who's standing right beside me, releases an annoyed sound. I've known her since we were eight and became sort of besties.

Mostly because the other girls were too intimidated by me to ever try and befriend me.

She's a brunette and has doe brown eyes that make her appear kind and peaceful when she's in fact the one who metaphorically lent me the "bitch manual."

"He's not her dad, he's her stepdad. Didn't you hear her calls him Uncle Henry? Keep up, Hannah," Chloe says with a plastic smile and I stop myself from wincing.

Yes, Uncle Henry isn't Papa, but I wanted him to be at one point. However, I knew early on that that was impossible. Despite what Mum used to say, he only ever cared about Astrid as his real daughter.

He might not buy her things, because she doesn't want them, and is stricter with her than he is with me, but she's the one he makes sure is asleep every night.

As if on cue with my thoughts, Chloe tips her chin to the entryway. "The real daughter is a bum with no grace."

The group breaks out in snickers except for me. My attention slides to the entrance and sure enough, Astrid is walking inside with her usual aloofness.

She's wearing shorts and fishnet stockings and has some tacky star pins in her light brown hair. Astrid is short, way shorter than me, but she never wears heels, or dresses, or anything that would bring out her natural beauty.

And still, Daniel is wrapping an arm around her shoulders and laughing out loud at something she said.

I'm caught in a trance—my lids slowly droop and my heart starts a war in my chest, then drops to my fluttering stomach.

It's a mayhem of emotions that keep mounting with each passing second like overstimulation.

Overflow.

Overdose.

Daniel has always been beautiful, but his beauty is much more severe now. He's beautiful not in an everyday-things kind of way, but as someone who's meant to become an actor, a model, or make a living by selling his looks.

He's grown tall and muscular over the years. Not in a buff way, but like a lean prince from a fairy tale. The blue Elites jacket complements his frame and envelops his wide shoulders like a second skin.

His hair has become darker, but there are still those streaks of blond like a natural balayage of latte and the rays of the sun.

The same sun that shines brighter in his star-filled eyes. They're sharper now, having lost all the boyhood that once made him mischievous.

He's just a player.

And not only on the football team, but generally. If someone had a shot every time he shagged a random girl, they would need their liver replaced by now.

He's become popular, but not in a "stuck-up, you're gross to even think you can talk to me" kind of way. But more like "I'm a bus and everyone is welcome for a ride" way.

Rumor has it, Daniel is the one person people need at their party if they want it to be a success. He's laid-back, welcoming, charming.

To everyone but me.

I tried to keep myself as disinterested as possible from that part of him, but I know he probably had sex with Royal Elite's entire female population and is branching out to other schools for up-and-coming vaginas.

I know because he's not shy to tell Astrid about his sexcapades, to which she calls him a pig.

I know because I heard a girl describe sex with him as "an experience of a lifetime."

I know because I had wet dreams that night and woke up touching myself and moaning into my pillow.

I know because I cried right afterward and it wasn't from pleasure.

Usually, I retreat whenever he's with Astrid. I give them space and pretend I don't care.

Not today, though.

Today, I have a plan.

"Maybe I should go teach her some manners," I say to the girls, plastering a smirk as fake as their daddies' wigs.

Chloe snorts. "Not sure if it will work on a hopeless case like her, but go for it."

"I'm in the mood for charity." I flip my hair, blinding them with a splash of natural blonde. "How do I look?"

"Ten out of ten," Hannah says, starry-eyed.

"A bad bitch." Chloe grins. "Show us what you got."

I flip my hair again, then walk to them while gently swaying my hips.

Before I reach them, I stop at the beverages table and grab two shots. I pretend to be adjusting my dress, then reach into my bra and retrieve the small bag of pills I bought the last time Chloe took me to a club.

When a random bloke asked me if I wanted to have fun and flashed me the pills, I told him, "Eww, gross." But then the wires in my brain connected together.

I know what ecstasy does, or at least, I read about its effects and how it makes someone mindless with pleasure.

I wanted that.

Needed that.

But not only for me.

So I bought the pills, behind Chloe's and the others' backs because I couldn't have them figure out my plan.

I couldn't have everyone figure out what good girls plotted behind closed doors.

There are three pills. Just in case I need the extra one.

Still pretending to fix my neckline, I pull out two of them and put each in a glass. Then I grab my pendant, the one I've never removed ever since I got it for my thirteenth birthday. The one that matches my eye color and calms me beyond anything else I've ever tried.

"What do we have here?"

I freeze, my heart catching in my throat. Christopher, another football player and the captain's friend, slides to my side.

His curly hair kisses his forehead and his eyes twinkle with mischief. Jeez. Please tell me he didn't see me put the pills in the drinks? I chose a corner on purpose.

"You look hot as fuck in that dress, Nikki. I bet you'd look even better out of it."

Phew. So he's just being his usual flirty self.

He reaches a hand for my arse, but I swat it away. "Gross. Not in this lifetime."

Then I grab the shots and head to where I last saw Astrid and Daniel. But my stepsister is nowhere to be found.

Daniel is all alone, standing near the balcony, but that's not all. Both of his hands are shoved in his jean pockets and he's narrowing his eyes on me.

Not anyone else, me.

Seeing Daniel alone is as weird as witnessing a flying unicorn toward England's nonexistent sun. But the fact that he's also looking at me is even stranger.

My nerves start to snap and attack the rest of my body. I can feel my feet getting cold and the tips of my fingers becoming numb. But I continue channeling the inner diva in me who's a glorified version of eight-year-old me.

Only, she has more issues now.

And they all start with him.

Daniel.

I don't have to keep walking to him, because he closes the distance between us in a few long, determined strides.

My feet come to an abrupt halt when he nearly crashes his chest against mine and brings us both tumbling to the ground.

"What?" I ask because he's looking at me weirdly.

More accurately, he's glaring.

Almost like he wants to split my face open and peer inside it. Or maybe punch whatever he finds there like he's always bruised my heart.

"Where are you going?" he asks.

"And that's any of your business because…?" Yeah, so I usually sound like this. Snobbish, mean, and completely detached.

It's a defense mechanism.

That sadistic gleam returns to his eyes. My chest hardens for the hit, for the attack that always leaves me emotionally crippled. "Thought I would check in case you decide to steal some peaches and ruin the party."

"Whether I eat peaches, live or die, or end up paralyzed is none of your business."

"It is if I'm forced to attend your funeral instead of going to summer camp."

"And who says you're invited to my funeral? Maybe I'll have a ban list and you'll be at the top of it."

That makes him pause, a muscle working in his square jaw. And did I just imagine that or did his arms become tauter?

A smirk breaks out on his lips, and although his dimples make a guest appearance, I don't like them under this light. They're sinister, projecting the sadism in his eyes. "Or maybe you won't have a say in it and I'll be sitting in the front row singing 'Hallelujah' in my head."

"Then at your funeral, I'll wear a pink dress, hold a matching umbrella, and stand on your grave, crying loudly. When people gather around, I'll say, 'Everyone says men with minuscule penises have short lives, but I never believed that until now.'"

His smirk widens, and I'd swear it's about to become a smile, but he clamps it down at the last second. "All the girls who had the pleasure of seeing my cock will testify otherwise. That's what it's called, by the way, Peaches. A cock or a dick, not a penis. What are you, a toddler?"

Heat rises to my cheeks, and it's not only because of what he called his thing. It's due to hearing him say that other word.

Peaches.

He has no business speaking it so naturally that it feels intimate.

"I'm not crude like you, Daniel."

"Oh, right. You're prim and proper and aren't allowed to say cock or dick. How about go down and fuck and a blowjob?"

"It's not that I'm not allowed to. I don't want to. They're beneath me."

"Then don't talk about my cock when you haven't seen it. Unless…you want to change that?"

"Eww, gross." I pretend to be disgusted when I'm in fact burning up from the inside.

Maybe I should just take the drug now to bring my guard down and say what I'm feeling for once.

"You're the one who brought it up first. Junior has a reputation to protect."

"Did you just call your thing Junior?"

"Did you just call his name because you want to see, after all?"

"You could be the last man on earth and I wouldn't come near you, even if humanity's destiny depended on us."

"Is that so?" His permanent smirk falls. "And who would you choose? The one you're taking those shots to?"

"Who I choose is none of your concern."

One moment I'm standing there cursing myself for ruining the chance to give him the shot, and the next, he snatches one from between my fingers and downs it in one go.

My lips fall open. "H-hey!"

"Oops." He wipes his mouth with the back of his hand, then in another swift move, he snatches the other shot. "Guess your plans are ruined."

And with that, he turns and leaves.

"Daniel!"

My voice is a bit high-pitched, definitely above the range I ever allow myself to speak.

Because I'm freaking out here. Is he going to drink that? What if something happens to him if he drinks a double dose?

Before I can think of a way to stop him, Daniel finds Astrid coming out of the toilet. He sweeps up another shot and gives her what was supposed to be my shot and they do a one-shot.

My shoulders fall as my lips tremble.

It doesn't matter what I do or the lengths I go to, I'll only remain invisible to Daniel.

Maybe it's time I finally give up.

So why does the mere thought fill my eyes with tears?

FIVE

Daniel

Age eighteen

MY HEAD BUZZES WITH A STRANGE TYPE OF ENERGY. AS IF I'm plummeting to earth and shooting for the sky at the same time.

It's a feeling I've never experienced before and it's forcing me to move, to jump out of my skin and just...go.

Somewhere.

Anywhere.

Like a shooting star—aimless, heartless, and absolutely destructive.

I parted ways with Astrid and told her I'm going to fuck one of the girls, which is usually her cue to give me the stink eye, call me a pig, then let me have my fun.

Then she'll call someone to drive us home, usually my brother. She's loyal and responsible like that. The "we can't drive while we're drunk" Astrid. The "please tell me you wear condoms, because I don't want to be an aunt this young" Astrid.

In short, the best wingman I've ever had. Except for the fact that she doesn't like partying and I have to drag her kicking and screaming as if she's heading to her hanging.

Actually, she doesn't like people in general and prefers to remain hidden like a stone that's camouflaging a diamond.

Unlike her flashy, seductive stepsister.

That's where I'm going right now—after Nicole.

Yes, I lied about fucking the other girl, because the moment I saw Nicole sneaking about, I knew she was up to no good.

Not that she was ever up to anything good.

If trouble were a club, Nicole would be their face, soul, and the inspiration for their name.

I shouldn't give a fuck what Nicole is up to. In fact, I made it my mission not to focus on her, not to get pulled into her manipulative web, where she lures her victims, then sucks their souls like the blood countess sucked young girls' blood to remain beautiful and ageless.

That shit is real. Look it up.

If Nicole lived in those times, she would've been her wingman and best advisor. Hell, she wouldn't even have been caught for it. Since, well, that countess had the brain energy of an aimless bird.

Back to the reason why I'm following Nicole with the persistence of a crooked detective.

She's been different today. Talkative, though still venomous. Dressed in a fuck-me dress and heels as if she was out to get some.

And why the fuck am I getting so bloody hot that I want to set my own clothes on fire?

So when I saw her gulping a drink, ignoring her holy circles of glorified bitches and slipping through the crowd, I followed her.

Just like I followed her that day ten years ago when she nearly died in my arms.

I shouldn't have.

Since that day, she's been a thorn in my fucking side.

Prior to that incident, she always had a smile on her pretty little face, and acted nice in an annoying kind of way. So seeing her sneaking about was an occurrence I've never witnessed.

It's why I left the game and tailed her. The I watched her stealing peaches, hiding them behind her white lace dress, and tiptoeing so no one would see her.

Now feels like a repeat of that time.

As if she's about to steal a peach, go eat it in an obscure place, and...die.

That's what the doctor said that time. Her allergic reaction was only oral when she was younger, but after she turned eight, it became respiratory, too. He said that the next time she eats a peach, she'll stop breathing.

She'll drop dead.

There will be no more Nicole and her fake smiles and dainty dresses.

I waited for her to wake up so I could ask her again why the hell she ate peaches when she already knew she was allergic to them.

I wanted her to explain if liking something was enough of an excuse to push herself to the brink of death.

However, I didn't get the chance to ask anything, because she's a fucking backstabber and got out of the whole situation by blaming it on me.

I've never seen Mum as disappointed in me as she was at that moment.

Not that she's been a model mother all our lives. Her mission has been, for as long as I can remember, a self-pity party, to mourn her youth for being with my cheating bastard of a father.

Anyway, Nicole is now avoiding everyone, walking in the background, almost as if she's floating on air.

She's the type who makes her presence known anywhere she goes.

Fucking anywhere.

She's hot and the worst part is that she knows it.

She dresses for it in her designer clothes and bags and heels.

Not only that, but she flings it all over social media, too. As if she's a model looking for representation.

Though it's beneath her. As she says in her snobbish fucking tone.

After all, she's an aristocrat who only knows how to look down her haughty nose at people. Unlike Astrid, who never embraced that side of her bloodline.

Nicole, however, breathes that life. The prim and proper side of it. The arrogance that comes with it. The extravagance that coats it like honey. And she has the looks that go with it.

She's a bombshell with legs that go for miles and hair so blonde, it's more blinding than the sun and just as burning. Her body is slender, with curves that are made for grabbing onto while I fuck her senseless.

I pause, internally shaking my head.

Did I just think about fucking Nicole? What in the bloody hell was that all about?

These ominous bloody thoughts should stay in my subconscious where I can't even reach them, let alone entertain them.

My attention, though hazy and a bit blurry, returns to the present when Nicole slips into a secluded room on the ground floor. Soon after, Chris throws a quick look around, then follows her in.

So he's the one she dressed up like a sin waiting to happen for. He's the one she's been taking those shots for.

I wish it was like ten years ago and it was about her weird fixation on peaches.

I wish I hadn't already painted a picture in my head about what's going on inside.

But I did.

And all I can see in the midst of my now red vision is Chris removing Nicole's fuck-me dress and heels and pounding into her until she's biting her lips and screaming.

That's fucked up. My thoughts. The accuracy of the image. The rage that's covering my vision.

The fact that I don't want anyone to see or hear Nicole while she's in the throes of pleasure.

I should find Astrid and leave. I'm in no mood to party or fuck or anything.

But that's not what I do.

My legs are leading me straight to the room and I can't stop them.

Or maybe I don't want to.

I jam the knob open and I don't know why my heart squeezes. Like that first time when I was thirteen and saw Dad kissing a woman that wasn't Mother, teenage style, while smearing her face with all types of food.

Or the time Zach was screaming at Mother for letting Dad get away with it and she admitted that she had to pretend she didn't know because her family didn't want her back and she had nowhere to go.

Oh, and he'll take us away from her.

I never hated the world more than at that moment.

Never wished I could gut-punch Dad and shove him in the nearest dumpster.

Not only for hurting Mother but for also turning her into someone so absorbed in her pain that she failed to see me or my brother anymore.

So in a way, we lost both parents.

It's the same feeling of betrayal now—as if someone I gave a piece of me to is burning it alive.

Which is fucking ridiculous. Nicole and I are nothing.

If anything, I hate how much of a bitch she's become. I hate her band of mean girls, who think being vicious is the new trend.

And yet, I can't chase away the bitter taste from the back of my throat.

Nicole is lying on the bed and Chris is hovering over her, his hand on his belt.

"Mind if I watch?" I'm taken aback by the slur in my voice.

Chris's attention slides to me, but Nicole doesn't even stir.

No idea why that makes me rage like a bitter fucker on pills.

"Get out, Sterling," Chris bites out. "Why are you ruining my fun?"

I lazily walk to a chair that's opposite the bed and that's when I get a glimpse of Nicole's face.

Her eyes are closed. Is she pretending to be asleep after she heard my voice?

Something doesn't feel right.

Instead of sitting down, I stride to Chris, who's now standing to his full height by the side of the bed. The tension in his shoulders resembles a bodybuilder on crack. He probably is, considering his unnaturally bloodshot eyes and the twitch in his fingers.

Why would she even choose this...this crackhead cunt who has more drugs in his system than an eighties' rock star?

Not that I have a say in who the fuck she chooses, but it's the weird buzzing in my ears coupled with the hotness in my chest that's acting now.

"Shouldn't she be awake for the fun to happen?"

"She likes being woken up with dick, what's in it for you?"

My teeth grind together and the unbearable heat burns up a notch. "So it's a habit of yours to wake her up with dick?"

He jerks his chin with a nod.

"Funny, because I don't remember you being her boyfriend."

"She's my side bitch. Are you done questioning your senior?"

"No, not yet." The fact that he called her a side bitch makes me ball my hands into fists.

Nicole isn't the type who'd settle for being anyone's side anything.

She's the main course. The highlight of a show. The film's premiere.

I'm about to punch Christopher in the face, out of pure crazy emotions that are raging through me, when a moan echoes in the air.

Nicole's.

She slowly gets up into a sitting position, her eyes drooping. She looks like a fucking goddess with her slightly flushed cheeks and dewy skin. I want to grab her by the throat and mess her up a little, ruin her a little so she's not so perfect anymore.

So she finally stoops to my level.

"What's with all the noise?" she asks with a slur of her own.

"Fuck this," Chris mutters. "And fuck you, Sterling."

Then, he storms out of the room, forcibly closing the door shut behind him.

Bloody cunt.

Everything in me is shouting to go after him and punch the bastard until his blood is dripping all over the ground.

"D-Daniel…?"

My attention slides back to Nicole. Her dress has ridden up to her waist, revealing her creamy pale thighs and a hint of her white lace knickers.

Her lips are plump and parted and a red flush covers her cheeks and neck.

No clue if it's the weird sensation I've been having since earlier or the rage I've been feeling since I imagined her with Chris or a combination of both, but this view of her gets my dick hard in an instant.

The traitorous fucker strains against my jeans until it's physically painful. Until the need to grab her is far more powerful and urgent than anything I've felt before.

It's an animalistic need.

An instinct.

Or maybe it's far deeper than that but I don't want to think of it as such.

"What are you doing here?" The slur in her voice matches mine—light, subtle but also magical.

Almost like none of this is real.

Maybe it isn't and this is one of my bothersome nightmares about her that I can't stop my subconscious from conjuring.

"Do you really like being woken up with dick?" I don't know why I ask the question, but I do, and I also keep approaching where she's sitting and watching my every move like a deer caught in the headlights.

"W-what?"

I didn't think it was possible, but my dick thickens even more at her soft voice. There's no haughtiness and snobbishness in it. It's almost as gentle as she looks.

"I said, do you like being woken up by dick? Is that why Chris was here?"

"What...? No..."

"Then is there something else you're into that I should know about?"

"Why?" She licks her lips, pauses, then lowers her voice until it sounds like something out of my deepest, darkest fantasy. "Will you make it happen?"

"Maybe."

"Even if it's a dangerous kink?"

I smile. "My, Peaches. I thought you were as prim as a princess and didn't even say crude words. Now you have a dangerous kink?"

"I...do."

"Let's hear it."

"I'll only tell you if you promise to make it happen."

I pause, contemplating the answer. I don't usually make promises unless I know what it's all about.

"If it's about eating peaches, then no way in fuck. You're not touching that shit for a lifetime." I breathe harshly.

Why the fuck did I sound so serious? Protective almost.

"No, it's not about peaches. It's something more dangerous."

"What is it?"

"Promise first."

I purse my lips, then say, "Fine, promise. Now, tell me what the kink is."

She gets on her knees and inches closer, bringing the sheets with her until she's eye level with me, then whispers, "You."

And I know, I just know I'm not only going to fuck Nicole Adler, but I'll also enjoy and regret every second of it.

SIX

Nicole

Present

MY HEAD IS ABOUT TO EXPLODE.

I'm overthinking everything, thanks to a certain jerk, and worse, the onslaught of emotions that I went through over the past two days is stronger than anything I've experienced.

It's like being waterboarded and I have to count fractions of seconds until I get my next breath.

It's like living on my toes for the next hit.

I have no doubt in my mind that it's coming. I have no doubt that Daniel will find a reason to chew me out or threaten to fire me.

It seems to be his modus operandi—wanting to kick me out. The arsehole has the power and he knows it. Hell, he's bent on showcasing it every chance he gets so I have no misconceptions about my position.

After the initial shock of meeting him again wore off, I googled him.

What? I needed to know my enemy.

Obviously, Daniel abandoned his family fortune. He left everything behind and came to the States at the age of eighteen. He studied law, passed the bar, and became one of the youngest solicitors to acquire the junior partner position. That's especially notable considering how big and influential Weaver & Shaw is.

Not only that, but he's also talented enough that some European sovereignty recently appointed him as their attorney in charge. That, aside from all the international business moguls that he represents.

All except for his own family.

Not many people drew the connection between him and the influential Sterling family back home. Probably because no one would think he'd abandon such fortune to become an attorney.

Still, he managed to become the media's sweetheart and photographers' wet dream. He has the looks anyone with cameras or eyes would want to freeze into an ethereal moment of perfection.

Over the years, Daniel gained everyone's attention with his quick wit and dripping charm. Or at least that's what the articles say.

They sing praises for him like angels hum hallelujah in the heavens.

But no one knows the Daniel I know.

The heartless, merciless jerk with control freak tendencies and egomaniac issues.

My gaze flits to his office, to where he disappeared with the lawyer named Knox.

They've been there for five minutes and I'm not sure if I'm allowed to interrupt him. But on the other hand, if I don't get him what he asked for on time, he'll just bring up the wanker parameter a notch.

Besides, I need to leave now if I want to get him his freaking "specific" lunch on time.

So I open my texts and grind my teeth at the long string of orders he sent at exactly three-second intervals just to distract me.

He can be such an unbearable fucking jerk.

But it doesn't matter what he does. If I put my head to something, no one will be able to stop me.

Not even him.

Me: I finished the report.

His reply is instant.

Bloody Idiot: What are you waiting for then? Email it.

Me: If you checked your inbox, you'd find it there.

Bloody Idiot: Drop the fucking attitude, Ms. Adler.

Me: It wasn't attitude, just a piece of information.

Bloody Idiot: Let me be the one to decide that. I need my lunch in exactly thirty-seven minutes.

I'm about to type that I was going to get that anyway, but I settle with, *On it, sir.*

I hate the flutter and the squeezing in my chest whenever I type or say that word.

I hate the wave of emotions that follows it.

But most of all, I hate this man.

I hate him with a passion that leaves me seething and constantly thinking about how to commit a flawless crime.

But I don't let the anger rule me or it would ruin everything else.

Grabbing my bag, I storm out of the office as if my heels are on fire. I wore medium ones today because my legs are still screaming at me from yesterday's torture.

After I take a taxi, I call Jay.

He picks up immediately. "What's up?"

"Heeey! Is that any way to talk to me when I didn't see you last night or this morning?"

"That's okay. I'll wait for you tonight if you prepare fish."

"You greedy little rascal. But fine, I'll bring some fish."

"'Kay."

"Don't forget your medication, Jay."

"I won't. Stop moaning."

"Did you just say I'm moaning?"

"You do that a lot. I'm a child genius, remember?"

He is. Last year, Jayden skipped two grades, which is why he doesn't have friends.

If I had the necessary means, I would've sent him to one of

Europe's prestigious schools for the youth, but that's a dream neither of us is capable of entertaining. At least, not now.

Maybe one day, when he's older, I'll be able to pick up the dream I've been secretly suppressing and I'll be well off enough to afford a better education for him.

"I'm just reminding you, Jay."

"Yeah, yeah. Shouldn't you be working?"

"Yeah. I'll see you later."

"'Kay. Oh, by the way, Nikki. There was a letter in the mail this morning and…I kind of opened it, sorry."

"What is it about?"

He pauses, gulping audibly through the phone which is not a good sign. "I'll send it over. I gotta go."

Then he hangs up, leaving me baffled.

The taxi pulls up in front of the restaurant and I pay the driver before I step out, practically jogging inside.

Katerina's is a high-end restaurant with a futuristic clean décor that looks kind of tacky instead of revolutionary. If I was responsible for this, I would've added a splash of color and removed the loud music that doesn't allow people to concentrate on what they're eating.

But that's just me.

"Menu du jour?" The cashier asks when I stop in front of him. His name is Jonas and he's a middle-aged man with a kind, welcoming smile. I think he's used to having dozens of different assistants come pick out Daniel's meals.

He always gets the "menu du jour" with coffee if he specifically asks for it.

I'm half panting when Jonas shows me the ingredients in the meal.

"Is that parmesan and pesto in the pasta?"

"Yes," Jonas says.

"I'll just take a steak then."

"Are you sure, miss? Mr. Sterling always takes the menu du jour."

Not when it has parmesan and pesto. I shouldn't remember that, but I know for a fact that he dislikes them.

"Yes, the steak will be fine. Medium cooked, please."

"I'll tell the chef." Jonas gives me a "you're out of line" look. "Not sure if she'll appreciate it."

"Excuse me?"

"You're new, so you probably don't know this, but the reason Mr. Sterling only eats here is because of our chef. She's a *close* friend of his."

I narrow my eyes, and it's not only because of the way he enunciated "close." What is he trying to insinuate? That I'm getting in the middle of his chef and Daniel? They can be all lovey-dovey for all I care.

"Listen, Jonas." I adopt my calm tone. "I'm merely an assistant who happens to know that my demanding boss doesn't like parmesan and pesto, so I'm trying to get him something to eat that he actually likes or else he'll call me incompetent, send me here again for something else, and force me to make up for the wasted time after work. And I can't do that, because I have a family and dinner to cook. So how about you do us both a favor and get me a freaking steak?"

His lips twist, but he nods. "Right away, miss."

I check my messages as I wait for the food. My stomach growls, rightly so since I haven't eaten anything since this morning in my attempts to get his majesty his damn coffee on time.

Once I get him his lunch, I'll be able to eat my measly home-made sandwich.

My hunger is long forgotten when I find the letter Jay sent me.

It's from the court.

And it's about Jay's custody.

No, no.

My fingers shake and moisture burns in my lids. This can't be happening.

The words blur in front of me and I lean back against the wall so as not to lose balance.

I latch my fingers onto my necklace for much-needed solace, for some semblance of calm.

However, neither comes.

Even my necklace seems useless in front of the ghost from my past.

"I assume you're Danny's new assistant."

My head slowly lifts at a woman's voice. She's wearing a chef's outfit, her brown hair is tucked neatly beneath the cap. Her brown eyes are big and currently judging me.

"Uh, yes. That's me."

She shoves a takeout bag in my hand. "Give Danny the pasta and tell him Katerina sends her love. Next time, don't interfere in our routine when you're just an assistant."

I grind my back teeth, calling for an extraterrestrial force of calm. "As his assistant, it's my duty not to give him something I know for a fact he doesn't like. And since you're his chef, shouldn't you have learned his eating habits by now?"

"And what makes you an expert on his eating habits?"

My old unhealthy habits. But I don't say that and conjure calm instead, "Can I please get the steak?"

"No. Tell Danny I sent him my menu du jour."

"You know what? I don't care." I take the bag and storm out of the restaurant.

When the traffic gets bad, I jump out of the taxi and continue on foot, practically stomping like a spoiled child. My mind is overcrowded, overwhelmed, and going on overload.

The court letter is playing in my head like a distorted record. Why now of all times? Why does he think he can get Jay now when he never wanted him?

When he freaking abused him to get to me?

I wince when I reach the office five minutes late.

A different emotion sinks in my stomach as I knock on Daniel's door. An emotion I've been actively trying to kill.

An emotion that I won't let revive again.

"You're five minutes and thirty seconds late, Ms. Adler," he barks as soon as I'm inside and I slowly close my eyes to rein in the need to lash out.

"There was traffic."

"I don't give a fuck about traffic. When I say twelve thirty, do I mean twelve thirty-five?"

"No."

"No, what?"

I stare at him. Or maybe it's something a bit more intense than a stare when I grit out, "No, sir."

His eyes meet mine and I'm trapped in a cage so wild and dark, I regret actually making eye contact with him.

What was my resolution about Daniel, anyway?

"Are you glaring at me, Ms. Adler?"

I shake my head.

"Then lose the attitude and lower your fucking eyes."

I purse my lips and stare at my shoes, chanting.

This is for Jay.

You need this job now more than any other time.

You can't throw the takeout bag in his stupid gorgeous face and leave.

"Are you going to get me the food or should I wait another five minutes?"

I walk so forcefully that I trip, but I catch myself and the food at the last second. That only makes Daniel impatient, because he's throwing poisonous arrows my way from behind his desk.

After placing the bag down, I straighten. "For your information, your chef, Ms. Katerina, refused to give me steak and insisted that you have her precious menu du jour, even though I repeated twice that you don't like pesto and parmesan. So I would appreciate it if you don't blame me for this. It clearly isn't my mistake and I don't want to pay for other people's stubbornness and lack of cooperation. Oh, and she sends her regards. Sorry, I mean her love. Now, if you don't need anything else."

I turn around to leave, realizing I kind of just had a mini-rant in front of him, which is possibly frowned upon in his stoicism dictionary.

But I can't help it. The accumulation of meeting him again, what happened earlier, and the custody suit are turning my head to mush.

"Stop." Daniel's authoritative word makes my feet halt. "Turn around."

I slowly do, my heart thundering in my chest. Please don't tell me he'll act on his threats and fire me this time.

"How do you know I don't eat parmesan and pesto?"

His question catches me off guard. Out of all the word vomit I just said, that's what he got out of it?

I clear my throat, summoning nonchalance. "It must be in the million requirements you sent me."

"No, it wasn't, and I told you to drop the attitude before I find an unpleasant way to extort it out of you. Now, tell me how you know about my preferences regarding parmesan and pesto?"

"I just know it. Why is that important?"

"I never shared it with you, so how did you find out?"

"I must've overheard one of the other assistants mention it."

"Liar." He stands up and my heart squeezes when he stalks toward me. The moment I smell him, the pine and lime and bergamot, I become drunk.

But not on his smell alone.

It's on his presence.

His nearness.

I quit my addiction to him a long time ago—I'm eleven years sober—so how come one hit is enough to make me backpedal into bad habits?

When he speaks, his voice is too close to my ear, I shiver. "Even my best friend isn't privy to that detail about me. In fact, no one is. So how are you?"

"I don't remember."

"Is that so?"

"Yeah, I kind of forget easily. Can I go now?"

I make a move to turn, but he grabs my elbow and I nearly shriek when he pulls me back against him. "No, you can't."

SEVEN

Nicole

It's been years since I was in this position.

No, over a decade.

It's crazy how much the passage of time can change someone's perspective about everything.

Eleven years ago, I would've melted if Daniel had so much as looked at me. If he'd touched me, I would've flown to euphoria land in no time.

Because of him, I was mentally and physically sick numerous times. Because of him, I hid in toilets and cried where no one could see the proud Nicole being weak.

And because of him, my life took a sharp dive for the worst.

But that's been long over.

That's in the past.

It's strange how years and events can change a person. How our perspectives can flip one hundred eighty degrees as if it exists in a parallel universe.

I wish that were the case. I wish I'd first met him now and he was just my boss. Maybe then, he wouldn't be such a jerk.

Maybe then, I wouldn't be thinking about the way his fingers are wrapped around my elbow or how they burn through my shirt and reach the skin.

He's always grabbed me by the elbow, almost as if he doesn't want to touch any other part of me.

But that doesn't lessen the impact of the gesture or how that small nook of my body is nearing the point of self-destruction.

I dare to slowly lift my gaze and search his in an attempt to wrap my chaotic mind around this.

But the moment my eyes clash with his, I wish I hadn't looked at him.

I even wish I'd never met him again. I wish our ill-fated connection had died the day he metaphorically killed me eleven years ago.

Because the way he's watching me?

It's nothing short of domineering. His square jaw is set and his nostrils are flaring and those eyes that I once found solace in? They're now judging me, worse than a criminal who's being prosecuted in court.

Just like everyone else did back then.

Daniel is no different than them. If anything, he should be offered the leadership of my anti-fan club.

Yes, he's a man now, but he's still the boy who punched my heart and stomped all over it as if my feelings meant nothing.

He's still the boy who gave me malevolent butterflies and caused my heart to be dangerously wild by merely existing.

He's still the one person I can't forget, no matter how much I attempt to.

"Can you please let me go?" I don't know how the hell I sound calm when a wildfire is erupting inside me.

"Why?" His voice drops to an almost sinister edge. "Are you uncomfortable?"

"Yes. Surely you know this is sexual harassment."

Daniel lowers his head so he can speak near my ear in a

whisper-like range. "You of all people shouldn't be talking about sexual harassment when you put a date rape drug in my drink."

I go still, cold sweat breaking down my back and across my forehead.

This is the first time he's shown an inkling of recognizing me. Ever since yesterday, I'd started to question myself and think that maybe he'd truly erased me from his life.

I thought that maybe I'd become invisible again and that I was only existing as a punching bag he could take his jerk attitude out on.

But no.

He remembers.

No clue why that fills me with equal parts dread and relief.

But that doesn't matter right now, because his words echo inside me like a hungry beast.

"Is that what you think? That I put a date rape drug in your drink?"

"It's a fact, not a mere thought. That night, you put a drug in a drink and I happened to take it, but you didn't stop me."

"You didn't give me the chance to. Besides, that was ecstasy, which has the purpose of making someone feel good. It's not a date rape drug, and I took one myself."

I have no idea why I'm explaining this to him. I shouldn't. I wouldn't usually, because it's useless. Daniel takes everyone's word as fact except for mine.

I get it, he labeled me a liar, manipulator, and backstabber when we were kids, but it doesn't hurt any less to know that whatever I have to say holds no value to him.

He tightens his hold on my elbow until it turns painful. "Why?"

"Why what?"

"Why did you take the drug? Was it so you and Christopher could have a good time? Did I happen to ruin your fucking plan, Nicole?"

A full-body shudder overtakes me, partly because of the way

he said my name when it's only been an impersonal *Ms. Adler* up until now. But mostly, it's due to the fact that I'm going through a shock reaction.

I recognize it, even though it's simmering in the dark corners I spent years burying and hiding from everyone's reach.

So how come one insinuation from Daniel, one sentence, and the feeling is banging on the surface, trying to claw it open?

The hairs on the back of my neck stand on end and my breathing sharpens, moving in sync with the flutters in my stomach.

All I can smell is weed, strong and potent, and it's mixed with cigarettes and the stench of musk.

I'm going to throw up.

Shit. Shit.

"Let me go," I whisper.

"Did I hit a nerve?"

"Please." I stare up at him at the same time that a tear slides down my cheek. "I know you hate me, and I'm fine with that. I'm fine with the way you treat me as if I'm a rock in your shoe. I'm fine with calling you sir and stomping on the last bit of my dignity to be your assistant, but I beg you, stop touching me."

Any decent human being would do that. Any normal person would at least pause at the sight of tears that came out of nowhere, in spite of my attempts to never show them.

Daniel isn't decent, though. Far from it.

Not only does he grip my elbow harder, but he also reaches a hand to my face.

I'm disoriented by the time his thumb wipes beneath my eye. Then he rubs them, his thumb and my tears, against his forefinger. But it's not the gesture that makes me pause. It's the fascination in his gaze, the way he looks like a researcher who just made a discovery.

It's so rare to see Daniel enamored by anything. He's always treated life as either a game or a chore—never a subject to be absorbed in. Never something to be fascinated with.

But he is now, as he crushes my tears between his fingers with both care and sadism.

"So you do cry."

Before I can react to his words, he grabs me by my nape, the pads of his fingers closing in on the sides. It's like a chokehold, but backward, and it's so familiar that I can't suck in air into my lungs.

Keeping me immobile, he leans down so his face is mere inches away from mine.

His eyes appear like a bottomless ocean in the middle of a night storm.

Dark.

Dangerous.

Deadly.

"Why the fuck do you think you can cry? Do you feel wronged? Victimized? Or maybe you still need sacrifices at your bitchy altar for old time's sake. No matter what's the case, know this, Nicole, I'm going to personally make your life a bloody hell. I'll destroy everything you build and ruin any goals you're aiming for. I'll smash you to pieces and ensure you don't have the ability to pick them up or mend them together. I'll make you wish you'd never fucking showed up in front of me." He releases me with a jerk. "Now get out of my fucking sight. I don't want to see your face unless it's absolutely necessary."

My feet falter with the force of his shove and my heart spills on the floor metaphorically covered with dark splotches of blood.

But instead of hiding and crying like when I was young, I force myself to hold my head high. "Do you think you hate me more than I hate you? Do you think I'd ever choose to see your face, let alone work for an egotistical prick with narcissistic tendencies? Do you think I would ever put myself at your mercy—or the lack thereof if I had the choice? I'm only doing this to keep a roof over my family's head. So you can show me your worst, but you won't be able to break me or force me to quit, *sir*."

He raises a perfectly thick brow. "Is that a challenge?"

"It's merely information."

"I can still fire you, Ms. Adler, so you best remember that the next time you choose to run your mouth or criticize me when you have no right to."

I'm about to argue, but he cuts me off by snapping his fingers. "You're still talking when you should have been out of my fucking sight a minute ago."

I glare at him, but I stop myself from saying anything because I know it will just come out wrong.

And I might get myself fired.

As a compromise, I close the door not so gently on my way out.

I head to the cafeteria to have lunch. This is the only time I'm able to escape the twat's orbit.

In the lift, two secretaries join me, but they ignore my existence as they chat among themselves.

Once upon a time, that would've bothered me, mainly because it meant I wasn't doing a good job being noticeable, but that's not the case anymore. I came to appreciate the lack of social interactions and being in the background.

It's where predators can't find you or hurt you.

I get my phone out to double-check what I should do for my jerk of a boss after lunch, but I can't help focusing on the conversation the two women are having.

"Did Knox decide on his next pro bono case?" The secretary wearing gold-framed glasses asks her much shorter, black-haired friend.

"Not yet. He has a lot of options because of his recent win. How about Aspen?"

"She's still deciding. You know how picky she is about which people she'll represent. Besides, since Kingsley came back, he's been interfering in her cases and making everything difficult."

"Really?"

"Really. I feel sorry for her. It doesn't matter that she's the only senior female partner in the firm or that she's close friends with Nathaniel. Kingsley is making her his target, and apparently, nothing will be able to stop him."

"That's so petty. Just because he owns the firm with Nathaniel doesn't mean he gets to treat people like dirt."

"Well, he is known to have a ruthless reputation, but the way he's making an enemy out of Aspen is weird."

"You never know what happens behind closed doors, girl."

"True." The secretary pushes her gold-framed glasses up her nose. "Anyway, because of the whole Kingsley drama, Aspen's workload has doubled, so she'll probably only offer pro bono legal advice, not representation."

"Makes sense…" the other woman's voice drifts off when they both get out of the lift.

It isn't until the doors close that I realize I should've gotten out on this floor as well to have lunch.

The conversation I just overheard was more important than eating.

So instead of pushing the button to open the doors, I punch the highest floor number that's dedicated to management and senior partners.

The lift asks for my access card and I swipe it.

Since I'm the assistant of one of the partners, I have limited access to the managing partners' floor. I can get up during business hours and only onto the floor, not into the rooms.

Once the lift dings open, I'm thinking about the best way to approach Aspen or ask her for advice.

But my thoughts come to a halt the moment I step out of the lift. Not far from it, Aspen Leblanc and Kingsley Shaw are fighting.

And I mean full-blown fighting with loud voices that echo through the entire hall.

I saw their pictures on the virtual tour HR offered me, but they didn't do them justice. Kingsley appears taller and more imposing in real life.

He's what I call the epitome of American beauty. He has a masculine face, a proud chin, and a muscled body that only adds to his intimidation factor.

This man, who's only in his late thirties, started Weaver &

Shaw with his best friend, Nathaniel, and it's known for its tremendous growth, not only nationally, but also internationally.

The New York branch is the biggest and the most important since the two founding partners use it as a home base.

Although Nathaniel Weaver is the managing partner, Kingsley still has equal power. So meeting him for the first time while he's having a fight is awkward to say the least.

"I told you to stop meddling!" Aspen is facing him. She's about my height but she couldn't be more different looks-wise. Her shiny red hair falls to her shoulders and she has high cheekbones that could cut stones.

Kingsley slips a hand in his trouser pocket, appearing as laid-back as a monk when his eyes tell a completely different story. "And when did I meddle?"

"Meeting my opposing counsel for dinner is the definition of meddling. In fact, it's treason."

"Treason? What do you think this is? Some medieval war?"

"Might as well be, considering your barbaric methods."

"Funny coming from a damn witch. You realize your kind were burned at the stake, right?"

"I'm so over your mind games, Kingsley. And I'm warning you to stay away from my work."

"Sorry to burst the delusional bubble, but I don't have time to waste on you, sweetheart. The counselor and I studied together, so I was just meeting an old friend."

"Old friend, my ass. I'm telling you, asshole, if you don't stop getting into my business, I'm taking you to the board."

He laughs, but it's malicious. And when it dies out, he looks like a demon, complete with metaphorical horns peeking from his head. "You can try, witch. I'm curious to see how far you'll go."

Okay, I really shouldn't be here.

Just when I think about the best way to get back in the lift, Kingsley's attention slides to me. Harsh and unforgiving. "And what do you want?"

I swallow. "I…came here to talk to Ms. Leblanc if that's possible."

"It is not. Disappear."

She jams a finger at his shoulder. "Who the fuck are you to tell me who I should and shouldn't talk to?"

"We're not done yet."

"Well, I am. So how about *you* disappear?" She switches her attention to me and I expect it to be as harsh as his, but it's calm, neutral almost. "Follow me."

I can tell Kingsley is displeased by the turn of events, but I choose to follow Aspen down the hall anyway.

This isn't a chance I'm going to miss.

Once we're inside her spacious office, Aspen pours two coffees from the machine, then sits on the dark red leather sofa and motions at me to do the same. "What did you want to talk to me about?"

"I…it's…"

"I don't have much time, so if you have a point, please make it so I can go to meet a client."

"I heard from the other assistants that you're offering legal advice."

"Why would you come to me for that? Don't you work for Daniel?"

How the hell does she even know that? I only started yesterday and Kingsley definitely looked as if he had no clue who I am.

"And if you're wondering how I know, I make it my business to vet every employee who comes into the firm, no matter how small of a role they play. Now, tell me. Why didn't you ask Daniel for legal advice?"

"We…don't get along."

"I'm still not convinced."

"We go back and he hates me, so he definitely won't help me."

"I see. The fact that he insisted that you work for him makes sense."

My head jerks up. "W-what? He insisted I work for him?"

"He put his foot to the ground like a child whose toy was taken."

The information sinks in like acid at the bottom of my stomach. He really meant to torment me from the beginning. I must've looked like a clown the first time I stepped into his office.

Aspen crosses her legs with the elegance of a model and the confidence of a queen. "So what do you need the legal advice for?"

"It's…for custody."

"Go on."

"The court mailed me from England because the child's father is suing for custody when he never even wanted him. I…don't even have the means to fly to England or leave Jayden alone. And if I do leave him with someone, wouldn't that be considered neglect? If I don't show up, can I lose custody?"

She's not fazed by my word vomit, merely listening with staggering professionalism.

"Slow down and tell me the story from the beginning. I'm not licensed to give legal advice about law in England, but my friends from the London branch will be able to help."

"You would help me?"

"Isn't that why you came to me?"

"I did…I just never thought you'd agree to this so easily."

A distant look crosses her eyes. "I know the feeling of losing a child, and I'll do my best to keep you from going through the same experience."

My heart warms. It's the first time a stranger has ever given me unconditional kindness and I don't know why that makes me want to cry.

I wish I had the courage to tell her how the whole clusterfuck with Jay's father started and see if it could help me.

That bastard has taken so much from me, to the point that I have nothing left.

He's almost worse than Daniel.

Almost.

EIGHT

Daniel

THIS EARLY MORNING, I WOKE UP TO A CONTINUOUS PING OF messages from my group chat with my friends from England.

We played football together back in secondary school and our lives kind of intertwined together. And by that, I mean they're the annoying bunch who like interfering in each other's lives like mothers-in-law on steroids.

Besides, since my best friend married one of the wankers, I was dragged into the middle of their unholy circle of demons.

Not that I'm an angel or anything holy. But there are degrees to that shit, and I'm pretty sure I'm the mildest of the bunch.

Anyway, Ronan and I are usually the heart of the group chat, so the fact that it was pinging while I wasn't in it was the first red flag.

The second red flag was finding that Knox was wide awake in the middle of the night just to catch their time zone.

What I found was enough to make me lose sleep altogether.

Knox: Remember when Daniel came here not long ago with some announcement about the state of my shagging life?

Ronan: Oh, yeah. Turns out, your dick wasn't broken, after all.

Aiden: And I was right and you were shagging one person. Next.

Knox: As they say, karma is a bitch and I'm here to expose him.

Xander: Don't tell me his dick is broken, too? What do they feed you in the States?

Levi: Ouch. I wouldn't know how to deliver that type of news to Astrid.

Cole: Is it just me who thinks this unorthodox fascination with each other's dicks is weird and should be frowned upon?

Aiden: Crawl back into your boring life and let us have our fun.

Knox: No, his dick isn't, in fact, broken. And no, this isn't fascination, it's payback time so Daniel will stop being a dick on Viagra. So here's the trivia moment. Guess who started working as his assistant?

Ronan: One of the blonde hookers you've been sending him?

Knox: Something close to that.

Xander: Fuck me, his assistant is really a hooker?

Knox: No, she's a blonde.

Ronan: Isn't he allergic to those?

Knox: He is, but this isn't just any blonde. She's the original blonde. You know, the one who broke his heart.

Xander: You don't mean…?

Knox: The name is Nicole Adler.

Levi: What the fuck? I thought she disappeared off the face of the earth.

Knox: Apparently not. She's right here at Weaver & Shaw and currently working as Daniel's personal slave. Sorry, I mean assistant.

Aiden: I didn't know Daniel had a thing with Astrid's stepsister.

Cole: Since when do you care about anyone but yourself?

Aiden: You fuck off.

Ronan: Me neither. I thought it was harmless flirting or whatever. I remember Danny boy saying she's a major bitch and that's it.

Xander: I saw them coming out of a room together once. Didn't think much of it. Who would have thought she was the blonde who traumatized him to all blondes?

Knox: He was pissed drunk during university and when I asked why he purposefully avoided blondes, he told me because one of them ruined everything. I had to stop him from hopping on a plane to England in his state. He said he wanted to find her, strangle her, and revenge-fuck her, and maybe do it all over again. And then he was spouting shit about peaches and whatever.

Aiden: Sounds like Daniel.

Xander: Now, I'm intrigued. Hey, Lev, did Astrid mention anything about them?

Levi: Vaguely. Apparently, Daniel is closed off about anything Nicole. He doesn't like any subject that includes her. But then again, Astrid and Nicole never liked one another.

Knox: I'll keep you posted on the state of things here.

Ronan: Send us pictures, dear brother in-law.

Knox: At your service, Ron. Here's to Daniel curing his blonde phobia.

Xander: Amen.

The guys break out in a fit of laughter and continue joking around at my expense.

So I send them screenshots of when each of them was making a fool out of themselves, but that only gets me in worse trouble since their sarcasm meter goes up a notch.

To say I'm grumpy this morning would be an understatement. Not only did the bastard Knox send me another blonde hooker last night, but he also went ahead and started this fucking circus.

The hookers are payback for how I called him out about not wrapping it up for the first time in his life, but now he's making it a damn habit because he's a cunt.

Or maybe I'm in a foul mood after what happened yesterday.

After I saw Nicole's tears for the first time and touched them.

After I heard her say she's only tolerating my despicable presence because she wants to keep a roof over her family's head.

Family.

When the fuck did she get a family? Her father is dead. She left her stepfather's house that fateful day, and her mother is gone, too.

So she doesn't have that. A family.

Or maybe she's not fucked up in the head like I am and made herself a family like normal people are supposed to.

Either way, I reach the office carrying all the demons that I've been hiding for years. They're proudly sitting on my shoulders now, on fucking display for the entire world to see.

And because I'm in a mood, I'm tempted to make someone else experience it, too. Specifically, her.

I stare at my watch, counting the seconds until she misses the eight a.m. mark, but she comes inside at that exact moment, carrying the cup of coffee in one hand and the files in the other.

She's wearing a tight dark blue blouse that's straining against her tits. That's not all, though. The first two buttons are undone so when she leans down to place what she's holding in front of me, I get a front-row view of the line between her creamy pale tits.

I grind my teeth with pure fucking anger at how my dick strains against my trousers.

Being attracted to Nicole or even seeing her as a woman should be the last item on my agenda.

"Here's your coffee and the contract drafts that you asked for. I also emailed you a digital version in case you need it."

"Are you a fucking whore?"

She jerks back at that, her eyes widening. "What is wrong with you first thing in the morning?"

"I should be the one asking that. Is seduction your next scheme?"

"W-what?"

I tilt my head to her chest and she slowly looks down, then

clamps her fingers around the loose buttons. Red covers her cheeks, and if I didn't know her better, I would've said she's blushing.

But Nicole fucking Adler doesn't do any blushing or most normal human feelings.

"That wasn't on purpose." She releases her shirt as soon as she buttons it, then stares at me. "And you're the last man I'd ever attempt to seduce."

"That's because I won't be seduced by you."

"Perfect. We finally agree on something." She fixes me with one of her haughty looks. "Now, if you'll excuse me."

Then she turns around and leaves.

I'm tempted to call for her again, just to annoy the fuck out of her as much as she's making my life hell.

Maybe it's not worth it, after all.

Maybe I should throw her out and continue living like I did before she showed her face in New York.

Then I'm hit with all the fucking things she did and the way she turned my life upside down and I instantly wipe those thoughts away.

Taking a sip of my coffee, I flip through the document. Red marker in hand, I underline any words and sentences that I want replaced and circle the ones that need to be removed.

Once I'm finished, I take it to her. I could call her over, but I like catching her off guard. She'll slightly jump in her seat and her lips will fall open as her green eyes widen.

It's a view I've been actively trying to recreate every chance I get.

Before I open the door, however, I see her leaning against her desk, facing the wall and holding a phone to her ear.

Although her back is the only thing visible, her shoulders are tense and her spine is snapped in a line.

Instead of my plan of forceful entry, I slowly open the door. She doesn't pay me any attention as she manically taps her foot on the floor.

"…I know. I'm sorry, hon. I promise to come a bit earlier today, so wait for me and don't fall asleep, okay? I'll make your favorite dish."

A red haze covers my vision and I'm close to punching the wall.

I don't, though.

I shouldn't be even thinking about such violence.

"Are you having personal calls while working, Ms. Adler?"

She startles and stumbles forward before catching herself at the last second. The phone falls to her side and she stares at me with that frozen expression again.

Only, this time, I find no pleasure in it. The usual feeling is muddying with something else entirely nefarious and somber.

"I…" she trails off.

"You're what? Does the firm pay you to talk on the phone?"

"I didn't think…"

"Obviously. Are you daft?"

"I'm not daft." She lifts her head. "Stop calling me that."

"Then stop doing daft actions. Have another personal phone call while working and it'll be your last. Are we clear?"

"Crystal."

"And drop the fucking attitude. I mean it, Nicole. You're not the one with superiority here."

She purses her lips, but she doesn't make the situation worse and remains silent.

I throw the document on her desk. "I need that back in twenty minutes. Get to it."

Then I return to my office and close the shutters before I act on the animalistic urge inside me.

Hon.

That's what she said.

Fucking hon.

And don't sleep. Wait for me.

And she'll make him his favorite dish.

Since fucking when does she even cook?

She's always been a princess. Always tended to and served

one way or another. So who the fuck would she cook for? Who the fuck would she hold in such high regard?

I pull out my phone and call the only person who can explain this clusterfuck.

She answers with a long, excited, "Bug!!"

Muse's music filters from her end. She's been obsessed with that band ever since we were teenagers.

"Hey, Bugger."

That's what my best friend and I have called each other since we were fifteen. Ever since I saw stars on her wrist and thought they were bugs. I asked her if that's what they were and she was offended because they were the last tattoos her mother did. She swung around to punch me, but we lost balance and fell together in the pool.

Then we were pushing each other while trying to climb out and fell into it again.

We burst out laughing and have been inseparable ever since. Astrid is the only one who's never judged me for being a trouble-maker, for being too flashy and fickle.

She says she understands I'm doing it for a reason. I'm acting out for a reason, and she's there to listen.

I could never find a more loyal friend than her. She's my ride or die. The one I would go to a survival game with and know we'll both come out of it riding our unicorns toward the sun.

Muse's music lowers in volume and she asks in a serious tone, "What is it? Are you okay? Should I fly to New York and beat up whoever is bothering you?"

"Easy there on the violence, Bug. This isn't the Vikings."

"The world would be much easier if it were, just saying. So? What's up?"

"Why do you think something is up?"

"You sound weird."

"What are you, my mother?"

"Well, I am a mother, so I have a different gut feeling. Speaking of mums, yours kinda misses you. It's okay if you call for more than a minute per decade." I can imagine the eye roll without having to see it.

Old pain resurfaces, but I clamp it down. "She has her favorite son with her and that's not me."

"How can you say that, Dan? You chose to go to the States and Zach chose to stay."

"I chose to go to the States after she chose Zach. But my mini family drama isn't why I called."

"Then what is?"

"I want to ask you something, but I won't unless you promise you won't be mad."

"Why would you ask about something that will make me mad?"

"Just promise you won't be."

"Fine. What is it?"

"Have you…heard anything about Nicole since she left?"

There's a pause on the other end and I grip the phone tighter. "Astrid?"

"Why are you asking about her all of a sudden?"

"Just tell me. Do you know anything about her?"

"She cut me and Dad completely out of her life. You know that."

"Surely Uncle Henry tried to get in touch with her at some point? He didn't hate her as much as he hated her mother."

"I don't know. Maybe."

"You sound annoyed right now, which means you're hiding something."

"Maybe *you* are."

"What?"

"Why would you ask about Nicole after eleven years of closing down any conversation I try to have about her? I thought you said she wasn't important when I asked about that summer party. What changed, Bug?"

Something.

Everything.

I'm not even fucking sure anymore.

"I'll tell you when I'm ready, Astrid. Now can you tell me what you know?"

She releases a long sigh. "It's not much, really. Dad once said that he searched for Nicole and when he found her, she was carrying a baby and ran away."

"A *what?*"

"A baby, Dan. You know, like my daughter, Glyndon."

"Nicole has a child?"

"I don't know. Even Dad was surprised by that. He tried to find her again, but it's like she disappeared off the face of the earth."

"How long ago was that?"

"I don't know…our second year in university, so about nine years ago."

My mind goes into overdrive. Nicole had a child nine years ago. That was also the same year she dropped out of Cambridge, per her résumé.

All her references after that are here in the States. Which means she probably left England after Uncle Henry found her with a baby.

A fucking baby.

My fist clenches.

"Oh, and, Bug," Astrid says slowly. "There's something else."

"What?"

"When Dad saw her, he said her face was badly bruised."

NINE

Nicole

Age eighteen

WHAT THE HELL AM I DOING?

There must be a rule somewhere that says I'm not supposed to say things like that in front of Daniel.

I shouldn't be calling him my kink or actually getting on my knees so I can get close and smell him. His cologne has always smothered me and clung to my lungs like smoke.

Lime and bergamot is the type of scent I search for in candles, bath bombs, and male perfume. I secretly keep a bottle, too, for when the feelings get too intense and I need to sense him beside me.

There must be a rule somewhere about how I shouldn't be this attuned to him.

But maybe I didn't read the fine print of that rule. Maybe rules are stupid, after all.

I'm not controlled by them.

Or the world.

Or how lucky I am.

Maybe, as Papa said, I can go after what I want with as much passion as I can conjure.

Or maybe I shouldn't have crunched on the remaining ecstasy pill like it was a sweet.

It only made me sleepy, and I meant to do just that until Mum came to pick me up.

But when I woke up, I saw a scene I thought was a mere translation of my many dreams.

Forbidden dreams.

Fantasies.

That can't be possible, however, because he's within touching distance.

Because the warmth radiating off his body is bouncing off mine and rolling down in the valley between my breasts.

It's creating a path to the bottom of my stomach and pooling between my thighs.

Just why is he so beautiful? Why did he have to steal from the stars and the sky—and me?

Why does he have the type of messy hair that falls over his forehead and begs for my fingers in it?

Why did he have the face and body of a model and the soul of a devil on his quest to win a popularity award?

And why, just why did I have to notice him?

It's become virtually impossible to not look for him anywhere I go as if he's bewitched me.

Maybe he has dark magic in his eyes.

Satanic rituals in his soul.

"I'm your kink?" he asks with slight bewilderment, but he's smirking, those beautiful dimples creasing his cheeks.

Ever since I said those embarrassing words, the air has been thick with tension. Sexual, to be more specific.

The last thing I expected to exist between us.

From his side, at least.

But I see it, in his pants, the bulge that's tenting against the fabric as a clear translation of his desire.

"I put ecstasy in that drink you had earlier," I say instead of giving an embarrassing answer to his question.

Like *you're my only kink.*

Or *you're the reason I even have kinks.*

That would be soul-crushingly humiliating. More than wishing for him to touch me, then stupidly proposing to him while I was dying of an allergic reaction.

"I had one, too," I blurt. "A drink with ecstasy, I mean."

I expect him to be mad, to glare at me like he usually does, but his smirk widens, and it's now laced with sadism.

"I didn't know you were the type who shags."

"Then what am I?"

"The bitch type with an unhealthy dose of mean-girl endorphins."

The sting of his words breaks the surface of my fogged-up head. And despite wanting him with every molecule in my DNA, I won't let him walk all over me.

"Then go find a goody two-shoes for your minuscule penis." I start to get up, but the world is pulled from beneath me.

Or more like, I'm falling backward.

Daniel has pushed me, I realize, because both his palms are on my shoulders. I have too many fantasies to count, but none of them are as real as the view from beneath him.

He's hovering over me, his chest rising and falling as hard as my heaving breasts. "Who said I want a goody two-shoes? Besides, that's the second time you've mentioned my cock's size today, so I'm under the obligation to prove you wrong, Peaches."

Daniel unzips his jeans, then lowers them and his boxer briefs before he sits on his hunches—on my legs.

My eyes must double in size as his penis pops out. No, cock. Yeah, that thing should definitely be called a cock. It's huge and hard and veiny and shouldn't be allowed near a vagina.

"I assume that reaction means you can't proceed with your plan for my funeral?" The amusement catches me off guard.

And I'm tempted to wipe the smugness off his godlike face. "It's not that special."

"Is that why you're licking your lips like you want to have Junior for dinner?"

"Maybe it's because I'm disgusted."

"Stop saying what you don't mean unless you want to get your mouth fucked."

"In your dreams—" I'm cut off when he grabs a handful of my dress and pulls me up by it.

His face is mere inches away from mine and it's red, probably like mine. But there's no smirk there, no taunting mockery, just pure tension that's currently wrapping itself around my neck like a noose.

"You were going to do this with Chris anyway, so don't act like a prude in front of me."

"I wasn't going to do anything with Christopher." *Just you.* But I don't say that, because my dignity took enough hits to break an Olympic record.

"Fuck that and your stubborn fucking mouth that I'll stuff with my dick in a second."

I want to ask why "in a second," but my thoughts are interrupted when he reaches for my back and undoes my zipper, then pulls the dress over my head.

My throat gets dry as I sit in front of him in nothing but my nude-colored bra and knickers. They're lace, too, and cost a small fortune and are so totally worth it, judging by the hungry look on Daniel's face.

It's like he really wants to have me for dinner.

Maybe breakfast, too.

Daniel doesn't open the clasp like a normal person would. His hand latches onto the middle of my bra and rips it open, then he pushes me back down.

My gasp is wordless and as silent as the ruined shreds that fall onto my lap like weightless paper.

He grabs a nipple between his forefinger and thumb, twirling, then pulling with a harshness that wets my inner thighs.

"I always thought you had beautiful tits, never thought they would be this pink and gorgeous. Your tits are made to be fucking worshipped."

Before I can be mortified at his words, his mouth swallows the other nipple, teeth tugging on the erect flesh with maddening expertise.

A loud moan echoes in the space and I soon realize I'm the source. Not only because he's devouring my breasts as if they're his first and last meal, but also because I'm finally focusing on a part of what he said.

"You always thought I was beautiful?" I ask with a voice so breathless, it almost doesn't sound like mine.

He doesn't answer, because he's sucking on my dusty pink nipple like he's in a race to extract my soul through it.

Is it possible to come from nipple stimulation alone? Because my thighs are shaking and I'm sweating. My blonde hair gets in my eyes and I can't push it away because I'm holding on to the sheets for dear life.

He releases one of my nipples, but only so he can lower himself and trail his hot lips down my stomach to my flat belly, lingering on the line that separates it from my core for what seems like an eternity.

"You have the beauty of a fucking angel, Peaches." He rests his chin on my stomach, his eyes clashing with mine for a brief second. "Too bad you possess the personality of the bloody devil."

My belly clamps and I'm not sure if it's because of pleasure, pain, or a combination of both.

I'm distracted, though, because his teeth are on the hem of my knickers. And like the animal that shone in his eyes a second ago, he uses his teeth to slowly slide them down, uncovering my bare pussy.

The act is so erotic that my hands barely keep me upright.

Is this too much or am I thinking that because of the ecstasy? For some reason, I don't think the drug would make me throw myself in someone else's arms.

"You're oddly responsive," he muses, releasing my underwear for a second before he shreds them with his teeth like he did to my bra.

I'm not prepared for what happens next.

Completely and absolutely taken off guard.

I couldn't have imagined it if I tried.

Daniel slides his hot tongue on my clit. One long, single swipe and all my nerve endings explode.

"You're dripping wet, Peaches. Did you know that you taste like a fucking fantasy?"

"S-stop saying things like that."

"Why?" He speaks against my folds, the rumble of his voice adding to the stimulation. "Still too prim and proper for crude words?"

"You don't have to include a commentary for what's happening."

"How else will I tell you that I'll be eating your pussy for dinner while you choke on my dick like a little whore?"

"D-Daniel!"

He chuckles, the sound vibrating on my sensitive skin. Then he lifts his head and licks his lips suggestively. "I have a lot to educate you on. Tell me, have you sucked a dick before, Peaches?"

I remain silent, my pulse about to jump out of my throat.

To say I haven't thought about this moment before would be a blatant lie, but never in my wildest dreams did I imagine that it would lead to this.

I'm completely and utterly out of my depth here.

"You did?" His eyes have darkened, turning pools of deep blue. Then he wipes his finger beneath my lower lip with sudden harshness. "Did these venomous lips open for a cock before? Did they get swollen and red like when you ate those deadly peaches because you liked them? Did you suck and deep-throat a limp dick with these same lips, hmm?"

I can't inhale air properly. His words have stolen my oxygen and sanity and everything in between.

Just how can he sound so damn hot when he says such filthy words? Under different circumstances, I would be saying, "Eww, gross," but I can't even speak now. And gross is the last feeling inside me.

He takes my silence as a challenge, though. Or maybe an acceptance, because his touch turns more explorative, harsh even.

"You won't remember any other cock once I'm done with you."

He releases me and before I can miss the contact, he pulls his shirt over his head, then kicks his jeans and boxer briefs away.

A sculptor couldn't have made a body as perfect as Daniel's. He has a cut abdomen that flexes with his movements, but he's not too buff, not too in your face.

A model through and through.

No wonder scouts kept asking his mother to sign him to their agencies.

No wonder girls fell to their knees in front of him with no effort on his part.

No wonder I couldn't move away from him.

I wish it was only because of his Greek god looks or charming traits. I wish I only saw his exterior and decided that was all I needed.

I wish I hadn't dug my nose into him as much as I did and learned shit I should've never been privy to.

But I did.

And now, I'm too hopeless. Too involved.

Too…obsessed.

With everything about him—from the flutter of his lashes to the flexing of the tendons in his muscular shins.

Everything.

I wish he saw something in me, too—anything.

But if the only thing he sees right now is my body, then so be it.

One day, it'll be more.

…Right?

Daniel flips me on my side and then lies opposite me. His cock juts in my face and his hot breaths are inches away from my pussy.

"This is called sixty-nine, Miss Prude. I'm going to devour your little pussy until I make you scream and you will open those lips and suck my cock like you do those lollipops when no one is looking."

My eyes widen.

How the hell did he see that when I only do it in secret?

I don't get a chance to think about it before he thrusts his hips so his thing is at my lips. *Cock*, I chastise myself. *It's called a cock, Nicole.*

I slowly open my lips and he drives all the way in. My mouth is so full of him and I still don't get it all in.

"Now, suck and make it good."

I hear the challenge in his voice loud and clear, and I rise up to it like a moth who's well aware that it'll burn to death.

My tongue creates friction and I'm rewarded with a grunt. In my haste to do it faster, I graze him with my teeth.

The sound that comes out of him is nearly animalistic. "Don't use teeth, Nicole. Hollow your cheeks, loosen your jaw, and do it faster."

His order is like an aphrodisiac. My movements are less awkward and more determined as I suck him with everything in me.

"That's it, Peaches. Good girl."

I'm surprised my heart doesn't spill on the mattress right here and now.

Shit.

Why did those two measly words coupled with that nickname feel as if he's thrusting inside my core instead of my mouth?

I'm still pondering on the strange sensation his words elicited when he places an open-mouthed kiss on my pussy.

It's so hard and intense that I physically jerk.

But I don't release him. My mouth is still wrapped around his cock as he rocks his hips, driving in and out in a measured rhythm.

His teeth nuzzle on my soaked folds and then he bites down, making me choke on his girth.

Holy...

Why are my teeth not good for him, but his teeth make me feel like I'm about to explode into a million pieces?

His hot lips wrap around the bruised, sensitive flesh and then he's sucking on it.

Licking, teasing, kissing.

The chain of events repeats again. Pain, then overwhelming pleasure.

And just when I'm about to get used to the rhythm, he thrusts his tongue inside my core.

It's intrusive, yet intimate and erotic and so damn intense that I feel myself being rolled to the edge of something. What, I have no clue.

All I'm sure about is that it isn't a mere orgasm. It'll be the mother of all orgasms.

But I don't allow myself to fall into it—not yet. I can't lose to him.

So even if my thighs are trembling and my heart is about to explode from its confinement, I keep on licking and sucking.

It's messy and awkward at best, but I don't fall behind. When he twists my clit between his thumb and forefinger, I reach out to touch his balls.

The more he grunts against my opening, the harder I moan around his dick.

It's a game.

A push and pull.

And we're both not playing by the rules. In fact, there's no such thing at this moment.

No codes.

No rules.

No words.

Just us.

And I'm losing, because his pace has become impossible to keep up with. I'm falling, shattering, and crashing on solid ground.

The orgasm is so hard and swift that I don't even get to think about it as it hooks against my bones and drags me under.

I scream and he pulls out of my mouth.

"W-what? No…" *I don't want to lose.*

"I can't wait anymore. I need to fuck this tight pussy like I need my next breath." Daniel flips around and lies opposite me until his face is mere inches away from mine.

The brightness in his eyes is nothing like I've seen before. Like a rare shooting star, the type people camp outside to see up close and personal.

I choose to think it's because this moment means something to him as much as it consumes me and not because he's simply drugged.

Daniel lifts my leg, places it on his hip and thrusts inside me.

My breath catches as his huge cock tears into me.

Literally.

Figuratively.

Then stops, meeting an obstacle.

"Fuck…" he breathes harshly, his ocean eyes drooping with lust and something else. "Relax, Peaches. If I didn't know any better, I would say you're a virgin."

I turn my face to the other side, biting my lower lip.

He goes still, his cock twitching inside me—probably, like me, needing him to move or do something. I can feel the tension in my thigh beneath my leg.

"Wait…are you a virgin, Nicole?"

Shut up. Shut up.

"Look at me."

I slowly shake my head. I can't bear the heat of his eyes. Can't possibly stand how he'll look at me.

Will it be with pity?

Mockery?

His usual sadism?

While I pretend I can handle that on normal days, I don't think I'm able to right now.

Lean, firm fingers wrap around my chin and turn me so I'm facing him again. So I'm held hostage in that star-like prison. Bright from the inside but dark up close.

"Answer the question. Are you a virgin?"

"Why are you asking?"

"Tell me, Nicole. Am I the first you've allowed to see you like this? The first dick you're letting tear into your tight little cunt?"

"So what if you are? Is that a problem?"

A strange gleam covers his face and takes refuge in his eyes. It's almost…like possessiveness. "Could be."

"What…what do you mean?"

"You're too tight and my dick is too huge." He thrusts another inch in as if to prove a point. "And if I'm your first, I'll probably tear through your virgin cunt and make you bleed all over my cock while I fuck you hard and deep."

"S-stop talking like that…"

"I'm just stating facts so you know what you're in for. It'll hurt."

"Do you think pain scares me?"

I've been in pain for years and I never shied away from it. If anything, I embraced it like a junkie with multiple addictions.

Hopeless addictions.

Up until now.

His lips tilt and I'm blessed with his dimples. For once, they're solely directed at me. "I didn't think it did."

"It doesn't."

"I'll fuck you now and I'm not holding back."

The first stroke nearly has me retracting what I said. The pain sears through me like wildfire when he's all the way in.

I feel him so deep inside me, it's kind of scary that he can even reach such a secret place I didn't even realize existed outside of romance novels.

The second thrust, however, leaves me panting with my lips parted wide. A zap of pleasure pools between us and it's wet, I realize, not sure if it's blood or arousal, but the effect is the same.

My nails sink into his chest and I think I start hyperventilating because he grabs me by my nape and slows his pace.

"Breathe, Peaches. Don't collapse on me."

I use his eyes as anchors and I focus on inhaling and exhaling.

"That's it." He thrusts deep and hard. "Mmm. Good girl."

I don't know if it's the way he's touching me, holding me, fucking me, or maybe it's the way his eyes are trapping mine.

But I come. Hard.

So hard that white dots form behind my lids and my whole body caves into his.

Daniel keeps on driving inside me over and over. And it's like he's elongating my orgasm.

He pulls out and I think he's done, but he flips me on my stomach and grabs my hips so my arse is in the air.

"Did you know that I have a perfect view of your dripping cunt from this position? You're so wet, it's staining the mattress."

"S-stop it…"

"Why? You look the most beautiful I've seen you, Peaches."

The position makes my cheek heat, but I'm unable to process that when he slaps my left arse cheek and thrusts in again.

Oh, God.

It's like being on a rollercoaster. And why the hell am I so turned on by being slapped on the arse?

His pace is more animalistic, as if he was only preparing me earlier. His thrusts turn deeper, harder, and out of control.

My body shakes on the mattress and my head spins as my moans are broken off by his maddening rhythm.

"Dan…slow…down…" The lust is apparent in my chopped-off tone.

"Why? You want me to stop?"

"No…"

"Then shut that mouth, Peaches. I call the shots now and I'm going to fuck you in every position. I'll fuck you for every time you made me want to grab you by the throat and back you against the nearest object. I'll fuck you for every time you screwed me over."

"Dan…"

"Shhh. And you don't have the right to call me that. We're not friends, Nicole. Never were and never will be. I'm not of your standing, am I? No one is."

"Bloody idiot…" I mutter, feeling moisture stinging my eyes, but I don't let it loose.

"You're a little bitch, but not when you're underneath me. Not so high and mighty when you're stuffed with my dick, are you?"

"I hate you."

"Not more than I hate you. But my cock loves your tight little pussy. Mmm. Do you feel how you swallow me in with every thrust?"

I close my eyes, but it's brief, merely a fraction of a second. Daniel wraps my hair in a fist and pulls me back by it until his lips meet my ear.

"Don't hide when I'm fucking you, Peaches. Next time you let a dick in you, I want you to remember how this feels."

He thrusts deeper, harder, hitting a place that makes me see stars every time. Seeming attuned to my body language, he keeps doing it over and over until I'm moaning again.

His grunts echo with my moans, creating a fucked-up symphony. And then he pulls out, slaps my arse again, and shoots his cum all over it.

It stings against my hot flesh.

By the time he releases my hair, I collapse on the mattress, arse still in the air.

I'm exhausted, my body aches, and I feel like I'll pass out.

A heavy weight falls on my back. His chest that's slick with sweat rubs off my heated skin as he whispers in my ear, "Don't fall asleep, Peaches. I haven't even started with you yet."

⚖

When Daniel said he hadn't even started yet, he meant every word.

I lost count of how many times he fucked me.

On the bed, in the shower. Even on the floor.

He put me in positions I didn't think were physically possible and took me to lengths I wouldn't have deemed humanly accessible.

It was the first time I had sex and he turned that into a marathon. But I think it was the drugs that kept me going.

At times, I thought I would faint, but all he had to do was stimulate me and I'd be chasing the pleasure right there with him.

Fucking like animals.

He has the stamina of a sex god, I swear.

No wonder the girls who've slept with him brag about it for anyone who'll listen. No wonder his reputation has reached other schools.

He would do so well as a porn star with a modeling gig on the side.

And that thought fills me with red-hot trepidation. It makes my blood go green with jealousy.

But I can push that to the side because this moment is more important.

We're kissing right now. Or more like, he's devouring me against the shower wall after he fucked me against it.

His lips taste rougher and sweeter than I've ever imagined.

They're like my custom-made drug, and I can keep kissing them until I take my last breath. He's a generous lover who always puts my pleasure before his own, makes me come before he does, and while he's my first, I know most men don't really care.

If I say I'm surprised, that would be a lie. Daniel might have been the founder of my anti-fan club, but he's generally a generous person. He volunteers in charities when other rich kids let their parents' money take care of it.

I'm not only happy that he's my first, but I'm also so utterly relieved.

Sex didn't really interest me. More accurately, sex with other people who aren't Daniel didn't interest me.

His cum trickles down my thigh with the water and that's when my brain that's been fogged with lust catches on.

My lips leave his with a jerk.

Annoyance contorts his handsome face, probably because I interrupted his fun.

His hair sticks to his temples and the droplets of water travel down his chest, kissing his pecs and licking his already semi-hard cock.

"You…didn't use a condom."

"Kind of late to point out the obvious, Peaches."

"Why didn't you?"

"I forgot."

"You *what?*"

He grabs my nape, which I'm starting to think is his sign for me to either shut up or pay attention.

Maybe both.

"Don't give me that attitude when you've forgotten yourself."

"But it was my first time."

"That was at least five times ago."

"And you forgot all those times!"

"I was kind of busy fucking your brains out, Nicole. Don't make a bloody event out of this."

"What if you give me some STD from your previous sexcapades? God knows you've probably dipped in half of London's available holes."

He flattens my back against the wall and I have no choice but to stare up at him. I didn't know he could be so domineering when he sets his mind to it.

"Are you keeping tabs on me, Peaches?"

"In your dreams. I'm just worried about my health."

"Not terribly worried if you didn't bring condoms for your fucking session with Chris." He sounds disapproving, angry even.

"I told you that was not my plan. Do you at least use protection with the others?"

"Why? Worried I'll become a teen dad?"

"One, that would be awful for Aunt Nora. She doesn't deserve your trouble. Two, I'm worried for myself."

"You won't get anything."

I narrow my eyes. "Are you sure?"

"Yeah. What I'm not sure about, however, is whether or not you'll become a teen mum."

"I'm on birth control! You're the last person whose spawn I would want inside me."

He twists his lips with apparent displeasure or exasperation, I'm not sure.

"And who's the first on your list?"

"None of your business. Maybe I don't want kids for the next ten years. Wait a minute, why am I talking about kids with you?"

"Because you secretly want me to be your baby daddy. I'm rich, smart, charming, and most importantly of all, I have the right equipment."

His cock brushes against my thigh, and a frisson jolts through me. He's looking at me like he'll fuck me hard and fast again.

Like he'll make me scream his name while he does it.

"No…no way, Daniel."

"Why not? You're trembling for it."

"Are you a sex addict?"

"You make me a sex maniac, Peaches, and I'll devour you for it. I'll fuck you until neither of us can stand anymore."

"Don't you…hate me?"

"I can still want you."

"That's all?"

His eyes meet mine, but it's brief before he lowers his head and sinks his teeth into the space between my collarbone and shoulder, then speaks against it, "Believe me, you don't want anything else from me."

"Why…not?"

"Because the world is beneath you, Nicole. Me included."

I shudder, and it's not only because his teeth are back to that sensitive place, biting and sucking like he needs to engrave something on my flesh.

A memory.

A memento.

Or a detail much more nefarious.

My body melts against his as I scramble for words to tell him he was never beneath me.

He was and will always be my darkest, most forbidden fantasy.

"Daniel, I—"

"Fire!" Someone bangs on the door as commotion filters through from outside.

Daniel and I look at each other and then he's pulling me out of the bathroom and into the room. We hastily dry ourselves and Daniel puts himself together in no time.

Then he sighs when he sees me fussing with my dress's ribbons.

"Give it."

He doesn't wait for me. He snatches the dress from between my fingers and puts it on me with staggering efficiency. I have no underwear on and my wet hair drips onto the dress, but that doesn't matter as Daniel grabs me by the wrist and drags me out.

A commotion greets us in the hallway. People running, others screaming, and fire extinguishers being used in the most amateurish way.

I'm slightly overwhelmed by all the chaos, the smell of smoke, and the shouts.

Daniel, however, seems more focused than me. He moves forward, pushing everyone out of his way as he keeps me firmly behind him with his warm hand wrapped tightly around my wrist.

And just like that, the whole turbulence loses meaning. The dread from the fire is now nonexistent.

He then brings out his phone and holds it to his ear.

"Pick up, Astrid. Come on."

I bite my lower lip the more his brows draw together when she doesn't answer.

As soon as we get outside, it's chaos. The left wing of the house is completely in flames. Students are taking videos, others are running or screaming or being loud for no apparent reason.

"Nicole!"

"What?" I realize Daniel is speaking to me when he snaps his fingers in front of my face.

"Do you have your car?"

"Yeah."

"Can you drive?"

"No. I feel a bit drunk."

"Fuck. Just wait here."

"What…where are you going?"

"I need to find Astrid. She's not answering her phone."

I grab onto his arm with both hands, and for the first time since I've known him, I say, "No, go back with me."

It doesn't matter that I already asked Mum to pick me up, I want him to be the one who does it.

His brow furrows and when he doesn't make a move, I do something else I've never done. I beg, "Please."

His eyes clash with mine for a second, and I can see his walls tumbling, but before I can peek at what's behind them, he pulls them right back up.

Daniel removes my hand from his arm. "I'll find Astrid and be right back."

And then he's running through the house again.

I fall to a sitting position on the steps, my heart hammering and my chest wounded.

It's dripping blood on the concrete; no one can see it, but it's right there.

Dark.

Red.

Lethal.

The need to cry hits me like a natural disaster that demands to happen, but I don't let the tears loose.

I stay.

I wait.

In the midst of the chaos, the fire, the firefighters.

I sit there and wait.

And wait.

But Daniel never came back for me.

And just like that, I've become invisible again.

TEN

Nicole

THE BASTARD.

The freaking cold-blooded, Machiavellian bastard with a villain complex.

I'm really starting to think that Daniel's sole purpose of existing is to turn my life into a 3D nightmare.

It's been two weeks since I became his assistant and he made every single day a rollercoaster ride. The type where you come out of it puking your guts up and cursing like a sailor on crack.

If I'm a minute late, he makes me work an extra hour. If one single thing isn't done according to his snobbish requirements, he makes me redo it a thousand times, then throws it away.

I tried taking the high road, tried to ignore his cold barks and harsh words, but it keeps getting worse.

Almost as if he wants me to snap.

As if he's provoking me to call him names and get myself fired.

But no.

I can do this.

Or more like, I have to.

Aspen got me in contact with one of her acquaintances in London. Andrew is an English solicitor specializing in family law and was most accommodating on the phone call we had. He told me that I have to be there for the court hearing in three months.

A no-show is bad for the records. He also said it's a lucky break that I have a stable job in a law firm. That, and everything I've done for Jay through the years, will play in my favor.

What won't, however, is how much I've moved him from state to state searching for better work opportunities. The fact that Jayden is a genius and should be treated as such means his father will argue that he has the means necessary to send him to the best schools out there. Not to mention that judges prefer biological parents if they prove they've redeemed themselves and want to take care of their children.

Last night, I stayed awake in bed, gripping my necklace and thinking maybe I should step on my heart and let Jay get the education he deserves. But I soon chased that thought away when I recalled who his father is.

There's no way in hell I'll let him live with an abusive predator, even if we have to sacrifice an elite education for it.

Aspen even said she'll finance my flight and accommodation in England until I save up the money to pay her back.

She'll also handle the solicitor's fee.

"This is only an upfront investment," she told me when I said I don't know how I'll pay her back. "You will go places, Nicole. I see it in your eyes and I hope you'll also be able to see it soon."

I didn't tell her that I don't even like thinking about or looking at myself. Not since that day at least.

But Aspen doesn't need to be burdened by that. She's my only ally at W&S and I intend to keep our relationship close.

When I asked her not to tell Daniel about any of this, she gave me a look, but she nodded.

The last thing I need is for Daniel or anyone from my past to get involved in my business.

I left England for a reason and I intend to keep it that way.

That is, if I don't end up killing my boss and being charged with second-degree murder.

Inhaling a deep breath, I carry the documents he demanded to his office. Now, I just need to knock and then go in. He doesn't demand I wait for his approval anymore.

He's on his laptop, typing at a rapid speed, completely and utterly focused on his task.

I try not to get ensnared by the view, by how his lean fingers fly gracefully over the keyboard or how his brows slightly dip when he's on a task.

I try not to ogle his masculine face or broad shoulders that nearly burst through his shirt. Or how the cuffs are rolled over his powerful forearms, which are now veiny, unlike when we were younger.

I really try.

But most days, I fail. Most days, I keep thinking there's no harm in looking.

I'm just…looking.

Not dreaming, hoping, or fantasizing.

That foolish side of me was brutally murdered a long time ago.

"Are you going to spit out what you're here for or do you plan to stand there like a second-rate statue?"

I'm used to his cold shoulder by now, but I can't help the heat that burns my cheeks or the clamping in my stomach. Thank God he's focused on his laptop or he would've caught me ogling the hell out of him.

He finally spares me a glance, his eyes closed off, frosty as arctic ice. It's as if he wants to shake me or choke me these days. I don't know which, or why he's awfully hostile.

I've been trying my best.

But that's never enough for the perfectionist jerk.

"Are you sick, Ms. Adler, or do you look like a dreadfully undercooked squid for sport?"

Inhaling a calming breath, I walk up to him and place the documents on his desk, resisting the urge to throw them at his illegally attractive face. "I finished the draft, proofread it, and sent it to the paralegal and emailed her a copy. I also squeezed in a ten-minute meeting with her tomorrow before lunch. Your dry cleaning was sent to your house and I emailed you a summary of the cases HR sent you."

He flips through the pages while I'm speaking. He usually skims any work I do and still finds mistakes and snobbish remarks to say.

This time, however, I'm sure he won't. I got Aspen's expert view when we had lunch together today. She offered to help when she found me foaming at the mouth and calling Daniel a thousand colorful creative names.

So I spent the entire afternoon doing everything else on the list he sent me through the day.

It's seven in the evening, two hours after the time I should've left, which is a record compared to the past two weeks. Since I used to leave extremely late, per his majesty's orders. Sometimes, after they turn off the lights in the whole building.

Today, at least, I'll be able to get back at a reasonable hour and actually cook something decent for Jay.

I feel like I barely see him these days and although Mrs. Potter watches over him, I'm still worried. Not to mention what he must've felt after he saw the court's mail. He doesn't tell me these things, but I know he hates his father as much as I do.

He's scared of him, too.

As much as I am.

"Are you waiting for an award, Ms. Adler?"

I focus back on Daniel. "What?"

"You're either slower than a vintage train or you prefer to play daft on a regular basis, both of which need to disappear if you want to remain in this position. Now, answer my earlier question, do you want a pat on the back or a biscuit for doing your job?"

"No, sir."

"Then what are you waiting here for?"

"C-can I go home?"

"Get the fuck out of my face."

I jolt at the abrasive tone. What the hell is wrong with him lately? He acts as if my existence is the work of the devil and he's the angel sent to wipe me out.

Or maybe it's the opposite.

I glare at him, then leave, biting my tongue so that I don't explode on him. I'm finally going home early, so I won't allow my temper to ruin it.

On my way out, I call Jay and tell him to get the ingredients for pasta out of the fridge.

He acts cool, but I can hear the excitement and glee in the little rascal's voice.

As soon as I get home, Mrs. Potter hugs me and tells me he's been such a good boy, then goes back to her place. Jayden and Lolli jump from the sofa and he hugs my waist. His face hides in my chest for a long moment. "Missed you, Nikki."

"Missed you, too, baby." I throw my bag on the floor and wrap my arms around him. Sometimes, it amazes me that he was a baby not so long ago, but now, he's all grown and will probably become taller than me in no time.

"I'm no baby." I can hear the scowl in his tone, but he doesn't pull back.

"Yeah, whatever." I ruffle his hair. "Have you taken your medication?"

"Yup!"

"That's my good boy. Want to help me cook?"

He looks up at me, showing me a toothless grin. "Hell yeah."

"Wait, look what I got you." I rummage through my bag under the watchful eyes of a curious Lolli, then produce a key chain.

Jay gasps, snatching it from my hand as his pupils turn into saucers. "Kevin!"

Is that the name of the Minion? Well, I guess. I found it at a stand on the side of the road and had to buy it for him.

Jayden has always been obsessed with the Minions ever since he watched *Despicable Me* as a toddler. The small collection he assembled over the years is the first thing he packs whenever we move and he even makes sure they're safe and sound by peeking in the drawer where he keeps them every night and morning.

"Thank you, Nikki." He hugs me again. "He's going to be happy to join the family."

I shake my head as he adds them to the "Minions drawer."

After changing into a comfortable woolen dress, Jay and I get to work.

He's more like my cheerleader and a sloppy salad chopper, but he oohs and ahhs over everything I do.

I'm more meticulous about cooking and I find great pleasure in it. Jay always tells me I should be a chef, but he's honestly the only one who has tasted my food, and he's a bit biased. Besides, just because I love cooking doesn't mean I should pursue it professionally. Though, a part of me has been secretly yearning for it.

Maybe after Jayden grows up.

Despite Jay's awful sous-chef techniques, we make it work in less than thirty minutes, and then we have our dinner.

He prepares the table, which is basically him lighting the cheap Walmart candle that we save for special occasions. Like his birthdays.

I stopped celebrating mine when I fell out of grace.

"What's the special occasion?" I motion at the candle.

He rolls his eyes. "You getting a job, duh."

I slide across from him. "Even if it means we don't spend much time together?"

"It's okay. I understand that you have to work so the court doesn't take custody away. I can be on my own sometimes or with Mrs. Potter. I don't mind."

"Oh, Jay." I fight the tears stinging my eyes. "I'm so sorry."

He lowers his head. "I'm sorry, too."

"Why?"

He moves the pasta on his plate. "Because you have to go back to England because of me. Because he…he's coming for me."

"No one is coming for you, Jay. Not when you're with me."

He lifts his innocent eyes to me, and they're wide and expectant. "Promise?"

"Cross my heart and hope to die." I smile and motion at the pasta. "Now, eat your food."

He digs in, appearing satisfied. "So good, Nikki."

"Eat up, then."

I'm about to take my first bite when my phone dings with a text.

My heart nearly reaches my throat when I see the name.

Bloody Idiot: Come to my flat. I need you to review a last-minute contract.

No. No, he doesn't.

Bloody Idiot: And bring me something to eat from Katerina's.

My fingers are basically punching the screen when I type.

Me: Excuse me, sir, but I'm off duty and spending personal time with my family.

Bloody Idiot: I don't give a fuck about your personal time or your family. And you're not off duty unless I say otherwise. Be here in thirty minutes or don't bother showing up to work tomorrow.

I release a frustrated sound that makes Jay pause eating and give me a "what's going on?" look.

"It's just my twat of a boss."

"Your typing sounded like you were about to punch someone to death."

"Him, preferably," I mutter, then sigh. "Sorry, Jay, can I take a rain check on the film? I have last-minute work."

His shoulders hunch, and I hate how he quickly fakes a smile. "It's okay. You'd fall asleep anyway."

"So sorry, baby. But I will stay for dinner."

Jay smiles genuinely at that and my heart bursts. What have I done to deserve this blessing?

I call Katerina's restaurant beforehand to ask them to prepare me the meal, but Jonas informs me that they're not accepting orders anymore.

So I tried to tell him it's for Daniel and even begged him to let one slide, but he snobbishly hung up the phone in my face.

He and his chef have never liked me since that pesto and parmesan incident, which Daniel threw away as I predicted.

My gaze falls on my untouched plate and I chew my lip as an idea pops in my head.

This way, I get to spend a few more precious minutes with Jay. Daniel will throw away anything that's not from Katerina anyway. He throws away half her dishes, too, because he's picky as fuck.

I really only witness him consume unhealthy amounts of protein bars sometimes.

Ten minutes later, I reluctantly kiss Jay's head, put the pasta in a takeout box, and head to Daniel's flat.

This isn't the first time I've been to his building. He gave me access to his flat on the first day I started working for him so I could personally deliver his dry cleaning.

This is the first time he's called me from his flat, though.

And for some reason, when I get out of the taxi, hugging my bag, the place doesn't feel familiar.

It's an up-and-coming building in the heart of New York City with security that rivals the Queen's palace.

A flat here is worth twenty-six million dollars. I know because I heard a lady bragging about it on the phone, and she only lived in a normal flat. Not like Daniel who's in a penthouse with special access.

The concierge, a kind old lady, smiles at me. We've become acquaintances over the times I've been running like a headless chicken and she's helped push the button for the lift for me.

She does it again and I thank her before I type in the code to Daniel's place.

The lift opens straight to his living area. The interior of his flat is black and blue and as impersonal as funeral services.

Yes, it's luxurious and screams money and status, but it's as cold and frigid as its owner.

And judging by his overloaded schedule and night fun, he barely spends time here anyway. It's like he keeps himself busy on purpose. Why, I don't know.

The sound of giggling reaches me and I pause, thinking I overhead something. Does he have kids over?

Who in their right mind would leave their kid with that insufferable jerk?

I step into the living room and pause when I realize it's not a kid that's giggling.

It's a woman.

Two, actually.

Each one is hanging on Daniel's arm like a hooker in a Christmas parody.

The green-eyed monster rears its head, filled with rage I've never experienced before.

Is this what he called me in the middle of the evening for?

Is this what I left Jay sad and heartbroken for?

You know what? That's it.

I've had enough.

ELEVEN

Daniel

NICOLE LOOKS AT ME AS IF SHE WANTS TO KILL ME THEN
throw me to rabid dogs.

I share the feelings.

Or maybe mine go a step further.

Maybe mine is mixed with an unhinged sense of hatred that
I don't usually allow myself to feel.

A hatred that's so childish in nature but also lethal.

The reason I chose to become a solicitor isn't because of a
warped sense of justice or even profit.

It's because I'm vindictive. To a fault. With enough black emotions to drown the Dead Sea.

And because I'm vindictive, I've become colder to Nicole. I've
turned her everyday life into hell and made sure she never goes
home at a reasonable hour.

Except for earlier today.

I had this thought that was basically "what the fuck are you
doing, Daniel?" and decided to let her go home.

Until I had a glass of whiskey—or two, that is—and started

imagining her with her "family." The same family she was on the phone with the other day and called "hon."

No clue why, but I became equal parts annoyed and murderous.

That's why I magically invented a contract and ordered her to come over.

The girls just showed up on their own because I sent a half-drunk text.

It doesn't even take effort anymore. They see my face on magazine covers and hop on my lap like kittens with separation anxiety.

It's all too easy. Too convenient.

Too fucking boring.

I don't have a goal in life aside from building a career, I guess. I don't even think about opening my own firm like Knox does, because…well, I didn't choose law because I could see myself practicing it for life. I chose it because it was the farthest thing possible from my beloved family affairs.

I don't have that, either. A family, I mean. Not after Father fucked every escort his assistant could get her hands on, then died while he was with one of them. Fitting as fuck, if you ask me.

As for my mother, she checked out years ago, not to mention she always preferred Zach over me. To say our relationship is stagnant would be the understatement of the century.

We barely speak. Actually, change that to never.

I haven't visited England since I left it.

Not even once.

If Astrid misses me, she makes a trip here, but those trips have become few and far between ever since she had three spawns.

I swear that fucker Levi keeps knocking her up for sport.

Point is, I might have subtly cut myself off from the family tree, but I've done well for myself and got everything I strived for.

The only thing that's not easy, convenient, or boring is the woman standing in front of me, her blonde strands about to catch fire from the flames in her eyes.

They're so light and green and fake.

She is fake.

Or was.

Either way, I want to fucking strangle her for it.

The feeling is mutual apparently, because she looks about ready to transform into a hulk and smash me into the nearest wall.

"You're here," I drawl the words nonchalantly with boredom in my voice.

"Obviously." She throws a dirty look at the girls who are still clinging to me as if they're extensions of my body. "I thought there was a contract to review."

"There is. Over there, on the table."

"You clearly have company."

"Doesn't mean you can't work."

"If you're too preoccupied with other things, surely this can wait until tomorrow."

"It can, but you'll work on it tonight. Now, sit your arse on that chair and proofread the contracts."

She purses her lips, which is her way to stop from spouting nonsense, then whirls around in a cloud of metaphorical smoke and forcefully sits down.

I expect to see ashes surrounding her, but none appear.

Yet.

The girls giggle, smelling of strong perfume that nearly bleed my nostrils. One of them kissing me on the cheek. "Let's go to your bedroom."

"We'll make you feel good," the other says.

Apparently, it's not quiet enough, because even though Nicole is focused on the documents and the tablet, her leg bounces under the table and her lips are set in a thin line.

I know because I'm watching her like a hawk. My attention isn't on the girls, it's on her.

The ice in my whiskey clinks as I swirl it and take a sip. "You can start right here."

They giggle again, and the sound is annoying. What are they, preschoolers?

Nicole never giggled. Not even as a child. She always had elegance and was the walking form of proper manners. Now that I think about it, I don't remember seeing her laugh either.

And probably never will, considering my status as the warden of her hell.

One of the girls lowers herself between my legs and I lazily open them wide, letting her settle in the middle.

She looks like a malnourished pubescent, which I know she's not, but the fact that she reminds me of a minor is a major turn-off.

Or maybe the whole fucking scene is.

I keep comparing them to Nicole's voluptuous body that's become sexier than a porn star's. Not that she wasn't hot back in school, but she's all grown up now.

All woman.

The girl brings my attention back to her when her fingers latch onto my belt and she meets my eyes with a seductive look. "I'll start. Remember when you told me I'm good at giving head?"

No, I don't, but I nod absentmindedly anyway. "You're a doll."

Nicole jerks up to a standing position, taking the documents with her. "I'll finish these in the kitchen."

I resist a smirk by taking a sip of my drink. "You'll finish them right there."

"It's distracting."

"I pay you to tune that out. Sit down."

She glares at me, but there's something else in there, hatred and a feeling I can't identify.

When she doesn't make a move to comply, I jerk my head to the chair. "Sit the fuck down if you want to keep your job."

"My job doesn't entail witnessing my boss receiving sexual favors."

"Sexual favors? What the fuck is this, a detective show? It's called a blowjob, and if I say your job requires that, then it does."

"Are you trying to prove a point?" she asks, her face red, whether with anger or something else, I'm not sure. "If that's the case, then I already know you get more pussy than Casanova during his prime and you love it. I get it, congratulations on the meaningless record. Now, can I please go home?"

"No." I slowly push the one kneeling in front of me. "Both of you, out."

"W-what?"

"Do you have hearing problems? I said get out."

They pale, but not more than Nicole as they grab their flimsy bags, give her a dirty look, and saunter out of my flat, huffing and puffing as if they have breathing issues.

I stand and Nicole watches my every move, closely, without blinking.

"Are you going to sit or should I throw you out as well?"

She flops down on the chair, her gaze glued to the paper.

"Where's my food?"

She fumbles in her bag and produces a container.

"Doesn't look like Katerina's."

"The restaurant didn't accept orders when I called so...I brought food from another place."

"Always going against orders."

"I couldn't exactly force open the restaurant or make her fix you something. You know, with the thirty-minute time limit and interrupting my quiet night."

I stare at her, but it's not because of the attitude. I'm starting to think she'll never lose that mouthy side, no matter how much I threaten to fire her. And for some reason, I don't want the fire to disappear either.

The reason behind my pause is the way she's speaking while reading from the document. Multitasking at its finest.

I slide across from her, abandon my glass of whiskey and open the container. Even I know drinking on an empty stomach is bad, and since food is the work of the devil, I wouldn't have come near it with a ten-foot pole if it weren't out of necessity.

I grab a fork and glare at the pasta as if it's my next battle. There's neither parmesan nor pesto, because for some phantom reason, Nicole knows I don't like them.

Fact is, I don't like all food, but those two were what made me vomit the first time.

Still can't figure out how she knows about my preferences, but that doesn't deny the sense of satisfaction that fills me at the fact. "Since when do you like quiet nights?"

She slowly lifts her head, appearing taken aback by the question. "I've always liked quiet nights."

"Could've fooled me with all the parties you made sure to become the center of attention at."

Her eyes glitter, turning a molten green, almost too bright to look at.

Too real.

Too…uncomfortable.

She's every obscure emotion that religions ordered humans to stay away from.

She lowers her head, allowing a stray strand to play hide-and-seek with her face. "Back then, I was chasing an unreachable dream."

"And now?"

She tucks the blasphemous piece of hair behind her ear and sighs. "Now, I'm just surviving, Daniel. I wouldn't have worked for you and allowed you to treat me like the dirt beneath your expensive Prada shoes if that weren't the case."

Nicole is not the dirt beneath my shoes. She's the rock in it. Always has been since the first time I saw her and thought she was a snobbish little princess.

She still is.

It doesn't matter if she wears cheap clothes from a department store. Being a princess is an aura and she exudes it from a mile away.

"You mean to tell me you didn't like the attention?" After enough procrastination to trick my stomach into accepting the devil's fruit, I take the first bite of the pasta and pause.

Usually, I don't.

Usually, I swallow my food without even chewing. It's only

a mundane thing I religiously do so I'll survive. I've never taken pleasure in eating.

Not since I saw my father kissing that woman with food all around them; then a week later witnessed him fucking another woman, by inserting all sorts of vegetables and fruits inside her arse while he had his limp dick in her cunt.

Place of the traumatizing event—the table we ate at every day.

Time—when I was twelve.

I told Astrid I loved my mother's scones and we often fought for them, but whenever I had a taste of those unfortunate things, I threw them back up when my friend wasn't looking.

It's a habit I had for seventeen years, so I became a professional at training my stomach on which times it's allowed to be a freak and which times it has to act as if food is the creation of heaven.

The taste of this pasta, however, is…peculiar. Simple yet exquisite in its ordinary ingredients.

"I didn't," Nicole replies to my earlier question. "Attention exhausted me. I always had to look a certain way, speak a certain way."

"Be a bitch in a certain way."

"That, too." She has the audacity to flip her hair and I'm tempted to pull her down by it. "Couldn't let anyone beat me in anything."

"Until you lost it all." I take another forkful, pausing to savor the taste. "Hurts to fall from grace, doesn't it?"

"Not really. It felt peaceful."

I narrow my eyes. "It felt peaceful to lose everything you ever owned?"

"It was never mine. I only enjoyed what I was given."

"Am I supposed to applaud you now? Be fooled by your "I'm a changed woman" speech?"

"I don't want anything from you, Daniel."

"Not even your job? Because the door is right there."

"Aside from my job." She focuses back on the papers, fingers digging into the edges as if she's stopping herself from ripping them to shreds.

It's then that I realize I finished the pasta, the first meal I've enjoyed in…forever. I don't even remember liking food all that much prior to the "Dad fucks with food" episode.

"What's the name of the restaurant?"

Nicole's head whips up so fast, I'm surprised it doesn't roll on the floor post-decapitation style. "W-why?"

"Give me a name."

"They're…nobodies. I mean, they're small. If you didn't like it, I promise not to get you anything from there anymore."

"On the contrary, I need all my future meals from there. What are they called?"

"Lolli's," she blurts, then winces.

"Bit weird name for a restaurant. Sounds like a stripper's stage identity."

"It is what it is." She pauses, then asks suspiciously. "You really liked the pasta?"

"It's fine." It's the best meal I've had since I was a teen, but she doesn't need to know that. "Just tell them to have more variety and I'll pay handsomely."

"Got it." She has a shit-eating grin on her face, and it makes her features happier, shinier—almost too girly.

Ever since she came back to my life, I've been so angry and pissed off, and a million other indefinable emotions, that I failed to notice just how much she's grown up.

In a way, she's still the same Nicole who made every male's head turn in her direction. The Nicole who left a cloud of cherry perfume behind her—the scent boys jerked off to in their lonely showers.

The Nicole who called every one of those sorry cunts gross, and other colorful synonyms for even attempting to breathe near her.

But then again, she's not the same. She's more reserved now, more introverted than extroverted.

And she's ten times prettier than she was eleven years ago. Her curves are that of a woman and her face has matured with age.

She stopped hiding the tiny beauty mole above the left corner of her lip with makeup. Every fashion magazine considers that a sign of beauty, but for Nicole, it was an unwelcome disturbance of her flawless face.

I always liked it, though. That small distinction made her perfectly imperfect. Prior to when she hid it like her life depended on the fact.

Before I realize it, I'm reaching out for her face, for that small imperfection that she's finally embracing.

The moment my fingers connect with it, she jerks, her wide eyes meeting mine.

"Why do you no longer hide this?" I ask, ignoring her disgust with me and the squeezing in my chest that I'm promptly chalking up to being half-drunk.

"Why...why are you touching me?"

I don't know either. Could be the alcohol or the way she grinned or the fact that she's even in my vicinity again when she shouldn't be.

It's over.

I erased her from my life.

I fucking got over her.

So why does she think she can walk back in and set each of my barriers on fire?

"Answer the question, Nicole. You started hiding this as soon as you hit puberty. Why do you no longer do it?"

"How do you even know that?"

"I just do. For the last time, answer the fucking question."

"Because I used to feel self-conscious about it."

"You don't anymore?"

"I don't really care now."

A heavy silence falls between us as I glide my index finger over the tiny beauty mark and accidentally—or not really—brush against her upper lip.

My skin refuses to leave hers, refuses to part from the warmth mixed with tremors.

So I don't.

Like an addict, I continue sniffing the forbidden powder.

Nicole inhales stuttering breaths, her lips parting.

"What happened after you left?" The question leaves me before I can stop it.

I'll blame that on the alcohol, too, even though I usually hold my liquor like a sailor.

Her compliant albeit confused expression disappears and a fire ignites in her eyes.

"You're eleven years too late for that question." She jerks to a standing position and slams the documents on the table. "I'm finished. So if you have anything you want to be changed, please let me know, sir."

"What the fuck got your knickers in a twist?"

"You and your useless questions. What do you care what happened eleven years ago when you never glanced my way?"

I never glanced her way?

What in the ever-loving fuck, and I mean this, type of crack is she on?

"Should I remind you of what you've done, Nicole? If I make a list, I'll break some fucking record."

"Just like you broke a record of being a stage-one bastard, you mean."

"Did you just call me—your boss—a bastard?"

"You're the one who brought up the past. Why would you? Do you like tormenting me for fun?"

"Maybe I do."

"Maybe you have too much time on your hands."

"Not nearly enough to turn your life into hell. I have a wish list of the things I'll do to you every day."

"I hate you."

"Careful, Peaches. Hate is a mixture of love and jealousy on steroids."

Her mouth falls open and I realize my mistake too late.

I called her Peaches after vowing to never use that nickname again.

Before I can retract it or think of an insult to erase it, she clears her throat. "I suppose the fact that you're not reading the file means you're not in a hurry. So, I'll take my leave."

Then she's practically jogging out the door, leaving her cherry perfume behind.

It's cheaper, not nearly as strong or authentic as back then.

But just like eleven years ago, I'm left confused, angry, and with a fucking hard-on.

TWELVE

Nicole

"**Y**OU'RE FIRED."

My mouth falls open in an O.

If I hadn't been a zombie who didn't sleep for the whole night and had to hug a small box I shouldn't have kept, I would've probably processed the words better.

Or maybe I did, but my brain is unable to catch up.

Jay has had a nasty fever and, even worse, asthma that made him wheeze for breath without his inhaler. I found him squeezed in a ball beside the sofa while Lolli fussed around him.

I had to take him to the emergency room at midnight and monitor his fever all night long.

Apparently, he's been feeling sick for a few days, which is why he went to sleep early. When I asked him why he didn't tell me, he said he didn't want to worry me or distract me from my "twat" of a boss.

My eyes are puffy from so much crying by his bedside. I cried for not being there for him, for making him an adult trapped in a child's body, and especially for not seeing the signs of his sickness.

The doctor told me his asthma will get worse with the fever and I should keep a better eye on him.

I only breathed a sigh of relief this morning when the temperature went down and Jay even got up and took a shower.

I made him food, gave him his pills, and told me I'll try to come back early today.

The chance to bring up the subject to Daniel hasn't even risen yet, and he just told me I'm fired.

Ever since that night in his flat a week ago, he's been colder than usual, standoffish. Proper insufferable.

However, I took it all in.

The jerk attitude and the snobbish tendencies.

I even became accustomed to it and his dark sense of sarcasm that he showers me with on an everyday basis.

It's become a routine, especially since he completely abandoned Katerina's restaurant and started to eat the meals I make. He even let me surprise him with what type of dish it would be.

Good thing is, I now bring in my food and his. Bad thing is, I shouldn't be feeling a sense of pride every time he licks the dish clean. Not once has he thrown out my food, unlike what he sometimes did to Katerina's.

The worst part of all is that I can't stop thinking about the way he touched me that night or his tone when he asked me what happened after I left.

A question that made me mad and sad at the same time. A question that I carried with me for eleven damn years and still can't find the answer to.

What really happened?

How did fate bring me to his doorstep to be his glorified slave just so he'd fire me?

I stare at his imposing presence behind his desk, clad in a dark gray suit and his groomed lawyer look. "Excuse me?"

"You are excused. Take your stuff with you on the way out. If you leave anything behind, I'll throw it away." Daniel shifts his attention to his laptop and completely erases me from his vicinity.

As if I were insignificant.

Unimportant.

Invisible.

If it were the past, I would've tucked my tail between my legs and left. I would've accepted my "not seen" status and just disappeared.

Or watched from afar.

Not now, though.

Not when Jay's future depends on it.

"Why are you firing me?" I ask in a clear, neutral voice.

"I don't need a reason to determine that you failed the trial period." His concentration is absorbed by whatever's on the monitor.

"But I want to know."

"I don't explain myself to you or anyone else, Ms. Adler. Don't forget to pass by HR so you'll get paid for the average work you've been doing these past three weeks."

A hot fire courses through me, and I have no clue if it's because of his scathing words or the fact that he completely ignores me as he says them, or maybe, just maybe, this is an overflow for all the pent-up energy that's been building inside me for weeks.

Slamming my palms on his desk, I lean over so my face is right above his stupid screen. "My work isn't average."

"You've been consistently late in some way. My coffee isn't always one gram of sugar—that is, if it came on time. You have the habit of talking back and offering your unnecessary opinions. I called your work average as a form of a parting gift. If you want the truth, your work for the past three weeks has been nothing short of disastrous." He checks his watch, then slides his attention to me. "And you're five minutes late."

"That's because I had an emergency. Jay had a fever and I had to nurse him all night long. He wouldn't have had the fever if you didn't keep me working until unreasonable hours."

"You won't have to anymore, because you're fired. And spare me the details about your love life." There's a bite in his tone, an ice-cold harshness that rattles me to the bones.

A frown etches itself between my brows. "That's not…"

"Out. We're done here."

My lips tremble and it takes everything in me to trap the tears of frustration from spilling free. "You never meant to employ me long-term, did you? It was a game of yours, all this time, you only wanted to play around with me, then chew me out as if I never existed. It didn't matter if I busted my butt for you, if I woke up at dawn to cook your freaking meals or bring your precious coffee on time. It doesn't matter if I endured your sadism or your abrasive behavior. If I sacrificed my personal time to tend to your demanding schedule and every selfish whim. No matter what I did, you would've found a reason to fire me."

"Congratulations for finally figuring it out."

My plans fall to pieces in front of my eyes, and all I can do is stand there and watch, then silently mourn the pieces. Without being able to pick them up.

"I hate you," I murmur before I realize it.

"Your feelings for me or the lack thereof mean jack shit to me, Nicole."

I knew that, ever since a long time ago, but I still wanted to hurt him. Still wanted to sink my nails so deep into him, he wouldn't be able to breathe without feeling pain.

"You were always a jerk wrapped in good-boy looks, Daniel. You might have charmed everyone, but I saw the ugliness in you. I saw the boy who was so disgusted with himself, he made it his mission to make everyone love him. Daddy issues, wasn't it? I saw you that day, when we were twelve. You witnessed your father with a woman who wasn't your mother and came out from the restaurant, then threw up your food. It's why you've hated pesto and parmesan ever since. Why you barely eat anything, why you're pickier than royalty and just as snobbish. Your little-boy dreams about your father were tarnished, so you decided to grow up into a worse version of him. You grew up into a cardboard imitation of a human. I pity you, I truly, most definitely do—"

My venomous words are cut off when he abruptly stands up,

erases the distance between us, and grabs me by the arm, then flings me against the wall. And it's a full-blown fling.

A yelp spills from my throat as my back hits the wall and he stands in front of me like a ruffled savage.

He's breathing so harshly, his dress shirt nearly rips from the abrasiveness of it.

Only an inch separates my breasts from his heaving chest. If I take a deep inhale, I won't only be able to smell him, I'll also become one with him.

As tempting as that option is, the expression on his face isn't. For the first time since that "night," he's not put-together or businesslike in his coldness.

Something is melting his ice. Anger, maybe, or rage—the black kind.

"How dare you say you pity me when you're the pitiful one? You came begging for a job as my assistant. A job where I can eat up your life for breakfast and throw out the leftovers for the dogs. You're no longer in your untouchable tower, Nicole. You're no longer a princess or a bloody fake goddess, so don't pretend a crown is sitting on your fucking head."

"Maybe you should stop pretending that the world revolves around you."

"Never pretended. My own world does revolve around me and you're a mere nuisance in it. One I'll crush before it becomes an issue."

I try to pretend his words didn't just cut me open, slide into my wound, and ruin its infected stitches. I try to pretend I'm not affected by his words or his accusations or his...presence that's enveloping me in a vise-like grip.

"I should've never given you my lollipops," I whisper quietly, lamely.

Every time he hid from people to throw up from the sight of food, I followed close, pretended I saw him by coincidence, and slipped one of my precious lollipops in his hand.

In his bag.

In his jacket.

On the bench beside him.

Anywhere.

Then I stayed behind to see if he'd throw it away like he does with food when no one's looking. But he didn't. Every single time, he stuck the lollipop in his mouth and then crunched it instead of savoring it.

He still ate it, which was all that mattered.

And I made it a habit to slip a lollipop or two in his bag every day.

He probably forgot about that, though. He seems to have crossed the past from his life.

"No, you shouldn't have. I hated them as much as I hate you." He leans close, so close that I breathe in his air. "You also shouldn't have come here after everything that went down."

"It wasn't on purpose."

"We'll rectify that then. Get out and don't ever come back. If we meet by chance, pretend you don't fucking know me. I'll do the same."

A hiccup the size of a ball gets stuck in my throat, but instead of bawling my eyes out in front of him, I run out of his office.

Out of his reach.

Out of his toxic presence.

Then I finally let the tears loose.

Just like I did eleven years ago.

THIRTEEN

Nicole

Age eighteen

THREE MONTHS.

It's been three whole months and two weeks since that night everything went terribly wrong.

Except for the popping my cherry part—yeah, that one went perfectly right.

It's probably the rightest thing that's happened to me after being born.

The only thing that's surpassed my every fantasy.

And that's where the problem lies. Due to being an experience out of magic land—or filthy land—semantics—I couldn't stop thinking about it.

Not even after Daniel ditched me like a used condom—that he didn't put on while deflowering me or the gazillion times after.

I still think about the people who looked at me as if I'm a nutcase and should be admitted to a psych ward for sitting at the step of a literally burning mansion.

The similarities weren't lost on me and they were probably right. After all, I sat on those steps, watching the entrance like a pole dancer watches the Queen's notes.

I didn't blink, didn't move, and definitely didn't pay attention to the chaos unfolding around me.

It's how unhealthy obsessions work. The world kind of ceases to exist, and the only time it does is when it's working as a vessel for the subject of my obsession.

Who, if you didn't gather already, didn't show up.

The one who did was my mother. She grabbed me by the elbow and kind of shoved me into her car, which was very unlike her. Showing any violent behavior, even while enraged, is very unladylike-like.

I chalked it up to the fact that she was mad for finding me in the process of killing myself.

Daniel didn't call or text that night. Granted, we don't have each other's numbers.

Correction—he doesn't have *my* number. I stole his from Astrid's phone when she was too careless to leave it unlocked three years ago.

He's gone through an excessive change of nomenclatures on my phone since then.

Lollipop.

Peaches.

Snow Globe.

Fantasy.

Obsession.

Unhealthy.

And the very latest is my favorite.

Bloody Idiot.

No clue why I had his number for years when I never called or texted him. I guess knowing he was in there was enough before.

Now, it's not.

So what if he didn't have my number? If he wanted to change

that, he could've asked Astrid for it. Despite my strained relationship with my stepsister, we do have each other's numbers.

But then again, she's the reason he ignored me all summer. That night, Astrid was involved in a hit-and-run whose culprit remains free.

They found ecstasy in her bloodstream, due to the shot Daniel snatched from me and gave to her. Uncle Henry has been mad at her for doing drugs.

To be fair, I'm sorry about that, but not enough to out myself in front of Uncle Henry. Mum would kill me. Well, not exactly, but being disappointed in me is no different than that.

After my peaches incident, she didn't speak to me for three months and only got back to talking to me when Uncle Henry started to notice. I still have nightmares about that.

If she hears I'm the one who unintentionally drugged Astrid, she'll think of ways to erase me from her existence.

And I'm kind of invisible to someone else so I don't need that double torture.

Besides, ever since her accident, Astrid has possessed Daniel's attention worse than his favorite tacky action films.

As a result, he hasn't looked at me, hasn't spoken to me, and certainly hasn't spent any alone time with me.

It doesn't help that he was at a football camp for most of the summer.

But even after we got back to school, he just ignored my existence as if I no longer existed.

He's back to being Royal Elite's heartthrob, a charming athlete, and Astrid's side piece.

I don't even recognize myself around her anymore. Sometimes, I catch myself genuinely wanting to hurt her. Genuinely wishing she never came around.

Genuinely wanting to push her into the pool.

Those thoughts were scary.

My feelings for Daniel were even scarier.

If I was willing to go that far to have him, what did that make me? Desperate? Obsessive?

An unstable lunatic?

Maybe it's a combination of all three.

And the worst problem is that I can't put an end to these toxic, hate-infested thoughts.

Or the emotions behind them.

It's why I'm wearing Levi King's jersey at tonight's game. Chloe is wearing Ronan Astor's because she's always after the hottest piece around.

I am, too.

Just differently.

Since that night when Levi's family holiday mansion went up in flames, he's been getting suspiciously close to my plain stepsister.

Sometimes I wonder what she has that I don't. What makes the hottest, richest boy in school and Daniel so wrapped around her tiny finger?

She's a bit tomboyish, weird, and entirely unsophisticated. She doesn't even like her own father's lifestyle.

That hasn't stopped Levi from following her around like he wants to strangle and fuck her at the same time.

And while I don't care about that, Daniel is getting in the middle of it.

I heard him when he was watching stupid Vikings—her favorite show—with her in our pool house. The same pool house in which he spoke to me, touched me, and held me for the first time since that peaches incident.

He told her she shouldn't get involved with Levi and that he would satisfy her sexual needs instead.

That was exactly three months and two weeks after he fucked me so senseless that I couldn't walk properly for a few days.

It doesn't matter what I let him do to me. Given the chance, he'd go to his precious Astrid.

But she's into Levi.

Which is how my plan comes into play.

After the game, the football team throws a party at Ronan's house.

Chloe and I tag along, then break up at the entrance. Since Ronan's father is an earl, he has the mansion that goes with the title.

When I first came here for a collector exhibition thrown by his mother, I was struck by how much the place seems out of a fairy tale with its high-end furniture and prim and proper servants.

However, since his parents often travel outside the country, Ronan has sort of turned this into a brothel/club/casino.

The number of ignorant fools walking past precious paintings and spilling alcohol over premium carpets is insulting.

Still, I ignore the chaos and any attempts anyone makes to talk to me.

I'm on a mission.

So I walk straight to it.

To a private room where Levi and a few team members have retreated.

The stench of cigarettes, weed, and alcohol wafts in the air like the stench of death.

But I keep my head high as I slide to Levi's side. He blows a cloud of smoke in my direction but looks at me as if I'm the dust on his shoes.

He's looking at me at least, so that's a good sign.

"On your knees," he announces out of nowhere and I want to smack that rich-boy smugness off his face.

"I'm not a whore," I bite out.

"On your knees or get the fuck out of here."

My eyes trail off to the door. *Papa, if you can send a sign, then please do that now.*

Preferably him.

But I'm just too naïve. I should've stopped believing in Papa and wishes made upon passing stars.

I should've stopped having the same wish for my past ten birthdays.

Wishes that never came true.

Wishes are meant for fairy tales, shooting stars, and imaginary worlds.

Biting down on my pride, I fall to my knees between Levi's legs. He jams two fingers in my mouth and I resist the urge to gag and throw up all over his limited edition designer shoes.

Imagine it's him.

It's not Levi. It's him.

I start to suck, but Levi tuts. "Stay still."

A bulge grows in his trousers and I reach for it, thankful that my hand doesn't shake. "Wow, you're so big."

Someone kill me.

What the hell am I doing with Levi?

He grabs me by the shoulder when a gasp fills the air.

Both Levi and I turn at the same time to find Astrid standing in the entrance, her eyes wide and sad and angry and every emotion I've been feeling for the whole summer.

When Daniel chose her over me.

When Daniel abandoned me and went to her.

I meet her gaze. How does it feel to be invisible to the one you like, Astrid?

"I…um…thought Dan was here. Sorry to interrupt."

She bolts out, jamming the door shut behind her and I break out in hysterical laughter.

It doesn't feel satisfying.

Not in the slightest.

It's humiliating and downright embarrassing for me to be between Levi's legs in the first place.

For me to be on my knees because of a man who didn't see me. This isn't me.

"Why the fuck are you laughing?" Levi snaps.

"The little Viking learned her place both at home and here."

"At home?"

"She's my stepsister, but not for long. Now…where were we?"

I reach for him again. I need to at least start it for when Daniel comes to see the show.

I have no doubt that Astrid will go cry in his arms like a damsel in distress.

He's her knight.

I'm their villain.

Levi shoves me away, telling me to go swallow someplace else.

He doesn't see my middle finger as he storms out of the room.

I stand to my full height with barely conjured grace and flip my hair. I can sense eyes on me, snickers from the rest of the players, but I don't let them get to me.

It doesn't matter what type of reputation I'll gain from this, especially since I used to reject boys faster than an audition.

The deed is done and I'm officially following the devil on my shoulder.

As for the angel, that one is strapped to a peach. I can't touch or listen to him unless I'm in the mood to die.

I feel high by the time I get out of the room. No, not high.

Miserable.

They touch the same emotions inside me. The emotions where I want to dive into a pool and drown or maybe eat a peach and die by the one thing that I love one-sidedly.

So I sneak into Ronan's kitchen. A stuffy middle-aged butler slides in front of me like Dracula in an inhabitable palace. "How may I help you, miss?

I adopt my very polite, very good-girl tone. "Do you have peaches?"

If the request baffles him, his expression doesn't change as he echoes, "Peaches?"

"Yes, the fruit."

"One moment, miss."

He disappears into another door and I stand there like an *Alice in Wonderland* character, trying to ignore all the crazy that's going on at the party around me.

Did that guy just hug a pillar?

"If you're in the mood to swallow, all you have to do is ask, sweets."

I shudder, but it's the bad kind. The *creepy* kind.

Chris needs to seriously stop sliding up from behind me out of nowhere. He grins at me, and I subconsciously step back.

His eyes are bloodshot red as if his blood vessels murdered each other in an epic battle.

"Heard you wanted to swallow for Captain?"

"No, I didn't." I wouldn't have finished the blowjob even if my life depended on it. I only wanted the rumors and to get either Daniel or Astrid so they could have a front-row seat.

"No need to be shy about it." Chris reaches for me. "I can satisfy you."

"Eww, gross." I slap his hand away. "Don't touch me."

His face hardens and before he can come near me, the butler returns with a whole bowl of peaches and hands it to me.

"This is…a lot," I say.

"In case you need them," he says, all serious.

I smile, then take my peaches and sneak to a small gazebo at the back of the garden, overlooking a fountain.

It has a devil and an angel.

Ha. Ronan's parents are as poetic as my two sides. Everyone knows the devil always wins. We're designed to be bad. Goodness comes with so much headache, stomachache, and most importantly, heartache.

Opening my small bag, I take out a lollipop and suck on it. Peach-flavored, of course. It's synthetic, so I'm safe with it.

This is how I've survived my craving for peaches all this time. But I have to do it in secret ever since Mum called it juvenile.

I place the bowl beside me and grab a peach, then hold it beneath the moon. It's crazy how a small fruit could send me to an early death.

Still, my mouth waters with the desire to have a bite.

One taste.

I'm kidding myself, though; one taste is never enough. Not even hours of that taste.

Not even multiple orgasms because of it.

"*Killed by a Peach* would look so fucking depressing on your tombstone."

I startle as a shadow falls over me.

Daniel.

Breathe, Nicole. You have to breathe.

I slowly stare up at him.

He has both his hands in his jean pockets and that causes his shoulders to stretch his Elites jacket.

Daniel always looked beautiful, but he's equally scary right now.

Like a volcano that's about to erupt. An allergic reaction slowly building in the background.

Ignoring his demeanor, I focus on his words, still clutching the forbidden fruit and sucking my lollipop. I feel defiant enough to do it in front of him.

I'm so badass that I'm sucking a lollipop.

"I'd still look pretty and unique and I would die doing something I love."

"What are other things you love doing, aside from sucking cock, I mean. Didn't know you were a whore."

My chest aches. I expected him to hear about the Levi fiasco and predicted his reaction. Didn't think it'd hurt like being stabbed with a peach-flavored knife.

"That's funny coming from a manwhore." I pull out the lollipop, then pop it in again, letting it snuggle in the side of my cheek.

A dark smirk tilts his lips as he watches the motion. "If you want dick, all you have to do is ask."

"That's the second time someone told me that tonight. You guys must be so desperate for these forbidden lips."

His eyes narrow. "Who asked you?"

"Don't remember. Don't care. As for your invitation, I'm going to have to decline. I'm still testing for STDs after that one time. You know, after you forgot about me."

A muscle works in his jaw, disturbing his otherwise calm face. "Astrid had an accident."

"Cool." I stand up, ready to nurse my bleeding heart with a dozen lollipops. "Why aren't you nursing her wounded heart about Levi, then? Oh, were you looking for her and found me, instead? It's a bit dark out here, so you might have mistaken us."

He grabs me by the shoulders and I yelp as he pins me against the bench. I'm on my back and the peaches are scattered around us like murdered shooting stars.

Daniel hovers over me, knees on either side of me, and glares down at me with the fury of a warrior. "You think I would mistake you for anyone when you're driving me fucking nuts?"

My heart starts to soar for the sky and have those misconceptions that left him with multiple plasters. So I clamp my feelings on its misplaced hopes and adopt my angry tone. "I'm driving you nuts? Who abandoned the other after fucking them senseless *without* a condom?"

"Astrid got into that accident because she was high on the drug I gave her." He speaks so low, I feel the hiss of it against my skin. "Do you think I was in the mood to shag the evil stepsister who was behind the whole fucking drug idea?"

"Who told you I would let you touch me again? It was a one-time thing, so don't flatter yourself." My voice drips with cool venom, but it must be as cutting as his words, because his jaw clenches.

"Is that why you're moving on to Levi?"

"None of your business."

"I'm making it my business. If you're doing this to hurt Astrid…"

I'm doing this to hurt you as much as you hurt me. But I don't say that, opting to remain silent.

"You're a fucking nuisance, Nicole."

"Your thing didn't think that when it was prowling inside me."

"A hot nuisance, and for the last time, it's called a cock and the act goes by the name fucking, Miss Prude." There's amusement in his tone. "You didn't really suck off Levi, why not?"

"How do you know I didn't?"

"Cole was there and told me the actual story."

I search his unreadable face. "Why did you ask?"

"Because." He tightens his hand on my arm. "You came on to Captain, but you looked disgusted, is what Cole said."

"Cole needs glasses."

"So you prefer being called a whore instead of telling the truth?"

"I prefer you leave me alone."

"I can't."

He pauses, eyes widening as if he's as surprised by what he said as I am.

"You…can't?"

He shakes his head once. "You're actively working to make my best friend's life hell, and I want to strangle the fuck out of you for it, but I can't leave you the fuck alone."

"The three months you didn't even look in my direction would testify otherwise."

"Maybe you're the one who needs glasses."

"What?"

He plucks the lollipop out of my half-open mouth. It leaves a sticky, wrinkled trace on my inner cheek and sweet drool gathers in my mouth.

Before I can think about what he's doing, Daniel shoves it in his mouth. The motion is so sudden and erotic that I gulp.

He sucks on the sweet candy, hollowing his cheeks before he pops it out and runs his tongue over it like he did to my pussy that day.

Over and over.

And over.

I gulp, my inner thighs clenching.

Then he crunches the lollipop in a few seconds, crushing the view as if it never existed.

"You're…supposed to savor it," I whisper, still unable to get the previous scene out of my head.

"I prefer getting to the sweet part faster." He leans down and captures my lips in a slow kiss.

The taste of peaches explodes on my tongue.

My forbidden fruit and my forbidden person.

My body goes into a shock reaction of emotions that leaves me breathless.

Daniel grabs me by my nape, his fingers sinking into my hair as he deepens the kiss.

It's madness and we're the only people in it.

The only two allowed entrance.

I lift my hand, about to touch him, to lick all the peaches off him, but something vibrates.

It's his phone, I realize. He groans but doesn't release me, but it vibrates again and again and he pushes off me with a grunt.

"Oh, for fuck's sake."

He stares at what I assume is a text, then back at me with lust and trepidation. "I have to go."

My heart that briefly revived to life shrivels again. "To Astrid."

"She called my brother over so he'd drive us home."

I shove him away, my limbs shaking so hard, I'm surprised they're working.

"Nicole." He grabs me by the elbow, spinning me around.

"What? You have your precious Astrid waiting for you. What do you want from me?"

A look passes his features and I wish I could use up all the wishes and lamp genies in the world to know what it means. "You and I…are impossible."

"Obviously. Good luck being Astrid's boy toy."

"Oh, please. It's not about Astrid. It's about you, Nicole. You're vindictive and vicious and a general bitch. I don't want that."

"Clearly. Judging by the tent in your pants."

"Physical reaction."

"Were the five times you fucked me that night also a physical reaction?"

"I was drugged."

"The drug doesn't make you want someone you don't, Daniel."

"Yes, it does."

I see it then. He desperately wants to believe that, he wants to believe that he wouldn't touch me with a ten-foot pole if he had a choice.

But he did touch me just now and he's sober, which is why he's frustrated.

I don't know whether I should laugh or cry.

So I settle for a smile. "What if I say that wasn't the case for me? What if I told you I wanted that night? That I felt it like nothing before?"

"Then you'd be lying, because your plan was Chris."

This bloody wanker.

I want to poke him in the eyes.

Instead, I settle with throwing a jab at him. "Maybe he's still my plan, and now that you ruined it, I have to work twice as hard."

A flash ignites in his blue eyes. It's so harsh and fast that I physically stiffen.

"So that's what the sucking Captain episode was all about? Getting Chris's attention?"

"Maybe it was."

"Best of luck attracting fucking losers."

"Seems I have a record with those." I flip my hair. "I consider it pro bono work."

His eyes flash again and he reaches a hand for me, but before it can touch me, his phone flashes and he shakes his head, then turns around and disappears.

Again.

Giving me his back.

Again.

And this time, I feel like I really lost a part of him.

One I won't be able to recapture.

Still, I lick my lips and the taste of the peach lollipop, praying for a day where I'll be able to eat actual peaches.

But that's probably as impossible as wishing Daniel would ever accept me.

Like me.

Want me.

And not feel disgusted by it.

FOURTEEN

Daniel

Present

MY FIST CLENCHES AROUND THE CUP OF COFFEE I HAVEN'T taken a sip from, even though I've been clutching it harder than necessary, then I throw it in the rubbish bin.

Fuck.

Bloody fucking hell.

It's been an hour since I fired Nicole, but the wildfire that's erupting inside me isn't close to dying out.

She just had to run her mouth about what never should've been spoken out loud. How the fuck did she even know all those details when my own mother, brother, and Astrid didn't?

Everyone thinks I'm picky with food because I'm hard to please or that I'm being a dick on purpose.

Everyone looks at the surface.

Except for fucking Nicole. The previous queen bee and the resident evil of my childhood and teenage years.

It doesn't make sense that she of all fucking people knows.

I'm tempted to go find her, grab her by the hair, and make

her talk. I'm tempted to do a lot of things while grabbing her by the hair.

There was a tremble in her body when she stood in front of me, even while she didn't cower away. Even when she met my malicious stare with a venomous one as if she was the wronged party in this.

As if she's the fucking victim.

Maybe making her work for me was a mistake. Plotting revenge against her was also a mistake.

I expected to feel triumph for tormenting her and turning her life to hell, but that's the last thing I'm feeling.

It's, in fact, nonexistent.

In fact, it might be the exact opposite.

But I have the decency to trick my mind into thinking I'm relieved and should ride some unicorn to the sun.

Maybe burn in the process.

It's what happened before, I got too close to the sun and it roasted me alive.

That's the thing about the sun.

I could look at it all I want, could even spin in its orbit, but the moment I touch it, my only destiny is to burn.

The door to my office opens and I stare back to find Knox standing there wearing a stupid fucking grin.

"What?"

"Looks like I'm going to win the bet."

My eyes track his movements as he rounds my desk and stands in front of me, facing the window. It must be my fucked-up mood and the need to fill it with anything that makes me swallow the bait. "What bet?"

"If you'd bothered to check the group chat today, you would've seen it."

Narrowing my eyes on him, I retrieve my phone and go to the group chat that I muted after they made me the joke.

After ignoring several of Ronan's one-man show texts, in

which he's promptly ignored but carries on anyway, I stumble upon Knox's text.

Knox: Who's in the mood for a game?

Xander: Hell yeah.

Cole: I'm bored, so why not?

Aiden: Did someone say a game?

Knox: It's more of a bet, actually. As everyone knows, our Dan the Man is traumatized by blondes because a bombshell who goes by the name of Nicole broke his heart. He says he's keeping her as his assistant for revenge, but I was neither born yesterday nor am I blind. I see the sparks.

Levi: Are you going to keep your one-sided monologue going or is there a bet in there?

Knox: I was getting there, if you had some patience, twat. Now, where was I? Right. I bet ten thousand dollars that Daniel will cave to Nicole like a hooker for an old rich man.

Cole: Ten thousand pounds, not dollars.

Knox: Call.

Xander: Count me in.

Levi: I'll raise you fifty thousand.

Aiden: Make it a hundred for me.

Xander: What? Why? Why are you and Levi raising? What did I miss?

Aiden: Your whole second year in school apparently, because Daniel used to watch Nicole like a kicked puppy who was crushing on the prettiest Chihuahua.

Knox: Did you just compare them to dogs?

Aiden: Your point is…

Xander: Explain the reason why you and Lev raised?

Levi: I know things, but no questions, please. I won't answer until the bet is over.

Ronan: I'm here! Miss me, fuckers?

Cole: As much as the desert misses the sun.

Ronan: Stop it, you. Don't make me blush.

Aiden: Astor, read Cole's message again. Slowly this time.

Xander: *laughing out loud emoji*

Ronan: Wait a minute. It's always sunny in the desert, so it doesn't miss the sun.

Cole: Exactly.

Ronan: Fuck you, Nash. You're not invited to my next party and the one after. Actually, you're on a three-month ban and working your way up to a permanent ban.

Cole: Be right back. I'll go cry in my pillow.

Knox: Focus, Ron. We're now in at one hundred eighty thousand pounds for Daniel caving to Nicole and announcing their wedding soon. Are you in?

Ronan: Sure as fuck. Let's round it up to two hundred.

Knox: Fantastic. If Daniel caves in a month's time, he pays us. If he doesn't, we pay him.

"Better start writing checks, Danny." Knox grins when I finish reading.

"You're the one who should pay me. I'll start with your check." My jaw clenches. "I fired her."

"Nice try."

"She's fired, Knox. Sorry to take away your change, but I'll gladly accept it."

He narrows his eyes, then searches her empty office. "You really fired her?"

"Her three-week trial is over and I don't wish to keep her as my assistant."

Knox watches me weirdly, as if I pissed on his engagement picture that he recently had taken with the mafia princess.

It's one step below how he looked at me when I made the mistake of suggesting she sleeps with me because I'm a better fuck.

I am, but nearly having my nose broken for it was not worth it.

This motherfucker might seem charming, but he's a criminal defense attorney. You should never trust someone who not only likes to get their hands dirty, but also strives for it.

"You sorry cunt," he lets out in a whisper laced with a small chuckle.

"Either say what you want or piss off."

"You're even angry about it. Fuck, I should've raised my bet and took more change from you."

"Do you have a point you're about to reach? Preferably in the next ten seconds, before I kick you."

"Don't you see it?" A smirk tilts his lips. "You're so into her, you fired her so you wouldn't have to suffer by seeing her every day. I could've slapped any label on you, my friend, but a coward twat was never one of them. Until today, naturally."

"I fired her because she's incompetent."

"She's the best assistant you've ever had. You know that, your few functioning neurons know that, and even your dick would know that, too, if you stopped fucking random brunettes and gave him what both of you truly want."

Before I can summon my dick-ish remarks, my office door is opened with a force that slams it on its hinges.

Aspen appears on the threshold, her red hair resembling flames from Satan's favorite lair. She crosses her arms and taps her shoe on the floor.

"What is this?" I stare between her and Knox. "Barging into Daniel's office day?"

"You fired her?" she asks in a slow, menacing tone that she usually reserves for the actual devil of this firm, Kingsley.

"I'm sorry, who's her?" I fake nonchalance.

"Adler. Nicole Adler, who you've been a dick to ever since she started working here."

"I don't remember inviting you to my employer-employee TED talk, Aspen."

"And I don't remember you having the type of small dick energy to actively ruin a woman's chances at custody."

I'm about to show her my actual dick size and risk a sexual harassment suit, but before I can go the crazy route, her words sink in.

My throat closes as if I'm sobering up. Or getting drunk. I can't tell for sure.

"Nicole has a custody case?"

"Yes. In England." Aspen taps her shoe more manically. "She didn't want to tell you, because, in her words, 'You hate her and would rather see her lose than help her,' but the least you could do is let her keep a steady fucking job. Now, she'll be at a huge disadvantage in front of that abusive jerk."

I want to hit the wall for very irrational reasons. Like why the fuck does Aspen know all this information about Nicole and I don't?

Because you made it your mission to erase her from your life. How is that working for you, by the way?

I shoo away the voice that's perched on my shoulder, even though I'm not sure if it's a demon or an angel in disguise.

He probably figured out I only listen to a creature with two tiny horns and, therefore, decided to start an up-and-coming fashion house that imitates an obscure section in hell.

"I'm bringing her back as my second assistant and you will stay the hell away from her," Aspen tells me. No, actually, she informs me, and I'm starting to realize why people find her insufferable. She's the reason redheads are stereotyped as hellions who only ride the devil's face.

"No you won't," I inform her right back, sounding calm and definitely not on the verge of throwing her and Knox out the window.

"Yes, I will. Stay out of my way or I'm calling a board meeting on your ass."

"Kinda bold coming from someone who's facing their own board meeting. Heard King is kicking you out soon, Aspen. Will my disciplinary shit happen before or after yours?"

"First of all, he's not kicking me out, not unless he wants me to haunt his nightmares. Second of all, if you don't let her be, I'll make sure to bring you down with me, even if it's the last thing I do."

"That's a good one." Knox grins. "I wish I'd brought some popcorn."

Aspen lifts her chin. "You have two choices, Daniel. Leave her alone or suffer. Which one will it be?"

"I choose the third."

"There's no third option."

"There will be after you tell me the whole custody fiasco."

"Why would I?"

I grind my teeth and catch Knox grinning in the background and throwing imaginary popcorn in his mouth.

An hour ago, I was contemplating burning my office and detaining myself for my foolish behavior.

An hour ago, I was burning with fire because she said she spent the night taking care of her lover whose name is Jay.

An hour ago, I felt no different than the teenage me who couldn't stop looking at her as she sucked on those damn lollipops where no one could see.

And I hated it.

All of it.

Now, I also hate it as I say, "Because I'm possibly the only one who can help her."

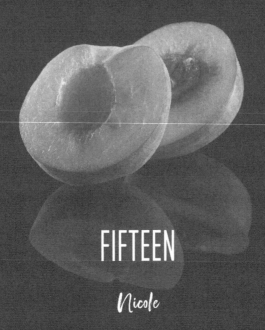

FIFTEEN

Nicole

"**N**IKKI?"

I sniffle, wiping my eyes on the back of my shirt sleeve. I'm glad I bought this thing at a store sale and wouldn't mourn it being ruined with blotches of tears.

The thing is, I kind of spent the whole morning and some of the afternoon crying like a crazy lady behind a tree in a nearby park.

I just couldn't go back to Jay looking like shit—though that's an epic failure on my part—and I had to think about a lot of things. Such as how desperate I am to beg Daniel.

And I am desperate.

Extremely so.

But I broke any semblance of professionalism between us by bringing up his wound. The wound he hid so well that normal people would never have noticed.

Hell. Even his mother didn't, and I suspect Astrid didn't either, considering how much she always liked to shove food in his face.

But then again, I was never normal when it came to Daniel. I was either obsessed, completely unhinged, or desperate.

Just not desperate enough to go beg him.

He wouldn't take me back anyway, not when he looked two seconds away from strangling me—and not in a fun way.

Maybe if he cools down, I can muster the courage to talk to him? That's the plan anyway. I think he's better to approach when he's not in his devil suit, channeling the Lucifer in him to make other people's lives hell.

And that time is usually at night.

For that, I need to make him a nice meal and take it to his flat—that is, if he didn't put my face and name on the "call the police once spotted" dial.

Trying to remain positive, I spent the afternoon grocery shopping for dinner and shushing my inner sinister voice that told me no amount of food will make him agree.

It's the reason behind these fresh tears, but anyway, screw that voice.

I won't know until I try.

Jay trots in front of me, wearing his Minions pajamas and socks, proudly displaying an obsession he never outgrew.

"You're back early." Instead of sounding happy, he frowns. "Are you okay?"

"Of course." I touch his forehead. I called him a few times and he said he was better, but I have to personally make sure. "Your fever is really gone."

"You thought I was lying to you?" He narrows his little eyes on me. "Are you sure you're okay? You called me so many times today and even came home early. Are you in trouble because of me?"

"What? Of course not." I take the shopping bag to the kitchen.

"You're lying to me, Nikki. I'm a man now; you can tell me if something is wrong."

"Oh, my little rascal is a man?" I turn around and attack his sides. "I didn't realize, knowing how ticklish you are."

He breaks out in laughter and runs away. I catch up to him

and wrestle him to the sofa, tickling him until he's about to lose his breath.

He loves this game a bit too much, but I can't do it for long or I'll aggravate his asthma.

"This is oddly domestic."

I freeze, thinking I'm probably losing my mind. That velvety deep voice can exist anywhere but here.

In my home.

My eyes must resemble a deer caught in the headlights as I stare at him. Wide. Unblinking.

He stands in the middle of the living area like the Grim Reaper with a sole target.

Me.

I slowly ease off Jay and smooth down my wrinkled skirt. "D-Daniel? What are you doing here?"

"The door was open. Might think about locking the thing in the future, considering you live in a shithole."

My cheeks redden at his easily delivered harsh words. He's not even looking at me. His entire attention is on Jay, who's straightening up and squaring his shoulders, which is extremely comical when coupled with his Minions outfit.

"No one invited you to this shithole." Jay stands in front of me like a protective shield. "And who are you?"

"Nicole's boss, who's pissed off at her."

"Does that mean you'll fire her?" There's a note of caution in Jay's tone.

"Already done, Minion."

I wince as Jay stares up at me with a hint of betrayal. "You said you had no trouble. Why did you lie?"

"That's kind of been her modus operandi since we were kids," Daniel supplies unnecessarily.

"You've known each other since you were children?"

"Since about your age, kid."

"Daniel!" I shake my head.

"It's sir to you."

"You're no longer my boss."

"Depends."

My heart skips a beat and I hate it. I hate how I'm irrevocably out of control when it comes to Daniel and his words and his actions and his presence. But what I hate the most is that there isn't a way to tame or tamp down my reaction to him.

It's always meant to cross every line.

Every limit.

Every logical barrier.

"You said you've known Nikki for a long time," Jay says in a contemplative tone. "That means you can let her keep her job."

"Again, it depends." Daniel continues staring at Jay as if he's contemplating what to do with him, and I'm not sure why the mama bear in me is demanding I protect Jay from his watchful gaze.

But I don't need to, because the blue of his eyes slides to me, slowly, suffocatingly. "A word."

I glance down at Jay, then back at Daniel again. I wish I had the luxury of telling him he can shove it where no one can see, but I don't, so I motion at Daniel to follow me onto the small balcony and shut the door behind us, locking out a curious Jay inside.

It isn't until I'm nearly chest to chest with Daniel that I regret my choice of place.

His bergamot, lime, and male scent envelop me with intrusiveness that steals my breath.

I can't help noticing how a few rebellious strands of his hair have left the rest and fallen over his forehead. Or how his suit looks as perfectly pressed as it did this morning.

His face, however, appears blank. It's nothing like the savage devil who fired me without listening to anything I had to say, but it's not welcoming either.

The rusty railing digs into my back in my hopeless attempt to keep as much space between us as possible. It's disastrous enough without us having to touch.

Daniel cocks his head toward the glass door. "Is he mine?"

I nearly choke on my spit. "W-what?"

"Is the boy mine?"

"No!"

"Is he yours, then?"

"What the hell, no! He's my brother."

"Official papers indicate as such, but maybe you had your mother adopt him to take the heat off you?"

"She was in prison, Daniel. How could she adopt anyone?"

"Just putting all the possibilities out there considering who his legal fucking father is." His eyes darken and his posture turns as rigid as the metal at my back. Heat creeps up my cheeks, and it's entirely due to the damn audacity of this man.

"Jayden's father and everything about him is none of your business."

"Are you sure you want to put it that way? I heard you're in the middle of a custody suit and need a steady job as much as scientists need to start searching for a stupidity cure."

"How did you…? Wait, was it Aspen?"

"Doesn't matter. Your employment status does."

I bite my lower lip but remain silent.

He watches me for a beat, maintaining merciless eye contact as if his reason for living is to make me squirm. I don't, holding my own and staring right back.

It's exhausting, though. Being Daniel's target, his nemesis, his enemy has always been so fucking tiring and I'm not sure just how long I'll be able to take this.

How long before that final nail is dug into my coffin?

Daniel raises a brow. "Aren't you going to convince me to take you back?"

"Are you willing to be convinced? I thought I was incompetent and the worst assistant you've ever had."

He lifts his arrogant damn nose in the air. "I'm in the mood for charity. So thank your lucky stars and start the convincing session. In case you've forgotten, my time happens to be the goose that lays golden eggs."

"Why don't you spare us both the trouble and tell me what you want? Surely you came all the way here for something."

A small smile grazes his lips and a hint of his dimples appear on both his cheeks. "You were always a clever little minx."

"Glad to shatter all the blonde stereotypes."

"Not all." He watches me closely. "What are you willing to do to have the permanent assistant position as well as legal advice?"

"Anything."

"Including becoming my sex toy?"

My heart drops to my knees and I clutch the railing behind me in a death grip. "N-not that."

His face remains unchanging. "Why? You have a boyfriend who would oppose the idea?"

"*I* oppose the idea. I don't want to sleep with you."

Or anyone for that matter.

"Why not?"

"It'd kill our professional relationship."

"We never had any sort of professional anything, Nicole."

"I just…can't do it." *Please don't make me do it.*

I nearly beg but swallow the words at the last second.

"Do I disgust you that much?" There's no accusation in his tone. It's flat, almost deadpan.

"Maybe tales of your endless shagging does."

"You might want to wipe that jealousy off your face. You're drooling with it."

"You're the last man I would feel jealous of, Daniel. You're nothing but a mere blip in my past." *Lies, lies, and more lies.*

I feel no different from young Nicole who spouted nonsense left and right. And that's dangerous.

That would lead me down a destructive path similar to the one from back then.

"I see."

He's still speaking in that toneless way, no inflection whatsoever. His face is just as closed off, an absolute mask that I can't read what's lurking behind.

A metaphorical weight squeezes my windpipe, and panic starts to settle in. For all of my brave talk, I can't lose this job.

Maybe if I close my eyes and pretend—

No. Nope. That's not going to happen.

"Daniel, I—"

"Start by making me dinner," he cuts me off. "You've been doing it for a week anyway. I should've suspected it from the Lolli name. Bit predictable, no? You had to include your lollipops."

My lips fall open, then closed. "*Start?* And then what?"

"We'll figure it out along the way."

"I told you I'm not going to sleep with you."

"It's called fucking. I doubt any sleeping will be happening. And we'll see about that."

"No, we won't. Why the hell do you even want me?"

His lips press in a line, but that slight show of affection quickly disappears. "No reason. It's just a business transaction."

I wish I could throw him over the balcony from this height and watch his gorgeous face get smashed to pieces. I hate how small he can make me feel.

How insignificant.

"Business or not, I won't be doing it. The sleeping or the fucking."

"You said a crude word. That's progress."

"That's a warning. Don't come near me."

"Not while you're so uptight about it, but you'll come around."

"No, I won't, Daniel."

"It's sir to you." He opens the balcony door. "And I'm hungry. Make the dinner quick."

I wish I could make his death quick, but oh well, it doesn't work that way in real life.

Jayden is waiting for us inside. He was pretending to do homework and play with Lolli earlier while he watched our every move.

Or Daniel's, to be more specific.

He approaches us while carrying Lolli as a weapon, which she can be under certain circumstances. "Are you going to let Nikki keep her job?"

"Depends on how well she does. And stop calling her that, it's juvenile."

"Maybe if you stop having her call you sir. It's demeaning."

I suppress a smile, impossibly proud of my baby brother. The little rascal is so mature for his age.

Daniel raises a brow. "Jay, was it?"

"Jayden. You didn't get the okay to call me Jay."

"Not asking for it in this lifetime."

My brother lifts his shoulder. "Your loss. When I become something important in the future, you'll want my favor."

"Doubt it."

"I'm going to make dinner," I announce, putting a halt to their bickering.

"Is he invited?" Jay cocks his head to Daniel like he's a fly that won't go away.

Daniel fixates him with a stare. "It's one of the conditions for her keeping the job."

"Nikki's food is a luxury that not just anyone can afford."

The corner of Daniel's eye twitches and I'm not sure if it's displeasure or amusement. "I can."

"Do you pay her extra for it?"

"He does," I answer on Daniel's behalf as I put on my apron.

"How much extra? As much as the expensive restaurant you dine at?"

"Jay!"

"Well, it's the same level. He has to pay well."

"I will." Daniel slides his gaze to me. "Double Katerina's."

My fingers pause on the strap and I stare at him, dumbfounded. Did he just say my food is worth double what Katerina—a professional chef with a few restaurant chains under her belt—cooks?

"Not enough?" Daniel muses. "Triple it then."

Holy...

"Still not enough?"

"No, it's fine," I choke on the words.

"Silly." Jay scrunches his nose at me. "You could've gotten more. Never say it's enough."

"That's right. You're intelligent," Daniel tells him.

"I know."

"How well do you do in school?"

"Genius level. Other kids can't keep up with me."

Daniel raises a brow. "I see arrogance runs in the family."

My brother crosses his arms over his chest after releasing a fussy Lolli. "How well did *you* do in school?"

"Not well, but that doesn't matter since I became a partner at twenty-nine. You just have to use the system to your advantage and fuck it over."

"And how do you do that?"

"By continuing to be smart about it. You have the brain; just direct it toward the right path."

I stand there in awe about the conversation between them. They're even sitting down now, on the shabby sofa that seems so small with Daniel occupying it.

Lolli hops between them and, surprisingly, Daniel pets her. No clue why I thought he'd be indifferent to animals. Probably because he never had pets.

Jay laughs when our cat flips over, showing her belly to Daniel, which is a sign that she not only trusts him, but she also likes him.

Someone is entranced after their first meeting.

A shiver goes through me at the view.

Is he mine?

Daniel's question from earlier strikes me again, and although Jay is neither his nor my son, I don't know why a twisted part of me is wishing for that.

It's the same part that I've been trying to purge from my life since I was young.

Stinging moisture gathers in my lids and I quickly whirl around and dab at my eyes with the back of my sleeves.

What the hell am I doing?

It took me years to tuck away those unrequited feelings and all the pain that came with them.

Years. Damn years. And it still feels as if I'm stuck at the same point.

I get busy making dinner, opting for fish today since it's Jay's favorite. I also make white rice balls and sprinkle them with a mixture of Indian spices.

Every now and then, I slide my attention to the living area to find Daniel engrossed in my brother's homework. It seems he's struggling, too, judging by the deep frown on his forehead.

He was always a slacker in class with a complete "fuck the world" attitude. He probably only passed them because he thought falling behind was a nuisance.

And yes, I shouldn't know this much about him, but it's a disease.

I've come down with the Daniel flu, and apparently, it's chronic.

Every time we make eye contact, a weird frisson goes through my body, as if it's about to possess me.

And I always break it first, desperate to escape his pull in any way possible.

"Dinner's ready," I shout once I'm done.

Jay shoots up from the sofa like a lithe tiger, followed by Lolli, who's mewing her head off.

I put some fish in her bowl and she gets busy eating and ignoring everyone else.

My brother and I transport the dishes to the living area, where Daniel is still sitting, legs crossed as if he's a king and we're his servants.

Twat.

I move to sit opposite him on the floor, but Jay snatches the position and I'm forced to take a seat beside Daniel on the sofa.

I try not to get sucked into his warmth or look at him as I reach for my utensils.

The keyword being *try*.

The air is always sucked up from my surroundings whenever he's in the room, the building, the school, city, country, world.

Sometimes, just the thought of him existing somewhere on earth is enough to steal my damn oxygen.

"It's so good, Nikki!" Jay exclaims, stuffing his face with rice.

I reach over and remove the rice grains that are stuck to his lip. "I'm glad you like it."

"I don't like it, I love it." My brother glares at Daniel, who's eating in an eerily silent manner. It's like he's afraid to make any motion or make any sound. "What about you, Daniel? Any comments?"

My boss swallows with difficulty. "It's food."

"It's not just any food. It's Nikki's and it's the best you've ever had. Admit it."

"It's good," he manages to say.

Lolli, who finishes her serving in record time, strolls into the room with the grace of a lioness and rubs herself against Daniel's leg.

I see the exact moment when his face scrunches up as if he's about to get sick.

And I see now why he never talks or moves and doesn't like to be interrupted while he eats. It's like he considers meals a battle he has to go through alone and with no external stimuli.

"Good isn't even a compliment," my brother grumbles.

Daniel starts to get up, probably to go throw up what he ate. I quickly pull a lollipop from my bag, open the wrapper, and stuff it between his lips when he opens them.

He stares at me for a beat, the lollipop still frozen in his mouth. And then for a moment, a brief moment in time, his expression softens.

For a brief moment, I see the stars in his shiny, bright eyes. The same eyes that looked at me and didn't hate me.

But it's gone when he crunches on the lollipop, not bothering to suck on it first. When he swallows, he throws the stick to Lolli who runs after it.

"Peaches."

My heart flips and falls to my stomach. I can't stop looking at him, at the dip in his chin and the small teases of those gorgeous dimples. Or what's between them, his glistening lips.

"The lollipops always have a peach flavor." He cocks his head to the discarded stick.

"I know right?" Jay says after chewing a mouthful of fish, seeming to have forgotten about the earlier subject. "She only ever buys those. Nikki is weird."

Daniel's gaze rakes over me with so much heat that it feels like he's melting my clothes while they're on me. "She is."

Then he goes back to eating, leaving me heaving.

Jeez.

He finishes the entire dish despite Jay's chatter. I try to talk to my brother instead of Daniel to not distract him from eating, but he's a very demanding rascal who doesn't like being ignored by our guest.

"Go take a shower, Nikki. Daniel and I will do the dishes."

"That's okay." I spring to my feet. "I'll do them."

"No. You prepared the food. It's only right that Daniel and I do the dishes."

"I paid for this food," Daniel says in his haughty tone. "I don't do dishes at a restaurant."

"Yes, but you also don't visit a chef's house, so this is a compromise," Jay counters and pushes me in the direction of the bathroom before Daniel or I can protest.

Suppressing a smile at my boss's knitted brows and narrowed eyes, I get some clothes and head to the bathroom.

Since the walls in this building are so thin, I can hear them bickering over soap and whatnot.

I catch myself grinning as the water sprays over me and I grasp my white gold necklace. It has a pendant the exact color of my eyes. It has a dainty oval shape and is emerald-colored enamel over gold. This is the most valuable item I own, or more like, the only thing I kept from my previous life, along with the box it came in.

And while I've been wearing the necklace since I first got it, I begrudgingly remove it and carefully hide it in a towel. I will put it in a box later.

Daniel can't see it or he'll get ideas.

Ideas even I don't want to entertain.

I end up taking a long shower, allowing the muscles in my body to loosen up.

Once I'm done, I throw on a cotton robe, dry my hair with a towel, then step out of the bathroom.

The flat is eerily calm and I suspect that Daniel had enough of my brother's antics and left.

But that's not the case.

Jay is sleeping on the sofa, his limbs flailing in all directions.

Daniel is on the floor in front of him, and his shirt sleeves are pulled to his elbows, revealing his strong forearms. His tailored jacket that must've cost a couple thousand dollars is currently being used by Lolli as a pillow.

He doesn't seem to care that it's covered with hair, though, because he's way too focused on Jay's textbook. I've only seen him this concentrated on work-related stuff.

I must make a noise, because he starts to lift his head. "What's this bollocks they teach kids these days…"

He trails off when his eyes fall on me. He takes me in from my feet, slowly dragging his gaze up to my waist and stomach, then lingers on my breasts before his eyes clash with mine.

They're dark blue—a dangerous blue that makes me squirm—something I haven't done for over a decade.

"Our education system is different from the American one," I say in a hopeless attempt to disperse his attention.

"Everything is different here—bigger, louder, and less stuck-up than in London."

"I still miss it. London." I don't know why I say it, and I resist the need to fidget under his scrutiny.

"Why did you leave it then?"

My gaze silently flits to Jay.

"Right. You were running away and still are apparently."

Not knowing how to reply, I go to the kitchen, grab two beers, and offer Daniel one.

"I assume you don't have premium whiskey here," he says while examining the can of beer with distaste.

"You should be thankful there's even beer." I sit across from him, tucking my feet underneath me.

"That dire?"

"Don't pity me."

"I have a lot of twisted emotions toward you, but believe me, pity is not on the list."

I gulp a mouthful of beer, sinking my nails into the can. I want to ask him what those feelings are, but I can't.

Not after I said what I said on the balcony.

"I couldn't raise Jay in England," I whisper, reverting the subject back to my brother. "He…was neglected by his father to the point of abuse. He got asthma from the conditions he was kept in. So when social services came knocking on my door, I couldn't say no. He was a few months old at the time."

"That's why you dropped out of Cambridge."

It's not a question, but a declaration.

"I had to use the rest of my trust fund to raise Jay, so I couldn't afford Cambridge anymore."

"You could've asked Uncle Henry for help."

A ball the size of my fist clogs up my windpipe. "Uncle Henry hated Mum more than he hated the devil."

"But he didn't hate you."

"Yes, he did. He couldn't even look at me after she was arrested. I reminded him of her and it hurt him. It's why I avoided his advances. I couldn't just ask him for help to raise another child my mother gave birth to."

I stare at Jay, thankful he's a deep sleeper.

Daniel jostles the can of beer, then takes a small sip. "Did you know I was in New York before you came?"

"No. If I had, I wouldn't have come here."

A sadistic smile tips his lips. "I never took you for a coward who would run away from their past."

"I'm not a coward. I just don't like unnecessary confrontations."

"So I'm unnecessary now? Not a very good sales pitch to get back into my good graces."

"Does such a place even exist?"

"What?"

"Your good graces."

"It does."

"Shocker, considering you're pickier than royalty."

"I can be reasonable."

"Not even if you were hit on the head with that word."

He smiles a little, or more like smirks, before he takes another sip of beer.

Silence falls between us, heavy with unsaid words and vindictive thoughts.

We've been at each other's throats so much that it feels wrong to have this small moment of peace.

But I don't break it.

Don't try to fill it.

Because I might have been drawn to his charming side, but I enjoyed Daniel's silence as much as his words.

What I didn't enjoy were his actions. Each and every one of them.

And he's watching me as if he's contemplating the best way to make me agree to his less than subtle offer.

Problem is, I can't stop thinking about it either.

Even though I've completely closed myself off to that side of me.

But I could never close myself off to Daniel.

SIXTEEN

Daniel

THINK I MADE A MISTAKE.

No, it's not a probability.

The fact that I'm even thinking about it is a clear indication that I did make the fucking mistake.

And I'm in the middle of an even bigger mistake.

Grabbing an empty glass of water, I stare over my kitchen counter.

If someone had told me I'd witness a scene such as the one in my living area, I would've paid their therapy bills.

Maybe this is an indication that I should start with my own therapeutic session. The reason is simple. As strange as the view is, it feels…fucking right coupled with all the wrong emotions I shouldn't entertain.

Nicole, who graduated from multitasking school with flying colors, is helping Jayden do his homework while going through her pending assistant tasks.

Her *brother*, Jayden.

A nine-year-old little fucker of epic proportions. He's almost like a younger Nicole but with more bite and less snobbishness.

As much as I hate to admit it, the little fucker has grown on me since I first met him a week ago. Not only is he as allergic to stupidity as I am, but he has a sassy mouth that nearly rivals his sister's.

Almost.

It's part of the reason why I opened my home to them. I told Nicole I wouldn't be driving back and forth to her shabby flat for dinner and demanded she bring it to me.

Although her place should be listed as a noise, danger, and life hazard, that's not actually the real reason I no longer want to go there.

The thing is, I couldn't keep seeing her in her skimpy robes and then have to get up and leave with a hard-on bigger than Mount Everest.

Naturally, she gave me a piece of her mind and blathered about how not everyone can afford a luxurious flat. She has this annoying tendency where she likes to express whatever's on her mind.

She usually goes red at my biting replies, though, so we're basically pushing and pulling with no strings attached.

Anyhow, after she agreed to bring me dinner every night—correction, after I gave her no choice—I provoked Jayden so he'd suggest that he'd tag along. I wouldn't have said it myself if I were on the brink of death.

Even I know that their shitty, humid flat is not good for his condition. Not to mention the endless noise that can be heard through the paper-thin walls.

Even the cat is constantly jolted awake by a sudden thud or scream in that hellhole.

The same cat that's currently rubbing against my sweatpants and leaving hair galore. In the span of a week, she ruined exactly five of my suit jackets and dirtied double that amount of the rest of my clothes.

And yes, even the cat, Lolli, had to come along. Jay insisted not to leave her alone.

Lolli.

Jesus fucking Christ. Nicole couldn't be more predictable than a criminal who's been caught red-handed pleading not guilty.

The cat mewls, probably trying to get my attention, so I sigh and lower myself to pet her. She purrs, headbutting my leg, and then she jumps on my knee.

"Give you an inch and you'll take a mile, huh?"

She just meows in response and it almost sounds like a whine.

What the fuck am I doing?

Jesus.

Not only have I opened my house to Nicole but also to her brother and cat.

And the worst part is that my flat feels…full. There's no emptiness echoing from the walls or the biting edge of loneliness.

Though that dreadful atmosphere does return after I drive them home later. Which defies the whole purpose of my not going to their awful neighborhood that could turn into a crime scene at any second.

Still, I couldn't let them take a taxi.

Not at night, when the psychos and predators come out to play.

It's enough that she ran away from England. However, something tells me that wasn't only because of Jayden.

Uncle Henry saw the bruises on her face, not the baby's. *She* was the one who was hurt.

I didn't ask, because she would've brushed me off. Which is her modus operandi for everything lately.

More specifically, ever since I casually mentioned that I would fuck her.

Well, not so casually, considering that I wanted to make it a condition to keep her job.

Harassment much? Probably.

I should be on the law circuit's black list, not on the front of every single one of its magazines.

The job was hers anyway, but the fucking part was my way to make her feel like she means nothing.

She doesn't.

Which is why I have to fuck her to prove a point. Ever since she barged into my life again, I've been constantly hard like a teenage boy with hormonal issues and abstaining like a fucking priest.

Now, I could've fucked a random brunette. Like those two girls I kicked out the day she came here and I touched her beauty mark.

I was positively hard at that moment, but not for them or their less than subtle advances. I was hard for her.

The woman who's driving me bonkers and becoming a problem in my scheme to take over the world. Sorry, I mean, to regain control over my life.

And I had to come all over my hand like a caveman because Nicole wasn't excited about my offer to fuck her out of my system.

She was disgusted by it.

I could see that emotion written all over her delicate features and could hear her say her famous line, "Eww, gross. Not in this lifetime, loser."

And I might've become a colossal jerk as a response. It was either that or bend her over my desk and take her from behind like an animal in heat.

I need to take care of this business as soon as possible. The more she lurks in my fantasies, the harder it'll be to chase her away.

And that should happen soon-ish. Today, if my dick has any say in it.

The trial for Jayden's custody is a few months away, and after that, I'm going to refer her to another branch of W&S in some other state.

I can't live with Nicole in the same city and also hope to be able to breathe properly.

That's simply not going to happen.

"She likes you." Jayden's voice interrupts my bewildered musings as he stands in front of me, motioning at Lolli, who's practically sleeping on my lap. "Even more than me, the traitor."

I smirk. "I'm the likable type."

"Not to Nikki."

This little jerk needs to be less direct about his words or I'm going to strap some duct tape to his mouth.

"Your sister has terrible taste," I say loud enough for her to hear me.

If she does, she doesn't show it, because she's still engrossed in the tablet. I doubt she's even noticed that Jayden left her side.

"No, she doesn't." He still takes offense on her behalf, crossing his arms over his awfully juvenile Minions T-shirt. "Just because she doesn't like you, doesn't mean she doesn't like others."

I narrow my eyes, then continue to pet Lolli. "Others?"

"Yeah, Nikki has a lot of guys wanting her."

A red-hot feeling forms a haze over my vision and it takes everything in me not to revert to the bitter cunt I was eleven years ago.

When a lot of fucking wankers wanted her, too. When they looked at her like they wanted their tiny dicks inside her every hole.

But I didn't have to worry about it much, because she always, without exception, told them, "Eww, gross," and looked at them as if they were dust on her pristine shoes.

All of them.

Every single one.

Except for the fucking cunt from that night.

Pretending I'm fascinated with Lolli's black furry head, I ask, "She introduced them to you?"

"No, she says she doesn't have time for them." There's a grim expression on his face. Guilt.

He feels sorry, probably figuring out he's the reason why his sister doesn't have time to live her life.

This kid is too sharp for his own good.

"She could have time for me," I announce out of nowhere. "Considering we work together almost every day"

It's Jayden's turn to narrow his brown eyes on me. "You still haven't proved yourself worthy, Dan."

"I make triple digits from the attorney job alone. I work with mega international corporations and a sovereign family in Europe, not to mention I have more money than ten generations would be able to spend, even if they flew first class to Mars. Oh, and I have a model's face and body that photographers won't stop moaning about. I'm the best choice you have."

His eyes widen, but then he clears his throat. "That's only on paper."

"What is that supposed to mean?"

"You're the perfect candidate except for one small detail. Nikki still doesn't like you."

"That is not true."

"Don't think I didn't notice that she avoids you every chance she gets."

I clench my fist, stopping myself from strangling Lolli and Jayden with her.

"That's because she's playing hard to get." *Or she's actually disgusted with me, judging by her horrified expression.*

"What does that mean?"

"Not so know-it-all now, huh?"

He lifts his small chin. "Either tell me or I won't support you."

"You'll support me anyway, because you know I'm the one."

"Keep telling yourself that, Dr. Evil." He places a hand at his hip, like Nicole. "Now what does playing hard to get mean?"

"That she pretends she's not interested so I'll chase her more. Girls do that all the time."

"Why?"

"No clue. Ask them."

He regards me for a bit. "In that case, I'll grant you a chance."

"*Grant* me?"

"Yeah, consider yourself on a trial period."

"I'm honored," I mock.

"As you should be. I don't do this all the time."

"Wow, Your Majesty. That's so benevolent of you."

He grins, showing me his missing teeth. Then he reverts to

his serious expression. "Hey, Dan. If you hurt my sister, I'm going to scratch your BMW and burn your luxurious apartment."

"I'll sue you for property damage."

"I'm a minor. You can't sue me."

"I sure as fuck can and you might go to juvie for it."

"Fine." He rolls his eyes. "I'll pay someone else to do it."

I can't suppress a laugh at how serious he sounds. "You can still get in trouble for it, and next time, don't tell anyone your plans or it could be used against you."

"Oh." He scratches his chin like an old man who's channeling wisdom. "Good to know."

"That would be legal advice and I get paid by the hour. Since your only fortune is your Minions collection, I'm not interested in it. I demand another currency. You'll help me."

"First of all, I didn't ask for legal advice, so I refuse to pay for it. But I will help you under one more condition."

"What now?"

"Can you tell me how to get away with murder?"

I pause at the serious tone in his voice, the sharp gleaming in his eyes. It's not a question he asked for the sake of asking or due to curiosity. He's actually harboring such thoughts.

"You have someone you want to murder?"

"No," he blurts. "I'm just wondering."

"You can't get away with murder, Jay."

"Yes, I can. Aren't you a lawyer who helps people get away with it?"

"That's a criminal defense attorney. I deal with international companies."

"So you're the boring type of attorney?"

"The richest type. I travel to a lot of exotic places, too."

His eyes shine brighter than light. "Really?"

"Yup." Though I skip the fact that I don't find pleasure in it.

He kicks an imaginary pebble. "Nikki and I have never been anywhere. Well, I was in London when I was a baby but I don't remember that, so it doesn't count."

"You never went back to England?"

"No. That's where my father is." Jay purses his lips.

"I assume you don't like him?"

"No, he's a twat."

"You met him?"

"Once. He came to visit us two years ago when we used to live in Colorado, and Nikki told me to hide, but I heard him saying bad things to her and—"

"Jay!"

He startles at Nicole's voice before his small body goes still. She's near us now and probably heard the last bit of the conversation.

Her face has turned a bright shade of red and her fingers tremble as she motions to the table. "Go finish your homework."

Jayden lowers his head, giving me an apologetic glance, and drags his feet back to where he left his homework.

Holding Lolli up, I put her near her bowl of food and stand to my full height. Nicole plants her hands on the counter and gets in my face, even though the surface separates us. "Stop talking about unnecessary things with Jay. Anything that has to do with his father is prohibited."

I try to ignore the way her tits strain against her white shirt or how a blush creeps up her delicate neck.

Try being the operative word since my dick is in a constant state of stimuli and is warring with my briefs and trousers as we speak.

I'm surprised I can speak in a human tone. "Are you sure prohibition is the best way to raise a child who's asking about how to get away with murder?"

Her eyes that resemble the most exotic plants widen. "He… he asked that?"

"He's a lot sharper than you think and happens to notice things, even when you try to hide them."

"What else did he say?"

"What are you willing to do to find out? I have an interesting currency I'd like to try."

Her cheeks turn a bright, shiny crimson that makes her resemble a tomato.

It's her cue to run in three, two, one—

"I'm not willing to do anything," she blurts, then whirls around and joins Jayden.

I grab the edges of the counter and curl my fingers around it so hard, I'm surprised none of my tendons snap.

If I was suspecting it before, there's no doubt now.

She *is* avoiding me.

Whether it's repulsion or something else, I have no clue. All I'm sure about is that it's provoking my nasty side.

Breathing in a harsh intake of air, I storm to my home office and make some international phone calls. Work always keeps me grounded enough to keep me from thinking about needless fucking things.

Like the goddess with a body of sin sitting in my living area.

Apparently, work isn't a solution either if all my brain thinks about is a Pornhub version of Nicole.

Jesus.

I retrieve my phone in a desperate attempt to find a distraction—that's not Pornhub.

The text I find on my screen allows me to breathe easier.

Astrid: Still alive?

I grin, typing back.

Daniel: Shagging the whole of NYC as we speak.

In my head. And not the whole of the city, just a fucking annoying someone in the middle of it.

Astrid: Have I told you that you're a pig lately?

Daniel: In as many colorful words as your palettes. I'm kind of desensitized to it after fourteen years of hearing it, little bugger.

Astrid: Wow. I can't believe we've known each other that long. Maybe we should start celebrating milestones.

Daniel: You sure you want to add more dates to the number of birthdays you have to keep up with, considering all the spawns you keep giving birth to?

Astrid: There's a thing called a calendar. And did you just call my children spawns?

Daniel: All children are.

All except for Jayden because he acts like a thirty-year-old. I contemplate telling Astrid that Nicole has a brother, but that will bring on a whole other line of questions that I'm not ready to answer.

Naturally, I'll tell Astrid about Nicole.

Eventually.

After she's no longer working with me and belongs in the past tense.

Or maybe I can get away with not mentioning her to Astrid at all. There's no love lost between the two women and…fuck, I don't want to see the disappointment on my best friend's face if she finds out I'm lusting after her evil stepsister.

It was that way in the past, too. I hated wanting Nicole despite knowing my best friend's feelings toward her.

Astrid: I'm going to throw this back in your face when you have your own kids, Bug.

Daniel: Not foreseeable for the next five to six decades.

Astrid: You'd probably be dead around that time.

Daniel: Exactly.

Astrid: You really don't plan to get married and have kids? Ever?

Daniel: Marriages are overrated. They're just a glorified contract for a socially acceptable whoring agreement. They're messy, full of betrayals, and usually end with sloppy divorces and a hefty check for the solicitor.

Astrid: Just because your parents' marriage was messy doesn't mean all marriages are. Look at mine.

Daniel: Three kids and thinking about a fourth? How is changing nappies going for you, Bugger?

Astrid: I can't believe you've become so cynical, Bug.

Always was. Just tried to hide it with a charming façade in the past.

Daniel: I'm a realist.

Astrid: How about kids then?

Daniel: Wrong number. Not interested.

Astrid: Damn you lol. I mean, who will inherit your fortune? Who are you making all that money for?

Daniel: A million and one cat organizations. I would've given them to your children, but they have the King surname and have been richer than me since they were fucking toddlers, so I'm going for the next best thing.

Astrid: I can't believe you're choosing cats over actually fathering children.

Daniel: Everyone has different priorities. Mine include not changing nappies.

But even as I text that, my mind reels to when Aspen first told me about Nicole's custody case.

For some illogical reason, I hoped—no, I wished—that Nicole had been raising our child. After all, I didn't use a condom that time.

It didn't matter that the maths didn't align and that if she actually had been pregnant, she would've shown during our senior year.

It didn't matter that in my head, she cheated on me with that fucker.

At that moment, I wanted Jayden to be mine and hers. A link that would connect us for years.

That was crushed to pieces once I saw the official documentation, but I asked her the question anyway.

It was worth it, if not for anything else but to see the surprised expression on her face.

Astrid and I text back and forth for half an hour, then she ignores me when Levi comes home.

Or he probably distracted her.

I lose count of the number of times he kisses her, open-mouthed, while we're on a video call, just to force me to end it. I try to give him the middle finger by continuing to watch, but apparently, hearing Astrid moan is my limit.

That's similar to imagining my mother having sex.

And now, I need bleach for my brain.

I stand up and go to grab a coffee, completely intent on ignoring Nicole's presence.

But the moment I step into the living area, I pause.

Because they're asleep. All three of them.

Jayden is holding on to the remote as a film plays on the TV. *Despicable Me*. No surprise there.

Lolli is curled up to his side and Nicole's head is lying on the sofa beside them while she's in a sitting position, the papers and the tablet snug on her lap.

I should wake them up and send them home, but the peacefulness of the whole picture keeps me rooted in place.

It's the first time in…ever that I've seen Nicole off guard. Looking almost soft.

And my dick hardens against my sweatpants.

Fuck.

I endure the discomfort for long enough to get some blankets and go back to them. I cover Jayden first, then take away the remote and switch off the TV.

Carefully, I remove the papers from between Nicole's fingers and move her so she's more comfortable on the carpet. It's thicker than the floor in her flat. The better option would be to carry her to a room, but she'd probably wake up.

Lolli peeks at me like a sneak as I place a pillow under Nicole's head, then cover her.

What? I glare at the cat. *If she gets sick, I'll be the one without an assistant.*

Lolli gives me a haughty glance as if thinking, *Whatever makes you sleep at night, mate.*

A moan mixed with a sigh rips from Nicole's bitable lips and I remain there, perched over her like a fucking devil.

My fingers latch onto the cover, then I slowly trail them to her frail neck, to the visible veins beneath her transparent skin and the delicate contours of her face.

She's like a fucking sin waiting to happen.

A sin I should've committed a long time ago.

Her lids flutter and I retract my hand before I act on some disturbing necrophilic thoughts.

I glare at Lolli, the only witness of my fuckboy moment, then stride to my room, shutting the door behind me not so gently.

I spend ten minutes pacing, another fifteen minutes doing push-ups, and another ten minutes contemplating Pornhub for real.

But here's the problem, I don't need fucking Pornhub.

It's not just any gratification that I'm after. My dick's tastes have become singular and pickier than my stomach about food.

After getting rid of my clothes, I step into my shower and hit the cold water button.

The state of my hard-on, however, updates from mildly annoying to I probably need to fuck the nearest object. Slamming one hand against the shower wall, I grab my cock with the other one and jerk off like a teenager with anger issues—hard, fast, and with the intention to get the bloody hell off.

I jam my eyes shut, feeling the snarl lifting my upper lip as I pump the length of my dick.

And just like that, her face appears in front of me. The same face she made when I fucked her that time when she made me her first. The same goddess-like body she had back then.

Her tits are round and full and tipped with dusty pink nipples that make my mouth fucking water.

Her pussy is smooth and waiting for me to fuck it the hell up.

I'm thrusting inside that pussy now, over and over, until her moans echo in my ears, bleeding into my veins and infecting my system.

This is the reason I hate blondes. I always, without exception, see them as her.

With brunettes, I can keep my distance. I can pretend that my type isn't the only woman with whom sex ever meant something.

Her moans echo in my ears and I up my pace, pretending that my brutish, callous hand is her inviting, delicate pussy.

A gasp reverberates around me and I frown. They're supposed to be moans, not gasps.

Slowly, I open my eyes and stare at the source of the sound.

Nicole stands in the doorway of the bathroom, her limbs shaking and mouth open in an O.

Fuck me.

What are the chances that I'll empty down that pretty throat that keeps bobbing up and down with her swallows?

Only one way to find out.

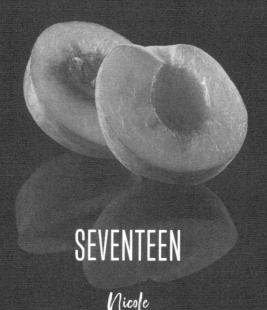

SEVENTEEN

Nicole

ARE THERE SIGNS OF HAVING A HEART ATTACK? BECAUSE I'M pretty sure I'm having one right now.

A nasty heart attack that's coming due to the bane of my existence.

My whole body trembles and my eyes widen as they take in the view in front of me.

Daniel is in the shower, completely naked, with his hand wrapped around his thick and very hard cock.

A view I wasn't supposed to walk in on or see.

A view that's currently paralyzing my motor and cognitive functions.

When I jolted awake from an extremely forbidden dream, I was disoriented and surprised to find myself sleeping on Daniel's carpet while Jay lay on his sofa. What was even more surprising was the fact that my brother and I were covered with blankets, and the papers I was reading through were neatly tucked on the table.

I meant to see if he was still awake and tell him we could take a taxi back home. He didn't answer when I knocked on his door three times so I let myself in and planned on leaving if he was asleep.

But he wasn't in his room either, and just when I was going to try his home office, I heard a grunt—or more like a growl—from the bathroom, as if he were in pain.

I must've been on drugs when I slowly pushed the door open. Or more accurately, I was showing symptoms of the "Daniel disease" and was inexplicably worried that something might have happened to him.

Something is happening to him all right, but it's not the dangerous type I was concerned about.

Or maybe it is dangerous but in a completely different way.

The rough, unapologetic way he touches himself is nothing short of an exhibition of domineering masculinity. The type that should revolt me and send me running for the hills.

The type that's been plaguing my nightmares and giving me sleep paralysis. When I open my eyes, the demon I find sitting on my chest always has *his* face. With that twisted sneer and mocking eyes.

But there are no demons now. Don't get me wrong, no angel is in sight either. The scene in front of me is my worst nightmare mixed with my best dream.

And I choose to hang on to the dream.

To the twisted reality.

My legs won't move anyway, not when my full attention is honed in on the way Daniel pumps his cock up and down with savage intent that makes me clench my thighs.

His muscled biceps contract and his hips jerk with the power of his movements. It's like he's angry at his cock for being hard, angry at what he's doing.

Angry that he has to get himself off.

Anger is the last emotion coursing through me, though. There's confusion, and it's due to other feelings. The longing and the desire I can't and shouldn't be experiencing.

The desire to slip my fingers inside my knickers and do something I only do once in a blue moon.

The desire to grab my embarrassingly aching nipples and pull until they're as painful as the expression on his face.

I must've released a gasp at my own thoughts because Daniel's head jerks in my direction, his eyes locking on mine.

They're darker, more hooded, as if the night sky abandoned all of its stars and decided to be bare. Crisp. Open for me to see.

His hand pauses on his cock; I'm not looking, but I catch the scene in my peripheral vision. The only reason I'm not staring at his cock is because I couldn't look away from his magnifying gaze even if I tried.

"What the fuck are you doing here?" His words are cold, cutting, but not enough to jar me out of my messed-up state.

"I…uh…I was…"

What exactly was I doing anyway? I'm pretty sure there was a reason I came in here in the first place.

"Looking for a live porn show? Working part-time as a Peeping Tom? Picking up voyeurism as a side gig? Which one exactly?"

"No…I just…" My eyes slide down to his fist on his cock and then I quickly avert my gaze.

"You can look. If you're so disgusted with me, you wouldn't have a reaction, would you?"

My head whips up to his face. "Disgusted with you?"

"Isn't that the reason you've been avoiding me?"

"I'm not disgusted with you." The reason I've been avoiding him is because of this inexplicable rush of tingles and unhealthy heart rate.

It's because I couldn't trust my reaction around him anymore.

A feral gleam shines in the depth of his gaze. "Prove it."

"W-what?"

He steps out of the shower, his muscled chest glistening with droplets of water that travel down his abs, over the V-line, and down to his still very hard and very unsatisfied cock.

There's a tattoo on his right pec, a script that's too small for me to read.

"Prove you're not disgusted with me."

"Why should I?" I try to keep my attention on his face no matter how tempting the other view is.

"Because I'm challenging you to prove it, Nicole."

My muscles lock at those words. He's challenging me.

Such a low damn blow. He knows I don't cower in front of a challenge, don't look the other way from it.

In fact, our whole fucked-up relationship, or lack thereof, was because I couldn't say no to a challenge.

I couldn't lose.

My feet are floating on air as I approach him, my head held high. I'm a lot of things, but as he said, a coward is not one of them.

The art of pain is an abstract form of vengeance.

That's what his tattoo says, in bold, neat letters that should belong in a museum.

My heart lunges, thinking about the reason he had this inked on his body.

The reason he's keeping it with him forever when he doesn't seem to be a fan of inking his body otherwise.

Once I'm standing in front of him, I reach my hand out and touch his chest. A zap of electricity goes through me at the contact, but I force myself to stare at his eyes.

"There. I'm not disgusted with you."

"Touching me doesn't prove anything." His lashes fall over his light eyes. "Getting on your knees does."

I bite my lower lip, but it's to suppress the need to smack him upside the head. He has me where he wants me and he knows it.

"Either suck my cock or get the fuck out, Nicole."

I fake a smile. "Repeat that nicely and I might."

"Nicely?"

"Oh, right, you wouldn't recognize the meaning of that concept even if you were slammed head first with it, so here's some middle ground. Add a please."

"A *what?*"

"A please, Daniel. A word people use to ask for something."

"Not fucking happening."

"Then I guess you should go back to your solo jerking-off session," I say sweetly, gliding my palm over his muscles. "It looked kind of violent, so you might want to be careful with that."

I hesitantly remove my hand and turn to leave, equal parts thankful I dodged a bullet and disappointed that it ends here.

"Please."

The low, strained word explodes in my ears and freezes my limbs. I slowly spin around to find Daniel glaring at me as if I'm an opposing counsel he wants to smash under his shoe like a cockroach.

But the lust from earlier still shines in the depths of his eyes.

"Repeat what you just said," I blurt, still not believing my ears.

"Fuck no. I did my part, you'll now do yours." He cocks his head toward the space in front of him. "On your knees."

I hesitate for a beat, then lower myself before him, my knees scraping on the hard tile floor.

"I want you to lick me first, then choke on my cock like a filthy little slut. And make it good, otherwise you'll lose."

"And if I win, you'll grant me something," I say, half calm, half shriveling, and dying due to his dirty talk.

"You already have a job. That's your something."

"Aside from that, and don't use the job to get your dick sucked unless you want a sexual harassment complaint."

"That's a lot of crude words in one sentence, Miss Prude."

"Maybe I'm not a prude anymore."

A light shines in his gaze. "Oh yeah?"

"If you want to find out, agree to my condition."

His head moves in a subtle nod, but that's all I need as I take his cock in my hand and lick the sides.

My eyes meet his hooded ones while I dart my tongue out and make a show of it.

I expected that I would need to shut myself down for this,

that I would need a pep talk, but it's more natural than I thought possible.

"That's it." His fingers thread in my hair. "Suck my cock like it's your favorite lollipop."

My core tightens and I slide the head inside my mouth, tasting the precum. Then I suck on it hard, just like a lollipop. Actually, I do it harder and it's nothing like the candy. It's more primal and definitely bigger.

"Jesus fucking Christ," he grunts, grabbing a fistful of my hair. He starts to thrust his hips, trying to get control, to hit the back of my throat.

But I fight for that control. I pull more of him inside and end up scraping him with my teeth.

"No fucking teeth, Nicole," he manages to get out, but he still sounds like he's in a pleasure haven.

I loosen my jaw to fit as much as I can of his huge cock.

The grunt that escapes his lips makes me more frantic in my movements, in my attempts to control the pace.

But then something happens. The tip of his cock hits the back of my throat, and although my gag reflex kicks in, so does something else.

Pleasure.

It's pooling between my thighs with a need for one single bit of friction to detonate.

One single touch.

"I'm going to fuck your mouth," he informs me and doesn't give me a chance to react as he uses my hair to keep me in place while he thrusts in and out.

He uses my tongue and lips for his own friction, groaning with each jerk of his hips.

My stomach revolts and the sensation is weird with the pleasure gathered in my knickers. It's so weird that I don't even attempt to stop it. My hands are on his muscular thighs, but I don't dig my nails in his skin or push him away.

I'm too struck by the feral look on his face, the raw power in it as he uses my mouth like it's the best he's ever had.

The thought of him doing this to other girls makes me want to throw up. So I push that idea away as fast as it appears, choosing to focus on him.

Only him.

I feel that he's close by the way his body tightens and how his thrusts turn jerky.

And then he empties himself down my throat. "Swallow. Every last fucking drop."

I try to, but there's so much cum that it leaks down each side of my chin. Daniel wipes the droplets with his index and middle finger and lazily smears it all over my lips.

They're bruised and puffy, but they fall open when he jams those two fingers inside my mouth and rubs them against my tongue.

Once.

Twice.

"That's your cue to suck, Peaches."

I do, curling my tongue around his lean fingers, trying to ignore the way my heart grows heavy at the use of my old nickname. A nickname that's stopped appearing, even in my dreams.

Why couldn't it just remain physical? Why did he have to make me feel so nostalgic by bringing up emotions?

He pulls out his fingers with pop, and a trail of my drool mixed with his cum hangs between his hand and my mouth.

"How did I do?" I ask in a breathless tone, even though I try to hold on to my nonexistent cool.

"You get your wish." He slides the two fingers that were in my mouth between his lips and sucks them as if they're his favorite meal. And that says something, considering he doesn't even like food.

I'm struck by the view, by how he licks me off him, not bothering to break eye contact.

In fact, he seems to be making it on purpose so I'll see what he can do with those fingers.

"Now, I want a chance to get my own wish."

One moment I'm on my knees, the next I'm on my back and Daniel is pulling my feet apart.

For a minute, I'm disoriented as to what's happening, but then red-hot panic crashes my windpipe.

I gasp, animal-like sounds escaping my throat before I start thrashing, hard, like a mental institute patient without tranquilizers.

My legs kick in the air and I bite skin. I don't know whose skin it is, but I do it, a guttural sound escaping with it. I also scratch somewhere, anywhere.

If I do it, he won't get to me, if I do...

"Nicole, stop!"

My wrists hit the ground with a thud and reality starts creeping into my vision.

Daniel's face greets me. He's hovering over me, his knees on either side of my stomach and his hands holding my wrists hostage on the tiled floor.

Salt explodes on my tongue and I realize it's tears. I'm crying and being the general mess I've been trying to hide from everyone, especially him.

The man who might as well have made me this way.

Daniel's brows are drawn together as he tracks my every movement like a hunter.

"What the fuck is wrong with you?" The authoritativeness in his tone would've had an effect on me on any other day but today.

I lick the sweat and tears off my upper lip. "L-let me go."

"Not until you tell me why in the bloody hell you acted as if you were possessed by Satan himself."

"Let me go, Daniel...please...just let me go."

A whole-body tremor goes through me, and I don't know if it's because of that, or my begging, but Daniel eases off me.

As soon as he releases my wrists, I crawl backward on my elbows and then jerk up so fast, I trip.

A strong hand keeps me upright, but I flinch away, my heart beating in my throat.

"Nicole—"

"You want to know what my wish is?" I jerk my chin up even as a tear clings to it. "Don't touch me, Daniel."

And then, I run out of the bathroom, my heart bleeding and my soul in flames.

Our relationship has never been the same after the running-post-blow-job incident last week.

We still have the same routine of my cooking in his chef's kitchen with Jay and Lolli as company. We even spent three out of four nights there this week.

But other than that, it's been strained.

Don't get me wrong, Daniel is still the worst boss-devil anyone can ask for with a diploma from the king of Hell himself, but it's robotic.

Almost as if he needs to be mean. As if not being mean will cost him a position on Satan's lap.

And I don't know how to fix it, save for going back in time and not agreeing to that challenge.

I should've forfeited and taken a hit like so many other hits.

Better yet, I should've never gone into his room in the first place.

If I hadn't, we could've had our weirdly domesticated life and just coexisted peacefully.

But maybe I'm tired of forfeiting and turning the other cheek. Maybe I wanted a challenge after so long.

Besides, who am I kidding? Daniel would've eventually seen my ugly side anyway.

He of all people would've witnessed it.

And I can't look him in the eye after that night. I don't even talk back like I usually would in response to his ludicrous commands. That would mean staring at him, and that energy is currently out of stock.

I can tell he's upping his icy cold behavior and adding some frost on top to get a kick out of me and make me talk, but I haven't taken the bait.

He'll eventually tire of demanding an answer out of me and move on.

Or at least, I hope so.

In the meantime, I try not to be in his vicinity unless absolutely necessary. The fact that we're practically in his house all the time doesn't help, though. I tried putting my foot down, but Daniel is surprisingly adamant about not letting us go back most days. He even made it a requirement to continue working.

My traitor brother is on his side, too. No surprise there. Jay hated our neighborhood and always said he'll become rich and buy us a house to get us out of that hellhole. A part of me is happy that his asthma has gotten significantly better since we don't spend much time in the humid flat, but the other part is both anxious and completely perturbed at being around Daniel.

I'm wearing a cracked professional mask, and I'm sure he sees right through it.

How the hell am I supposed to be professional after I sucked his cock like a first-class whore?

Then had an epic meltdown when he touched you. Don't forget about that part, Nicole.

Releasing a sigh, I step out of the lift on the managing partners' floor. It's lunchtime and I usually spend that with Aspen—when she doesn't have work outside the office, which is as rare as peaceful days in my life.

She's the only person I consider a friend around here. And I think I'm also her only actual friend.

Most people, including her assistant, are either intimidated by her or scared of her.

She's even lonelier than me. At least I have Jay and Lolli—and, yes, Lolli counts. Aspen is a true lone she-wolf through and through. Despite her senior partner status and tough bitch persona, she has no one on her side. Aside from Nathaniel Weaver, maybe.

And because she's not particularly close to anyone but me, I'm surprised to find a young intern standing in front of her office. From what I've learned during my time here, her name is

Gwyneth Shaw Weaver, daughter of *the* Kingsley Shaw and wife of *the* Nathaniel Weaver.

She's tucked into her father's side, her face red as Aspen stares at her with an expression I've never seen her wear.

Vulnerability.

She says something, but Gwyneth lowers her head and Kingsley smirks as he guides his daughter away.

Once they're out of view, I approach a stiff Aspen slowly. "Are you okay?"

She goes inside with rigid steps and I follow after her, closing the door.

Aspen grabs her glass nameplate and throws it against the wall. "That motherfucker!"

Then she straightens and puts her navy blue jacket in order, composing herself as fast as she had lost her cool.

"Sorry." She smiles at me as she picks up her nameplate, which is surprisingly still in one piece, and puts it back on her desk. "I had to get that off my chest or I would've had a stroke."

"No judgment here." I place the lunch boxes on the table and sit down. "I hope you like lasagna."

"I like anything you cook. No one's ever made me homemade meals."

"Well, I'm your girl in that department."

She slides onto the chair opposite me and we eat in silence for a few moments. Despite her small fit of rage, she doesn't seem relaxed. Just…uptight.

It's so unlike her to be agitated for long. Yes, she's in a sour mood after every fight with Kingsley, but she usually forgets about it soon after.

"She's my daughter," she whispers.

I take a sip of water. "Who?"

"Gwyneth."

I choke on the water and Aspen is by my side, patting my back. "Jesus, Nicole. I tell you something and you nearly choke to death? Thanks for the moral support."

I clear my scratchy throat. "I'm…surprised, is all. Isn't she in her twenties?"

"She's twenty."

"And you're thirty-five. When did you have her? At fourteen?"

"Going on fifteen, yes."

"Wow."

"Kind of a reassuring reaction." She digs her fork in the lasagna and takes a large bite that she can barely fit in her mouth.

"It's not judgment. I'm just processing all of this." I touch her hand. "It must've been so tough."

She pauses chewing and stares at me as if I'm a clown in a horror film. If I didn't think it was so unlikely, I'd think tears were shining in her eyes. "You're…the first person who's ever said that to me."

"That's because other people are scared to tell you anything."

She swallows the bite of food. "Doesn't matter anyway. She… *Gwyneth* doesn't like me or consider me her mother, and that fucking asshole Kingsley is turning her against me every chance he gets. He's not even allowing me the chance to be a part of her life."

"Isn't she old enough to make her own decisions?"

"She is, but she's also too attached to him considering he raised her on his own. I told her I thought she'd died and that I didn't abandon her on purpose, but she still hates me for having to grow up without a mother. Which is understandable, but still…"

"How about asking for her husband's help? You're friends with Nathaniel."

"Nate told me to give her time. But with her jerk of a father in the picture, no amount of time will help." She pauses, narrowing her eyes on an abstract painting on the wall. "Maybe I should do the world a favor and hire someone to kill the motherfucker for real this time."

"Are you sure you want to say that out loud?"

"Pretend you didn't hear anything." She smiles and I smile back.

Then we fall into a silent companionship. Now I know why Aspen helped me the first time I knocked on her door, no questions asked.

She's experienced what it feels like to lose a child, and judging by how guarded she's turned out to be, the pain must've been immeasurable. It probably shaped her into the woman she is today.

I can't imagine my life without Jayden. He's my second chance to do better, to do something good.

And I'll fight for him until my death if I have to.

My phone pings with a text and I startle, then my heart skyrockets when I see the name on the screen.

Bloody Idiot: I have a last-minute job. Book me a flight to Singapore and a hotel room for two days.

Singapore? Two days?

I don't know why my stomach churns at the news. Even though he's in his office every day and mostly handles things remotely, Daniel is still an international solicitor, and traveling for work isn't a novelty.

Nicole: Right away.

Bloody Idiot: Stay in my flat with the kid and the cat.

Nicole: We're fine in our flat.

Bloody Idiot: That's an order, Ms. Adler. I don't want to hear your annoying neighbors through the phone when I call for work.

I purse my lips. He either likes being a jerk or he's terrible at being nice without the jerk part.

Nicole: Got it.

Bloody Idiot: Oh, and take this as your deadline. When I come back, you better tell me what the fuck was wrong with you the other day or I'll find out myself. Either option will give me the same result, but you can choose whether or not you'll pay for keeping information from me.

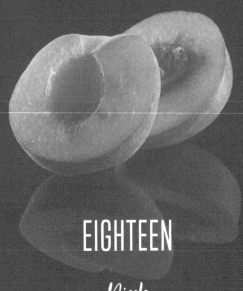

EIGHTEEN

Nicole

"D IDN'T YOU SAY HE'LL BE HERE AT NINE?"

I wince at the accusation in Jay's tone, then pretend to check the huge Roman numeral clock on the wall. "I did."

"Well, it's three minutes past nine and he's not here yet."

"Flights can have delays, hon. And three minutes is hardly late."

"Then call him, Nikki." He shakes me by the hem of my dress, channeling the clingy four-year-old version of himself.

How to tell him that the thought of calling Daniel is no different than putting a finger in my mouth with the intention of throwing up?

I've been a bundle of nerves the past two days, thinking about the best lies to tell when he comes back.

There's no way in hell I would bring up my screwed-up condition willingly. Not in this lifetime.

Two parts of me have been equally at war with each other concerning how to feel. A part of me wishes he wouldn't come back anytime soon. But the other part is as eager as Jay, if not worse.

It doesn't help that we stayed in his flat. Not only that, but my twisted cravings led me to his room late at night and I slept hugging his pillow that's soaked with his scent.

And I might have touched myself to it too. I slid my fingers into my soaked knickers and pictured his face as I thrust in and out of my pussy. When I came, I cried into the pillow for being so irrevocably dysfunctional.

"He has his phone turned off inside the airport," I lie through my teeth.

The thought of hearing Daniel's voice makes me a nervous mess. I could barely talk to him about work-related things these past two days. Let's say I'm thankful for the twelve-hour time difference.

"Can't we go to the airport?"

"No, Jay. We can't." I release a breath. "Just go watch TV."

He sulks as if I told him there will be no fish for a week, then hugs a fussing Lolli and throws himself on the sofa.

To give him credit, he really tries to stay awake by shaking his head and widening his eyes, but thirty minutes later, he's out.

I cover him and Lolli, who's sleeping on his leg. She whines and gives me the side-eye, drama-queen style, then goes back to her slumber.

"You miss him, too, huh?" I whisper to my brother, feeling a weight the size of a brick push off my chest.

I shouldn't miss that damn jerk. Not when he's made it his mission to turn my life into a colossal hell. But the emptiness I experienced these past two days are worse than a tomb's silence.

With a sigh, I cover the food I made, then slip into his office. Another place where I can smell him.

Sometimes, a smell is enough. There needn't be a touch or anything.

Just a smell.

One that's composed of bergamot, lime, and maddening masculinity.

I would've gone to his bedroom, but I don't want to get caught there if he comes in.

The space is large, clean, and has a vintage quality to it. The shelves and the desk are sturdy dark wood and the lounge area has one of those tall chesterfields that appears to be out of a historical show.

I get to organizing the files on his desk, even though there isn't much of a mess. Then I move on to the drawers and pause when I open the first one.

My fingers tremble and my heart nearly spills at my feet.

I blink once, twice, unable to believe what the hell is in front of me.

The object doesn't disappear.

My fingers shake as I wrap them around the smooth surface and lift it up.

This is not a dream.

Tiny glitters of fake snow jiggle around the girl, and my chest rattles just as hard.

I flip the snow globe, just in case it's a lookalike, but the initials Papa had engraved at the bottom nearly send me weeping.

N. A.

But why?

Why would Daniel keep this snow globe…for twenty-one years? He clearly said he didn't.

Never in my wildest dreams would I have thought that he actually kept it.

"Picked up a snooping habit, I see."

My head jerks up and my throat closes.

Daniel stands in the entryway like a dark warrior in a dashing navy blue suit.

The clashing color of his clothes with his eyes would've been mesmerizing if he weren't in the process of eating me alive with those eyes.

Tearing me to pieces.

Scrutinizing every part.

"Why…" My voice is an airy breath and I swallow in a helpless attempt to speak properly. "Why do you have this?"

He strides to me in a few quick steps, erasing the distance between us along with any semblance of sanity I was holding on to with chopped off, bloodied fingers.

Daniel grabs the snow globe, but I don't release it, so it remains suspended between us.

"When I thought I lost it back then, I asked you if you've see it and you said you threw it away. You told me to get over myself because this thing meant nothing."

"It doesn't." The icy coldness of his tone doesn't fool me anymore. I'm starting to think he uses it as a camouflage for something much deeper.

"If it means nothing, you wouldn't have kept it for twenty-one years, Daniel."

"It must've ended up with the rubbish."

"Bullshit." I square my shoulders.

"You might want to watch your language if you want to win the Prude of the Year award."

"You're not changing the subject." My lips tremble. "Tell me why you still have this? Why did you lie about throwing it away?"

He purses his lips and a muscle tics in his jaw, but he doesn't say anything.

"Did you lie about other things?" My voice is broken, thick with too many emotions. "Are there other lies I need to know about?"

"Let's start with yours first." He pulls the snow globe from between my fingers, throws it in the drawer, and slams it shut.

Then his big, hot hands wrap around my waist and the world slips from beneath my feet. He's lifting me up, I realize, but before I can react, my butt meets the solid surface of the desk.

"W-what is this?"

"I specifically mentioned I was going to need answers when I got back. Start talking."

My palms find his shoulders and I push, but I might as well be attempting to move a building. "Why do you want to know?"

"Don't concern your smart brain with that. All you have to do is spit out the reason you acted that way when I touched you."

I stare to the side. "Maybe I don't want to talk about it."

"Maybe I don't fucking care about what you want." His fingers dig into my sides. "Now look at me and speak. Don't make me repeat myself again."

I don't think about what I do next.

Although, I probably should've.

I came up with a million lies to tell him, but as I look at his face, I can't utter any one of them.

So I move on to something else.

Distraction.

Using my hold on his jacket, I pull him close and slam my lips to his. It's just that at first, my mouth on his in the silence of the office.

Then a growl echoes in the air. *His.*

My thoughts scatter and wither into nothingness as one of his palms forcefully grabs my nape and the other remains on my waist. Big, warm, and…safe.

It's the last thought I should have about this situation or him, but it's there, in the back of my screwed-up mind—this is safe.

Completely and utterly safe.

He kisses me slowly as if, like me, he doesn't believe this is happening.

After years.

Eleven, to be exact, but who's counting, right?

I try to be in control, I really do. I'm the one who started this and it should be on my terms and mine alone. So I keep my lips shut.

"Let. Me. In." He accentuates every word with a bite against my lower lip and when I don't comply, he traps the sensitive skin between his teeth and bites down so hard, I'm surprised there's no blood. "Fucking. Open."

My mouth parts with a whimper and he uses the chance to thrust his tongue inside. My insides liquefy at the raw passion and unapologetic strength he holds me with.

He kisses me like he wants to ruin me and worship my body at the same time. He kisses me like I'm his arch-enemy and only friend.

My head swims with the conundrums, and it blurs the signs of the panic attack I usually get under similar circumstances.

His tongue toys with mine, licks it, and renders it completely helpless. A moan reverberates in the air and I'm not sure if it's his or mine.

I'm not even sure what I'm doing anymore. I only meant to shut him up, but it's turning into so much more.

It's turning into something I can't stop or control, not even if I wanted to.

My legs part wide when he settles between them, and that causes the arousal I've been helplessly reining in to smear my core.

At first, I don't put two and two together, but then I sense the emptiness of his hand on my waist. Not long after, two long, calloused fingers trace the line of my underwear. They slip beneath the fabric, teasing my clit, then thrust in my opening.

All in one go.

I gasp against his mouth, my stomach clenching. Despite the pleasure, despite the sloppy sound of the in and out of his fingers, I feel like throwing up.

No, not only feel. *I am* going to throw up.

I wrench my swollen, battered lips away from his and grab his wrist over my dress, causing his hand to stop.

The shake of my head is as frantic as what he must see in my unfocused eyes. "D-Daniel…"

"What?" There's a cutting darkness in his tone, a challenge that he's baiting me to take. "If you want me to stop, tell me why."

"Why would you care? Why do you even want me?"

"Why would I even want you? Isn't that the million-dollar question? I don't fucking know, Nicole. I don't know why you're the only woman I see despite having hundreds at my disposal. I don't know why I'm blind to them and not you. Never you. Did you put some bewitching mojo in my food?"

A tear slides down my cheek. "You'd rather be bewitched than admit you want me?"

"And you prefer hiding over wanting me back." He curls his fingers inside me and darts his tongue to lick the tear from my eye to my cheek, then he bites the droplet that got stuck on my lip.

My grip loosens on his wrist and he takes it as an invitation. Daniel thrusts his fingers inside my pussy hard, fast, and couples them with sliding his thumb back and forth on my clit.

The pleasure is so strong that my hips jerk and I ride his fingers, my lips pressed in a line and my eyes rolling back.

When the orgasm hits me, it's as intense as his touch. As damning, too, because I can't stop releasing sounds that I usually muffle with the back of my hand. I can't now, because he's licking my face, nibbling on my lips, and tasting the pleasure he triggered off my skin.

He releases my neck and unzips his trousers to free his cock. I'm mildly aware of it, but I only feel it when he slides out his fingers and replaces them with his cock with one brutal thrust.

I scream as the still fresh orgasm bleeds into another one. It's much stronger this time and my eyes slam shut.

Blurry gray images form behind my eyelids like vengeful shadows. Drops of black ink stain my vision.

Drip.

Drip.

Drip.

The stench of cigarettes and weed suffocates me. The violence they promise condenses in the distance like distorted lines.

It's pain now.

Raw pain.

And I can't say anything, because it's my fault. I started this. I deserve the pain.

The panic attacks.

The sleeping paralysis. All of it.

Please don't hurt me…

It stops then. The sensation of being trapped. He's not thrusting inside me.

He stopped.

It's over.

"Peaches…"

My eyes slowly open to find Daniel staring at me with a furrow in his brow.

We're still joined, his cock filling me until I can no longer tell where he starts and I begin.

It's Daniel.

Daniel.

I don't know why I want to cry from both frustration and joy.

"You think I would ever hurt you?"

"W-what?"

"You said 'please don't hurt me' just now."

Shit. I spoke that out loud?

"Say it, Nicole. Am I hurting you?"

I slowly shake my head.

"Then why did you beg me not to just now?"

I wasn't talking to you, but I can't say that and expose how much of a freak I actually am.

So I use my earlier tactic and kiss him. I'm more aggressive this time, biting his lips and tasting him on my tongue.

He tastes of peaches and impossible addictions. Logically, he shouldn't. Logically, he's not supposed to be a replica of my lollipops and my coping mechanisms.

But I welcome it anyway.

I need to be anchored in this moment. To Daniel and his mythical eyes and euphoric touch. I can't allow the shadows to creep in again.

Daniel pulls out a little, then drives back in, hitting my G-spot. I shake with the force of his thrusts and moan against his mouth.

My eyes get droopy once more and I can feel myself slipping into that other realm.

A hot hand grips my nape, squeezing the side of my throat. "Eyes on me when I fuck you."

My pulse skyrockets as I let Daniel's eyes trap mine. They're full of stars, galaxies, and planets.

They're otherworldly, overwhelming even, but they're also safe.

The safest thing on earth.

Even if I could only look at them from afar.

Even if being too close may blind me.

Both my palms find his cheeks and I stare at his face as he fucks me deeper, taking his time to hit that pleasurable spot over and over.

By the time he ups his rhythm, I'm on the brink again. A wordless gasp shapes my lips and he devours my mouth as he pulls out of me and I feel his thighs quivering against mine.

My mind is hazy as I stare down and see him coming all over his hands. His cum smears my clothes and his before dripping on the ground.

It's then I realize he actually fucked me without a condom. Shit. If he wasn't thinking straight and pulled out at the last second, we'd have more complications on our hands.

And why the hell am I disappointed about that?

Wake the hell up, Nicole. You had unprotected sex with a womanizer and you're disappointed he pulled out?

I release his face, frantic to disappear from his vicinity. Maybe I can dig a hole and hide in it for the foreseeable future.

It was only a kiss. Just how the hell did it end up being mind-blowing sex?

Daniel grabs my chin with his hand that's still coated in cum, aborting my mission. "Where do you think you're going?"

"Aren't we done?"

"We haven't even gotten started." He smears his cum on my parted lips, then thrusts two fingers inside like he did the other day. "I'm going to fuck you again, once in the shower and once on my bed, and then…you will tell me all about the fucking skeletons you're hiding in your closet."

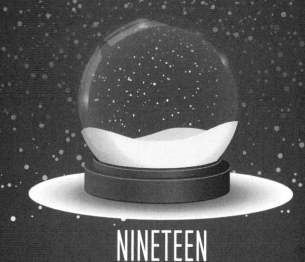

NINETEEN

Daniel

N MY ATTEMPTS TO GET MY HEAD OUT OF MY ARSE—OR MORE accurately, my dick—I'm entertaining the mayor in a golf game this weekend.

He invited most of the partners at W&S. Most, as in, the ones he deems worthy of his precious games. That includes the two owners, Knox, and me.

Knox, being a twat on borrowed time, promptly declined. Mayor Jefferson, an old man with a shock of white hair and brows that should see scissors, couldn't even take offense.

Not when Knox is engaged to a Russian mafia princess. The same mafia whose drug-filled arses he kissed to get to where he is.

Corrupted wealth in a corrupted city in a corrupted world.

Just my scene.

Nate and King showed up, though, clad in their tailored slacks and polo shirts.

This whole thing is part of their networking schemes so their firm keeps representing pigs like Mayor Jefferson and extorting

"This is more boring than monogamy," King says, hitting a beagle.

Nate side-eyes him as if he's speaking an alien language. "You don't even know what that term means."

"Your point?"

"How would you know it's boring if you've never tried it?"

"You're going backward. I know it's boring, which is why I avoid it as much as Switzerland stays out of war."

"Flawed logic, King. You like war."

"There will definitely be war on your motherfucking ass if you think about anything outside of monogamy."

"Never said I would. I happen to be happily married."

"To my fucking daughter." He swings his club in the air. "Even your happiness depends on me. Better keep that in mind next time you take sides, my dear son-in-law."

"Will do when you check your ego into a mental institute."

A silent war of glares and stares starts between them.

I tactfully slide to their side. "Excuse my bloody French and interruption, but Jefferson can probably fucking hear you calling his game boring."

"That old tool has hearing problems." King smiles and waves at him to which he waves back. "He wouldn't hear a whore calling his son's name."

"You're one to know." Nate takes a sip of water. "Considering all the whores you fuck on a regular basis."

"They're called escorts, and I swear to fuck, if you bring that up to Gwen…"

"A little misleading that she still sees you as a saint when you're a demon, but I won't be the one who breaks her heart. You know she still holds out hope that you'll settle down, right?"

"Make her abandon it then. I won't give up sex for the white fence nightmare." He wraps an arm around my shoulder. "Isn't that right, Danny?"

A few months ago, I would've hollered "Fuck yeah" and taken

my car to the nearest club. Sometimes, the riding happened during the drive.

Now the words can't even leave my lips. They're stuck between my teeth like annoying fish bones.

A week.

It's been a week since I fucked Nicole again.

A week of constant sex every time I could get her alone.

A week of bribing Jayden with *Despicable Me* merch—holy fuck, who knew there was tons of that shit?—so he could beat it to his room and let me fuck his sister.

In my flat, naturally.

I didn't let them go back to their place from hell, so we're all stuck in that "Are we living together?" phase.

Though, I'm going to make her break the lease for that hell-hole sooner or later. Even after I'm out of the picture, I'll find her a better place to stay at.

That's too many depressing thoughts about the future—or not, depending on how I should look at it.

Back to more cheerful news, on top of which is fucking Nicole.

The downside is, I can't fuck her when Jayden is out and about in the flat like her third-class bodyguard. So I have to do it at night, thankful as fuck for soundproof walls.

There are the occasional Peeping Tom sessions from Lolli, but she soon remembers she doesn't give a fuck and stalks to her next cat adventure.

Touching her in the flat isn't enough, though, so I lock us in my office and take her against the table, wall, floor. Any surface that's available to shove my cock in her warm pussy, basically.

For the sake of my sanity and my dick-shaped ego, I have the decency to pretend that I'm getting her out of my system.

The plan is still ongoing and working like a charm.

It has nothing to do with how much my dick only comes alive around her or that I've been obsessed like a second-rate creep with her peach-smelling blonde locks while she sleeps.

Or the fact that I've been diligently undergoing one sex

marathon after the other as if she's an assignment and I'm studying for the bar all over again.

And it definitely has nothing to do with the way her body fits around mine like a vise.

But maybe it does have to do with the way she stiffens whenever I start to touch her. Only at the beginning, though. She attempted to close her eyes at some point, too, but I fucked that habit out of her.

Now, I need to make her less freaked out about oral sex when she's receiving it and figure out why she withdraws into herself every now and then.

"Daniel?" King's voice brings me out of my mini dark fairy-tale musings.

"What?"

"You didn't answer the question."

"That's because rumor has it, he's screwing his assistant. And by rumor, I mean Knox and Sebastian."

"Sebastian?" I echo. Knox is privy to my life like a power-hungry FBI agent, but Sebastian, Nate's nephew and another junior partner, has the attention span of a bird about everyone who's not his girlfriend.

He's the personification of devil-may-care, complete with tiny red horns and a tail peeking from between his legs. Knox says that's his dick, but that's not the point. Nor is the fact that we discuss each other's dicks during breakfast.

"You're lucky there are no rules against in-house romance or your ass would be with the board as we speak," King tells me with disdain.

"Jealous that monogamy's train is leaving you behind?" Nate grins.

"More like I'm ecstatic there's natural selection for idiots. The world needs less of them."

"I'm not in a monogamous relationship," I announce more to myself than anyone else, ignoring the fact that my dick refuses to touch another woman with a ten-foot pole.

"Tell that to the blinds that are rarely open in your office nowadays." Nate stares down at me. "I'm going to need to check if you're actually working."

"Don't give me that. Judging by the number of times Grace said you were unavailable while you were locked in your office, I'd say you fuck Gwen like you're a teenager on his first sex marathon. I doubt any work is involved."

"Thanks a lot for the unnecessary imagery about my fucking daughter, Sterling." King pushes me away but directs his disgust at Nate. "While I was in a coma. Really, Nate?"

He digs his club into the ground. "You're still alive."

"You, however, won't be once I change my mind and decide to kill you."

I hold up a hand. "For any future criminal case references, I didn't just hear that threat."

"I did."

The three of us turn to the source of the feminine voice. Aspen stands there in a short white skirt and a blue polo shirt with a hand on her hip, looking ten times younger out of her usual suit.

"I'll bring you justice and make sure this crazy jerk is locked up for life." She stares at King. "If you do us all a favor and commit a homicide in, say, Florida or Alabama, I'll even sit on the front row as they electrocute you."

"Maybe I'll be the one in the front row when your witch blood pushes you to commit first-degree murder. Now, can you grace us with the reason behind your unwanted presence?"

"Jefferson invited me for golf."

"You?"

"A senior partner last time everyone checked."

"You're late," Nate says amicably.

"Probably couldn't be bothered for the first hour?" I ask.

"You knew?" King stares at us as if we beheaded his favorite puppy à la guillotine style.

"The question is, why don't you? Jefferson invited the partners. Aspen is high on that list." Nate checks his watch, probably eager to go back home. The only reason he agreed to be here is because Gwen is studying for her exams.

"His sexist dick hates the idea so much that he forgets about it. Often."

"You happen to be the forgettable type, *sweetheart*."

She glares at him as if he jammed his feet against her ribs and crushed her nonexistent heart, but she soon smooths out her expression. "Not more than you, *babe*."

It's his turn to regard her like she's a wild stallion he wants to tame. Flipping her hair, she faces me and Nate. "How do we go from here?"

King laughs. "You wouldn't know how to play golf if you were spoon-fed, amateur."

"You're on." She starts to follow my and Nate's instructions.

By the time we're done with golf, King and Aspen are seconds away from slitting each other's throats or fucking on the grass. Not sure which one is more pressing.

Nate wears the expression of "what have I done to deserve this?" and I'm more than ready to go home.

Usually, I don't. Go home, I mean. Except to sleep or pretend I have some semblance of a nice life.

But today, I can't stop thinking about who I left back at the flat.

And I might have bought a shitload of unnecessary shit on my way home. Like a Minions jacket, a cat toy, and a premium fish.

When I get there, I'm greeted by so many fucking colors, they explode in my face.

Some pop song is playing and there's dancing. By Nicole and Jayden, to be specific. They're jumping with the energy of a stripper on a pole. Lolli is joining in on the fun, too, running from one end of the room to the other, seeming to search for her own dose of whatever these two are on.

Ignoring my knee-jerk reaction of pissing all over their fun, I lean against the doorway and cross my legs at the ankles. The scene in front of me plays out like a clichéd scene from a Disney film. Nicole twirls a giggling Jayden, her own laughter echoing in the air with the grace of a fucking angel.

No, Daniel. You're not thinking about throwing a nine-year-old out the window so you can take his place.

"Dan!" The same person I've been having serial killer thoughts about calls for me, a grin showing his missing teeth.

Nicole's attention finally slides to me and she pales, then flushes like a virgin. Correction, she didn't flush when she was a virgin.

She was an angel with a devil's appearance. Now, she just looks like a broken angel. A devil on his second try of "Knockin' on Heaven's Door," the Guns N' Roses version.

Her movements are flustered as she turns down the music from the speaker. "Sorry, I…thought you weren't returning until later in the evening."

That was the plan until I came to a perturbing realization that the outside world doesn't have what I want.

My boring—ex-boring—flat does.

I don't offer that explanation, though. Instead, I toss Jayden the Minions jacket that he oohs and aahs over and even hugs me.

The blasphemy.

I pat his back anyway, because spawn or not, children kind of need all that affection shit. He might be smart, but he's as lonely as his sister.

They've been each other's world for so long that it feels intrusive to even be in the middle of them.

But they let me in anyway, Minions, Lolli, and all.

"I'm going to take a picture of it with my other collection," he announces, then runs to his room as if his arse is on fire.

His room.

The little rascal has a room in my flat. It's actually a guest room that no guest has used before him.

Nicole has the second guest room that she doesn't sleep in, because the fucking happens in my bedroom.

"You should stop getting him stuff," she tells me when I'm in the kitchen, pouring myself a glass of water.

I lean against the counter and face her. "Is that your way of saying, 'thank you for taking care of me and my brother. Let me suck your dick to show how grateful I am'?"

Her cheeks turn a deep shade of red, but to her credit, the haughty expression doesn't disappear. I guess having aristocratic blood in your veins never changes, even if your mother turns out to be a psycho on steroids.

"You're spoiling him." She completely ignores my "suck my dick" suggestion. "He'll find it hard to adjust when this whole thing is over."

"This whole thing?" I try to pretend she didn't metaphorically stab me with her favorite kitchen knife.

Yes, the plan—that's currently searching for therapy—is to kick her out once the custody battle is over, but that doesn't mean she gets to think that as well.

Nicole releases a frustrated breath. "Whatever vendetta you have against me."

"There's no fine print that says this will be over anytime soon. Might want to rest that busy brain from thinking about unnecessary things."

"How long do you intend to keep this going?"

"Bored already?" I grab her by a handful of her hair, my fingers digging into her nape. "Didn't sound like it when you were screaming the room down last night."

Her delicate hands land on my chest as she peeks behind me. "Stop it. Jay's awake."

"So is my cock."

I nudge my erection against the soft flesh of her stomach to prove a point. It's been in this state ever since I walked in and saw her dancing and laughing like a fucking goddess.

Her thighs tremble against mine and then it happens, the slight shudder, the closing of her eyes, and the whole body stiffness.

When she opens them, she relaxes a little and stares at me

like a nymph. Either she is one or I really need some therapy for being a sex addict.

I even did my own diagnosis and can spare the psychotherapist the trouble of naming it. I'm sexually addicted to Nicole.

Have been ever since I found out what fucking means, and the fact that I couldn't have her, then shouldn't have had her, turned me into a bitter fucking dick.

My emotions have always been mild, controlled, absolutely regular. Except for when it comes to this woman.

With her, they're a tsunami of toxic shit and bring an immeasurable need to inflict pain.

I rub my cock against her stomach and she shudders.

"Oh my God, here?" she whisper-yells.

"Good a place as any."

"You're insane."

"Heard worse. Now make that mouth useful and wrap it around my cock, Ms. Adler."

"Don't call me that." She scrunches her nose.

"The inferiority pisses you off?"

"Feeling like a stranger does." Her hand wraps around my cock through my trousers and I nearly come like a pubescent amateur.

"We are strangers, Nicole. Eleven years would testify to such. Oh, and the ten years before that weren't exactly a splash of color."

"Still doesn't make us strangers." She wanks me slowly, taking obvious pleasure in how my cock twitches in her hold. "See? Junior recognizes me."

"Why the fuck do you remember that name?"

"I have a strong memory. Besides, he's telling me something, Junior."

"Didn't know you were a dick whisperer."

"Junior only whispers to me," she says with a bright smile that makes me as hard as the Statue of Liberty.

"Let's go with your crazy shit. What is he telling you?"

"That you dipped him in too many holes and he's tired."

"Is that so?"

"Yeah, he thinks he should take some downtime."

"You must have hearing problems, because downtime doesn't exist in his limited vocabulary. Shagging is his way of survival as a healthy twenty-nine-year-old male."

She squeezes me until I grunt. "He doesn't mean downtime from sex, just downtime from the other girls."

My lips tilt in a smirk. "That's too many words and a tacky tactic to tell me you want us to be exclusive."

She reaches into my trousers and gives me a real hand job, up and down until all my blood rushes to my groin. "I want us to be exclusive."

"And I want to be the Queen's solicitor. We don't always get what we want."

Nicole pulls her hand out of my trousers just when I'm about to decorate it with my cum.

The lust slowly vanishes and her haughty expression returns. "Then I'll go fuck other men."

"You do that. Don't forget to not use your teeth when giving head." I want to kick the fucking arsehole in me who even uttered those words when the prominent feeling is to stab whoever comes near her.

Or whoever she goes to.

"You'll really sleep with other women?" There's hurt in her tone, a brokenness that fucking guts me.

"We're not in a relationship, Nicole. This is called fucking. No strings attached. Google it."

"I won't let you touch me then. Go to your side pieces for your erection problems."

"Why the fuck are you being dramatic?"

"So asking for basic human decency is called dramatic now? Fine, I'm a drama queen then. You might want to rub one out, because my mouth won't be touching that dick."

And then she storms to Jayden's room, leaving me there, hard with both rage and the need to strangle the fuck out of her.

Now, I have to reacquaint my dick with my hand and hope their love-hate affair will hold up for some time.

For the rest of the day, Nicole ignores me. Flat out. Like she's the queen and I'm a pageboy at her disposal.

It's one of her loathsome traits that I've hated since we were young. She has this tendency of making those surrounding her feel like less than fucking dirt.

During dinner, Jayden, my only ally aside from a fickle Lolli, asks, "How did you guys meet?"

Nicole stares at her brother, then at me. "We went to the same school."

"That wasn't the official meeting. We didn't even talk at school." I sip the soup, half amazed that I can talk while eating, half tempted to throw it all up.

"When did you start to talk then?" Jayden asks.

"When I saved her from an allergic reaction. She would've died if it weren't for me."

"That's not true," Nicole says.

"Want to call the doctor? You were asphyxiating."

Jayden's eyes widen. "Because of peaches?"

"That's right, mate. Your sister knew she was allergic to them but still stole them and hid to eat them."

"I didn't use to have that strong of an allergic reaction," she grumbles around a bite of food. "I've never eaten peaches since that day."

"You just suck on those lollipops instead and slap the color anywhere physically possible."

"I do not."

"Your phone case is peach-colored."

"It was the only one available."

"Your Post-it Notes are also peach-colored."

"Coincidence."

"Debatable."

Jayden stares between us half oblivious, half curious about

the tension that's about to catch flames. "Did you become close after that?"

I snort, "Not after she ratted me out as the culprit who gave her the peaches."

"I never said that," she blurts. "Mum and Aunt Nora deduced it on their own."

"Nice try." I drink a whole glass of water, amazed I don't choke on it. "Now you'll tell me you didn't snitch on me the dozen times that followed."

"I did not."

"Then why did you follow me around with the devil swinging on your shoulders?"

Her lips purse, but she doesn't say anything.

"That's what I thought."

"You always do that," she spits out. "Assuming things and confirming them without even asking me about them."

"You never offered an explanation."

She lifts her chin. "I have nothing to explain to you."

"Fantastic."

"Brilliant."

Jayden releases a long sigh, shaking his head like an old man. "Should I go to my room now? Are you going to start kissing?"

"Not in this lifetime," Nicole hisses.

"Never," I say at the same time.

"Thank God." Jayden lifts a shoulder. "It's gross anyway."

No, it's not.

But I don't say that and, instead, choose to stuff my face with repulsive food that suddenly doesn't feel so repulsive anymore.

Nicole glares at me and I glare right back.

Play all you want, Peaches. I've already won this game.

TWENTY

Daniel

CELIBACY IS A CRANKY BITCH WITH WITHDRAWAL ISSUES.
My dick hates me. My body hates me.
I hate me.

Not enough to crack, though.

I survived a week and a half without sex before. What's four days?

Apparently, around four decades in human years according to my teenage-level hard-ons whenever that fucking woman is in sight.

It doesn't matter what she's wearing, a hot as fuck dress, simple jeans, or a long robe. All I feel is the need to fuck her until neither of us can breathe properly.

That night, right after she told me the E-word and I said in no uncertain terms that she could go suck it, I ran into her in the kitchen while she was making some apricot juice. I'm going to bet my career and left nut that she drinks it because it's the most similar fruit to peaches. But anyway, when my hand brushed against hers not so accidentally, she glared at me with that snobbishness that made me both hard and irritated as a fireball.

She motioned at herself and said, "This is off-limits." Then she flipped her golden locks and stalked back to her room.

I needed to stop myself from going after her or else we'd have second-degree murder on our hands.

My dick and I still haven't decided what we think about her newfound confidence. She's glowing with it like an angel flying above God's shoulder. Not that she didn't have it a few weeks ago, but she was keeping it under wraps, bowing her head and biting her tongue to keep her job—and Jayden.

Lately, however, her old self is starting to peek through the cracks. And as much as I wanted to fuck that Nicole into oblivion, I didn't really like her.

She wasn't confident. She bordered on arrogant with mean-girl tendencies and a bitch sign slapped on her forehead.

And I'll be damned if I don't clip those wings before she morphs back into her old self.

"Your coffee," she says sweetly, bending over so half her tits are nearly hanging out of her blouse.

I grab the edge of the desk.

Down, Junior. It isn't your time to shine yet.

Pretending she doesn't exist—which is as successful as ignoring global warming—I take a sip of my coffee and listen to her enumerating today's schedule.

I throw the coffee in the rubbish can.

She pauses her anchorwoman presentation. "What's wrong now? There was exactly one gram of sugar. I weighed it myself."

"Too hot."

"No, it's not. You're just being difficult for no reason."

"There's a reason."

"Enlighten me."

"My dick is throwing a tantrum for the lack of lips around him. If you want to fix it…"

Red creeps up from her pale cleavage to her neck and even to her ears. To her credit, though, her expression remains stuck in that snobbish stage.

Now that I think about it, Nicole has never been expressive. Not even on that day when everything shattered to pieces.

It's why I like the new version of her better. At least I can read some reactions she leaves unguarded. Maybe, just like she couldn't be bothered to hide her beauty mole anymore, she couldn't care less about sealing everything inside.

She smiles and it's as fake as A-list celebrities' laughs and just as bright. "Sure thing."

"Really?"

"Of course. You just have to say the magic words for it. Repeat after me, *no other people*."

My lips twist, then I snap my fingers in her face. "Get the fuck out."

She lifts a shoulder. "As you wish, *sir*."

Her walk to the door is the equivalent of a strip show, minus the most important part—taking her clothes off. Her hips sway in that gentle, alluring way only she is capable of.

Stop looking.

Stop looking—

Once she reaches the door, she turns around. "Oh, and what would you like for dinner tonight?"

The sodding thing knows she has a hold on me through that, too. Even though I consider food the most disgusting thing ever created, hers doesn't fall under that category.

Ever since she became my personal chef, I don't eat with the sole purpose of survival. I actually enjoy the activity, especially with Jayden being a clown and Lolli sticking her head anywhere she deems fit. That includes the top of the table and Jayden's shoulder.

But if Nicole thinks she has me as a ring on her finger, breaking news will hit her upside the head soon.

"I won't be dining at home."

"Oh?"

I don't fall for her prompt to keep me talking, and just like that, her gleeful expression disappears.

That's right, baby. You've got to work for it.

She clears her throat. "Where will you be dining?"

"It's a bit out of your scope of skills."

"I'm just asking if you'll need me in a business meeting or something."

"It's a charity event."

"So you need an assistant."

"Not really, but you're welcome to pass me condoms or join the orgies that I plan to take part in tonight."

Her lips press in a line before she steps out and slams the door.

Good. Now, she feels a sliver of the fucking frustration she's been shoving down my throat with a spoon.

Later that evening, I dress in a tux, ignore her glares over the kitchen counter, and let Jayden hug me goodbye, then head to the charity ball.

Calling it that is a bit of a stretch, considering this is the rich's way to write off taxes.

King and Nate included.

They're both here. Nate is accompanied by his young wife who's pretty much half his age, but looks at him as if he's her knight in a shining Mercedes.

King is solo because hoes aren't for the public, and he's actively glaring at Nate whenever he touches his daughter or makes her laugh. If a crime happens, I swear to fuck there will be no dragging me in as a witness into this mess.

Knox joins me with a gorgeous blonde on his arm.

Jeez, did I think of blonde and gorgeous in the same sentence? *Get a grip, Sterling.*

Anastasia doesn't look the part of a mafia princess. She's soft, demure, and extremely in love with my sod of a friend who, until a few months ago, thought he didn't have a soul.

Like me.

Turns out, I'm the only one on that merry-go-round. Aside from King, maybe.

Scratch that. King doesn't have a heart, a soul, and a whole lot of things I pride myself in owning.

Anastasia's continent-sized engagement ring was probably made by the blood of a mafia's enemies.

Not a good thought to have when I'm kissing the back of her hand. "Looking good, Ana."

Knox kicks my shin. "Hands off my fiancée."

"Whom you got because of me." I kick him back when no one is looking.

He stares at me as if I'm a pope who cursed. "How exactly did you contribute? Was that before or after you almost ruined everything?"

"Right in the middle, actually. Ana, let this wanker know that I played a vital part."

"Daniel was a good sport." She laughs, her expression lightening, and I get that queasy shit in my stomach that happens when I'm about to throw up.

This is why I don't like blondes. They always, without a sliver of fucking doubt, look like her in my mind's screwed-up eye.

"You're misunderstanding something, beautiful. Daniel is anything but a good sport."

"Your jealousy is flooding the floor, Van Doren. Every individual on planet Earth knows I'm more charming than you'll ever be."

"Is that why you yelled at two people this week?"

"Three, and they were being idiots. Being charming is not a synonym for pushover, and I'm allergic to stupidity."

"But Knox is right. Gwen said you're different," Anastasia supplies needlessly. Gwen, Nate's wife, is her bestie, and apparently, they've taken up gossip as a side hobby, because she says, "Ever since you got a new assistant. Blonde, too. I always thought you hated us."

"I do. No offense."

"Taken."

Knox levels me with a glare. "Apologize."

"I'm sorry you were born with a disgusting hair color, Anastasia. I liked you better when you dyed your hair black."

"Are you sure that's an apology?" She shakes her head.

"The only version you'll get." I smile, showing my dimples since they evidently make people drop their guards or drop to their knees. Except for one fucking person, obviously. "Now, if you'll excuse me. I have a few clients to greet."

The round of socializing is equal to liking random posts on social media and commenting that people look good when they're actually potatoes in the form of humans.

I might be on the extrovert spectrum, but over-interaction with people makes me feel...empty.

Maybe even lonely.

But my nonexistent therapist doesn't need to know about that.

"Danny!" A shock of gold throws itself in my arms like a hooker in a strip club.

"Katerina." I kiss her cheek as my cue to pull away, and she subtly rubs her stomach against my dick.

No sign of life.

Bloody perfect, Junior. We're going to the ER in a bit.

Katerina has a rich daddy that helped her get on her feet, but she's a hard worker, too. Which is what I respected about her the first time we met during our university years.

She's wearing a golden dress that could compete with a drag queen's clothes. She's tall with generous curves and a fuckable arse and...well, that's all I remember about her.

And the fact that my stomach tolerates one-tenth of her food.

"It's been a minute, stranger." She drags her red nails over my bowtie.

"I've been kind of busy." Trying to shag my assistant on my terms and failing miserably. Not that anyone needs those depressing details.

"Then it must be fate that we met here."

"We run in the same circle, Kat. Fate is the last thing you should be giving credit to."

"Oh, don't be a bore."

"Don't be a hopeless romantic." It's disgusting.

All emotions are.

Especially the sappy type that many are surprisingly fond of.

"A romance is the last thing I want," she purrs. "I'm opening a new restaurant in Paris."

"Congratulations."

"Care to take those congratulations somewhere more private?"

No. But I don't really have a reason for refusal, so I say, "Lead the way."

I want to stab myself with a ten-inch knife and hope the pain will wake my Sleeping Beauty dick up.

Katerina takes us to a supply room on the far end of the ballroom and locks the door behind us.

Leaning against it, she starts toying with her barely-there straps.

She's beautiful, hot, with a body I can lose myself in for hours, and she's a brunette.

Perfect for a quick shag, a forehead kiss, and a rain check for a Paris redo.

And yet, my dick continues his slumber, waiting for another princess's kiss.

The same princess he almost started a journal to memorize the first time he got to tarnish her.

Take her innocence.

Be inside her.

On the other hand, Katerina does nothing for me.

She didn't in the past either. None of the other women did.

They were just a necessity.

I'm about to leave, find Nicole, and agree to her condition with my hand on her arse as I fuck her, when a bang echoes in the silence.

At first, I think we've been bombed.

Hello, terrorists and world disorder.

But it happens again. A knock on the door. More like a damn fist on it.

"Someone is here," Katerina whines.

The knocking sound comes again, stronger this time.

"Did you not hear me?" she shrieks.

The bang comes again and I suppress a smile. I think I know exactly what type of terrorist this is.

Katerina opens the door with more impatience than a toddler's. "You!"

The "you," a terrorist with the most gorgeous face God has created, is none other than Nicole.

She shoulders past Katerina, her stance tense and face similar to sovereignty on paintings.

But her body is a myriad of motions. Her legs shake. Her fingers twitch.

It's hardly noticeable, but it's there. How come I've never detected the change in her body language before?

She stands between us, in her simple black dress and heels that I want off her.

Actually, the heels can stay.

Nicole doesn't need to be flashy or even make an effort to look pretty. A second-rate dress, a delicate chignon, and some makeup, and she's ready to walk the runway.

"Aren't you the assistant?" Katerina spits, obviously angry at Nicole for pussy-blocking her.

"The one and only." She smiles with dripping sweetness.

"Care to share what you're doing here?" Katerina asks.

Nicole glares at me, then reaches into her bra, and my dick kind of resurrects from the ashes like a cheap phoenix.

A packet is nestled between her fingers. "I thought I would give you a condom so he doesn't give you the STD he passed to me. Chlamydia. It's nasty shit and we girls have to look out for each other."

Katerina pales. I burst out laughing.

Fuck. This woman.

"Is this some sort of a twisted joke?" Katerina stares between Nicole's poker face and my extremely amused one like a spectator in a tennis match.

"Want to see the results?" Nicole starts to lift her dress.

"Disgusting. Both of you." Katerina glares at us and runs out of the room with a speed that cracks her heel.

Nicole makes a show of releasing the condom with a mic-drop motion. "Heard she has a big mouth. Have a nice life convincing anyone to touch your chlamydia dick, *sir*."

"You're too obsessed with my dick, did you know that?" I'm still smiling. "First, you suck it like a gorgeous slut, then you ride and touch it whenever it's near you, and you can't help looking when it's not inside you. And now, you're starting rumors about it. I'm guessing you still won't say I had a small dick at my funeral, huh?"

"That plan is in motion, thank you very much."

"Liar. You even brought the right condom size. Large."

"Part of my job."

"Passing out condoms?"

"Stopping my boss from polluting the world with his sperm."

"Cum, Peaches. It's called cum." I wrap my fingers around her nape and pull her flush against me. "And you better be ready to choke on it after you cock-blocked me."

"*Moi?*" She plays innocent even as her body quivers around mine.

My thumb finds her plump lips and I thrust inside. She darts her tongue around it, licking the sides and sucking on the single digit like it's my cock.

Her eyes meet mine with a challenge mixed with a feral type of lust that turns me fucking insane.

The Sleeping Beauty syndrome has released my dick from its clutches and he's currently upgrading to Hulk status.

Nicole grabs my wrist with both hands and bobs her head up and down, making a show of sucking my damn thumb.

What are the chances of it magically switching places with the other part of my body that's in dire need of her technique?

"Better stop that if you don't want to be fucked against the door." I have the decency to sound casual, almost bored.

Nicole doesn't take the bait, her eyes continuing to drill holes in my face and communicate something that should've been extinguished with the Nazis.

"Have you heard the part where I'll fuck you, door style, without the exclusive clause?"

She releases my thumb with a pop. "You can't touch other people anyway. Katerina is probably blabbing about the chlamydia episode to anyone that will listen. So I guess you're stuck with me."

"And you'd let me touch you with a *supposedly* STD dick?"

"You already passed it to me, so it doesn't matter. Consider it pro bono for old times' sake."

"Maybe you're the one who passed it to me."

"Says who?"

"My medical report and the condoms I've never fucked without."

"You fucked me without a condom."

"Slipped my mind."

"You wouldn't let an ant slip your mind… Oh my God, you were too rattled by me, weren't you?"

"Sorry to break it to you, love, but you don't have a golden pussy."

"No, it's better. Made of diamonds, hard enough that they penetrated your steel-like control. Did it hurt?"

"What?"

"Wanting me and denying it?"

"No more than your twisted version of jealousy."

"I'm not jealous."

"Oh, please. You just strapped an 'I own you' on me in front of Katerina and made sure she'll talk about it."

"I wouldn't have had to go this far if you'd just said no other people. So I had to improvise and make it happen on my own. Now, you have no choice."

I smirk and she stiffens. "Says who? I can always fuck escorts."

"You…you'd rather pay whores than be exclusive with me?"

"*Escorts*, and yes. I don't want to accidentally cut myself on your diamond pussy."

A tremble overtakes her locked jaw and moisture gathers in her eyes, flooding the green like a deadly hurricane.

"Why?" Her question is a haunted whisper as she closes her hand into a fist and hits me with it across the chest. "Why them and not me?" *Hit.* "Why is it never me?" *Hit.* "No matter what I do, you don't look at me." *Hit.* "I'm right in front of you, why can't you see me?"

Hysteria.

Breakdown.

Meltdown.

I've witnessed it in the courtroom when someone reaches their limits and their mind collapses.

When it gets to be too much and the only way out is losing their shit.

I just never thought I'd see Nicole in such a position.

She's hitting anywhere and everywhere she can reach, her face a mess of snot and tears and sweat.

The worst part is, I don't think she knows what she's saying or doing anymore. Her eyes have turned glassy and she seems numb, like that time she begged me not to hurt her while I was fucking her.

"Nicole," I call calmly, but she might as well be deaf.

I clasp both her wrists in one hand and push her until her back hits the door. "Nicole!"

"No, no, no…" she chants, her eyes staring right through me, and for the second time, I see fear in her gaze.

Raw, pure fear.

I'm about to let her go but think better of it. I'm such a lowlife for taking advantage of her weak moment, and God will probably call up Satan to dig me a lower hole in hell, but if I don't do this, I'll never know.

"Please…please…" she begs.

I tighten my hold on her wrists, grabbing her throat with my other hand. "Please what?"

"Don't hurt me…I didn't mean to."

"Didn't mean to what?"

"Be a cock-tease, I didn't mean to! Please, please…I'm sorry, I'm so sorry."

My jaw clenches and my hand trembles with rage. "What's going to happen now?"

Her glassy eyes turn into a waterfall of tears as she murmurs, "You'll hurt me…"

I know I'm the one who came up with this fucked-up idea and Satan is taking notes in the corner, but I wish the earth would crack and swallow me into its hell right this moment.

"Who am I?"

Her lips shake and tears stream inside her mouth.

"Who the fuck am I, Nicole?" I roar.

The name she whispers back smashes my world into bloody pieces.

TWENTY-ONE

Nicole

Age eighteen

WHAT ARE THE SIGNS OF "ALMOST" LOSING IT, DISCARDING the "lucky" badge, and galloping to the sun on a faulty unicorn?

For weeks, I've been hanging on the edge that separates sanity from its more destructive antonym. Maybe years.

Is it too late to sign up for therapy?

On second thought, Mum will probably disown me, so that's not an option for…a lifetime.

Unless I do end up revolving around the sun on my unicorn, after all, and get roasted alive.

Do they have a therapist in hell?

I have no doubt that I'm heading there on the expressway considering all the voodoo I've been doing in my head.

Every single imaginary spell is directed at the girls who keep hanging on to Daniel's arm as if it's made of gold.

It's not.

He's just a manwhore, and I hate that and him, and every girl who gets to touch him when I can't.

Jealous much?

No, it's way worse. I'm bordering on extremely obsessive.

It's unhealthy, toxic, and all the other terms my imaginary therapist will have a field day with.

I did my research and it said that the best way to get rid of an unhealthy obsession is to stay away, exercise, and keep my mind preoccupied.

Done, done, and done.

Now, best of luck telling that to my wet dreams about Daniel.

Ever since he expressed being disgusted with wanting me, he's made it a point to flaunt all the girls in my face as if they were Prada bags.

I never gave him a reaction, always staring down my nose at him and his tool for the hour as if the dirt beneath my shoes was more precious than them.

I'm many things, but an emotional mess was never one of them. Always composed, always elegant.

Always…detached.

Sometimes, I stared at my doll and talked to it as if it were Papa. If his soul happens to be there, we're all doomed.

But anyway, I asked Papa if I stopped being lucky, would Daniel have me?

The doll stared at me with its droopy eyes and remained silent. Which is my sign of a "no."

But my faulty brain didn't understand the concept. It doesn't relate to words like "giving up" and "letting go." It's just not in me.

Maybe it's because I usually got what I wanted, whether by working for it, asking for it, or manipulating my way to have it. It's not arrogance, it's pure determination.

Sometimes I wonder if I'm too fixated on Daniel because I can't have him. But I did have him during the night of the fire, and it only made my emotions flare to a dangerous level.

I didn't know it before, but turns out, I'm the type who

correlates sexual and emotional intimacy together. They're one, undivided entity.

Which is why everything he's done afterward hurt more than I'll ever admit.

One thing's for certain, though. Daniel isn't the only one who gets to play this "you mean nothing to me" game.

I got into his circle of friends and got close to the football players. Not only that, but I also allowed them to touch me and get handsy with me.

While he watched.

Daniel isn't as good as I am at controlling his emotions. They usually spill like ink on paper and he glares or flares his nostrils.

The other day, Daniel saw me laughing with Chris on a mini date in the school's garden. When we got back inside, Daniel waited for him to approach the classroom, then slammed the door as he was walking in, hitting him in the nose.

I didn't believe the scene at the beginning. The way Daniel apologized and smiled was like he really didn't mean to.

But as soon as Chris walked away, I saw the sly smirk on Daniel's face.

Then, when Chris was watching football practice from the benches because the captain and team manager were punishing him, Daniel kicked the ball straight at him but pretended it was Ronan's fault.

Before now, Daniel had no problems with Chris, so I knew it was because of me and how close I'm getting to him. He said something similar the night we first had sex.

Why did you take the drug? Was it so you and Christopher could have a good time?

I didn't think much of it then, but the fact that he mentioned it a few times says something.

So I'm testing a theory.

If Daniel thinks I have a thing with Chris, maybe he'll get his head out of his arse and accept me.

See me.

Make me visible again.

After I had that taste, it's safe to say I'm utterly addicted.

For the first time, Daniel only looked at me. Not at Astrid, not at the girls who worship at his Casanova altar.

Me.

The fire that ate the property was a few degrees below the one that feasted on my heart.

Daniel liked me.

He liked spending time with me.

He helped me put on my clothes and dragged me out of danger first.

I don't care that he blames all of that on being drugged. Or that he wants to erase that night with a red marker.

It's already engraved in my heart and no natural force will be able to tamper with it.

It's only a push.

All Daniel needs is a push to realize that he's meant to be with me.

Not anyone else.

Me.

That's why I invited Chris over. I heard Astrid talking to Daniel on the phone about meeting up here for some burgers at Alli's. One of the few places where he actually eats without throwing up. He sometimes acts like a pig in front of Astrid and steals her food, then as soon as she's out of sight, he vomits it all back up.

Maybe he's trying to impress her.

Maybe he actually likes her and you're just a side piece, Nicole.

I shush the demon on my shoulder as I put on a short white dress with peach-colored lace. Then I let my hair fall straight to my butt and do a kissy motion with my red lipstick.

It's reserved for special occasions. Like making Daniel jealous.

I complete the outfit with my golden heels that make me look like a beautiful goddess. Or that's what the girls say.

Chris shows up right on time, dressed in denim and expensive shoes. He's the son of the Metropolitan Police's deputy commissioner and is known to stir up more trouble than black magic.

He used to be friends with Levi, who's pursuing my stepsister with the determination of a bull, but they kind of fell out of each other's graces at the beginning of this year.

Rumor has it, Chris started following the wrong crowd, as in meth heads, and Levi hates druggies with the same passion he loves football.

Anyway, I've never seen Chris high. He's good-looking with a strong bone structure and a buff build.

Not as good-looking as the boy from my happiest dreams and most forbidden fantasies.

I'm starting to think no one can measure up to Daniel in beauty, wit, or charm.

I'm biased, sue me.

"Come in." I lead Chris to the pool house.

Mum and Uncle Henry are at a charity ball and will probably come home late.

Aside from some staff, the mansion is empty.

Well, I'm pretty sure I caught Astrid preparing to get out, probably with Daniel, but I'm one hundred and one percent sure that she'll bring him back here later.

Good timing to burn Daniel with the fire he's been melting me with.

"Do you want to drink something?" I motion at the mini-fridge in the corner of the room.

Chris throws his weight onto the sofa and pats the space beside him. "Would rather drink you."

Eww. Someone call the cringe police.

I smile anyway and stroll to his side, holding a bottle of water.

My skin crawls as I sit beside him. I've only ever spent time with Chris at school or in crowded places. Something feels different now, otherworldly even.

I place the bottle on the table and pick up the remote control. "We can watch something."

He clutches my hand. "You're much better to look at than TV."

Before I can comment, he dives in for a kiss. His lips feel like dry wood on mine, lifeless, and so wrong. At first, I'm stunned by the sudden attack, then I try to pull back.

The look in his eyes straight out brings out chills from the depths of my soul.

I stand up on shaky legs, maintaining my cheerful façade. "I…I remembered I have to do something. I'll see you out—"

"Fuck that." He clutches my arm and yanks me down on the sofa, all his pretty-boy smiles disappearing. "You've been cock-teasing me for weeks, Nicole. It's time I get a taste of the cunt you've been taunting in my face."

"No, let me go!" I try to shriek, but he clamps a heavy, strong hand on my mouth.

I thrash and manage to bite him.

"Fuck you, bitch!"

My mind is a frantic mess of emotions as I use his disorientation to run.

This was an awful mistake. One I'll regret for the rest of my life.

But in order to do that, I have to run—

Chris grabs me by the ankle, but I kick him as hard as I can.

He's bigger than me, though, stronger, and no amount of adrenaline can help me.

"Seems you chose violence, and I will deliver." He crawls atop my frail, thrashing body and slaps me so hard, my head hits the ground with a thud.

My vision blackens out and white dots start forming in my head.

I think I have a…concussion.

What happens next is a blur of motions. I'm disoriented, and my body feels like it's a different entity from mine.

The assault.

The violation.

The burning pain.

Sometimes, I think I'm lucky I don't remember most of it.

I'm lucky I only remember lying on the ground after he's done and thinking everything's going to be all right.

I think I saw Astrid in the middle of it all, but I also saw Daniel coming to save me, so it was probably a play of my imagination.

I hope the blood that's on my white dress is also a play of my imagination.

My body still feels like an alien entity as I crawl to the bathroom on my stomach. My nails break on the floor in my attempts to get there faster.

Or maybe they broke when I tried to scratch him. The stench of weed, cigarettes, and male musk clings to my skin, and I need it gone.

I also need the blood on my dress gone.

I need all of this gone.

It's a compulsive reaction, a need to get rid of it all, which is why I crawl faster, break more nails and scrape my knees against the ground.

Once I'm in the shower, I strain to hit the water button.

Cold.

Like my soul.

I sit against the wall in my clothes and pull my knees to my chest.

I don't cry, though. I don't have the right to.

My eyes lift to the ceiling and I whisper, "Papa… Please take me with you."

I spend hours under the spray of water until I think I'll surely get pneumonia.

Then I scrub my body until it turns red and painful, but I still can't get rid of his rotten smell.

Of the stench of cigarettes and weed.

No idea where I get the force to rip the bloodied white dress to pieces and change into a pair of jeans and a tank top, but I do.

I have to get out of here.

I have to forget.

My whole body shakes as I drive my car. I have to stop on the side of the road every five minutes to keep myself from hyperventilating.

But I don't abandon my plan. I don't turn around. I keep driving until I reach my destination.

Daniel's house.

Or more like a mansion.

His family is loaded and since his father is somewhat eccentric—and a horrible parent to both Zach and Daniel—he designed the house in a peculiar way. From the outside, it seems like a dome donned with different geometric shapes of windows and doors.

As soon as I step out of the car, the heavens open, and heavy rain soaks me in a second.

I feel nothing, not the water and not my steps. I'm floating on air until I reach the gate.

Aunt Nora appears, holding an umbrella, and lets me in. She's a short woman with dreamy gray eyes and a soft bone structure.

"Oh, dear. You're soaked. Are you okay?"

I must look like an injured puppy caught in the rain, and while looking less than pristine would've bothered me on other days, it doesn't now.

I don't think it will ever again.

"I…I'm fine," I breathe out, having trouble speaking past the lump that's been in my throat for hours. "Is Daniel home?"

"Yes, I heard his car earlier. He's probably in the guest house."

The house that's as far away from his parents as physically possible. I know that because he's been telling Astrid that he's going to move out as soon as he's done with school.

"Can I go see him?"

"Sure…" I don't wait for her to say anything as I storm past her.

"You should drive your car inside, Nicole," she calls after me, but I don't hear her.

I don't even care about the car that I left unlocked on the side of the road.

My pulse roars in my ears as I walk, then jog, then break into a full sprint under the rain, letting it wash away the rotten stench that clings to my skin.

By the time I arrive in front of the pyramid-shaped guest house, I'm panting, my hair covers my eyes, and my clothes feel heavy sticking to my skin.

My fingers spasm as I hit the doorbell.

A few seconds later, a light comes on from the inside and the door opens.

I take my first real breath in hours the moment my eyes clash with Daniel's.

He's my safety. The person who always made me feel calm and happy and…me.

And maybe I went the wrong way to have him. Maybe I should've just told him that I like him and I'd wait until he liked me back.

I love you. I think I've loved you since we were kids. I know you think I'm a bitch, but that's only because I don't know how to express myself and I was taught to never show feelings. But I promise to change if you teach me how.

I open my mouth to say just that.

"Daniel, I—"

"What the fuck are you doing here?" There's a slur in his speech, a troubled look on his face, and a dark gleam in his usually bright eyes.

They look gloomier than the gray sky and the pouring rain.

His fingers twitch and I'm not sure if it's because he's drunk or something else.

"I had to see you and tell you that—"

"You fucked Chris in your pool house? Astrid broke the news. Congrats and fuck off."

"That's not—"

He grabs a handful of my hair at the nape, stepping in the

rain with me. His fingers are harsh, unforgiving, as he speaks so close to my lips, he's almost kissing me. "I always knew you were a conniving, manipulative fucking bitch. *Always*. But I kept finding loopholes and conjuring excuses for you, kept thinking that maybe it's your survival tactic after losing your father. I kept being drawn to you and seeing you and watching you, and it drove me fucking insane to even think of you as someone other than the bitch you were. And yet, I couldn't help being attracted to you and wanting you more than my next breath. I've even abstained from fucking anyone else after that first night I had you.

"But now I realize it was all for nothing. The excuses, the twisted feelings, and my sappy thoughts that you'd change. Every. Fucking. Thing. You just like to toy with others, to manipulate them, then laugh in their fucking faces. Well, guess what, Nicole? I'm off that list, effective immediately. Don't come near me, talk to me, or even look at me. I'll pretend you don't exist and erase the mistake of touching you from my head. From now on, you're nothing."

He releases me with a shove and I nearly fall to the ground. My tears mix with the rain and I don't think he sees them. I don't think he's even seeing me right now.

But I crush my murdered pride and step toward him, my chin trembling. "D-Daniel…it's not…not…what you think… Let me…"

"What's going on…" a brunette peeks from behind Daniel in nothing but a bra and knickers.

Without sparing me a glance, Daniel grabs her by the throat and slams his lips to hers. His eyes meet mine as he drags her inside and slams the door in my face.

I crouch in the rain and let the tears I couldn't shed earlier loose.

Everything is over.

And it hasn't even started yet.

TWENTY-TWO

Daniel

Present

I'M GOING TO PUNCH A WALL.

Or a door.

Or better yet, myself.

The only thing that stops me is the way Nicole is shaking and chanting, "Please don't hurt me…don't hurt me, Christopher."

That lowlife *Christopher*.

The motherfucker that I should've nutted that first time I saw him hovering over her while she was pumped with E.

When I thought she meant to have sex with him.

Jesus fucking Christ.

What have I done?

I stare at Nicole's tear-streaked face, at the tremor in her body and the glassy look in her light eyes. They appear lifeless. Dead.

She came back into herself earlier, cried the worst I've seen her, and fessed up everything as if she couldn't stop. As if she waited her whole life to talk about that horrible experience. From the bits and pieces she told me just now, Christopher raped her in her pool house.

I told him to stop.

I begged him to stop.

That's what she said. He hit her, too, and she recalled everything that happened to her afterward.

The pain.

The helplessness.

Everything.

All that took place when I was broken to fucking pieces after I heard from Astrid that she saw Nicole having sex with Christopher.

When, in fact, he was raping her.

When, in fact, she'd been silently screaming for help.

And because my ego is dick-shaped, I told Nicole she was nothing when she came to find me.

Just after she was brutalized by that fucking scum.

The small supply room's walls close in on me, and I have to breathe deeply so as not to agitate her further. That's what I do with clients with a fragile mental state—I become the anchor they can hold on to. The only difference is that I'm detached enough to do that with them.

I can't be fucking detached with Nicole.

Not when her pain is bleeding in my fucking veins.

"Why didn't you ask Astrid for help?" I ask, my jaw clenched so hard, I'm surprised it doesn't dislocate.

"I wasn't sure I saw her. I think I had…a concussion, and uh…I don't know, but I was bleeding after he was…done."

"Did you go to the hospital?" My voice imitates the calmest monk while my insides roar with a burning fire.

She frantically shakes her head. "I got better after a few days on my own."

"Fuck, Nicole, fuck! Why didn't you file a report?"

"I couldn't!" Now she's the one who's screaming while she sobs. "Mum would've been so disappointed in me."

"Your mother was a fucking criminal. She had no bloody right to be disappointed in you."

"She was my mother. I didn't know anything about what she'd done at the time, and what did you expect me to say? I asked a boy over and he raped me? Who would've believed me?"

"They would've believed the medical rape kit the doctor would've made. You said you were fucking bleeding."

"It wasn't worth it."

"*What?*"

"Dragging Mum and Uncle Henry's names through the mud wasn't worth it. Christopher was a deputy commissioner's son. He would've gotten away with it. They would've said I asked for it."

"But that's not the case."

"Maybe it was!" She pushes me away, wiping her face with the back of her hand. "Maybe I was stupid and obsessed and was blind to invite a predator to my house. It happened, okay? It all happened, so what was the point of making a report?"

"Fucking justice, Nicole."

"I didn't need that."

"Clearly. Judging by the way you have panic and anxiety attacks whenever you're touched sexually."

"Then stop touching me!" She turns around and flings the door open. "I was doing just fine before you came back into my life."

And then she's running outside.

I catch up to her in no time and practically pick her up and shove her into my car. I remind myself that I need to be more gentle. That she just shared a traumatic experience she never told anyone about.

She tried to tell you back then, too, but you rejected her like a sorry cunt.

Is there a way to reach out to eighteen-year-old me and choke him to death? To make him aware of who stood on his fucking doorstep that night?

It wasn't only Nicole. It was Nicole in need of help. It was

Nicole traumatized, vulnerable and weak, and the last thing I should've done was shut the door in her face.

The evening Astrid told me she saw Nicole and Christopher having sex, I remember seeing black. I remember it so well.

It's the moment that shaped my arsehole self and turned me into a blonde-hater.

But as the world blew into smithereens in front of my eyes, I pretended nothing was wrong and even teased Astrid about her relationship with Levi.

I acted normally while my heart was bleeding on the floor.

I smiled while I was ripped open from the inside.

Then, when Astrid, my brother, and I got together to go bowling, I remember the doomsday-like feeling that crowded my spine.

I remember not hearing a word they were saying. The sounds and colors became gray and I was seconds away from snapping.

So I told them I was getting drinks. Instead, I drove straight to Astrid's house. To Nicole.

I had to talk to her.

To ask her why the fuck she chose someone else.

Then I recalled that I'd flung girls in her face like they were shiny toys. I remembered that she often called me Astrid's loser friend and looked down her aristocratic nose at me.

I recalled that I was nothing.

But I stood there like a creep for a whole hour, until I was sure one of the neighbors would call the police.

Then I went to the liquor store, got drunk on the cheapest whiskey available, and called the first girl on my contact list.

That's when Nicole found me.

Drenched in the rain, her eyes deep and dark and a little lifeless, now that I think about it.

That's how we ended.

When I told her she was nothing to me.

A few weeks later, her mother got arrested for killing Astrid's mother and nearly murdering my best friend in that hit-and-run.

Nicole disappeared soon after.

And I left England the same calendar year.

"I never fucked that girl," I say slowly as I drive.

Nicole, who's leaning against the door with her knees pulled to her chest, flinches. "What girl?"

"The one you found me with that night. I kicked her out soon after you left." I got drunk on more cheap whiskey and stared at the fucking snow globe she gave me all night long.

It was the first and last time I knew what a broken heart felt like. Excruciating pain, epic hangovers, and model-like blondes with vicious character.

It also included living with a heart that had a hole the size of a fist in it.

I filled it up with booze, sex, and a social life fit for Victorian courts. But it was never full.

Not really.

"Doesn't matter," she whispers, her voice haunted, a bit hoarse.

"It matters to me. I didn't fuck her the night you were hurt, Nicole."

"I believed it." She laughs, then breaks down in tears. "That night, all I could think about was you with her. Guess I should thank you for the distraction. God, I was so stupid."

"You're not stupid."

She folds more into herself, using her hold on her knees as armor against the world.

The people.

The injustice.

I'm too close to driving my fist into the steering wheel and inevitably getting us both killed.

If I'd listened to her back then, if I hadn't been so shoved up my own arse and so attuned to my naïve heartbreak, I would've seen it.

I would've seen her brokenness and silent plea for help.

But I didn't.

And I spent the following weeks actively pretending she was a pest.

She didn't look at me either. Not even her usual glares or haughty remarks.

The day Victoria Clifford's mask fell off and the police arrested her, Nicole broke down and maybe that wasn't only for finding out her only parent is a monster. Maybe she let the world see her rare tears because of the pain that was festering inside her for weeks.

After the police escorted her mother out of the room, I wrapped my arm around Nicole's shoulder and led her to the hallway. Even though the wound I thought she caused was fresh, bleeding, and refused to get better, I still felt a twinge in my gut at witnessing her state.

I still wanted to get her away from a furious Uncle Henry and a heartbroken Astrid. Despite my loyalty to my best friend, a part of me wanted to protect Nicole from her wrath if she or her father decided to blame Nicole for her mother's actions.

And for a few minutes, Nicole allowed me to hold her, to silently console her while she sniffled and trembled like a leaf in a violent storm.

But then I broke the spell and asked like a first-class idiot, "Do you need anything?"

What could a girl who just realized her mother was a murderer need, Dan? Maybe you're the one who needs a more functioning brain.

Obviously, I was on a kick of being daft back then because when her lips trembled, I lowered my head and brushed my lips against hers.

In my simpleton mind, I only wanted her to get better, to forget even for some time, but I ended up ripping my heart's stitches open and kissing her with the desperation of a madman. I swear she kissed me back for a brief moment. For a second in time, we were so in tune that I had no clue where she ended and I began.

But then, she swiftly pulled from my hold, and stared ahead. "I need you away from me, Daniel."

And then, she marched out.

A few days later, she packed her suitcases and left.

She hadn't even looked at me. Not once. And I'd thought she was done with me.

I'd thought I was done with her, too.

All these years later and I'm learning the hard fucking way that I was never done with her.

Not when I never really got started with her.

"How did that fucker…" I trail off at my strained tone and start again with a cooler one. "How did he become Jayden's father?"

A chin tremble. A jerk. Silence.

"Is he…actually your son?"

"No! Do you think I would've let that monster have more hold on me?"

"I'm just asking."

"Well, don't."

"I'm on your side here."

She huffs. "Could've fooled me."

"I really am, Nicole. Tell me…" I purse my lips and add, "Please."

More silence. More huffing. I swear the interior of my car is a thousand degrees and it's a miracle I don't drive straight into a wall at this point.

Nicole opens her mouth a few times, then stares out the window as she speaks in a soft, choked tone. "After Mum was arrested, I couldn't bring myself to go see her. I felt so sorry toward Uncle Henry and even Astrid. I was planning to study in Cambridge and then, maybe a few years later, I would ask for his forgiveness. He was like a father to me after I lost mine, and I loved him, in my own way, even if he was blinded to anyone but Astrid and her mother. I just wanted to start anew, build my life from scratch.

"I was doing well, pretending my classmates didn't murmur behind my back that I was a murderer's daughter, that the aristocrats were rotten to the bone. It was fine. *I* was fine. I didn't care about friends or parties or being a normal university student. I was just building my life. In the process, I ignored Mum's mail. Until two years later when I got a visit from a police officer who informed me she'd died due to cancer. She'd been writing to me about that. Her cancer and her battle with it.

"I cried at her funeral, which I attended on my own. I cried for how she'd shaped my life and I cried because she was no longer in it. Then, in the middle of all that, I saw Christopher holding a baby. Apparently, he'd married my mum soon after Uncle Henry divorced her and was seducing her long before she was arrested. He said, 'I only fucked you because you look like her. Now that she's gone, you'll do.' I bolted out of there and fell down the stairs and broke my arm. I had an epic panic attack and nearly got myself hit by a car. I didn't think seeing him again would spur such a reaction, but it did, and I hate that version of myself, the scared, faulty version. So I wanted to disappear, but he found me, he hit me."

My fist clenches. "Did he…"

"He wanted to, but I blinded him with pepper spray and kicked him. It felt so good…so liberating. He left me alone for a while. A month later, social services asked me if I could take custody of Jayden. He was abused, had blue marks on his back, and he developed asthma from the conditions Christopher was keeping him in. I couldn't say no, I just…couldn't. He found me soon after, beat me to a pulp, and if it hadn't been for a neighbor, he would've killed me and Jay. Uncle Henry found me around that time, but I couldn't face him."

That must've been what Astrid told me about.

"I had to leave the country and escape him. I dropped out of university and used the rest of my trust fund to raise Jay. It was tough at the beginning, and we moved a lot trying to find a good paying job. That's how we ended up here."

In New York.

Where I am.

My heart is thumping so loudly that I think she can hear every beat.

"Jayden said Chris visited you while you've been here."

She slides her attention to me. "Did you ask him that?"

"Answer the question, Nicole. What happened?"

"He wanted us back. I kicked him out and moved the next day. That was two years ago." She sniffles. "I never thought he'd sue for Jay's custody. He never wanted him."

But he wants you.

I don't say that, because I doubt it will have a positive effect. I'm sure his whole mother-and-daughter fucked-up fetish is only that, a fetish. The one he actually wanted was Nicole, not her mother. She's the one he used force to have, and she's the one he's been trying to keep a link to whether through her mother or her brother.

If he was actually after Victoria, he would've kept the last memory she left behind, Jayden, and raised him well. But he let Nicole have him just so he'd have an excuse to bulldoze into her life again.

That motherfucker is using his own son as a tool.

We arrive at the building's parking garage, followed by a gloomy cloud, but thankfully no accident happened during the ride.

Nicole's movements are mechanical and stiff. She looks so broken, so distressed, that I wish I could make it better.

Somehow.

Someway.

Once we reach the lift, she wipes at her face. "I don't want Jay to see me like this."

I lift her up in my arms and she gasps. "W-what…"

"I'll tell him you're asleep. Close your eyes."

She blinks once, twice, and then her body goes slack against mine and she closes her eyes.

Her hands are snuggled in her lap and she looks so vulnerable, like a child. And I can't resist the urge to smell her hair and breathe her in. To hold on to the reality that she survived.

That she found her way back to me.

Sure enough, Jayden and Lolli come running to the lift as soon as it opens.

He watches his sister, then narrows his eyes on me. "What's wrong with Nikki?"

"She's tired."

"She's never tired."

"She is, brat. Go watch your Minions."

He continues to eye me suspiciously even as I carry Nicole to her room.

"We're alone," I tell her.

She doesn't stir, probably has fallen asleep for real. I place her on the bed, remove her heels and cover her to the chin.

My lips meet her forehead and I whisper a promise against them, "I'll fix this."

Or whatever is left of this.

I step out to get water and find Jayden standing there statue-like in a trainee demon's stance.

"A word, Daniel."

He never calls me by my full name anymore. That, and the fact that he's not annoying Lolli to compete for the dick award should be a warning sign.

"Can it wait until tomorrow?"

"I'm afraid not."

Sighing, I close the door behind me and follow him to the living area, where he has a basket full of Minions merch.

He sits on the sofa, crossing his arms. "You can have these back."

"Are you sure?"

"No...I mean yes. I like them, and you, but I don't need both if you hurt my sister."

I would've smiled if I weren't two seconds away from exploding. "I'm not hurting her."

He swallows. "Promise?"

"Promise."

"If you do hurt her, I'm gonna kick your ass."

"I'm sure you will." I ruffle his hair. "Now, go to sleep."

"Can I have my things back?" he asks sheepishly.

"Never took them away from you."

"Thanks, Dan!" He drags the basket and a whining Lolli with him.

I head to the kitchen and resist the urge to get drunk. That's not a solution. Instead, I down a cup of water and dial Knox.

"Bit of a bad timing, mate," he says, breathless.

"I need a favor."

"Of what kind?" His voice sobers up. I'm never the type who asks for a favor.

Never.

"I need you to hook me up with a member of Anastasia's family."

"The fuck you need the mafia for when you're an attorney?"

"I need them to tie up some loose ends the law couldn't."

When I'm done with Christopher Vans, he'll wish for the fucking Grim Reaper.

He'll wish he'd never touched what's fucking mine.

TWENTY-THREE

Nicole

"We're going to London."

I choke on the orange juice I've been obsessing over like a fangirl with her idol for the sole reason of avoiding Daniel.

Until he dropped this bomb, of course.

We're sitting at the kitchen counter on a Friday morning, having breakfast in a setting as strained as the Cold War.

The only one speaking is Jay with his hyper energy and endless stories. Even Lolli has chosen the silent treatment.

"We're going where?" I echo Daniel's words, needing double confirmation.

Clutching an iPad in hand, he stares at me over the rim of his coffee cup with that cold streak that he wears as a badge around me.

One part of me is glad he doesn't pity me after the mess I was in last night, but a bigger part wants to rip open his exterior and see what he's thinking about.

Maybe he does pity me.

Maybe he's even more repulsed by me than ever before.

While he said it wasn't my fault, he was angry that I didn't file the report. He was angry that I didn't ask for help, forgetting that when I showed up at his door, he cut me open so deep, the wound is still unable to heal.

The jerk.

So what if he didn't fuck that girl back then? If I didn't ruin his evening with my epic chlamydia plan, he would've shagged Katerina all night long.

With a dash of orgies, as he informed me.

My fist clenches against my stomach and I fight the bitter taste of tears building behind my eyes.

I can feel myself stumbling, backpedaling, and falling back into a deep, dark abyss.

Into my old stupid, unhealthily obsessed self.

And just like then, it'll only end in disaster and heartache as harsh as Daniel's coldness.

"London," he repeats as if I'm a child. "England. The United Kingdom. Great Britain."

"I know where London is," I spit back.

"Congratulations for having the geographical knowledge of a toddler."

"Don't talk to my sister that way." Jay glares at him. "That's mean."

Daniel grunts, but he doesn't reply. Instead he glances at me. "Book the tickets for the trip. We're leaving today and returning on Monday."

Jay's eyes bug out as he swallows his pancakes. "We're really going to London?"

"No," I say with a force that rattles my body and causes Lolli to jump away from the seat next to me. Inhaling deeply, I stare at Daniel. "Can I have a word with you?"

"Make an appointment for it." He doesn't look at me as he reads the news on his iPad.

I show Jay my fakest smile. "Can you have the rest of your breakfast in your room, baby?"

He sighs. "I can't continue living with you guys if you keep kissing every second. At least tone it down until I have my own place when I'm eighteen."

"That's not…" I trail off, lost for words.

"Are we really going to London, Dan?" my brother asks, completely ignoring me.

"Yes. Start packing," he tells him, still lost in his iPad.

"Okay!" My brother trots to his room, holding a plate full of syrupy pancakes.

Daniel ordered them but didn't eat a bite.

"I'm not going to London," I tell him.

"Good thing you don't have a say in it."

"I have no reason to be there when the trial is weeks away."

"I do."

"Good for you. That doesn't concern me."

"You're my assistant, so I say it does concern you."

"Is this work-related?"

"In a way."

"You only have golf and a few international calls this weekend. There was no fine print about London anywhere."

"Emergency work."

"Then go on your own." I pluck the iPad from his hand, breathing as harshly as a cornered animal. "And look at me when you're talking to me."

He slowly lifts his head, his face a blank slate of emotions. A void with no intention of ever being filled.

And the worst part is that he looks like he's in his element, extremely handsome in his khaki trousers and a white polo shirt with his brown hair styled and his face clean-shaven.

Why was I so worried about telling him again? It's not like he cares.

Never did and never will.

"I know your face, Nicole. No need to worship at its altar all the time." He pauses. "If I didn't clarify it yet, you have no choice and you're coming with me as my assistant."

"It's the weekend."

"Your point?"

"I don't want to go to England."

"What you want means jack shit to me. We're going and that's that."

"And if I refuse?"

He tilts his head to the side. "There's no refusal option in your job contract. Unless you quit, of course."

"I can't leave Jay alone."

"Which is why he's coming with us. The time you've spent moaning could've been spent booking our flight tickets."

He slides the iPad from my fingers and goes back to scrolling through BBC's website because I heard him mention once that American news outlets are unreliable.

I hate that I hoard everything he says, that I remember the first word he said to me—peaches—and every single interaction we've had since.

I hate that I used to search for his gift for my birthdays first. His mum chose them and it was obligatory, but I still counted them as coming from him.

Still stared at them whenever it got hard and the world closed in on me.

Especially at the one item that I've hidden so well.

He reaches for a glass of water at the same time as me. Our fingers brush for a second, two—

He suddenly jerks his hand away, stands up, and stalks to his room.

My hand shakes as I pick up the water and down it all. But no amount of water could douse the fire inside me.

Or the familiar feeling that's rearing its ugly head from the past.

The fact that no matter how much I showered or scrubbed my skin clean, I'm still filthy.

⚖

Several hours later, we're on our way to London.

I avoid a panic attack by watching Jayden nearly piss himself with excitement from being on a plane for the first time—technically, second, but he doesn't remember that trip. First class, because God forbid Daniel travel any other way.

He ignored me most of the flight, opting to have a fixation with his iPad.

Whenever Jay talks to him, however, he engages him and even smiles, dazzling the whole crew with his dimples.

So the problem is me.

I'm the one he doesn't want to spare a glance.

The one who needlessly and embarrassingly told him everything, hoping he'd finally see my side of the story.

Not anyone else's. Mine.

After two hours, Jay collapses into sleep, his neck lolled awkwardly. I shake my head as I maneuver him to a more comfortable position.

All while trying to ignore Daniel, who's sitting across from me, still ignoring me.

When the attendants bring food, he flat out refuses it.

I rummage through my bag and retrieve a small sandwich I made, then place it and a lollipop on his table.

"Take them back," he says without looking at me.

"I didn't bring them for you. I just happened to have them, so you might as well eat."

"No."

"Then I'm not eating either."

He tilts his tablet to the side to stare at me. "Did you abandon your common sense in a different time zone? Why the fuck would you starve because I'm choosing not to eat?"

"I like company when I eat."

"The whole plane is your company."

"I don't know the whole plane. So if you don't want me to starve, you might as well pick up that sandwich."

"Whether you starve or stuff your stomach with food has zero effect on me."

I pretend his words don't create holes inside me as I fake a smile and act like I'm scrolling through my phone.

But I don't eat.

Masochism is apparently one of my traits. Or maybe I'm trying to see if he really doesn't care about me.

The wait is exactly ten minutes. With a grunt, he unwraps the sandwich and takes a big bite. He pauses, probably his nausea hitting him, but then he chews slowly and swallows.

I can't help but grin as I grab my fork and knife.

"Wipe it off," he growls.

"What?" I ask innocently, taking a bite of the meatballs.

"That fucking smile on your face."

That only allows it to widen and he releases a sound, but he doesn't say anything as he finishes the sandwich in a few more bites.

"I didn't do it for you."

"Then who did you do it for?"

"Myself, so I don't have to carry you when you faint."

"Whatever you say, Dan."

His lips twist. "Don't call me that."

"Why? It disarms you?"

"More like it revolts me. That sandwich is trying to find its way out in a less glamorous way than how it went in."

I see it then. The reason behind his cold, cutting words. It's clear in the depth of his eyes, right below the surface, there's a vulnerability, a weakness he's going the extra mile to hide.

"If you say so," I say sweetly, which clearly pisses him off. But before he can come back with his sarcastic, hurtful remarks, I change the subject. "When was the last time you went back to London?"

"Never."

I pause eating. "Really?"

"Want a look at my travel history?"

"But why?"

"Why what?"

"Why have you never gone back?"

"England is too small for me now."

"Bullshit."

He lets the iPad drop on his lap and glares at me. "Getting fluent in cursing, I see."

"I learned from the best. And you're not changing the subject. Why have you never gone back to England?"

"I don't like the people there. That once included you, by the way."

I ignore his attempts to egg me on. "What about your family?"

"My last words to Mum before I left were, 'Grow a fucking backbone, Nora.' Dad died in an accident with his mistress of the month after I told him to go fuck himself. My brother hates me because of all of the above."

The food gets stuck in my throat. I was completely unaware of this, but I did hear about Benedict Sterling's death during my first year in university. His gruesome accident was all over the news.

I remember the itch to check on Aunt Nora. She sent me chocolates and food after Mum's scandal and was the only one out of the community who didn't treat me as if I were a monster.

When her husband died, I wanted to visit her and be there for her. But the possibility of running into Daniel made me shrink back into my unwelcome university setting faster than a turtle into its shell.

"So you're estranged from your family?"

"Congratulations on your newfound deduction skills, Sherlock."

"You…don't even talk on the phone?"

"Not really."

"Even to Zach?"

"Especially to him, he speaks to me like a robot ever since

he became the head of the family business. And the name is Zachariah."

That was definitely annoyance in his tone, but I'm not entirely sure of the reason behind it.

"But you guys were so close."

"Not enough, apparently." A grim shadow covers his face and I'm not sure if it's because he hates how much he grew apart from his brother or something else.

"What about…" I clear my throat. "Astrid?"

"What about her?"

"You don't visit her?"

"She visits me about twice a year and bugs me the rest of it with video calls and random texts about her annoying husband and loud spawns."

My grip tightens on the fork. I knew he was still close with Astrid. I often heard them talking on the phone, and it was the only time he sounded carefree…happy. The only time his dimples were on display.

Doesn't hurt any less.

The old, ugly pain has morphed into a knife and it's currently stabbing at the surface, but I swallow the blade down with its blood.

"Good to see you're still friends."

"My turn to call bullshit, Peaches. You never liked Astrid." He studies me closely. "Why?"

Because I was jealous of her. Of how easily she could make him laugh.

I still am.

"Stepsisters aren't known to get along. Have you read *Cinderella*?"

"Boring and unrealistic."

"It's still true about the stepsisters part. I might have thought myself a princess, but I was the villain all along."

"A gorgeous one at that." He pauses. I pause. And it seems as if the entire plane pauses at his words.

Did he just call me...

"Did you just say I'm a gorgeous villain?"

He clears his throat. "You're evading the actual subject. Was there any other reason why you didn't like Astrid?"

"No." I take a sip of my water.

Daniel unwraps the lollipop and sticks it in his mouth. It should be comical that a solicitor with as much charm and charisma as he has is sucking on a lollipop, but it's the exact opposite.

He looks hotter than the sun and all of its planets and I have to stop myself from gawking like the teenage idiot version of me.

"How about you?" he asks.

"How about me?"

"Are you keeping in touch with any of your, and excuse my bloody French, pathetically vain, irrevocably selfish bitch friends?"

"They were never my friends."

"Not even Chloe?"

"Not even her. She blocked me faster than cancel culture after Mum was arrested. Being acquainted with a murderer's daughter was bad for her daddy's business."

"Her daddy is bad for his own business. He went bankrupt, so she got herself a sugar daddy instead."

"Really?"

"Yeah, saw them in Boston once. Seventy years old and with a heart condition that can't handle Viagra. Anyone can see her soul evaporating from her body, probably thinking about sucking that wrinkly dick for her next Rolls-Royce."

It's wrong, but I chuckle, unable to hold it in. "You're bad."

"She said that, too, when I gave her my card and informed her that once he's dead, his sons will sue her for everything, including the Rolls-Royce. So all the dick sucking is for nothing. She had other choice words for me as well, but they're as important as her existence. I don't remember them."

I smile, but it must appear sad, nostalgic. "She was the one who tattled on you, you know. She was always jealous of me and slept with every boy who showed interest in me. She told me so herself before she blocked me."

His eyes narrow. "Maybe I'll find her husband's sons, after all. Do the world a favor and get rid of gold-diggers."

"Are you serious?"

"Hundred percent. Though letting her suck wrinkly dick for a few more years is also tempting."

"Aren't you the vindictive one?"

"Never claimed otherwise." He pops the lollipop out and I realize he was actually sucking on it all this time.

He didn't crush it like he usually does.

My blood turns hot and a crazy idea materializes in my head.

Pushing my tray to the side, I lean over and wrap my lips around the candy.

My eyes remain on his as I suck on it. Fire erupts in his blue gaze, but then he releases the lollipop, a sheen of indifference covering his features.

I'm the one who crushes the candy this time, to match the havoc wreaking in my chest.

He doesn't want to touch me, doesn't even want to see me in a sexual light.

When he was the one who demanded to fuck me.

When he was the one who lit my world ablaze after years of being apathetically numb.

He really is disgusted with me, isn't he?

Just like back then. It's ending before it even started.

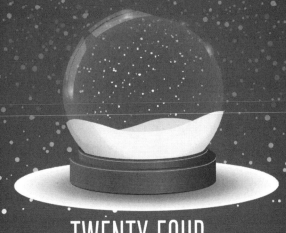

TWENTY-FOUR

Daniel

NICOLE HAS BEEN SILENT FOR EXACTLY THIRTY MINUTES. It's not only a record, but it should also be kept in a "warning signs" ledger.

At first, I pretend I'm utterly and completely fascinated with my iPad—despite not doing anything with it. Then I glared at the damn lollipop stick that I let fall to the ground and quietly questioned the object; *what the fuck have you done to sour her mood?*

Might want to ask yourself, mate, is what it silently communicated back.

Or maybe that's the demon-like angel swinging on my shoulder.

Finally, I let the iPad fall to my lap and direct the glare at her phone that she's fixated on as if it's her new lover. What are the chances that I can switch places with that phone in the next three seconds?

I clear my throat, but she doesn't even show a sign of acknowledging me, and rightly so.

Thing is, I might have been a fucking arsehole ever since she poured her heart to me, and it's entirely due to the fact that I have no clue how the fuck I should treat her. If I soften, it'd be no different than pitying her and neither of us want that.

So I played the dick card. Admittedly, not the best card I have, but it's the only card I know how to play so well.

But right now, it feels imperative that I shake off this gloomy cloud hanging between us. I search our surroundings and soon find a way to break off her affair with her phone.

"Jay's sleeping in an awkward position."

That successfully gets her attention and she drops the phone to her side before she straightens him up, then covers him with his Minions blanket he insisted to bring along. He whines, and it makes me smile, imagining him huffing and being a cranky Minion.

"He seems like a deep sleeper," I say when she picks up her phone again, probably intent on ignoring me for the rest of the flight.

"Thankfully," she says tonelessly.

"Was he always stubborn?"

She slides her attention from the fucking phone and stares at me blankly. "Why are you asking?"

"I'm trying to strike up a conversation so you won't get bored the entire flight."

"We both know that's not true, so either tell me the real reason or go back to your jerk persona and leave me alone."

"I just want to talk to you." I let out in a sigh. "Happy now?"

I swear her lips twitch in an almost smile, but she doesn't let it show. "That wasn't so hard to say, was it?"

I grunt as a response and this time, she does smile. And I find myself closing my mouth to not drool like a fucking dog.

Jesus.

Nicole is beautiful under normal circumstances, but when she smiles, her entire face brightens and the universe pauses.

At least mine does.

She places her phone beside her and leans forward, gracing me with her full attention. "What do you want to talk about?"

"Everything. Anything."

"Like what?"

"Like…eleven years back."

Her lips tremble and she fingers her phone case, absentmindedly digging her nails in. "I already told you…"

"I don't mean that. I'm interested in everything before it."

"What do you mean?"

"That Nicole…the bitchy, horrible person who made people feel less than dirt wasn't real, was she?"

She stares at Jay, the window, her lap—anywhere but at me. "I don't know what you're talking about."

"You know exactly what I'm talking about. The old Nicole was a persona, a defense mechanism of sorts."

Her long lashes flutter over her cheeks before she stares up. "So what if it was? Will I be forgiven and given a golden medal now?"

"No, you were still a bitch and your actions hurt a lot of people—namely Astrid." *And me.* But I keep that to myself, because emotional doesn't look good on me.

"I know that, which is why I don't offer excuses. What I did was wrong and that's that."

"But I want those excuses."

"Why would you?"

"Why do you think? Because I want to understand you."

She swallows, her delicate throat moving up and down and she stares at me funny. As if I'm a different Daniel from the one she's used to. And maybe I am. My perspective about her is as fickle as England's sun and just as obscure.

Ever since she told me about the past, I have no fucking clue where to place her anymore. My reasons for revenge are null and void. My need to touch her feels fucking wrong right now. As for my feelings…fuck.

I have no bloody clue what to feel right now.

One thing's for certain, though. Nicole is the only

woman—person—whose sole presence is enough to provoke the most reckless, passionate side of me.

I fully expect her to ignore me, but she whispers, "I was taught early on to never show emotions. They're a weakness, a hindrance, and would lead to my downfall. My father was an emotional man and that didn't get him too far in life, so I assumed sealing it all in was the right way to go."

"Let me guess. Your mother?"

She sets her lips in a line and nods. "Sometimes I hated her for it, but other times I couldn't blame her. It's the only way she learned to survive."

"Are you seriously defending her when she was the reason you were scared shitless about going against Chris? When she turned out to be a psycho?"

"She was still my mother." Her voice shakes. "Yes, she separated Uncle Henry from his first wife by playing on his parents' feelings and toyed with her brakes with the intention of killing her. But that was because Uncle Henry meant to leave us. Mum felt threatened and in her mind, getting rid of the problem was the right thing to do. I naturally don't agree with her or her methods or what she did to Astrid, but I can see where she came from. She wasn't a psycho; a psycho wouldn't care, but she did. She loved me in her own screwed-up way and I choose to hold on to those moments instead of when I saw her arrested."

"You said you didn't visit her in prison."

"It's because I refused to see her that way. Just like you refused to sit down or talk to your father after you found out about the mistresses."

"As disgusting as my father was, he didn't escalate to murder."

"He still shaped who you are, Daniel. As much as my mother shaped who I am. I'm assertive enough to admit that."

I pause, watching the light in her eyes—it's dim, but it's there. And at this moment, I know it'll never go away. That no matter what happens to this woman, she's strong enough to dust off her shoulders, stand up and start all over again.

She got a redo once and she'd do it all over again if she has to.

"You've matured, Nicole." *More than I ever did or will.*

"I had to." She stares at Jayden and smiles. "When I had to raise a stubborn, incredibly intelligent, and asthmatic child like Jayden, I needed to leave all naïvety and privilege behind and dedicate my life to him."

"I assume it wasn't always easy."

"In the first years, yes. Especially on the financial level. I could hardly find an affordable babysitter and I kept thinking about how he deserves a better education that I will probably never be able to provide him. But most of all, I'm lucky to have him. I seriously wouldn't have survived this far without him."

My fist clenches on my trousers and it's out of self-loathing more than anything. It's out of knowing that I could've prevented all of this if I could just go back in time.

"Jay even believes in my dreams more than I do."

I raise a brow. "How so?"

"He said once he grows up, he'll help me open my own restaurant."

"You want that? A restaurant?"

"I only ever thought I loved making food, but I also discovered that I love bringing joy to people through it. So yeah, I guess. Not now, though. Probably when Jay doesn't need me as much."

The information is new but not surprising. She has the talent to have not only a restaurant but a dozen of them. And I might be imagining a million different ways to cut the tongue of every person who will eat her food. Because I'm extra like that.

"How about you?" she asks softly.

"How about me?"

"Did you live the life you always envisioned since your player days in secondary school?"

"It was fine." *Plain, empty, and fucking meaningless,* but I have the decency to keep the embarrassing details to myself.

"Was it worth abandoning your mother and brother for?"

"For the thousandth time, I did *not* abandon them. Nora

Sterling is addicted to tears, drama, and wine—in that order. My name doesn't belong to her list of priorities. As for Zach...he was the one who abandoned me."

And I might have been more bitter about that than a loser in a presidential election.

She gives me a look as stern as when she's scolding Jay about his homework. "You're the one who didn't attend your father's funeral and told your mother to not contact you."

"I didn't extend the invitation to him, but he took it anyway."

Sometimes, I think I'm extracurricular in my family. Zach is the firstborn, the holy messiah of the Sterling name, and the only thing they need to keep selling our souls to the devil in a buy-one-get-one-free sale.

Even my father cared about him sometimes, but never about me. My mother always went to cry on his shoulder. Admittedly, I never allowed such blasphemy, but anyway.

Zach and I, however, were different from the rest of our family. We were close.

Until we weren't.

"I'm sure it's not what you think," Nicole tells me with a smile.

"How would you know that?"

"I just do. Not everyone is as cynical as you."

"I'm cynical?"

"Hello? Do you look at yourself in the mirror?"

"Everyday. I'm too gorgeous not to."

"Your arrogance is staggering."

"I'll take that as a compliment considering your ex-queen bee status."

"You give me a run for my money."

"I beg to differ. You walked around as if you had a crown on your head that no one was allowed to touch."

"You were." Her voice softens. "But you were never interested."

"That's not true."

Her lips part and a light I've never seen rushes to her eyes.

I wish I could take a picture of her right now and keep it with me forever.

I wish I could trap her fascinating expression somewhere between my rib cage and bruised heart.

"You...were interested?"

I take a sip of water and still fail to soothe my dry throat.

"Daniel!"

"What?"

"You were interested?"

"Maybe."

"Maybe isn't an answer."

"It's the only one you'll get."

That still paints a smile on her lips; one with blushing cheeks and glittering eyes, and I make it my mission to preserve that smile for as long as I can.

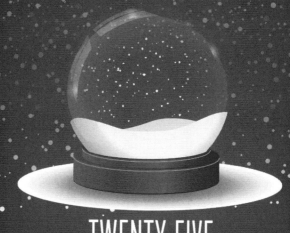

TWENTY-FIVE

Daniel

OUT OF SERIOUS CONCERN ABOUT LOSING MY COOL, EGO, AND probably dick, I leave Nicole and Jayden as soon as we land in London.

I even scheduled for a driver to take them to my mansion in East London. I didn't have to prepare it to be habitable overnight because its live-in staff takes care of it better than they would their children.

It's the only property I kept after I left. My graduation gift, not from my father, because fuck that guy. Grandpa had it in the will in my name for when I turned eighteen. Zach, who holds the sacred title of the firstborn and leader of the Sterling clan, received a small island in the Pacific.

No shit.

Our family is extravagant like that.

Of course, Zach now owns the family business—as in, a multitude of companies I lost count of. Or more like, he manages it. I own fifty percent of its shares and have the ability to kick him out and become acting CEO if the attorney gig doesn't work out.

Not that I would.

I chose not follow engineering for a reason.

The family business disgusts me more than food.

This land revolts me, too.

Every fucking thing in it.

As soon as I'm done with what I came here for, I'm leaving and never returning. I'm taking Nicole as far away as possible. To Mars, even, if they opened trips to there.

Talking to her on the plane was no different than pulling teeth and choking on my own blood while simultaneously flying to heaven.

Ever since last night, I can't look at her without experiencing that crushing feeling of "I could've stopped it." I can't talk to her without tasting that bitter pill of "what-ifs" or seeing the hazy color of guilt.

But at the same time, I couldn't *not* talk to her, listen to her voice, make her laugh.

Fuck. I'll never get used to the sound of her laughter. It's like a fucking siren in a mythical story that I'm willing to let harvest my soul.

And the fact that she can still laugh is similar to squeezing my own heart with sharp nails.

So I did more. The whole fucking seven hours. I didn't let her sleep, I got her talking about the years she spent raising Jayden on her own, and the story of how she found Lolli.

On her balcony, pretending the flat was her house.

Sounds like her.

The cat came with us, naturally, because both Nicole and Jayden threw a tantrum about leaving her behind.

Lucky little shit.

Anyway, talking to Nicole gave me a sense of peace I didn't even dream of having since the day she left my life without looking back.

She can be oddly sarcastic and fluent at talking back any chance she gets.

And I was wrong. It's not the old Nicole peeking through.

Did I even know the old Nicole beyond the image she plastered for her mother and stepfather's sake?

Did I even see Nicole when she was deliberately leaving me lollipops and letting me be the one who had taken her virginity?

Or did I only see my fucked-up prejudice of her?

Last night, after I put my plan in motion, I couldn't sleep. So I rewound every single interaction I'd had with her since that day she nearly died because of fucking peaches.

And every line I thought was set in stone is getting blurry, undecipherable.

And bloody confusing.

But I'll deal with that.

After I deal with *him*.

The man who's been living on borrowed time since the day he fucking touched her.

Knox gave me the phone number of a hitman in his future wife's family. He's married to Anastasia's great-cousin and has killed more people than he could count or remember.

"He's British, Irish, or maybe Russian. No fucking clue. His name is Kyle Hunter and he's the only one who understands my sarcastic humor at their dinner table. Anyway, he's your man. But don't tell me what the fuck you need him for. I'm out of this mess."

Kyle agreed to meet me here and even said he'll have Christopher waiting for me.

He only needed his full name and that's it.

When I was on the plane, he sent me a text with a location.

That's where I am right now. In an abandoned warehouse in an old industrialized area.

I walk straight in and sure enough, the fucker whose life is on a fast hourglass mode is sitting on the chair, head lolled to the side.

A black figure comes from the shadows, and I'm slightly taken aback.

He's tall, wears black like a Gothic model, and has the looks that go with it. Doesn't strike me as a mobster at all.

"Kyle, I presume?"

"Daniel." He tips his head. "I delivered your package. Do you need a bullet in his head? Or heart? Junk, maybe?"

"I'll take care of it."

"I'll be outside in case you need anything." He shoulders past me. "Oh, and you can make him scream, the area has been carefully chosen so no one can hear."

"Got it."

"Next time, try to pick someone in the States. England is a hassle for hiding your tracks."

The door screeches open, then closed, as he steps out.

Blood roars in my ears, then nearly spills all over the floor like fucking lava.

I stalk up to Christopher, rolling up the sleeves of my shirt. I abandoned my jacket in the car and my phone, too. I need zero distractions when I deal with this piece of shit.

My fist finds his face first. I was never a violent person, not when I was young and definitely not when I grew up.

Yes, I was a troublemaker, but not in a violent way, more in a mischievous way.

I'm the fun-loving Daniel.

The heart-of-the-party Daniel.

The charming Daniel.

But now, I'm channeling the vengeful spirit of a fucking warrior.

Christopher jerks from his slumber. At first, he blinks as if he doesn't know on what planet or decade he exists.

Then his attention falls on me and he squints before recognition settles on his sickeningly good looks.

It's people like him that get away with it. Sons of men in power, sons of men who taught them that women are only good at spreading their legs.

"Daniel?" he croaks.

"The one and only, motherfucker." I punch him again, sending his face flying backward.

A splash of blood explodes on his face and drips down his chin. Next, it will be his goddamn teeth.

"What the…what in the bloody fuck…?" He shakes his head, blinking rapidly. "Why are you doing this?"

"You don't know, huh? Probably had it written down in your memory as a good fuck, then moved on to your next victim."

His eyes widen a little and then he laughs, loud, in a bark. "It's about Nicole, isn't it? I knew you were a puppy in love when you almost hit me that day you found me with her. Ruined my fun that night, but I got her anyway, Danny. Here's a little life lesson for you. If you leave something behind, someone else will pick it up."

My jaw clenches and I feel myself about to lose control, about to strangle him to death. But that would mean he'd get away with it easily.

So I erase his words, the fact that I pushed her to him by being a brainless fucking twat, and square my shoulder. "Is that why you seduced her mother and married her while she was in prison?"

"I told Nicole I only fucked her because she looked like her mother, but it's the exact opposite. I went to her mother to relive a fetish of sorts. Have you ever fucked a mother and a daughter? The feeling is exquisite. She didn't bleed like Nicole, though. Pity."

"What the fuck did you just say?"

"She was as dry as a desert, Nicole, and I guess she started bleeding. I never liked lube as much as I did at that moment."

A roar echoes in the air and I realize it's mine as I kick him, sending the chair and the scum in it tumbling backward.

His deranged laughter echoes in the empty space. "And you know what the funny part is? The bitch kept calling your name like a fucking chant. *Daniel…Dan…help…* You weren't there to do that, were you, Prince Charming? And guess fucking what? She'll never forgive you for not coming to her rescue."

I grab him by the collar, then crash my head against his. Blood explodes on my temple and slides to the collar of my shirt.

The physical pain is nothing compared to the searing injury that's ripping my soul apart.

She called for me.

She came to me right afterward.

And I wasn't there both times.

Fuck!

Christopher shuts up for a second, then grins like an unhinged psycho. "I'm gonna have her back, Danny. With my kid. We're a family."

"Death is all that you'll have." I take his head and jam it against the dirty floor. "Did it feel good to hit her head on the floor, Chris? Did you feel so powerful by taking her power away? Did you get high on it? Hard for it?"

I stand up and before he can move, I slam my Prada shoe on his head. I wore them today for their sturdy soles, and is that a crack of bone I hear?

"You fucking—"

"Doesn't feel so good when the tables are turned, huh?" I kick his head until he drools blood and his eyes slip out of focus.

"Then what did you do? Ah, right." I'm surprised by my calm tone considering the fucking need to rip his teeth from his skull. Still stepping on his head, I squash his dick with my other foot like it's a useless cigarette. "You used this thing to rape her. To hurt her. Make her bleed. That will happen to you, too, not in that particular order, then I'll put so many objects in your arsehole, you'll wish for death. Maybe then you'll know how it feels to be violated. By the end of tonight, you'll be dickless, raped by a metal rod and other stuff. On Monday, you will withdraw the custody case and live in fear, Christopher. That man who got you here, I'll pay him extra to keep you in his sights. If you raise your head from the gutter you live in, I'll have it cut off. If you go to someone for help, I'll have you erased off the face of the earth. Remember, Christopher, you'll stay alive, not because I can't kill you, but because death is too easy of a punishment for you. I want you to stare at where your dick once was and wish you never fucking touched her."

"You will…" he croaks. "Have another man's waste."

"The only waste of air is you. As for being a man, you won't be one in about five minutes—not that you ever were." I jam his head harder, so he eats the dirt and stops talking. "Nicole, however, was and will always be a fucking queen."

One I don't deserve, but can't move away from either.

By the time I'm finished with the fuck, I want to throw myself off a bridge.

Not because of what I did to him—I would repeat that in a heartbeat. His wails and screams and blabbering like a baby didn't affect me, not one bit.

I would do it all over again.

I would restart if I could. Every day. Until the day I fucking die.

Kyle joined me some time later, offering a hand, but I refused, so he just hung around to watch.

He told me he'll keep him on a leash with the help of his friends here. I didn't ask who his friends are and I couldn't give a fuck as long as Christopher never sat right, peed standing, or breathed clean air.

I would pay them the billions in my name if I had to. Every single last dime.

As long as Chris's life turns miserable.

This brings me to the reason behind the emptiness.

Despite what I previously thought, this doesn't fix it. Doesn't bring back what Nicole already lost.

Doesn't erase the fact that I'm part of the reason she was traumatized.

Not anyone else.

Me.

I take a sip of the cheap whiskey bottle I kept in my rental car for this purpose.

Two hours. That's the amount of time I spent in my car on the opposite side of the street, unable to go inside the house.

Maybe I should leave now, sign over the mansion in Nicole's name, and threaten Zach to provide her and Jayden with rich oil princes' lives.

That would be the right thing to do.

But that would involve actually talking to my brother and me pushing her to another man.

Fucking again.

I retrieve my phone, all three hazy versions of it, and type out the ant-like letters.

Daniel: Asleep?

The reply is immediate.

Astrid: Currently painting for a fussy Glyndon. She's nothing like Lan and Bran.

Those are her spawn. Landon, Brandon, and Glyndon. The reason they have preppy names is the fact that they're Kings and will lead royal-like lives better than their father.

Daniel: I think I fucked up big time.

Astrid: Concerning?

Daniel: Someone. I hurt them. Badly. What should I do?

Astrid: Apologize.

Daniel: I don't think 'sorry I screwed up your life' would pay the bill.

Astrid: You'd be surprised at the power of a genuine apology, Bug.

Astrid: Is this about Aunt Nora and Zach? Will you finally talk to them?

Daniel: No.

I throw the phone away before she starts nagging and acting like my surrogate mother.

My fingers are unsteady, because of being drunk and pissed the fuck off as I drive the car the small distance inside the mansion.

The doorman opens the front gate, doing a spectacular job at ignoring my sewer rat appearance.

I practically throw myself out of the car as soon as I stop the vehicle in front of the house—or in the grass. What-the-fuck-ever.

An angel appears to welcome me home.

Or I'm drunk.

I really hope it's that and not that I actually need psychic therapy.

The nausea that I usually get from the sight of food creeps in my stomach. Or maybe it's something different that involves my stomach and the thing beating behind my rib cage.

Nicole stands in the middle of the garden, wearing a white dress with peach-colored lace and a fluffy shawl covers her arms.

Her blonde hair falls straight to her arse with the brightness of the sun. One that's going to burn me alive but I'd still approach anyway.

Touch it.

Fucking breathe its fire.

Her head is tilted back as she watches the moon with her biteable lips slightly open.

A sun that's in love with the moon.

Isn't that thing doomed in some tragedy?

Her attention shifts to me as if she could naturally sense me around her.

A gasp slips from her as she runs toward me, and fuck.

Fuck it.

Fuck me.

The sight of her coming to me nearly brings me to my knees.

I have fucking PTSD from the way she turned her back to me the day she packed her suitcases and disappeared into the night.

The air crackles with tension and shifts with her smell. Cherries, pain, and fucking heartache.

Joy, too. As small as it is.

"What happened?" Her voice trembles as she palms my face, her fingers dabbing on the dry blood from my temple.

"Pub fight." I don't sound so drunk. But then again, the sight of her always sobered me up. "You should see the other tool. They're performing CPR as we speak."

"Since when do you ever fight?"

"Since today." I lean into her hand like Lolli does when she pets her, and no, I'm neither jealous nor mimicking a cat. "Were you waiting for me, Peaches?"

"Don't flatter yourself. I just couldn't sleep after Jay was out."

"You know…your cheeks become the same shade of red as your lips when you're blushing…or lying. Which I assume is both right now."

"Shut up. Let me clean that." She takes my hand and leads me inside.

I let her guide me in my own house, watching her from behind, unable to take my gaze off her.

My hand itches to touch her, fucking grab her by that gorgeous hair and kiss her.

But something stops me.

She'll never forgive you for not coming to her rescue.

My jaw clenches.

My fist tightens.

And I wish I had finished that bottle of whiskey.

Actually, I should go back to the car and do just that. Maybe crash it against the gate this time.

Nicole sits me down on a sofa and produces a first aid kit from a side table as if she played Sherlock and learned this mansion's every nook.

Which I wouldn't be surprised if she did.

She has always been curious, intuitive, and the smartest woman I've ever met.

Nicole dabs the cotton at my forehead, a delicate frown on her brows. "You're not a kid or a teenager. How can you even get in a fight at this age? You're a solicitor, for God's sake, fighting shouldn't even be one of your options."

Her voice is like my favorite symphony and most distorted nightmare.

But no matter how much I want to close the distance between us, it's already too deep.

Too fucked up.

You screwed it all up, Daniel. You think you have the right to touch her?

I swiftly pull the cotton from her fingers and stagger to my feet. "I'll do it on my own."

Her shoulders drop and her face scrunches as if I stepped on her chest.

But I don't allow myself to look at that soft face, at the only lips I remember the taste of. For eleven years, I haven't kissed other women, never found the reason behind it. Not after I kissed her the day her mother was arrested. In a way, I kept her taste with me until her lips found mine again on the day I fucked her in my office.

Nicole is the only woman I want to kiss until we're both out of breath and sharing each other's air.

Wrong train of thought, fucker.

I turn around, not bothering to take the first aid kit as I stalk to the stairs.

But before I can take a step, her brittle, broken voice stops me. "Do I repulse you?"

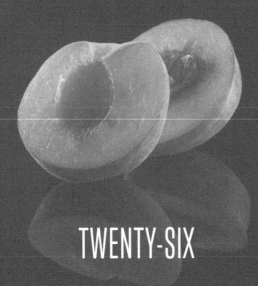

TWENTY-SIX

Nicole

I F HEARTS WERE ABLE TO SPILL FREE, MINE WOULD BE splashing on the floor.

My fingers dig into my shawl to stop myself from reaching out to his back. Seems that's all I ever have of Daniel.

His back.

His cold shoulder.

His ignorance.

Eleven years didn't change that. Probably nothing will.

He slowly turns around and I physically flinch at the tightness on his face, the raw anger covering his features like a warrior's helmet. That and the dry blood on his temple make him appear savage.

Primal, even.

"What the fuck did you just say?" The air carries his calmly-spoken words like a whip that meets my skin with a *thwack*.

I raise my chin, despite the pain that's bleeding in my soul with the lethality of a poison. "Are you repulsed by me because I'm damaged goods?"

"Shut the fuck up, Nicole."

"Tell me." I walk to him, my speed slow and faulty like a crippled animal. "Tell me you don't want to touch me anymore. Say it, Daniel. Just off me already so I'll stop having these delusional thoughts about you—"

My words end in a gasp when he grabs me by the throat and slams his lips to mine. It's a hungry kiss, animalistic in nature and with so much heat that I'll probably suffer from second-degree burns—make that first-degree.

His fingers squeeze the sides of my neck, turning me light-headed, and his other hand grips my chin with a possession that leaves me breathless.

He leaves me breathless.

Always has since that day I nearly died in his arms.

His lips devour mine and his tongue slips inside with the pure intention to conquer.

The magic breaks when he wrenches his mouth from mine as suddenly as he devoured me. The fire in his eyes is nothing short of lava spilling from a volcano.

"Don't you ever, and I mean fucking *ever*, repeat that. You're not damaged goods, never were and never will be. Are we clear?"

Is it wrong that I think he's the most attractive I've seen him right now? Even the trail of blood on his temple makes him ruggedly handsome in a fallen angel type of way.

The one who's able to take it all away, to give me the support I thought I didn't need but turns out I do.

A squeeze on my throat pulls me out of the dreamy phase. "Are we clear?"

I nod.

"Use your voice."

"Yeah. I just…thought you were repulsed by me since, well… you didn't want to touch me."

He slides his erection up and down my stomach, spreading a violent wave of arousal between my thighs. "Do I seem repulsed?

I can be disgusted with the whole world, but never you, Peaches. Fuck. You must know what you do to me."

"No," I blurt. "Tell me."

He drops his forehead on mine, briefly closing his eyes before they trap me in a shock of pure intensity. "You're the only woman I wanted with a desperation that bordered on both pleasure and pain. The only woman who drives me fucking insane but I still can't look away from. My fixation with you made me hate all blondes because they reminded me of you. Brunettes aren't my type, Peaches. You are. And you know what, your condition about exclusivity is bloody useless. Ever since you came back into my life, I haven't been able to see another woman, let alone fuck her. It's you. Only you."

Is it possible to have a heart attack due to happiness?

Is it possible to free fall deeper than I already was?

All the words he just said echo in my head round and round, making me dizzy, disoriented, and on my way to cloud nine.

I didn't think I could get high on words alone.

Not any words.

Daniel's.

I lick my dry lips. "Then…why did you vehemently refuse to be exclusive?"

His thumb strokes my cheek back and forth, like the rhythm of a soothing lullaby. "I wanted to push you away, to prove to myself that you meant nothing."

"How did that work for you?"

"In a miserably awful way, and stop smiling like that unless you're up for me to fuck you like an animal."

My grin widens. "You can. If it's you, I'm up for anything."

A grunt spills out of him. "You're killing me, Peaches."

"Not more than you were killing me all this time." I get on my tiptoes, grab a handful of his shirt, and whisper my deepest secret. "You're the first one who made me enjoy sex again after what happened."

He physically flinches at that as if I slapped him. "Really?"

"Really. I admit, at the beginning, it felt too much sometimes, which is why I got panic attacks."

Daniel searches my eyes, the lines of his face scrunched in pain. "Did I hurt you? Even unintentionally?"

I shake my head. "You always took care of me and put me first. Didn't you notice that I've become more comfortable touching you with time? I'm sure it'll get even better if we keep doing this."

When I get back on the soles of my feet, Daniel is groaning, and soon after, I join when his lips claim mine again.

He lifts me up in his strong arms, pulling the world from beneath my feet. I moan and smile and laugh against his mouth as he carries me up the stairs as if I weigh nothing.

I don't know where he's taking me and I don't care.

I can kiss Daniel for a lifetime and not be bored. He tastes of alcohol, a hint of the lollipop's peach flavor, and desperation.

He tastes just like my favorite things.

My back meets something soft, a mattress. We're in his bedroom, I know because the caretaker of the house told me so during the tour I insisted on taking while I was waiting for Daniel to return.

London scared me. London was filled with fake façades, broken dreams, and irreversible traumas.

But not when he's in it.

Now, it thrills me. It makes me want to return to the time where the highlight of my day was bickering with him.

I wish I could tell him, you're a loser meant you're the only person who rattles me.

Piss off meant come closer.

I hate you meant I like you, I miss you, I love you.

Still kissing me, he throws my shawl away and sneaks his hand behind my back to rip my dress open.

Then it's on the floor, my dress, and soon my bra and underwear follow. I'm entirely naked in front of his ferocious eyes, but that doesn't even spring a hint of a panic attack.

There's a different attack happening in my chest. Heart. Life. Everywhere.

And the way he looks at me? It's nothing short of both lust and passion. I feel stupid for even thinking he'd be repulsed by me, that he didn't want to touch me.

Daniel basically rips his shirt open, revealing his muscled abs and smooth chest.

This beautiful man is mine.

All mine.

And he seals that thought when his lips find my nipple. He sucks the tight bud between his teeth until I'm writhing and arching off the bed for more.

"Oh, Dan…"

He slowly lifts his head, nuzzling his chin against the soft flesh of my breast. "Say that again. My name."

"Dan…"

"Say you want me, Peaches."

"I want you. I always wanted you."

"Fuck." He slides his fingers down my stomach and to the warm place between my legs. "You're soaked, baby."

I press my lips together, unable to utter a word. And I don't need to. He brings me to orgasm within minutes, his fingers expertly working my core and clit. It's like he knows the right places that drive me mad.

While I'm still coming down from it, Daniel removes his trousers and boxer briefs. He flings my legs over his shoulders and drives into me slow, but so deep, hitting my pleasurable spot.

The orgasm elongates as he fucks me tenderly, taking his time to fill me whole before he moves.

My gasps and moans fill the air as the rhythm drives me insane. It's so similar to the way he fucked me that night eleven years ago.

After the first hard and ruthless ones, he took his time fucking me slowly, savoring me, and I was stupid to think he was making love to me.

Seems I'm stupid right now, too, because I can't erase that image out of my head.

That word.

That sensation.

My heart soars and my body detonates to life after so many years of being dormant.

My stomach churns and every limb falls into the same pace as his, my hips rotating to meet the power of his.

And just when I think I'll come, Daniel flips us.

I gasp as he ends up on his back with me on top. The position gets him so deep inside me, I can feel him in my belly.

My palms are on his chest, on his pain and vengeance tattoo, as I stare at him questionably.

"Ride me, Nicole."

"W-what?"

"Use my cock to get off. I want to see your tits bouncing and your hair flying with how much you fuck me."

Holy shit.

My heart can't take this. And neither can my body, but I do it. I lift myself up, then fall down on his cock.

It's so hard and thick that it hurts a little, but I welcome that burn, and I repeat it over and over again.

Once I find my rhythm, I release his chest and grip his thighs for balance. At first, Daniel watches me with that fire, with that lust, and want, that mirrors mine.

He rakes his eyes over my bouncing breasts, to my wild hair, and finally on where his body meets mine.

Then, he grabs my hips, his hooded eyes focused on mine, and thrusts in me from the bottom.

The rhythm is mad and the friction is so intense that I think I'll black out from the promise of pleasure alone.

"You look like a fucking goddess, Peaches."

I come then, my chest squeezing with all the words and touches and everything in between.

But it doesn't end. Not when he keeps driving in me from below and playing with my nipples as he chases his own orgasm.

I bite my lower lip, watching his face contort as he releases deep inside me.

I can feel his cum pouring out of me and I release a sigh as I collapse on top of him, my head colliding with his thundering heartbeat.

As if it's planning to leap out of his chest and slip into mine.

I love you, I want to say, but I can't.

What if it ruins this moment? What if I lose him again?

If my feelings scare him, then there's no need for them.

There's no need for stupid emotions that only got me in trouble before. I'm fine with just this.

Or at least I try to think that I am.

Unrequited love hurts. No matter how much I try to hide it, it escapes to a deeper part of me and remains hauled in there, festering, turning to a bitter pill I swallow every morning.

Every day.

Every year.

I tried to cure myself of the Daniel disease. I truly did, and I thought I succeeded all those years I was busy raising Jay and surviving in a world that spat me out like chewed gum.

But seeing him again, being with him, reaching to a secret part of him is just too much.

I'm not strong enough to resist that.

To resist him.

"The art of pain is an abstract form of vengeance," I read his tattoo in the silence of the room. "Who said that?"

"Me."

"I didn't know you were a philosopher."

"I'm not. I dreamt about it."

I prop my elbows on his chest to stare at him. "A dreamer, too. You keep surprising me, Dan."

A grin paints his lips and that's really not good for me because his dimples appear and they're so mesmerizing and beautiful and dangerous for me. "Mission accomplished."

"Do you still want revenge against me?"

"No. I don't think I even wanted that in the first place, I just… channeled those negative thoughts into that specific jar."

"Does that mean you'll stop being mean?"

"Was I?"

"You were a dick."

"Happy to see you have colorful language in your dictionary, Miss Prude."

My fingers find the blood on his forehead and I try to wipe it away. "I curse internally sometimes. What I showed was never what I felt."

He breathes heavily. "I'm starting to see that."

"You do?"

"Yeah. I'm going to need some time to wrap my head around it all."

"There was an exception."

"An exception?"

"The day we had sex for the first time, I showed what I felt."

A heated look covers his features and I think he'll fuck me again, but he kisses me.

Sweet and tender, then raw and violent.

"Tell me you're mine, Nicole," he groans against my lips.

"I'm yours." The words are the easiest I've ever said.

"Only mine?"

"Only yours."

Probably since we were young.

But I don't say that because apparently feelings are not Daniel's forte.

Hell. He's still wrapping his head around the past.

If I give him time, he'll come back to me, right?

He'll heal. I'll heal and he'll love me.

I shiver at that.

That's the exact thought I had eleven years ago. That with time, he'll come to me.

But it was never the case.

If anything, it ended with a tragedy.

I try not to think about that as I kiss him and sleep tucked in the curve of his body with his legs and arms swallowing me in a cocoon.

It's like he can't touch me enough, entwine his body with mine enough.

Be with me enough.

A small gasp startles me awake. At first, I'm disoriented by the morning light coming from the window.

I'm pretty sure the curtains were closed last night, and I don't think the mansion's staff would waltz into Daniel's bedroom.

Oh, shit. Please don't tell me Jay found his way here.

I jerk up to a sitting position, pulling the covers around my chest.

Fortunately, I don't have to worry about traumatizing my little brother for life.

Unfortunately, I'm staring into the green eyes I wished to not see again for a lifetime.

My stepsister—ex-stepsister—glares at me with a hand on her hip. "What the hell is going on here?"

TWENTY-SEVEN

Nicole

O NE OF THE FEW THINGS PAPA TAUGHT ME IS THAT WATER and oil never mix.

You can jam them together, shake them for eternity, but the moment they're in a static state, they each retreat to their respective worlds.

That's what Astrid and I are. Water and very flaming oil.

Ever since I first met her when we were fifteen, she was this free spirit who rebelled against what was expected and couldn't care less about her aristocratic blood.

She has Uncle Henry's fortune, name, and connections at the tip of her fingers, but never made use of them.

If anything, she abhorred them, and our life, and me—rightfully so considering I acted like a bitch toward her.

All because of the twat sitting beside me.

We dressed up, or I did anyway, pulling a dress over my head and covering my arms with the shawl.

Daniel is only in some shorts he grabbed from the wardrobe.

His hair is a beautiful mess of light brown locks, falling over his forehead haphazardly.

His expression is still sleepy, bored even. His stance is definitely the latter judging by how his long legs are stretched, crossed at the ankles, and he has both his hands interlinked behind his head.

In this position, his abs contract, visible for anyone to see. Namely Astrid, who's been pacing for the past ten minutes.

Is it wrong that I want to momentarily blind her so she doesn't look at him? Yeah, it probably is. Doesn't mean I'm not thinking about it.

"Sit down, you're giving me a headache worse than my hangover."

Astrid comes to a screeching halt and glares at him. She's shorter than me, has long brown hair, and eyes so green they compete with the brightest grass.

She's wearing simple short overalls and white tennis shoes. Nothing fancy, nothing flashy. This has been her fashion sense since we were teens.

Even though she's now a renowned artist and married into the richest family in the country, nothing's really changed about her looks or how she handles herself.

"Oh my God, look at that. You actually have a voice that you could've used to, I don't know, call and tell me you're in England after eleven years of leaving the country. That's a decade and one year. Not a big deal or anything."

"I didn't know you added drama queen to your hobbies. As your friend, I must tell you it doesn't suit you."

"And it suits you?"

"I'm not the one screaming the whole house down and scaring my staff away, Bug. They'll drink tea in your honor and call you a crazy hag behind your back."

"I'm talking about your endless excuses to not come home."

"Home is overrated."

"And so is your reason for not coming to England." She flops on the chair opposite us, crossing her arms like a stern teacher. "Now, let's talk about another important issue. Have you grown tired of shagging your way through the States so you settled for her?"

My cheeks heat. For some reason, I remained invisible from their conversation and I'm not sure why I thought that would continue until she screams her head off and leaves.

I don't know why I was slightly relieved that Daniel extended his lash of sarcasm to her as well.

"Her is Nicole," he says and I startle, then I smile, fighting the urge to get up and kiss him.

Astrid be damned.

She narrows her eyes on me and speaks with pure mockery. "Don't I know it?"

"Then use it." There's no hint of sarcasm in his tone as he straightens, cradling his head, probably because of both the hangover and the injury.

Astrid twists her lips in disapproval. "Are we really not going to address the elephant in the room?"

"Your drama queen tendencies, you mean?" Daniel asks with an innocent smile that creases his cheeks with gorgeous dimples.

"Her!" She points at me. "What is she doing here? And why are you fucking her of all people?"

"For the last time, her name is Nicole. She came with me—more accurately, I dragged her here against her will. And who I fuck has nothing to do with you last I checked."

My lips tremble and I tighten my hold on the shawl, my fingers digging into my palms.

I'm checking to see if I'm dreaming.

If this is one of those fantasy subconscious things where I picture Daniel picking me.

There's pain in my palms.

So this is real.

He's actually taking my side over Astrid's. His *best friend* Astrid.

The Astrid who always came before me. Whom he befriended upon minutes of meeting her while he glared at me for years.

"Are you listening to yourself? She's the bitch Nicole, Dan! The 'you're a loser, go wank a pole' Nicole. The 'you're not good enough to breathe the same air as me, try in two decades' Nicole. The 'I'm going to suck off Levi to get back at Astrid' Nicole. Have you forgotten what she's done?"

I wince at the reminder of my mean track record. And I'm once again struck by how much I changed and she didn't.

Oil and water. That's what Astrid and I were and will always be.

"Obviously, you haven't." Daniel isn't the least bit fazed. "And here I thought those spawns of yours deleted some of your memories."

"I'll never forget *her*."

"Kinda obsessive, but okay, Bug. Are you done?"

"I'm not done until she leaves."

"Stop talking about me as if I'm not here." I stare at her, my voice surprisingly calm.

"I'm not talking to you."

"Yes, you are if you keep throwing jabs my way." I straighten my spine. "If you want to say something, say it to my face. You never shied away from that before."

"Okay then, we're doing this." She pauses for dramatic effect. "What the hell do you want from Daniel when you always considered him worse than dirt under your Louboutins? Did you hear about his success and picked up gold-digging as a side job?"

"I never asked for a dime of his money. I'm his assistant, not a gold-digger."

"She's your assistant?" She directs her question at Daniel, then stares at me. "You're an assistant. Wow. How the mighty have fallen."

"If you intend to make me feel small, it won't work. I already adjusted to my new life and nothing you could say or do would have an effect on me."

"That's good and all, but why Daniel? You hated him. You fucking spiked his drink and raped him!"

I can feel Daniel stiffening beside me as my fingers turn clammy. I stare at him, dumbfounded.

He told her I raped him?

I…*raped* him?

My limbs start shaking and my throat closes. It's an unconscious reaction whenever the R-word is mentioned.

It's probably unnatural. Such as my panic attacks, and broken spirit.

A spirit that's only getting back to life recently.

A spirit that I thought I lost a long time ago.

"I told you that wasn't the case, Astrid." His voice raises for the first time. He calls her by her given name for the first time, too.

"Then what was it? You drugged him and me that night, Nicole! Levi saw it on the cameras. You told me so yourself."

"It's not…" I trail off, unable to get the words out.

"Then what was it?" Astrid asks.

"I fucked her." Daniel jerks to a standing position. "I followed her and kicked out Chris because the bloody thought of him or anyone else touching her put me in a murderous mood worse than a serial killer's. Because she'd been driving me fucking crazy for years and right then, I could pretend it was the drugs that made me do it. And that night? The night you had an accident and nearly died was the happiest night of my fucking life up until that point. Up until I abandoned her in the middle of the fire and found you drowning in your own blood. So she didn't rape me, Astrid. She didn't even come after me. I followed her, kicked out the lowlife who was there, and I fucked her until I lost count because I wanted her since I knew what wanting someone fucking means."

Astrid's lips open in a wordless gasp. I'm two seconds away from crying like a baby.

The words he just said have gone past the confinements of my ears and are slashing their way to my bleeding heart.

He grabs my hand and I feel like I'm floating on air as he

pulls me to his side. To his strong, hard, and very warm side. His arm wraps around my waist, fingers digging into my hip as if he's making sure I remain there.

"She's with me now and that's that."

I can't stop looking at him, at the seriousness in his features and his tone. At the way his jaw is set and his lips are in a line.

I want to kiss those lips.

To get on my tiptoes and let the world see that I'm with him.

That I'm his.

That he's mine.

I can tell Astrid is lost for words, as much as me.

Before she can formulate an answer, Jay trots down the stairs. "What's with the commotion? Some of us are trying to sleep."

Astrid's head whips toward Jay and she narrows her eyes on him. Then at me. "Is he…"

"My brother." I begrudgingly rush to him and put my arm around him, scared something will happen to him.

"And who are you?" Jay peeks past me, his inquisitive eyes studying her.

"Daniel's best mate," she says assertively, apparently not having revoked Daniel's friendship rights after all he said.

"In that case, you're fine. Dan's friend is my friend." Jay pushes past me and offers her his hand and a wide grin. "I'm Jayden, nine years old. I already skipped a few grades and will probably skip more and become a genius who finds a cure for cancer or human stupidity. I haven't decided which one is more urgent yet."

Daniel and I smile, but my ex-stepsister laughs. "You sound like you'd have fun with my children. I'm Astrid."

"Nice to meet you, Astrid. I have an important question, do your kids like Minions or not? Because that's a deal-breaker."

"They actually do. The majority at least."

"Let's go meet the majority then."

I squeeze his shoulder. "Another time, okay? Astrid must be busy."

"No, I'm not." Astrid's face is unreadable as she watches me. "Let's have breakfast together."

"All of us?" I ask, unsure.

She gives me a strange look. "Yes. I insist."

I'm not stupid enough to think Astrid invited us to her house as a peace offering.

She might not have been the bitch type, but she was always the "protect who I care about" type. The "mess with who I love and I'll cut you" type.

No clue why I think she'll dress me in a clown's clothes and tell her kids to spray me with her precious paint.

It'd make so much sense, seriously.

The whole twenty-minute trip to her house doesn't.

A big, warm hand grabs mine that I've been hiding with the other one between my thighs. I stare at Daniel as he interlinks his fingers with mine, keeping his attention on the road.

He stays there, between my thighs, eliciting pleasure, warmth, and the most important feeling of all.

Peace.

He peeks at me and I smile. It's not forced or remotely fake.

If he's with me, I can do this.

Or at least, I try to think of it as such.

He's changed into khaki trousers and a polo shirt that gives him that preppy yet hot look. Daniel always hovered on the line between good and bad.

He can be the most mischievous troublemaker and the coldest jerk, depending on who he's dealing with.

We arrive at Astrid's house—or more like, mansion. Pretty sure this was an old castle and they renovated it into this modern setting.

Jay is practically jogging to Astrid's side as soon as the cars stop. He doesn't stop talking to her on and on like a chatterbox. I envy his easy-going nature sometimes. How he finds it easy to express himself. It's so different from when I was a child—reserved and acting by the rules.

I'm glad he, at least, gets to live his childhood to the fullest.

"Mummy!" A small figure with light brown hair slams into her leg, then stares at Jayden with awe. "You found a prince, Mummy!"

"Sort of." She laughs, then leans down so she's almost eye level with him. Her expression is soft and loving as she kisses his cheek. "Brandon, this is Jayden. He loves Minions, too. Do you want to show him your collection?"

"Yes!" Brandon grabs Jay by the arm and practically drags him inside, then stops and waves at us. "Hi, Uncle Dan and beautiful lady from Mummy's pictures."

Then he disappears with Jay in tow.

I stare at her. "You have pictures of me?"

She clears her throat. "Some old things in the family album."

"I thought Uncle Henry would've gotten rid of them."

"Only the ones with your mum," she says dismissively, leading us out back.

However, I can't stop thinking about what she said.

Only the ones with your mum.

As in, the ones where it was only me stayed?

I never thought I would face Astrid again, but now that I am, I can't help feeling the crushing guilt about the past. I caused her accident, although unintentionally, made her feel unwelcome in her own house, and competed for her father's love.

Not only was I insufferable, but I also made it my mission to hurt her. And I hate the past me, I hate how much I went at her throat because of how insecure I was.

I want to apologize, not only for my behavior but also for the fact that Mum stole Uncle Henry from her and her mother, killed her mother, then attempted to kill her. I have so much to apologize for, but I'm not sure if that will have any effect on her.

She was always assertive in who she hated and I was at the top of that list.

My thoughts are scattered when we reach a gazebo in the

garden, painted with a shock of colors. Transparent stars dangle from the ceiling like fallen angels.

That's where the breakfast table is set up with all types of food that could feed an army.

Something travels in our direction at supersonic speed and I flinch. Daniel, however, catches the ball with his foot and even dribbles it.

"I see you haven't lost your touch, Sterling."

"Nice shot, Captain." Daniel grins at Levi who's approaching us while carrying Brandon.

Wait. Didn't he go with Jay just now? How is he—

As Levi gets close, I can see that the child is a spitting image of Brandon, but he has a small mole beneath his left eye. And he's wearing a sports jersey, unlike Brandon who was in light green shorts and a button-down.

Levi has grown up into a hard man. His boyish beauty has become all masculine, but his mane of golden blond hair is still as bright as ever.

He leans down and kisses Astrid on the lips, openly, with tongue.

Jeez.

My cheeks heat and I try to stare anywhere but at them.

"Get a fucking room." Daniel wrenches the child from Levi's arms and whispers, "Don't you hate this, Lan?"

"I'm used to it." Brandon's clone, Lan, lifts a shoulder. "Uncle Aiden says Mummy and Daddy like making babies."

"Your uncle Aiden is right."

"Your uncle Aiden is a twat, Landon," Levi says, finally pulling away from his school style make-out session with Astrid.

"Uncle Aiden isn't a twat. He only says the truth. Besides"— Landon furrows his brow—"you made Glyndon, who's spoiled and unnecessary."

"I told you to not call your sister unnecessary, Lan," Astrid says in a teacher's voice.

"But she is."

"Go to your room and reflect on that." She pulls him from Daniel's arm and puts him to his feet.

Landon shakes his head and stalks away with his hands linked behind his back like an old man, grumbling, "She's still unnecessary."

"He's definitely taking after Aiden." Daniel laughs. "My condolences in advance for when he becomes a psycho."

"How could you say that, Bug?" Astrid sounds mortified and rightfully so. Even though Levi was the wild card, Aiden was the one who exhibited destructive energy in everything he did. He was silent, broody, and with clear sociopathic tendencies.

Still is, from the rumors I read online. His wife and son might have tamed him a bit, but something tells me Aiden King will never change.

"Just the truth that you're refusing to see. He just called his sister unnecessary," Daniel says. "Where's that ray of sunshine anyway?"

"With Jonathan," Levi answers. "And you're on limited time, Sterling. One more snarky remark and I'm kicking you out of my house."

"Your jealousy is cute, Captain. Now, are you going to sit us down or do you need to keep watching Nicole like a fucking creep without actually talking to her?"

"So it is Nicole." Levi scratches his chin. "I thought she was a ghost following you and was contemplating whether or not to tell you."

"I found her at Daniel's house." Astrid crosses her arms. "*Bed*, to be more specific."

He bursts out laughing. "I knew I was right to bet more."

Daniel's lips twist and for once, he doesn't have some sarcastic comeback.

My spine, however, jerks into a line. "What...bet?"

"Knox told us you were Sterling's assistant and we bet on whether or not he'd cure his blonde phobia by falling for you again."

There was a bet going on?

About us?

"You knew about Nicole and didn't tell me?" Astrid asks, astounded.

Levi grabs her by the waist. "Didn't want to worry you, Princess. Besides, there was a fifty percent chance she would've gotten out of his life."

"Still…" She stares at all of us, shakes her head, then goes to the gazebo, glaring over her shoulder at Levi and Daniel. "We're not on speaking terms until your majesties decide whether or not I'm part of your life and should be privy to information like this."

"Was she always a drama queen or is this a new habit, or maybe you fucking impregnated her again so she's becoming emotional?" Daniel whispers to Levi.

"Call my wife a drama queen again and I'll hit you on the head hard enough to knock out your few functioning neurons," he tells him, then catches up to Astrid, puts his arm around the small of her back, and whispers something to her.

At first, her face is blank, but then her lips break out in a smile. I always envied the connection they shared since we were in school, and to see how strong they're still going is heartwarming and heartbreaking at the same time.

They had their differences and familial feuds, but they stood up for each other.

Which can't be said about me and Daniel.

But then again, our circumstances weren't the same.

A few minutes later, we're sitting at the table.

While Daniel, Levi, and Astrid bicker, I spend the entire breakfast silent, trying to force down bites of food.

This setting isn't for me. The itch to bolt out of here and run the fastest I can is more urgent than anything I've ever felt.

Maybe I can go to another country and not be forced into a place where my only ally is probably Daniel's dick.

Okay, maybe Daniel, too, but a part of me is unable to believe his sudden change of heart. Maybe this is a trick and I'll be dragged and laughed at in front of everyone American-high-school style.

"Why aren't you eating, Bug?" Astrid stares between him and his full plate.

"I only eat Nicole's cooking nowadays."

Her eyes flash to me. "You cook?"

I clear my throat. "Yeah."

"And her food is the best thing you won't have the luxury to eat." Daniel lazily wraps an arm around my shoulder, killing the few centimeters between us. "Be jealous."

Astrid twists her lips. "Why would I?"

"You can't cook an egg to save your life. If Captain doesn't feed you, you'll be a skeleton."

"That's not true. Right, Levi?"

"Kinda is, Princess."

"Hey!"

Both Levi and Dan burst out into laughter and continue teasing her until Levi reminds Daniel of his earlier threat.

Me, on the other hand? I'm caught by the weight of Daniel's arm on my shoulder. By the way he glides his fingers up and down the bare part right beneath my short sleeve. By the ease and possessive way he does it, making everyone see instead of hearing about us.

If it's only for this, coming to London, to home, to Astrid and Levi's house is worth it.

I would go through a thousand awkward meals if he's right by my side.

That thought soon vanishes and so does my small smile when a shadow falls upon us.

"Long time no see, Nicole."

My throat dries and I feel myself falling.

Not even Daniel's hold can keep me anchored in place.

One of the reasons I left and was ashamed to even look back is staring down on me with his usual calm that I only saw shatter once.

When he found out that my mother caused his first wife's death.

Uncle Henry.

"I called him on the way here," Astrid offers and her voice sounds far away, as if it's underwater. "He wanted to see you."

Why? Just so he'd blame me? Kick me while I'm down as she likes to do?

I can take that from her but not from him.

Not from the father figure who taught me how to ride my first bike and put a plaster on my knees when I fell down.

Only so I would realize I was only a substitute for his dear Astrid. A silver medal. A second choice.

Maybe that's what I am to Daniel, too. Levi has his dear Astrid, so he settled for me.

I jerk up so fast, four pairs of eyes focus on me. I try to keep my composure but I have a feeling that I fail as I blurt, "I have to go."

My movements are stiff and uncoordinated as I practically jog out of the gazebo and to the house.

Where did Jay go again? We need to leave, like right now.

I spend a few minutes contemplating if going upstairs would be rude, then recalling I shouldn't even be worried about that.

Steps echo behind me and I wish Daniel followed me and will now take us home.

No, I don't mean that his flat or mansion have become our home. They aren't.

They shouldn't be.

When I turn around, however, it's not Daniel who's staring at me. Uncle Henry has followed me and is now closing in on me.

I turn around to run.

"Nicole, please."

My chin trembles and I grab the handrail for balance as I slowly whirl around to face him.

Seeing Uncle Henry again is nothing short of being

electrocuted. It's been nine years since I last saw him, but the hands of time didn't touch his strong bone structure and tall, broad figure.

Even the few white strands give him an elegant edge more than a sense of old age.

But the thing I could never forget about Uncle Henry? The way his green eyes hold the calm of Buddha, the wisdom of Confucius, and the kindness of Mother Theresa.

He made me feel safe.

Until safe wasn't on the list of things I could have.

"How have you been?" he asks, oblivious to my near freak-out state.

"I'm f-fine."

"Are you sure? If I make you uncomfortable…"

"That's not it…"

"Then what is it?" He places a hand in his pocket and I'm glad he doesn't invade the distance between us. "Last time you saw me, you ran away and I couldn't find you again."

"I had to protect my brother."

"Jayden, right?"

"How… Did Astrid tell you?" She practically gave him a report on the drive here.

"It was Daniel, actually. He called me two days ago, told me he found you and your brother. He also told me that he's bringing you to London, in case I wish to meet you."

"He…did that?"

"Yes, and I'm grateful. I've been searching for you for years."

"But why? Don't you hate me?"

What resembles pain crosses his features. "I never hated you, Nicole. I admit that after I found out Victoria toyed with Jasmine's breaks, caused her death, and nearly killed Astrid in that hit-and-run, my sole purpose was to make her pay."

"She…died of cancer after giving birth to Jay."

"I know. I visited her often."

"You did?"

He hated her with a ferociousness that scared me, so to say I'm surprised he's the one who visited her while she was in prison would be an understatement.

"Yes. I wanted to see her suffer. But it wasn't the imprisonment or cancer that ate her alive, Nicole. It was the fact that you turned your back on her."

"She turned her back on me first." I fight the tears gathered in my eyes.

The main reason I let Christopher roam free is because I was scared of her, of the sacrifices she made for me, of how people would see us.

I was terrified of her reaction to even consider mentioning it.

If it was Uncle Henry, he would've fought for me. He wouldn't have told me to swallow the knife with its blood.

"She hurt you when you only took care of us," I continue in a broken voice. "She made me lose you for good."

He takes one step forward. "You never lost me, Nicole. The day I let you walk out of my house is one of the worst regrets of my life."

A bubble-like pressure deflates in my chest and I can't control the lone tear that escapes my eye. "I'm sorry, Uncle. I'm so sorry I'm the daughter of the woman who caused you so much pain. So sorry."

He erases the distance between us and wraps me in a fatherly hug. Uncle Henry is an aristocrat through and through, so showing any emotion is blasphemy, but he's patting my head now.

And I cry like a baby.

I cry for losing him. For thinking he always wanted to get rid of me.

"It's not your fault, Nicole. I'm the one who's sorry I let hatred blind me from what's important." He pulls back, smiling. "It took losing you to realize you're my daughter as much as Astrid is."

"Uncle…"

"You can call me Papa or Dad, as Astrid does, whenever you're ready."

"You really forgive me?"

"There's nothing to forgive. What Victoria has done is on her. You were a victim, too."

"But…but Astrid doesn't like me."

"It's because she only saw the mean side of you. She'll get around as Daniel has."

I bite my lower lip. "I don't think he's come around."

He just likes the sex. He said it himself, that he enjoys fucking me out of his system.

A knowing smile covers Uncle Henry's lips. "Yes, he has. But if he hurts you, just let me know."

"Thank you."

"No, thank you for giving me another chance." He kisses the top of my head. "Welcome back home."

My heartbeat roars in my ears and that's not good for my stupid heart because it's starting to believe this happiness is real.

TWENTY-EIGHT

Daniel

TAKE A SIP OF THE HORRIBLE COFFEE THAT DEFINITELY doesn't have one gram of sugar and obsess over Astrid's house with the impatience of a toddler.

It's been exactly two minutes since Nicole and Uncle Henry disappeared in there, and yes, I'm actually counting the time, because that's also how long I kept myself from following after and making sure she's fine.

"You're drooling."

My eyes meet Astrid's narrowed ones and I resist the urge to grunt because that will definitely give her the reaction she's asking for, and that shit won't be happening.

"And you're heading to the old hag category faster than an express train."

Searing pain explodes in my leg when Levi kicks me under the table. "No talking to my wife that way unless you want your head hanging on her art studio's entrance."

"Glad to see you're still a crazy motherfucker, Captain. Let's hope the spawns don't inherit that."

Levi shares a look with his wife. "Did this cunt just call our children spawns, Princess?"

"He's jealous." She glides her fingers through his hair.

"Of what, exactly? Giving birth as a sport or changing nappies?" I take another sip of the coffee.

They ignore me and Astrid kisses his lips.

"Some of us are trying to drink some coffee. Disgusting." I push the cup away.

My friend doesn't even spare me a glance as she pulls away and whispers to Levi, "Can you go check on Lan? You know he shouldn't be left alone for long."

He strokes her cheek and nods. Then he glares at me. "Behave."

"Yes, Captain," I mock salute, and he flips me the bird.

As soon as he's out of earshot, Astrid practically lunges to my side with the lethality of a coup d'état. "Explain."

"What?" I grab hold of my cup of coffee and take a sip of the revolting thing, pretending it's actually exquisite.

"Don't give me that, Bug. You're with Nicole, of all people, and that needs explanation."

"I already told you…"

"You slept with her that night eleven years ago, okay, but how can you forget about everything else she did?"

"I didn't. Which is why I couldn't be in a relationship with her." I release a breath. "I had feelings for her long before you came along, but I fought them harder than anything I've done in my life. I just couldn't believe that I'd be into a bitch, especially after the way she treated you."

Her lips part. "You…have feelings for Nicole?"

"*Had*. Did you miss the past tense?"

"You're with her now after you're all grown up, so don't even dare to deny it."

I grumble but say nothing.

"I'm still wounded." She sighs, her voice lowering to a murmur. "She seduced Levi, Daniel and it hurt me so bad at the time."

"She didn't do it for the purpose of seduction or out of interest in Captain. It was her fucked-up way to get attention." I can at least admit that now. She did a lot of twisted shit to get my attention and I chose to see her in the exact opposite light.

"Wow. You're actually defending her."

"She's not who you think, Bugger."

"Obviously. Am I speaking to you or your dick right now?"

"It's not about my dick."

"It obviously is! Did you forget that she had sex with Christopher Vans in our pool house while you were having these feelings for her?"

My jaw clenches and I slam the coffee cup on the table. "She didn't have sex with Chris, Astrid. He raped her. What you saw that day was fucking rape."

She gasps, her eyes widening. "W-what?"

"He took her against her will and hurt her. I'm not even supposed to tell you this, but I won't tolerate it if you mention that word in front of her or insinuate that's what she did to me."

"But…but…she didn't say anything…"

"She had a concussion."

"Oh, God. Now that I think about it, she looked in pain."

My fist clenches.

"I…" Moisture glitters in her lids. "I could've helped her but didn't. I…was more disgusted than anything."

"You didn't know."

Gloomy silence falls over us as we both think of all the ways we could've stopped it but didn't.

Nicole must've felt so fucking lonely with no one to turn to.

"She didn't show anything." Astrid frowns. "After that night, she acted normal around the house."

"Because she was taught by her bitch of a mother to not express emotions. She was too scared to disappoint her, which is why she didn't report it either."

Astrid jerks up. "This won't do. She has to report it, even now. That lowlife can't roam free after what he's done. I'm going to talk to her."

I grab her by the wrist and pull her down. "Don't you dare talk to her about this. I only told you so you'd understand her better and mind your words around her, not so that you would pressure her into anything."

"But Christopher…"

"He's taken care of."

"How?"

"You don't need to know."

Her eyes widen in slow recognition. "Is that why you came back to England after eleven years?"

"Yes. Just promise to…at least give Nicole a chance. She's changed."

A soft smile covers her features. "Apparently, she's changed you, too."

"What type of blasphemy is that?"

"She brought you back to London, you're defending her like a die-hard solicitor, and you're taking care of her brother, who under different circumstances, should be a spawn."

"He's a smart spawn."

"You're missing the whole point." She grabs me by the shoulder. "But hey, I'm glad you're changing for the better, even if she's the reason behind it."

"She's not the reason behind anything."

"Keep telling yourself that, Bug."

Astrid laughs and I want to kick her and make her take back what she said. Because, fuck no, I'm not changing because of Nicole.

Right?

TWENTY-NINE

Daniel

"IF YOU TELL ANYONE ABOUT THIS, I'LL SAY I WAS DRUGGED."

Nicole laughs, the sound drifting in the chilly afternoon air and doing strange shit to my chest that I refuse to honor with a name.

There's other shit happening to my dick, too, but it's neither strange nor vague. I'm not ashamed to admit that I want this woman with the desperation of a sex addict, an incubus, and a nymph combined.

It's borderline obsession at this point.

Yesterday after we had breakfast and lunch with Astrid and her loud family, I couldn't wait to get Nicole all to myself. However, as the little shit Jayden would have it, we accompanied him on a London tour like some sodding tourists.

He took more photos than an egomaniac celebrity. And fine, it might have been fun, too.

I love watching how carefree Nicole becomes around her brother or how her motherly instinct shows up at any hint of danger. She was the one who was vehemently against coming back to England, but she was more eager than the tourists and Jayden united.

Thankfully, he's spent all his energy and some and therefore, was out soon after we got home, which gave me a chance to fuck Nicole until dawn.

No kidding.

But this time, I made sure to tell my staff if someone interrupts us in the morning, they're fired. Since they love Grandpa's mansion more than their children, they paled and swore on their sacred tea that it wouldn't happen again.

So I fucked Nicole again in the morning until she whined, then laughed, then sighed into my chest. I love how she snuggles up to me as if I'm her favorite person. As if we're the only people in the world.

But what I love more is how much she likes the way I touch her, how she doesn't escape in her head anymore and meets me stroke for stroke.

It's as if she...trusts me.

My short honeymoon phase came to a halt when Jayden came knocking on our door. He demanded to visit his new friend, Brandon.

Nicole was skeptical about that, but when Uncle Henry offered to take him to Astrid's and spend the day there, she couldn't say no.

My schedule for the day was fingering her sweet pussy, eating it for breakfast, fucking it, then doing that all over again—not in that particular order—until we board the plane tomorrow.

Nicole, however, had other plans. She gave me the sloppiest blowjob of all blowjobs that may have transported me to another realm then told me to take her to the cinema if I want another one.

She's a smart little minx and knew I couldn't say no to having my dick sucked by her full pink lips.

So we go to see the fucking film. A sappy romantic one that makes my eyes roll to the back of my head.

But it's fine, I can handle this shit, because another blowjob is waiting for me.

Best currency ever invented.

"It wasn't that bad." She shakes her head as we walk through the nearby park. Since it's early afternoon and the weather is bloody miserable with clouds upon clouds of gray—no surprise there—not so many people are out and about.

Nicole is fucking glowing in a simple white dress and a light peach-colored sweater. Her hair kisses the wind and replaces the non-existent sun, flying all over her face like an angel's halo.

I can't even look at her without being blinded, stabbed in the chest, and all these other chaotic emotions.

So I choose to focus on the current conversation instead. "No, it wasn't bad. It was horrible and fucking cheesy."

"All good love stories are."

"All good love stories end in tragedy, Peaches."

She peeks at me from beneath her lashes, then stares ahead. "I like to reimagine their endings. The tragic love stories, I mean. It used to make me feel giddy when I was younger."

"I didn't know you were a hopeless romantic."

"The worst kind."

"No wonder your favorite films are romance."

"Not only romance. I don't mind action, historical, thriller, or fantasy as long as there's romance in the midst."

"You graduated from hopeless romantic and entered the category of a creepy romantic."

"You have no right to judge when your taste in cinema is boring."

"Say what now?"

"Quentin Tarantino's films are your favorites. Can you get any more obvious?"

"Excuse you, Ms. Adler, but his films are nowhere near as boring as your cheesy romances."

"Shoot. Shoot. Bang. The end." She rolls her eyes. "I mean, come on."

"It's entertaining."

"No, it's cheesy in the other sense."

"We'll agree to disagree on that." I pause, bringing us to a stop. "Now, hold on. How did you know I liked Tarantino?"

A blush covers her features. "I know a lot of things about you."

"Like what?"

"You like Muse's music and want "Resistance" to be played at your funeral. You thought reading for assignments was boring and barely turned them in. You're grumpy in the morning and used to only drink black or iced coffee. Now, you only consume black with one gram of damn sugar."

I smirk. "And you still managed to mess it up a few times."

"It was on purpose because you're a jerk, in case you didn't know."

"Shocker. Might want to report that to someone who cares."

"Do you channel the twat tendencies or do they come naturally?"

"A little bit of both." I stare at my watch. "Time to go home for that BJ before I'm cock-blocked."

"Not yet." She bites her lower lip.

"Not yet? What else do you intend to do in this sodding weather that made kings and queens give up these lands?"

"Just walk."

"You sound more suspicious than a traitor with a torch."

"Just do as you're told or my mouth won't show you some love."

"I already paid for that. The cheesy film, remember?"

"Don't care. This is part of the bargain."

I groan, inwardly kicking my pussy-whipped dick for agreeing to this in the first place. I could've taken her back to the house and had not gotten a BJ but the whole package.

But when she said she wanted to spend time outside, I couldn't say no. In a way, this is our first date.

Fuck you, Junior. Are you on my side or hers?

"Also"—she glares at me—"you should've told me about Uncle Henry. I was so flustered."

She was. But when she came back, she looked the happiest I've seen her in recent memory.

"You both needed closure," I say simply.

It was one of the things that bothered her, and apparently, I made it my mission to get rid of them one by one.

What happens next completely takes me aback.

Nicole gets on her tiptoes and kisses my cheek.

Well, fuck. Is it wrong that I want to grab her by the throat and kiss her against the tree while everyone is watching?

"What was that for?" I ask instead.

"A thank-you." She swallows. "I thought I'd lost him for good, but turns out, he was always searching for me."

"If you want to really thank me, that kiss can go somewhere down below."

She fixates me with a playful look. "I said later."

"Later isn't a measurable time so it's meaningless. In fact, later could be the fifteen minutes we'll spend on the drive home."

"Nice try." Nicole's laughing now and I can't get enough of the sound. Of the carefree nature of it.

The fact that it shines through pain is what makes it even more special.

I would sell both my kidneys in a buy-one-get-one-free package if that means I'll see her laugh more.

So I try to keep it on her face as we take the fucking stroll, twice, while I'm holding her hand. Because fuck it, I'll be sappy if it's with her.

Once we sit on the bench, she fingers the healing wound on my temple, her brows knitting together. "Does it hurt?"

"Not really, but I'm seriously worried about the fact that it'll scar. My magazine cover status is in jeopardy."

She laughs. "It's their loss. Besides, scars are beautiful."

"How so?"

"We're humans, we're not supposed to be perfect."

"Aren't you the philosophical one?"

She leans back on both her palms and stares at the sky, as

shitty and cloudy as it is, I wish I'm that sky right now. "I just learned to appreciate things and erase others."

"Was it hard?"

"Sometimes. But I didn't let it bring me down." She smiles and I want to trap that smile in my chest. Better yet, I wish I was there all these years she's been struggling on her own.

I wish I didn't let my dick dictate my actions and how I felt.

"I need to check on Jay." Nicole rummages through her bag. "Ugh, I can't find the thing. Can you call me?"

I would rather not. I like the peacefulness of this moment too much to ruin it, but I do so anyway.

She pulls it out and releases a sigh. "Found it."

I pause at the name she saved me as and snatch her phone away. "Are you calling your boss a bloody idiot, Ms. Adler?"

A blush spreads over her cheeks and neck. "All assistants do."

"When did this start?"

"When we were eighteen."

"This won't do." I tell her to unlock the phone, then change the name to Daniel surrounded by two hearts. Then I take a selfie while I kiss her lips and put it as the designated picture.

Nicole calls me silly, but she's smiling like the hopeless romantic she is.

We spend some more time in the park before she insists that we buy groceries.

"You know I have staff who keep the fridge stocked, right?" I push the trolley as she throws all sorts of things in it. "They'd have a mini-stroke and call you Americanized behind your back as they sip their Earl Grey tea."

She throws a smile at me over her shoulder. "I'll drink with them. I love tea."

"Congratulations for being one of the many Brits who consume unhealthy amounts of it."

"You don't. You prefer coffee."

"Which is why my staff call me the Americanized Sterling

behind my back, too. So we're mates, you and I. Congratulations again."

She stares at me while squeezing a packet of something green floating in a snot-like liquid. Please tell me she's just checking it out of curiosity and not actually going to take that.

"Have your staff stayed in the mansion all these years?"

"All eleven Christmases of them without a single present from yours truly."

"But why?"

"They come with the mansion."

"But they're people."

"Extremely annoying ones with a sense of loyalty that resembles a samurai's second hand. You know, the one that finishes them off after they disembowel themselves. In my case, if I choose to go, they would poison my coffee."

"Why?"

"They hate that stuff. Last I heard, it's considered blasphemy to prefer it over tea."

"No, I mean why did you keep them?"

"I didn't. They were technically fired eleven years ago, but they're more stubborn than my 'I couldn't care less' attitude."

"Who pays them, then?"

"My brother, through my owned shares. He's been managing the whole thing and probably bribed them with premium Chinese tea to be a thorn in my side."

"They must've been so lonely, serving a mansion without a master."

"Uh, hello? Did you miss the part where they drink tea to gossip about us?"

"You disappeared for eleven years, then came back out of the blue. You should be thankful they even welcomed you in."

"There was a keyword you missed. It's *my* mansion."

"That they lived in more than you. It's such a beautiful property, but you abandoned it without looking back."

"I don't particularly get attached to places."

"I noticed that." Her tone softens. "I bet you don't even consider your penthouse a home."

"It's just a house."

"Then where's your home, Daniel?"

Right in front of me.

Wait. What?

What in the actual fuck was that thought all about? I didn't just think of Nicole as my home.

I simply didn't.

"Nowhere," I grumble, my grip hardening on the trolley.

"That's just sad," she says with a far away look in her eyes then quickly sobers up. "Anyway, I have to count your staff in for dinner."

"You're not cooking for Mary Poppins's spawn, Peaches."

"Yes, I am." She slides the snot-like thingy into the basket.

And I'm hoping they will choke on it.

Nicole wasn't kidding when she said she was counting them in. The doorman, the cook, the maid, the butler, and the gardener. All five snobbish tea monsters of them.

I had to reschedule my BJ more times than I could count, then I ended up helping her in the kitchen, despite how much the smell made me want to throw up all over the stainless-steel equipment.

She told me she could handle it with the cook's help, but it was either keeping myself busy or bending her over and fucking her with a manner that will provide my staff with tea talk for decades to come.

While accidentally traumatizing them.

Nicole even serves them food in the kitchen and tells me to help her set the dinner table for four.

Me, her, Jay, and I suppose she invited Uncle Henry for dinner so she can spend as much time with him as possible before going back to New York.

Double cock-block.

But I can't have that if I want to function normally during the fucking dinner.

So when she says she'll go change then come back, I follow after her like a professional stalker.

I pass the staff that are fawning over her food with awe that must disgust them deep down.

That's right, tea monsters, be impressed.

The sound of a shower reaches me as soon as I step into our room. She didn't go to the guest room that was designated to her, she came to the one I took her to that first night.

If Astrid didn't use her creepy/drama queen card, I would've stayed with Nicole in bed two days in a row, coming up with creative ways to make her come.

Now, I need to tiptoe around in my own house.

I kick my clothes away, retrieve a small object I bought earlier when she wasn't looking, and step into the bathroom.

The steam invades the space enough to create a mystic smoke-like aura around Nicole.

And the conundrum doesn't escape me. She's like smoke now, I can touch it, but it'll eventually vanish.

Like she did before.

I banish those poisonous thoughts out of my head and rake my gaze over her sublime curves, smooth waist, and her peach-like arse.

She's facing the wall, tilting her head back and letting the water cascade over her. And I'm almost sure I trapped an angel, one I don't intend to ever let go.

I slide behind her and grasp her chin that's tilted back. She startles and I can't resist pushing a finger inside her mouth.

She sucks on it, stirring my dick to life with each pull of her lips.

"About that BJ, Peaches." I grab her arse and squeeze until she moans. "I'm upgrading it to a shower fuck. And by that, I mean your pussy, then your arse."

A gasp escapes her delicate throat, her biteable lips falling open around my finger.

The pads of my fingers dig into the flesh of her arse cheek and I slowly part it. "Did someone touch this?"

"No…" She stares at me over her shoulder, and I nearly come then and there.

I always wondered about the meaning behind the way Nicole looked at me. It was blank, annoyed almost, so I settled on the fact that she was a bitch, but I never thought that she's not actually annoyed with me.

She was probably annoyed at herself for watching me.

For feeling the need to leave me her seductive peach lollipops and being around me whether she liked it or not.

And now, that look is back, the slight annoyance mixed with deep lust.

"You hate it, don't you?" I jam my knee between her legs, intentionally brushing my skin against her core. "You hate how much your little cunt wants my dick."

She mumbles what seems like a "shut up."

I chuckle against her ear, earning a shudder, then bite down on the outer shell. "You hate that we're so compatible, you probably touched yourself to the memory of us late at night, under the covers, in one of your cotton robes. But it never felt real, did it? Not like this."

I wrap an arm around her waist and drive into her from behind. She gets on her tiptoes, slightly biting my fingers.

But she pushes back into me, bending her back slightly as she slaps both her hands on the wall for balance.

A wave of possessiveness drags me to a dark hole and I remove my finger from her mouth, then grab her hair in a tight ponytail. I pull her back and lick my way from her tantalizing throat to her ear. "I want you to scream, Nicole, not hold it in."

She shakes, due to pleasure or something else, I have no clue. It's probably both.

"I…don't do that."

"You will now. You'll scream for me when I fuck you."

"D-Daniel…" she strains, staring at me from underneath her lashes and I can feel her stiffening. "I can't do that…"

"Do you trust me?"

I hate that it takes her some time to nod her head, but again, I didn't have a great track record with her thus far.

"I'll make it good." I kiss her deep but fast. "I promise."

The moment I release her mouth, her lips find mine again, then she whispers against them, "Make me forget, please."

I do just that.

I fuck her hard, my hand gripping her jaw, kissing her anywhere and everywhere I can reach. On her eyelashes, cheek, nose, throat, beauty mole, and those delicious fucking lips that taste like peaches.

Nicole explores me as well, her fingers getting lost in my hair as she kisses the line of my jaw and whatever she can reach of my neck.

She even sucks the skin there and I do the same, leaving my mark on her as deep as she engraves her mark on me.

The water beats down on us like a violent participant in our intense fucking. It's a witness of how much this woman drives me bloody insane.

Like I'm seriously considering seeing someone about my damn unhealthy tendencies when it comes to her.

The blonde who made me hate all blondes.

The woman who broke my heart and is slowly mending it back together again.

Her breath hitches and I know she's getting close. So I release her hair, part her arse cheeks and drive the butt plug in. Her moan echoes around us like the most sophisticated music.

"Does it feel full, Peaches?"

"Yes…oh, God…"

"Don't push it out, if you can't handle that, how will you take my cock?"

I up my rhythm until she's gasping with her mouth wide open.

I fuck her harder until I feel the thin line separating my dick from the plug.

Then, the most beautiful thing happens when she comes. Her eyes meet mine and she screams.

It's not a sound.

It's my name.

I kiss it out of her lips as I keep my unhinged rhythm, then I wrench my mouth from her. "I'm going to fuck your arse, Nicole."

"O-okay."

"It might hurt. Scratch that, it'll hurt like that first time I tore through your virgin cunt."

"I don't care if it's you," she speaks against my lips, then whispers in the most erotic voice I've ever heard. "Fuck me, Daniel."

It's all the invitation I need.

I pull out of her at the same time as I jostle the plug out and throw it on the ground.

Grabbing Nicole by the hips, I bare her to me and use her juices to coat her inviting hole. She whimpers, then moans, and I slide in the first two inches. She gets on her tiptoes, her eyes closing shut.

I release one of her cheeks and grip her chin. "Look at me, Nicole."

Her eyes slowly flutter open, they're drooping with pleasure and something else I can't put my finger on.

"Relax, let me in."

Her muscles loosen around me and I'm able to thrust a few more inches. She moans this time, her mouth falling open, and I can feel her welcoming me to her warmth.

So I kiss her, stimulating her nipples and her clit until I'm all the way in.

"Fuck, baby. I love your arse as much as your pussy."

"It…feels so full."

"Do you like it?"

She nods a little, her mouth open and her eyes drooping with hazy desire.

I become unhinged and thrust into her with the urgency of an animal. I can't stop or get enough. The sound of her moans and gasps is my aphrodisiac.

And when she comes, I keep going and going at my ruthless pace until I release deep inside her.

Fuck.

Sex with Nicole will either suck me dry or become my cause of death.

An option I'm not entirely opposed to if not for anything, then to see how she talks about my dick at my funeral if she's the one who murdered it.

I slowly slide out of her, reveling in the sight of cum that trails down the back of her thighs.

Is it wrong that I want to see this for the rest of my life?

That way, she'll be mine.

Only mine.

My lips find hers and I'm flat out making out with her pubescent style, waiting for my dick to resurrect to life so I can pick up where I left off.

I might have an obsession with kissing Nicole. I like to think I'm a healthy man without serial creeper tendencies, but deep in my mind, I know I'd kiss her any chance I get for all the times I couldn't.

For all the times I wished I could trap her in a room and kiss her until she looked at me the way she did that day she almost died.

Like I'm the only one who mattered.

After a few minutes of kissing me like in one of her cheesy black and white romance films, Nicole pulls back with a gasp. "Oh my God, we're going to be late."

"For the second round? Don't worry about that, it'll happen in about two minutes."

"The dinner." She pushes me away.

"That can wait. In fact, I'm not hungry."

"Well, I am." She wraps herself in a towel and winces when she steps into the en-suite room.

I guess having dinner wouldn't be so bad.

And yes, I'm trying to pacify my urges and keep up the "I'm not a sex addict" façade. Stay out of it.

Nicole tells me to hurry up and meet her downstairs.

By the time I put on some trousers and a shirt, I'm ready to shove food down both our throats so we can go back to a much more fun activity.

How much Minions merch should I buy Jay so he goes to bed early tonight?

A commotion of voices scatters my master plan.

My steps to the dining room turn heavy, instead of light, and the snap of emotions jerks my spine into a line.

This isn't real.

I probably frustrated the tea monsters enough that they put something in my water.

Maybe this whole thing ever since Nicole showed up at Weaver & Shaw has been a dream and I'll wake up to find myself dashing, every girl's wet dream and so fucking alone, authors should write nihilistic books about my brain.

But the moment I step into the Victorian-like dining room, I know this is, in fact, real.

The two people I only wished to see at my funeral while I was in a casket and they threw skulls at me are here.

My mother and my fucking brother.

THIRTY

Daniel

MY CHILDHOOD IS A PHASE THAT I LIKE TO CONSIDER nonexistent.

It was a splash of eating disorders, a loss of faith in my cheating father, and a deep-seated hatred for the woman who allowed him to get away with it.

The woman who chose misery for herself and her sons instead of walking away about…thirty-one years ago, before Zach was even born.

The Zach who held her hand and couldn't care less about her status as a meek woman who didn't mind being used any way Benedict Sterling saw fit.

Both of them are staring at me now.

Mother is grabbing the napkin that's on her lap with long, skinny fingers that reflect the rest of her body. She's an abstract of bones and flesh wrapped in a designer dress and jewelry that cost a small fortune.

She doesn't even wear the known brands; the actual rich get to dress from obscure brands only people like us know about. Brands that sell you a shirt for twenty thousand pounds to make you feel more important than the mainstream brand people.

Her red lips part before she reaches a hand and pats her perfectly styled French twist. Her hair is a dark shade of blonde that she passed me a portion of.

But I always had my father's eyes. A fact we both hated but never voiced out loud.

"Daniel." It's my brother who speaks, his voice toneless, and his stance is upright but not rigid.

Zach is two years older than me, has my father's dark hair and my mother's steel-gray eyes. He used to be broader than me, the type who slaved at the gym for a perfect body, but it doesn't seem that he kept that dedication now. He's leaner, which makes him appear taller even when he's not standing.

"That's my place." I point at where he's sitting, at the head of the table, as if this is his damn house.

"Nonsense." He already has the napkin tucked neatly into his shirt which means he's ready to eat. "You forfeited your leading position eleven years ago and you have no right to demand it now."

I narrow my eyes, but despite the tension in my spine, there's something off about the way he speaks, the way his stance is.

It's almost…robotic.

Zach was more fun than me—if you can believe that. I let my father's behavior get under my skin and ruin my perception about things, namely food and relationships. My brother, however, tucked it all in a neat box, threw it in the rubbish, and lived the life he wanted to.

So his tone and voice are grating me the wrong way.

A soft hand touches my arm before Nicole stares up at me with enough brightness to light a whole fucking room. "You can sit down anywhere."

"You did this." It's not a question, because I'm sure it was all her idea.

The fact that she was stalling for time, made dinner for an army, and prepared the table for four.

"You can't possibly ignore your family forever."

"Watch me." I glare at them. "Have the food and get the fuck out. Better yet, leave without eating."

"Daniel." Nicole gasps, watching me as if I grew a few more horns than what a devil is allowed.

Well, surprise, baby. I'm still the jerk who made your and everyone else's life hell.

"Dan…please." Mother's voice is brittle, which means she's probably about to cry. That's what she used to do every day, every night.

It's her side gig. Aside from giving us prophets' names in a vain attempt to save our arses from hell.

"Too late for begging, don't you think, Mother? Here's a thought, how about you do us both a favor and leave?"

Zach interlinks his fingers on the table. "Since we're all here and there's food, we might as well eat."

"No thanks," I say.

I'm about to leave when Mother blurts, "Zach had an accident."

"Nice try, Mother. Next time you'll tell me his arm is artificial and he's surviving on Viagra to shag. Can't you hear how desperate you are?"

I expect Zach to spar with me, verbally or physically. He was always the number one defender and the founder of Nora Sterling's fan club. Even when she neglected us both for her husband-related issues.

However, my brother is sipping from his soup, his expression unchanged. "I like the chef. I'm moving him to my estate."

"Like fuck you will." I wrap an arm around Nicole's waist, a blinding sense of possessiveness gripping me by the throat.

"We'll see about that."

My urge to punch him snaps my shoulder blades together.

And why the hell is he saying that with a perfectly straight face? Is this a joke?

"Get out of my fucking house, Zach. Take Mother with you."

"I decline. I made a dent in my schedule to accept Nicole's invitation to dine here and I'll only leave when that's done." He dabs his mouth with a napkin, staring at me with soulless eyes. "And I'm taking the cook with me."

I lunge at him then, grabbing the collar of his shirt and the stupid fucking napkin.

A long time ago, we used to wrestle for sport. It was also our way to get our parents' nonexistent attention. Zach never, and I mean *never*, allowed me to win, or take a punch at him.

He was the sort of older brother who made sure I knew who held the power and frustrated me beyond belief.

But right now, he doesn't even attempt to fight as I hit him. "You're taking no one!"

Blood explodes in his nose, but he doesn't even touch it. Or me. His hands are still on the table with the spoon in his fingers.

"Oh my God, Zach!" Mother runs toward us like a shotgun, getting a napkin and wiping his nose.

Nicole grasps my wrist and pulls me back, but she doesn't need force for it. I was already letting go of him.

I saw something in his eyes just now.

Or more like…nothing.

There was no trace of the Zach I've known most of my life. It's like a ghost exists on his behalf.

Tears glisten in my mother's eyes as she dabs away the blood from his face. He seems more pressed to go back to eating as if that's his sole purpose for being here.

"Can you please hear me out?" Mother asks, fawning over him like the doting mother she rarely was.

I remain silent, but I take a seat to Zach's right.

"Alone?" Mother gives Nicole an apologetic glance. "This is a delicate matter."

"Yes, sure." Nicole starts to leave, but I grab her hand and force her to sit beside me.

"If you want to talk to me, she'll be here."

Mother twists her lips like a child having a tantrum, then she releases a deep sigh and retakes her seat, then neatly places the napkin on her lap. "The thing is…I never thought you'd come back, Daniel."

"We actually agree on something. Shocker." I pick up the spoon to keep at least one of my hands from fisting. The other is at my thigh, slightly curling.

The reason why I'm estranged from the two only family members I have left isn't only because of my father's fiasco.

But mostly because they remind me of a weak version of me. Of the young Daniel who was desperate enough to cause trouble so his own parents, the people who should've been forced by nature to nurture him, would finally see him over all their shit.

Spoiler alert. They never did.

Mother pours herself a glass of wine, then drinks half of it before meeting my gaze. "Zach was in a crash seven years ago and suffered from a traumatic brain injury. I tried to call you, but you told me, "Wrong number," and hung up."

"Sounds legit."

Nicole gives me a side-eye.

"What? I told them to forget about me. Not my fault they have trouble moving on."

And Astrid did mention that Zach had an accident, but I ignored her once I knew he was alive.

"A mother can't forget about her own child." Her eyes fill with tears again. She likes to paint herself as the victim, to be completely and utterly pitied.

"Oh, so now I'm your child? Sorry, kind of lost sight of that during all the years of emotional neglect." A small hand wraps around mine, and I force myself not to look at Nicole, not to get trapped into her again.

It's because of her that I'm even in this predicament, facing a part of me I wished to keep buried until I was six feet under.

The woman who gave birth to me swallows thickly. "Daniel, please…"

"Save it, Mother. Tell me about Zach. Why is he barely even blinking?"

"I don't know how to say it…"

"I'm over here and can tell you about myself." My brother's eyes meets mine, and once again, I'm caught in their ghostly quality and the black hollowness inside them. "Due to the head injury, I have Alexithymia. That means I don't recognize emotions anymore and I'm considered a heartless bastard, or that's what I've been told by the incompetent executive directors I fired."

Mother starts weeping, always, without doubt, turning the attention to her. Nicole releases my hand and goes to comfort her as if she's a baby.

Zach—who's the cause of all the distress—continues sipping his soup with no care in the world.

And for the first time since I left England, I think maybe I made a mistake.

Maybe if I stayed, if he didn't have to take care of Mother's dramatics and Father's death on his own, he wouldn't have had that crash. He wouldn't be a ghost of his previous self.

I would still have the Zach who laughed more than necessary and taught me how to touch a girl right and bring both of us pleasure.

The Zach who stayed by my side whenever I got sick because my mother was too busy throwing a self-pity party to take care of me.

"We're trying to hide his condition," Mother says in a brittle voice. "Since he refuses to get married or have children, people will eventually find out and the shareholders will kick him out. Oh, you don't know how much I've suffered."

"Shut up, Mother," I say calmly.

"Excuse me?"

"Shut the fuck up, Mother." I'm louder now, unhinged by all the emotions that have been running rampant in me. "Stop turning everything about you when Zach was the one who had an accident. This is about him, not you, not me. *Him.* So stop making it about you!"

Her wails turn up in volume and the only reason I'm not going full on aggressive mode on her drama queen antics is because I can't keep my attention away from Zach.

My brother watches us like we're the dullest animals in a zoo.

Now I recognize the emptiness in his gaze. It's complete and utter apathy, as if being alive is the most boring thing he's ever had to do.

My hand fists on the spoon. "Are you struggling?"

He meets my gaze. "With what?"

"Anything? Everything?"

"I've never been better, but Mother likes to act in such…an overly expressive way."

Tell me about it.

"I'm just looking out for you," she sobs while Nicole holds her shoulder. "I'm doing my best to protect the family name and company."

"Which I'm doing an excellent job at by doubling its profit," Zach says.

"But if they find out…"

"They won't, Mother. You're making an event out of nothing."

Something she likes to do, but I keep those words to myself out of fear that she'll burst into another wave of tears.

The rest of the dinner is strained to say the least. Mostly because Zach's lack of empathy makes him not only stoic but also kind of evil. His thoughts, principles, and perspectives have taken a one hundred eighty-degree dive and he's now a true nihilist.

Nothing is important and everything is senseless and useless.

By the end of the night, he says he'll drive my drunk mother home.

She had too much wine, no surprise there, and she's the type who bursts into tears when drunk. No surprise there either.

"Thank you, Nicole." She pulls her into a long hug. "Thank you for bringing my baby home."

"I'm neither back nor am I your baby." I resist the urge to inform everyone that I'm the one who brought Nicole back, not the other way around.

But then again, if it weren't for the fucker, whom Kyle informed me that he can't take a piss without crying like a whore, I wouldn't have returned. I wouldn't have learned about my brother's condition.

So I guess Nicole did bring me back.

That doesn't mean I'm less pissed off at her.

"You can hate me all you want, but you'll always be my baby." She releases Nicole to grant me one of her rare hugs. One I don't return. "I'm sorry I wasn't a good mother, Danny. I'm sorry I never grew a backbone, but if you give me a chance, I'll try."

I say nothing, and she eventually lets me go and sways on her feet, her tears cascading down her face. Zach grabs her by the arm and nods at me. "If you intend to stay, let me know."

"I don't. And Zach?"

"Yes?"

"You hated me back then."

"Back when?"

"When I left. Why?"

"I suppose I disliked the fact that you were running away.

You're not a coward, Daniel. But you acted like one, and that probably grated on my nerves."

"Past tense?"

He smiles a little, then taps the side of his head. "The benefit of this brain is that I couldn't care less anymore."

Then he drags my mother who's blabbering about her sons and herself and how much she regrets everything.

As soon as the driver speeds out, I want to hit something.

Anything.

And just right then, Nicole comes in front of me, in her white dress and a little smile. "I'm glad you guys could finally talk."

"That makes one of us."

I turn around and head to the kitchen. One of the tea monsters, the gardener, sees my face and bolts out with a bow.

Good choice because I'm contemplating drowning him in his tea.

I swing the cupboard open and wrench out a bottle of whiskey, the expensive type, the one that will get me drunk slower but deeper.

Nicole comes to my side while I'm popping the bottle open. Or trying to, anyway; the thing is stuck as if mocking me as well.

"Are you mad?" she asks cautiously.

"Am I mad? Oh, let me see. You invited my mother and brother over when I'm barely on speaking terms with them and forgot to mention that detail. On a scale of zero to ten, I'm one hundred at being mad."

"You had to speak to them eventually."

"I wasn't planning to."

"So you're okay with not knowing about your brother's condition?"

"He's fine. He's not paralyzed or incapacitated. Stop channeling the Nora Sterling in you and making this into a big fucking drama that it isn't." I forcibly pop the bottle and drink straight from it, dousing my throat with burning liquor.

"Well, I'm sorry that I tried to bring you close to your family."

"Apology accepted."

She glares, then crosses her arms over her chest. "You know what? Screw you, Daniel. I'm retracting that apology, because I know I did the right thing and you would know it, too, if you weren't too busy being a dick."

"The right thing? Since when are you a saint, Nicole? You like using people, so let's hear it. What did you intend to gain from this? My mother's favor? My brother's attention? Did you put all that effort into the food so that he'd decide to keep you as his warm hole?"

The sound comes first, loud and deafening in the silence of the house. Then the sting of her palm against my cheek follows. There's an unnatural shine in her eyes, but the tears don't escape. "I'm no one's warm hole, including yours. And I only put in all that effort for *you*. To make you happy as you made me yesterday by bringing Uncle Henry, but apparently, I made a mistake. I always make mistakes when it comes to you and it's time I learn to not make them anymore."

And then she strides out of the kitchen like a storm.

I slowly close my eyes and take a sip of the whiskey, knowing full well that I screwed it all up.

Not that it wasn't meant to be screwed eventually.

THIRTY-ONE

Nicole

I SLAM THE DOOR TO THE BEDROOM SHUT, WALK AWAY FROM it, then storm toward it again.

My hand hesitates on the handle before I release it with a loud puff.

The lava that's been building in my bloodstream is now roaring to the surface and I can no longer trap it inside.

I can no longer pretend that I can keep on doing this and feel nothing.

It's only been me, ever since I first saw Daniel when we were damn kids. Ever since I envied him for being mischievously free when I couldn't dream of it.

I grab a lollipop that's lying on the dresser and jerkily remove the stupid wrapper, then crunch it so hard, my teeth hurt. Now, even my lollipop sucking habits are changing because of him.

My weight falls on the bed and I pull my legs into my chest, but the usual self-comfort doesn't work this time.

So I walk to the bag I brought and retrieve the emerald necklace. I haven't been wearing it lately, but I always keep it close.

This time, I put it around my neck, then get the small box I always keep with me.

The box that the little girl in me used as a form of consolation. The adult in me continued to use it as a source of peace.

My fingers glide over the small wooden exterior that's accentuated with a metallic lock. I took this box with me everywhere after Mum was arrested. I hid it under my bed and stared at it when it got too hard. When Jay was sick. When my nightmares and panic attacks rendered me crippled.

I used to try and hide this part of me by any means necessary, but it's different now.

Now, I meant what I said. I'm not going to keep making the same mistake named Daniel.

If I want to move on, to pick up the pieces of my life and survive, then I need to deal with this once and for all.

It's not about why he's angry, which he vehemently believes is that I invited his family without telling him—a fact that he'll thank me for later.

He's angry because, like back when we were teenagers, he doesn't like that he wants me.

He loathes it with passion.

And if that's the case, then he's going to say it to my face and spare me a stronger heartache.

Not allowing myself to change my mind, I carry the box close to my chest and stride to the door. The moment I open it, I pull Daniel inside, because he's gripping the handle.

My heart does that strange flip that I only ever experienced when he's in sight. When I first met him, when I gradually fell in love with him, when he touched me, when he hurt me afterward, and eventually when I thought I would never see him again.

Until I did.

Until he slowly became an undivided part of my world.

The bottle of whiskey that he nursed like it's his baby is gone, but he still appears rugged, his hair tousled and haphazard in a glorious warrior kind of way.

"I said a few things that I regret," he says, one of his fists clenching beside him.

The box digs into my chest as I hug it tighter. "Like what?"

"Like the warm hole part. Won't happen again."

"And?"

"There's no and."

My tempter that I almost felt deflating due to his not-so-explicit apology flares again. I push the box at his chest. "In that case, take this."

A frown appears between his brows, then morphs into recognition as he flips the box. "Is this…?"

"The present you gave me for my thirteenth birthday." I reach behind my nape and unclasp the white gold necklace. When I pull it, the emerald pendant opens to reveal a small key that's designed for the box.

I push it into Daniel's bigger hand. "I saw you the day you went into a vintage shop and asked the old man for a custom-made necklace. You even gave him a picture of me so the color would match my eyes. That day was one of the happiest in my life. And when my birthday rolled around, I opened your present first. You said, 'It's called a box of secrets and you're the only one who can get access to it due to that key necklace.' But before I could say anything, you told me that Aunt Nora picked it out and then you left the party.

"You always lifted me up just to bring me down harder than before. You touched me just to stop touching me. You kissed me only to never do it again. Did you know that your smiles disappeared whenever you looked at me? That you always looked in the other direction? You ignored me to the point that I wondered if I was invisible. But I'm not, Daniel. I'm right here, I was always right in front of you, looking at you, watching you, being so unhealthily obsessed with you, it ruined me.

"I stepped on my pride to love you. I crushed my bleeding heart, then gave it to you. All I wanted was for you to see me, to not make me invisible. All I wished for was a tiny piece of your heart, a sliver of your attention, but you never gave me that. You never fought for me as I fought for you!"

My heart hammers in my chest and I feel myself on the point of hyperventilating.

I don't know what I expected his reaction would be, but the clenching of his jaw and the tightening of his fist until his knuckles turn white is definitely not what I had in mind.

Why does he get to be angry when I'm the one who should be?

His reaction disappears as quickly as it appeared. Instead, that sadistic gleam rushes forward, the frigid coldness wrapping over him, like when he's about to wear his dick hat.

"You were that desperate, huh?"

I ignore the jab of his words and suck in sharp intakes of air through my mouth. "I was that in love with you."

He bursts out laughing and I feel my heart shattering into pieces at his feet, with all of its blood and longing and stupid damn feelings that I harbored for years.

"Oh, I'm sorry." He slowly puts a halt to his maniacal laughter. "That wasn't supposed to be funny? Because the only thing I recall about you from back then is your bitchy, entitled fucking self, Nicole. You were just a fuck but you went ahead and made it into some love story. Hopeless romanticism does suit you since you're so fucking naïve."

"You don't mean that," I argue more to myself than him. "You liked me, Daniel, you always did. You just didn't like that fact. I know it."

His voice that was mocking a moment ago lowers in tone while being loud in volume. "You know jack shit about me, Nicole. You might need to see someone for your delusions and other issues."

A lump catches in my throat. "Are you trying to push me away? Again?"

"I'm trying to make you understand that I'm not your Prince Charming, nor your white knight nor anything remotely noble. We used each other and that's it. Keep the girlhood dreams where they belong."

His harsh words and tone don't faze me as much as the realization that's been creeping up on me but is finally hitting me across the face. "You'll never see me, will you? No matter how much I look at you, give you, or be there for you, I'll only ever be someone you despise to want. Someone who's meant to only ever be invisible."

"You have a stunning talent at figuring things out. Therapy will make it even better." He hands the box and necklace back to me. "I'm no professional, but I'm sure they'd recommend that you throw these little girl things in the nearest rubbish bin and move on with your life."

I grab them and do just that. The rubbish topples over from the force of my throw. Daniel barely glances at it, his expression blank, bored almost.

That's when I see what we are. I've always been the upper half of an hourglass while he was the bottom. Sooner or later, he was meant to empty me until nothing was left.

My shoulders droop and a lone tear escapes my lids. "I'm done with you. I'm done with your cowardice, with my unrequited feelings. I'm done, Daniel. So please, let me go. Please let me be free. Let me breathe air where you don't exist."

He gives a curt nod, then turns around and leaves.

The world splinters to pieces around me as I fall to the floor and cry the hardest I ever did.

I don't grieve us, not when we didn't even exist.

I finally grieve myself.

⚖

I don't know how long I remain on the floor then somehow end up on the bed, a mess of unstoppable tears, twisted fantasies, and impossible feelings. I might have fallen asleep at some point, I'm not sure.

But it's long enough that a lone ray of sun slips through the curtains and a new day sneaks its way through the harsh, merciless night.

It doesn't matter what happened during that night—whether

it's the shattering of hope or the scary reminder that I wasted my youth loving someone who would never love me.

Who would look anywhere but at me.

The need to pull myself off the floor and get out of his house prickles on my skin like a spring allergy but the will to actually do that is nonexistent.

Then I recall something, or more specifically someone.

Jay.

I spring up to a standing position and hobble to the bathroom so I can wash my face. I refuse to look at my reflection in the mirror. It's no different than facing that ghostly part of me.

I retrieve my phone from the nightstand, contemplating if calling Uncle Henry this early is a good or a stupid idea after we exchanged numbers and I left my brother with him and Astrid.

The text that I find on the screen breathes some life into me.

Uncle Henry: Jayden is fast asleep after playing with Landon and Brandon all day. Astrid insisted on him staying the night. I'll bring him over as soon as he wakes up.

At least one of us is accepted by Astrid.

Not that it matters now.

I need to pack my things and leave with Jay as soon as he's back.

If I have to beg Aspen to take me in as a second assistant, so be it. Although I'd still work in the same building as Daniel, it'll get easier with time.

Or so I like to fool my future self into believing.

It didn't get easier the past eleven years, but I at least managed to numb the pain and focus on raising Jay. But now that I've gotten a glimpse of the other side of Daniel—the cold yet caring side—I don't think it'll be as easy to numb anything.

When I finish packing my and Jay's bag, I resist the urge to cry. And it isn't until I've gotten downstairs that I realize I might run into Daniel and cry for real.

Pathetic.

"Morning, Ms. Adler," a gentle feminine voice calls. It's Sophie, the maid. Upon seeing my face, a delicate frown appears between her brows. "Are you unwell?"

If having my heart broken repeatedly is unwell, then yeah, I must be suffering from the worst type of unwellness.

"I'm good, thank you."

"Do you need anything? Perhaps some tea with your breakfast?"

If I didn't hate Daniel so much, I'd be laughing about how he calls his staff tea monsters. To their faces, even.

"No, I'm good. I'm just waiting for my brother so that we can leave."

"Leave?" Her frown deepens. "That's not what the master said."

I hate how my heart that's been ripped to shreds by his bare hands attempts to gather whatever's left of the pieces and beat for him.

Being with Daniel isn't only an experience, but a bloody battle with more losses and casualties. And that's all I'm suffering from right now.

Casualties.

"What did he say then?" I'm glad my voice sounds casual enough.

"That you'll be staying here for a while."

I'm…*what?* Does he really think I would stay at his house after all that's happened? Or maybe he still thinks of me as his assistant that he can order around for his one-gram-of-sugar coffee.

"Well, tell him that I'm not staying."

She winces. "He doesn't exactly take our calls and whenever he does he'd say, "Wrong number," and hang up."

"Wait…he's not here?"

"No, miss. He left early in the morning. I saw him coming out of your room."

"You must be mistaken…"

"Of course not, miss. I saw him leaving the room when I was on my way to get my cup of tea with milk and he motioned at me to stay quiet, then he gathered all of us to tell us to serve you as if you're him."

My head is unable to wrap itself around all the information tossed my way. Why would he do that after all he said?

"He had a box in his hand, too. And it's the only thing he took with him. I told him I would pack his bag, but he said there was no need."

The box…?

I run upstairs to the room and sure enough, the box isn't in the rubbish bin where I threw it. And neither is the necklace/key.

Did Daniel personally throw away the box?

A sense of panic floods the back of my throat and I start searching for it like a maniac. *Please don't tell me that box is gone.*

Fresh tears spill from my eyes as I drop to my knees, searching underneath the console and the bed.

I'm supposed to be getting it together, but losing that box is no different than losing a part of me. I didn't mean it about completely getting rid of it.

Just when I'm about to have an epic meltdown. I find a folded paper fallen by the side of the bed. My heart skips a beat as I slowly open it and find Daniel's messy handwriting.

Nicole,

The mansion is yours. I told my English solicitor to transfer it to your name and signed the appropriate documentation.

I also asked Zach to give you an apprenticeship in one of our biggest hotels in London. You have a formidable talent and as much I hated sharing it, the world deserves to have the experience of eating your cooking.

Jayden's education will also be taken care of.

Make London your home again as you always secretly wished.

You don't have to worry about Christopher or the custody case anymore. The cunt got what was coming for him and won't be bothering you going forward.

And neither will I.

I'm sorry you loved me.

Daniel

THIRTY-TWO

Daniel

MY FIXATION WITH NICOLE STARTED THE DAY SHE NEARLY died in my arms.

She was the weirdest fucking little shit I've ever met, and that says something considering I used to think of her as an "I'm better than you and your grandma" kind of snob.

At school, she was prim and proper. Always smiling, always looking down her nose at the peasants who dared to be in her vicinity.

Always…far.

But that day, she was herself. A thief, a sneak, and someone who liked to hide.

That day was the first time I actually met her.

Strange, outspoken, and generous despite her weakness. She gave me her precious snow globe. I know because she sometimes brought it with her to school and stared at it when no one was looking as if it was a part of her.

But then she decided to give me that part of her.

She gave me the snow globe and the girl trapped inside it. That girl takes her shape in my head whenever I stare at that snow globe.

It's a reminder of the little girl who smiled up at me with pure awe and adoration while she was slowly dying.

But her manipulative side ruined it all afterward. Or maybe it was my fragile pride that couldn't take the idea of being wounded by her disinterest over and over again.

I felt played.

Stomped upon.

And the first thing I had in mind is taking revenge. I wanted her to suffer as much as I did, but I had no effective method for that aside from ignoring her.

In doing that, I had hoped I'd manage to move past her intrusive eyes, her unmatched beauty, and addictive presence.

I had hoped wrong.

Nicole is the only woman I wanted with the same force that I hated her with. And if I weren't kidding myself, I would call it more than wanting her.

So much more.

However, she existed in another world than mine, like a queen. You can look at her on her throne, you can reach close, but you can never touch her.

She was also a bitch, not only to me but to everyone. She wore her mean girl persona as a crown and made sure everyone saw her adjusting it over those blonde locks.

No one had access to the Nicole that lurked within, not even her mother, her stepfather.

No one.

I got close once, so close that I kissed her and unleashed all the desire I've been suppressing for years.

But it was soon gone. Soon dissipated.

Then I thought she cheated on me. Don't judge—my dick-oriented brain categorized it as such since I didn't fuck anyone after her. I even went through all the trouble of making everyone—Astrid included—believe that I shagged something other than my hand so they wouldn't think I was broken.

But when I thought she willingly slept with Christopher, it

fucked me up worse than when I first saw my father fucking a woman who wasn't my mother. Worse than thinking Nicole somehow got ecstasy to fuck another man.

It was the first and only heartbreak I've ever experienced, and the pain I had from it still beats inside me like a different being.

So I moved on, or pretended to, for a whole eleven years.

I made it my mission not to look for her, ask about her, or even mention her name. Whenever Astrid did in a fleeting manner, I would change the subject faster than her next words are out.

And I was doing so well, avoiding blondes like the plague and filling the hole she left behind with fucking and working, and pretending I'm living the best life possible.

Until she came back into my life.

The moment I saw her again, everything, every single fucking coping mechanism I tried over the years smashed right in front of my eyes.

And the vicious cycle restarted.

I wanted to get revenge, to hurt her as much as she hurt me, but I'm the one who's in pain.

I'm the one who's all alone in a park, like some lonesome old man who lost everything and is reminiscing about the past.

The same park I walked through with Nicole yesterday.

No. I'm not going to think about her laughter or the way she blushed when I held her hand.

I simply won't.

It's been exactly thirty-five minutes and twenty seconds since I've been sitting here staring at the box that she threw away and told me she's done with me.

I stood right in front of the room as she cried, stopping myself from going in there and wrapping her in my arms.

I couldn't.

I didn't have the right to.

Not when I'm the one who ruined her life. I almost forgot about it during the bliss I felt these past three days. Almost.

But her words slapped me back into the reality that, as the

scum Christopher said, she will never forgive me for pushing her into his arms.

One day or another, she'll wake up and be grossed out with me.

And I can't do that to either of us.

But I did go into the room when her cries subsided. I carried her to the bed, my gut wrenching at the tears on her face.

Then, I picked the box and key and left. I should be at the airport for my plane back to New York, but I won't be able to leave without knowing what's inside this box.

Slowly, I insert the necklace key and turn. The sound of the lock penetrates my skin instead of my ears like a life-changing premonition. The feeling is tenfold heightened when I find what's inside the box.

The first thing I see are pictures. Of her birthdays and mine that our mothers forced us to attend. From our eighth birthday until our fifteenth—since then, they couldn't force us to do anything. In every single group picture of my birthdays, she was always looking at me. All eight pictures of them.

In all her birthday group pictures, I was always looking at anything but her. The boy in front of me. The camera. The cake. The presents. Anywhere she wasn't.

The contrast between the two sets of pictures isn't only obvious, but it's also a little sad. From her perspective, at least.

Because she doesn't know that I didn't look at her for the sole reason that she unnerved me, threw me off balance. The fact that I avoided her of all people isn't because I hated her.

It's because I wanted to hate her.

And sometimes, I thought I did but that never lasted.

I put the pictures to the side and find a single peach seed. It appears old, dry, and ugly. Why would she keep the seed of the fruit that could kill her…?

Wait a minute.

I bring it up to the sun and stare at the plain thing.

It can't be.

I clearly remember that the doctor told her to never go near peaches again, and even though I saw her with a basket of them at Ronan's party, she never ate them. I know because I lurked behind a tree and made sure she walked out of that gazebo empty-handed. What? I had to make sure she didn't have any suicidal tendencies.

The last time she consumed a whole peach was the day she had that strong allergic reaction.

So this must be from back then.

Fuck. She kept it for twenty-one years.

Underneath it, there's a lollipop wrapper. I remember this one. Peach flavor with the brand design that goes back to over seventeen years ago.

The first lollipop she left in my bag.

Then there's a pen. One she lent me once.

A few rings that I gave her for her birthdays because I once heard her telling a friend she likes the special edition ones.

It's how I discovered that vintage shop hidden from view that had custom-made jewelry. The reason I needed her to believe they came from my mother and not from me was because she was a damn mean girl and young-me's ego couldn't take being ridiculed by her if she didn't like the presents.

Then there's my bracelet. The one I lost the night I fucked her for the first time. The night she stole a part of me that I'll never get back. The night I realized fucking had a deeper meaning than mere sex and I could only feel it with Nicole.

I stare at the contents of the box, at the memory of us that she preserved with a key around her neck.

The need to go back to her burns hot behind my eyes, nearly blinding me.

I slowly close the box and stand up.

There's no way in hell I'm backpedaling on this. I already gave her a clean start, showing up again is no different than stomping all over it.

No matter how much I want to see her, going back to New York is the right thing.

Since when are you the right thing kind of person? The devil on my shoulder whispers in his "let's be selfish" voice.

But I shut it down, walk to my rental car, and put the box in my small bag. I'm closing the boot when I feel movement behind me.

My chest aches.

Did she follow me here? I told my staff to keep her in the mansion until Zach came over. He's the only one I could confide in knowing full well that he'll keep a level head about the entire situation.

Still, my smashed-over heart resurrects from the ashes at the thought that she's here.

Maybe she wants the box back.

Maybe I don't want to give it away.

I turn around and the first thing that registers is a slash-like sound as a dark figure slams into me.

"Chris sends his bloody regards," he whispers near my ear, then pulls back.

That's when a blinding pain explodes in my abdomen and a hot liquid soaks my shirt. My hand grabs the area and it's drenched in dark red.

Fuck.

I've been stabbed.

Before I can wrap my mind around the information, the world is pulled from beneath my feet.

THIRTY-THREE

Nicole

I'M STILL REELING FROM THE LETTER DANIEL LEFT ME.

I finally sit down after pacing the extravagant living area like a lunatic under Lolli's judgmental eyes.

My hands shake and my mind crowds with so many theories and questions.

Like, what was he thinking?

How dare he?

And most importantly; what the hell am I supposed to do now?

The thought of stepping on my pride again makes me nauseous, but that doesn't compare to the pain of never seeing him again.

Lolli bumps her head on my side as if knowing exactly the amount of distress I'm going through. I pet her black head and stare into her shiny black eyes.

"What should I do, Lolli?"

"I don't think a cat can offer advice."

Both Lolli and I jerk up at Zach's distinctive voice.

I stand on wobbly feet, hiding the letter and all its mysterious contents in my jean pocket.

"I got a call from the London branch lawyer and he was notified that Christopher Vans pulled the custody claim," is what Aspen told me half an hour ago over the phone, sounding as perplexed as I am.

What did Daniel do to make that lowlife give up Jay…and me?

I was so sure he'd want a claim on my brother just so he'd get to me. That was the whole point behind the custody case because I know for a fact he doesn't care about his son.

Then, there's the chef apprenticeship.

The mansion.

Jay's education.

The staying in London bit.

Just what was Daniel thinking and when did he plan all of this?

Unless he was planning to leave me anyway and this was always the course of action he intended to take.

My lips tremble as I focus on Zach. He has always been attractive, athletic, and so outgoing, he gave Daniel a run for his money when we were younger.

Whereas the old Zach was the charming and handsome type, he now appears detached, bored. The cold and lethal type.

"Do you know where he is?" I don't recognize the brittleness in my voice.

He checks his thick Rolex watch. "On his way to New York."

My lips tremble. "But why? Why did you let him?"

"Why not let him? It's his choice and as much as I don't understand the sentiment behind it, I can't exactly lock him up here." He pauses. "Although that could be arranged."

"Did he tell you to come to find me?"

"Yes. He wanted you to know that you have a small fortune to your name extracted from his shares that you can use to open your own restaurant. Not to mention that this old thing is being processed to be in your name as we speak. You take the staff that comes with it, too, or you'll have to do some satanic ritual to be able to fire them."

"Why?"

"I'm sure they would prefer to work here for free rather than leaving the place."

"No, why did he do this?"

Zach appears perplexed. "I believe the right word would be that he's an idiot, but I hope for your sake that you're not. I'll be watching what you do with his shares and if I smell a gold-digger who used my brother, I'll make sure you eat dirt for the rest of your life."

"I don't want his money! I only ever wanted him, but that's never been reciprocated. And now he's doing this and confusing me…"

"Are you daft?"

"Excuse me?"

Zach's expression doesn't change. "You're either daft or too oblivious to notice. Daniel has been following you like a lost puppy ever since we were kids. He'd ask Mother to lie and say she got you the birthday gifts and he never asks Mother for anything. And he's now leaving you a fortune that will make your grandchildren live like kings, not to mention that he beat up the scum who assaulted you and cut off his dick like a noodle, then made him drop the custody case for your brother. So please enlighten me, which part in that sounds like he never reciprocated?"

My jaw hurts from how much I clenched it and all I can think about is the last bit he said. "Daniel beat up Christopher?"

"Yes, he didn't tell me so himself, but I found out on my own. See, he might have chosen to stay away, but that doesn't mean I'll let that idiot run loose. When he bought his penthouse in New York City, I made the owner sell me the building so I can get daily reports about him. I did it under another company name, of course, so he doesn't catch up. Since he landed in London, I had a skilled PI watch him from afar. And before you ask, he didn't tell me about your assault, I found out about that myself as well.

Apparently, Christopher likes going around telling stories about the women he takes advantage of."

Daniel beat up Christopher and probably threatened him, which is why he dropped the custody case. It must've happened that night he came back bleeding and with a devil's expression on his face.

An onslaught of emotions attacks me and I grab the chair for balance.

The arsehole.

How dare he do all that for me, then leave me behind?

How fucking dare he?

The course of action I have to take clearly materializes in my head. "Zach?"

"Yes."

"You have a private plane, right?"

"I do."

"Please let me use it so I can wait for him in New York with a sledgehammer."

"I will not allow you to hurt my brother."

"It's a figure of speech. I'm not actually going to do it."

He narrows his eyes. "Fine."

I'm just about to get ready when his phone vibrates. He answers with, "Sterling."

He listens for a bit, then hangs up. Zach's expression doesn't change when he smashes my world to pieces. "Daniel was stabbed."

My heart has been stuck in my throat ever since Zach told me the news about Daniel's stabbing.

As in, Daniel is hurt.

As in, he was bleeding on the streets.

The only reason I held on to my cool during the drive to the hospital is the innate need to believe that it's not as bad as I think.

He will be fine.

He has to be fine.

Or else…

I shake my head, my fingers strangling each other. Zach remains completely detached, typing on his tablet and replying to emails as if his younger brother couldn't be dead as we speak.

It's probably his condition, but the need to punch his chest and ask him to do something creeps under my skin like a wildfire.

When the hospital comes into view, I practically leap out of the car before it properly stops. My voice is surprisingly calm when I ask the nurse about Daniel. She asks me if I'm family and I want to strangle her.

I might not be Daniel's family, but he's mine. He did so many things for me that my own family didn't.

He did something no one did.

Like making me feel alive.

Wanted.

Protected.

"I'm his brother," Zach says, stopping beside me. "She's his… significant other."

I stare up at him with wide eyes, but he seems more interested in his phone, whatever he has on that thing.

As soon as the nurse directs me to Daniel's room, I half jog there, then my rhythm falls into a stroll.

During all my life, I lost people because they tried to protect me.

Papa drowned because he tried to save me.

My mother, as power-hungry as she was, married a lord to secure my future. She killed an innocent woman and attempted to murder her stepdaughter so the field would be free for me.

My younger self lost her dreams and self-respect so I can move on.

Survive.

The thought of Daniel being added to the list physically nauseates me and I have to shake my head and blink my blurry eyes to remain on the right path.

During every disaster that befell me, it was Daniel or the thought of him that pushed me to stay afloat and do better.

This time, I won't be able to move on with my life.

This time, it'll be the end.

Zach told me his guy caught the one who stabbed Daniel. He was some low-rent thug and admitted to being paid by Christopher to stab Daniel.

So Daniel is hurt because of me. Because he beat up Christopher for me.

My heart nearly drops to the floor when I reach his room.

Please.

Please let him be all right.

If he still hates me, I'll disappear. If I'm a bad omen to his life, I'll never search for him again.

As long as he's alive.

And well.

And healthy.

My unsteady fingers push the door open and I freeze in the doorway. Daniel sits on a hospital bed, only wearing trousers as a male nurse wraps a bandage around his midsection.

He's…sitting.

Although his brows are knit together in what I assume is pain, he has his eyes open and he's conscious.

The nurse clips the bandage, then tells Daniel something, gives him a pill and water, then waits for him to drink it before he shoulders past me.

That's when Daniel looks at me.

And the emotion on his face shakes me to the bones. I expected surprise, anger, maybe even coldness, but the one I find?

It's relief.

The encompassing type of it.

The tears I've been holding spill on my cheeks as I step inside. "Are you okay?"

He runs his fingers through his hair. It's a bit tousled, a bit imperfect, just like him right now. "Some pesky stitches, but I'll be good as new soon. Besides, I've been told scars are beautiful so I'll be rocking that look."

Despite his light tone, the fire still burns hot and bright inside me. I stop a safe distance away because his closeness would turn that fire into a volcano.

"If that didn't answer your question, I'm really fine. Stop crying, I hate it."

A sob bursts free and I cry even harder.

"Oh, for fuck's sake." Daniel grunts as he reaches a hand and pulls me to him, his warm, big palm wrapping around my hair, keeping me nestled to his side.

"Why?" I sniffle through the tears. "Why do you hate to see me cry, take revenge against Christopher for me, leave me your mansion and your money, but still refuse to be with me? Is it so hard to love me?"

He grabs me by the shoulders, pulling me away so his blue eyes, the mixture of the stars and sky, are staring deep into mine. "I became obsessed with you since you gave me that snow globe and laid your head on my thigh. That obsession turned to hatred and fascination over the years. I hated myself because I wanted you more than I wanted anything. I hated myself for never being able to move on from you, for avoiding all blondes because they reminded me of you. So the thing is, you never gave me a choice. The memory of you followed me everywhere like a ghost, or an angel, I'm not sure which. It's hard to hate you and even harder to forget you, but loving you was the easiest thing that I've ever done. It was natural, inevitable, and fucking infinite."

My lips part open and my brain struggles to process every word he said, but I heard them all. Every single one.

And I still can't believe it.

I think Daniel said he loves me.

No. Maybe he didn't.

"Did you… Did you just say you love me?"

"Always fucking have, Nicole. I only figured it out late, as in when you broke my heart, and I was stupid enough to let it rot inside me and not express it."

"Then...then why do you want to leave me?"

He drops his hands from around my shoulders and I want to grab them and put them there again. I want him to keep touching me, to keep telling me things I would've never thought his beautiful mouth would say.

Daniel breathes so harshly, his abdomen contracts and his nostrils flare.

"Tell me," I insist. "And don't even think about channeling the cold jerk lurking inside you because I know everything you said last night was to push me away."

I wasn't entirely sure earlier, but I'm certain now. If he really didn't care about me, he wouldn't have left me his money and took vengeance for me.

He's not that selfless.

"You said it yourself," he speaks with a calm that contradicts his disheveled demeanor.

"I said what myself?"

"That I ruined you, Nicole! If I wasn't a fucking idiot and noticed the signs, if I didn't choose to see you as the image you projected, I wouldn't have pushed you into that cunt's arms. You wouldn't have lost a part of you that you'll never get back. And I get that now, I get that no matter what I do, you'll never forgive me for what happened to you. Which is why I chose to hurt you and myself and fucking leave."

"You didn't push me into Christopher's arms, my unhealthy obsession did. And you know what, I used to blame you sometimes, but I had no right. I also have no right to blame myself. It's not my or your fault, Daniel. It's Christopher's. Okay? And I didn't mean you ruined me in that sense, I meant emotionally, you arsehole. You keep playing hide-and-seek with me, the moment I think you're mine, you slip from between my fingers like sand. I'm tired of hoping, pining, and being so irrevocably in love with a man who never looked at me."

"I did," he whispers. "When you thought I wasn't looking. You were the only person I had trouble looking away from."

"You were glaring at me."

"Because I loathed how much you affected me even though you were hateful, not only to me but to everyone else."

I snort out laughter mixed with tears. "Looks like we both misunderstood everything."

"And we paid for it dearly." He sighs deeply, painfully. "The years you were out of my life were so empty and desolate, I tried to fill them up with anything available. I didn't realize I failed until the moment you walked into my office."

"I was empty, too. And that box is what kept me feeling full enough to survive." I smile a little. "I want it back, by the way."

"Including the peach seed?"

"That, too."

"It can kill you."

"I always wanted what I shouldn't have."

He wraps an arm around my waist, pulling close so his lips are mere inches from mine. "Does that include me?"

"You're the first on the list."

A beautiful grin appears on his face. "What if you hate me down the line?"

"Then I will just fall in love with you all over again. I'm persistent like that."

"You're fucking weird, did you know that?"

"You told me so when we were eight."

"I did. But here's something I didn't tell you. Since that day, I don't eat peaches."

"Why not?"

"I don't like things that can harm you."

"Is that why you assaulted Chris?"

"It's eleven years overdue, but I finally got the righteous type of revenge."

"You got stabbed for it."

"It's worth it," he speaks against my lips. "You're worth it, Peaches."

My palm finds his cheek and even though I can't believe what he's telling me, I want more.

I've always been greedy about anything that involves Daniel.

"Tell me we're together. Tell me I'm yours as much as you're mine."

"Fuck right we're together. And I don't only belong to you, but you're too deep into my soul, I'd have to die to remove you. And that's just tragic, so you can't leave me."

A lone tear slides down my cheek. "I won't. I can't."

He brushes his lips against mine. "Remember when you asked me where my home is?"

"You said it was nowhere."

"I lied." He taps my chest. "My home is wherever you are. You're my home, Nicole."

"Oh, Daniel. My heart can't take this."

"Stay with me. I haven't gotten to the most important part."

My chest squeezes. "And what is that?"

"Remember what you asked me back when we were children?"

"What?"

"You proposed to me."

My cheeks turn hot. "I was…a kid."

"It still counts and it's my turn to propose." He struggles to his feet, then awkwardly gets on his knee. "You're the only woman I can imagine spending the rest of my life with. The woman I want to wake up next to every single day. You don't only make me a better man, but you also give me the urge to be more for you. Nicole Stephanie Adler, will you marry me?"

I choke on my tears. Not just because his proposal feels surreal, but also because he actually knows my middle name.

He knows a lot about me that I thought he didn't.

I take his arm, trying to pull him to his feet, but he refuses to. "You'll rip out your stitches."

"You better say yes then."

I smile through the tears and open my mouth, but he cuts me off.

"Before you shoot me down, I want to tell you that my dick is now monogamous for you and refuses to be functional for anyone but you, so if you say no, he'll have to kill himself."

"How is that possible?"

"No clue, but he'll find a way. He's resourceful that way."

"There's no need." I palm his cheek as I drop to my knees in front of him. "The answer is yes."

"Yes, as in you'll marry me, or yes to watching my dick come up with a way to go down in history as the first junior to kill himself?"

My laugh is loud and carefree. "I'm marrying you, Daniel. Like I dreamt twenty-one years ago. I loved you then, I'm in love with you now."

"I loved you then, too." He grabs me by the nape, pulling me close to him. "I'm mad about you now, Peaches."

"Why do you call me that when you don't eat the fruit?"

"You still love it, and I'm low-key glad the thing, as dangerous as it is, brought us close together."

EPILOGUE 1

Nicole

Two years later

THE WAILS OF SCREAMING PULL ME FROM DEEP SLUMBER. I stumble out of bed, rubbing my eyes as I head to the nursery. My feet come to a halt when I find Daniel already holding his fussy son and rocking him back and forth.

My heart leaps with a mixture of adoration and complete bliss. Suppressing a yawn, I lean against the doorframe and rub the sleep out of my eyes.

I'm tired, absolutely exhausted from working all day. Those who say being a chef is easy didn't try having their own restaurant and branching out to other parts of the world.

It's a full-time job, just like being a mother, and a wife. While I should use the chance that Conrad has his father with him, I can't force myself to move.

I love the view more than sleep, more than rest, more than anything.

If I thought Daniel was attractive before, he's downright

mouthwatering as a father. It doesn't matter that he's only wearing a pair of boxer briefs—although it does add to the hotness. There's an edge of maturity to him. A part that's touched by time and experience and everything in between.

At first, he admitted that he never considered having children of his own. He was so cynical about it that I thought it would take some convincing.

I always wanted children, and even though I raised Jayden, I wanted to be a mother, not only a sister.

So color me surprised when, in the midst of a very intense fucking session during our honeymoon, in Zach's island, my husband flipped me on the sand and said he wants to put a baby in me.

It was his show of possessiveness, I guess. He tends to be jealous of any man I know, including his own brother, so I thought he probably wants to stake his claim.

But after we talked about it, he said he meant it.

"I never wanted children before because I didn't care for procreating for the sake of procreating," he told me while we were lying on the sand, staring at the million stars.

I rolled around to face him. "It's different now?"

"Fuck right it's different. They will be *our* children, they will be a mixture of you and me. More importantly, you will be their mother."

Then he proceeded to fuck me again and again. Nine months after that honeymoon, a little miracle called Conrad Sterling was born.

He has my eyes, his father's hair, and the stubborn attitude of the two of us combined.

Just because we're married doesn't mean we don't have our differences. We drive each other crazy like every healthy, passionate couple. We still fight about our differing points of view, but I'm starting to think Daniel does it on purpose for the make-up sex.

He turns my life upside down in every way possible. After I got into therapy about my past trauma, my life took a leap for the better. I became more body-positive, though Daniel played a major part in that.

Sometimes, he'd spend hours on end kissing me from head to toe and lighting my libido on fire until I beg him to fuck me already.

Other times, he'd let me have the control by telling me to ride him until I reach that peak.

He knows I need it sometimes, and even though he's the dominant one, he lets me have a sliver of it once in a while.

And I love him for it.

I love him for forcing me to see myself again.

For making my chef dream real.

For taking care of Jay's education.

My little brother is indeed a genius and is currently studying in one of the most elite schools in Europe. He comes home once a week and chatters nonstop about his friends and how he's called a prince there.

He never asks or talks about his father after I told him he dropped the custody case. If anything, he was more relieved.

Christopher has checked himself into a mental institute a few months after Daniel incapacitated him and he admitted to hiring that thug. It was a last-ditch attempt to get revenge for what happened to him.

I don't feel the least bit sorry for him.

It took me some time, but I got over the memory of him. I no longer get panic attacks or meltdowns. Nothing could erase what happened to me, but I learned to cope with it.

To accept it as a scar and live with it.

And the reason is the man who's rocking our baby while his muscles contract with every movement. He looks like a fucking god with his tousled hair and killer physique.

Not to mention how powerful he is.

Daniel quit being an attorney soon after he was stabbed. He told me that he picked a different career from what his family expected as a jab to his parents, to not follow in his father's footsteps, but that was the wrong thing to base one's future on.

He's now the CFO of Sterling Engineering, a pillar, and the reason for Zach's stoicism.

If I thought Daniel was cold when I worked for him at Weaver & Shaw, then Zach takes the cake. He can really be a heartless devil.

Aunt Nora, who was over the moon when I gave birth to Conrad, cried while holding him, because she probably will never be able to hold Zach's children.

Both her sons called her dramatic.

Daniel learned to make peace with his mother, and by learned, I mean that I forced them into enough dinners together that they both nearly choked on their food.

Papa and Astrid also join us. My stepsister and I don't paint each other's toenails, but she respects Daniel's choice and me whenever we meet. Uncle Henry became my papa soon after I moved back here. He makes it his mission to include me in all familial occasions.

But my small family is right here.

With that man and that four-month-old baby.

Daniel places him in his crib and quietly backs away, steps on a toy, and curses under his breath, but he swallows the sound.

I suppress my laughter and he turns around, narrowing his eyes, before he grasps my waist and slowly pushes me out, closing the door behind us.

"Are you laughing at my misery, Mrs. Sterling?"

My heart flips and my muscles loosen at the sound of my new last name. I don't think I'll ever not have this reaction at being called Daniel's wife. "Who? Me?"

"Don't give me that tone, you little minx."

"What tone?" I drop my voice, running my fingers across his chest.

"The tone that will get you fucked until the morning and you'll walk funny tomorrow."

"Why do you think I'm using it, husband?"

A squeal leaps out of me as he carries me to bed.

I'm obsessed with this man as much as he's obsessed with me.

I'm his.

He's mine.

Probably since we were kids.

EPILOGUE 2

Daniel

One year later

"I THOUGHT YOU CONSIDERED CHILDREN SPAWNS."

I take a sip of my apricot juice, ignoring Astrid's all-knowing smirk as she chugs on her cocktail. "I still do."

"Is that why Nicole is pregnant with your second child when the first one is less than eighteen months old?"

It's my turn to smirk. "I said children are spawns. Mine and Nicole's don't belong to that list."

"Oh, screw you, Bug." She laughs, stretching her legs out on the chaise lounge by the side of our pool.

One of the tea monsters, the maid, replaces Astrid's drink and silently judges her for not choosing tea.

They would judge me, too, but Nicole has been making sure they see me drink at least one cup of tea a day.

"You have to do this so they'd respect you, hon," she told me, and then she proceeded to convince me with our favorite currency—a sloppy blowjob.

That's the only reason why I drink tea. Aside from the way

she sweetly calls me 'hon' whenever she wants something. She's the sneakiest, smartest little minx and she knows it.

Out of fear of drooling like a toddler at the mere thought of my bombshell wife, I focus on Astrid who's talking about Glyndon's latest adventures at her grandfather's house.

That little girl is on the road to be a spoilt troublemaker with a crooked princess crown.

It's not a coincidence that she's Jonathan's favorite. The ruthless, merciless Jonathan who couldn't care less about anyone other than his second wife.

Even Aiden and Levi were only his 'heirs' until they gave him grandchildren.

Landon and Brandon and even Eli, Aiden's only son, don't compare to Glyn. Which is why the twins joined their parents today, but she's snuggling with Jonathan and his wife.

We invited Astrid and her family for a barbecue at the pool. Lan and Bran are making a mess in the water and Levi watches them with a proud expression as he grills some meat.

And fine, I had nothing to do with the inviting part, Nicole did. If it were up to me, I would be lost between my wife's thighs all weekend, praying to never be found.

The two stepsisters' relationship isn't roses and unicorns, but it's been improving over the years. Jayden and Uncle Henry played a big role in that.

Astrid cares for him like a true stepsibling in a way she never cared about Nicole. And Uncle Henry has been bringing them together every chance he got—with mine and Levi's reluctant help.

I finally understand why Captain is so possessive of Astrid's time. It's bloody miserable whenever I have to spend time without Nicole.

When I think back on the years I lived without her, I can't fathom how I survived.

She's always been the missing piece in my life, the calm to my storm, and the peace to my wars.

I've always seen her as a queen, but it took me years to realize she's the queen of my kingdom.

The years I've been married to her have been the happiest I've ever been. It's when I found the balance I couldn't reach before her.

As if reading my thoughts, Nicole appears on the house's threshold, holding Conrad's little hand as he does the drunk walk on his unsteady feet.

He recently started walking and he's been laughing uncontrollably since.

Nicole watches him with a soft smile that penetrates the walls of my fucking chest and settles in the organ that's beating for her and the family she gave me.

Seeing Nicole smile is no different than floating in the orbit of the sun and soaking in its warmth.

She's come a long way since her traumatic experience and became the woman no one can mess with. A woman with purpose, a successful chef, and the most doting mother I've ever seen.

And I'm the lucky bastard who managed to have that woman.

The one who got the queen.

She's wearing a simple peach-colored dress that falls to her knees. The only jewelry she has on is the wedding ring that I had made from the most expensive emerald available and the necklace I gave her when we were thirteen.

She's never removed it since the day we got engaged.

And that box? She replaced those depressing pictures with new ones. Our wedding picture, her birthday picture, where we celebrated with all our friends and I kissed her senseless. There's also our first family picture with Conrad, and last but not least, the ultrasound of the upcoming member of the Sterling family.

Nicole still doesn't show, but she glows with the pregnancy. She's so beautiful, it fucking hurts to look at her sometimes.

"You might want to wipe that drool, Bug." Astrid's voice, as mocking as it is, doesn't break my fixation on the woman slowly approaching us.

My woman.

"Might want to practice what you preach, Bugger."

"Me?"

"Your kids would testify to the unhealthy amount of PDA they witness on a daily basis."

"That's called giving a positive parental example."

"Obviously. With tongues!"

"You have no right to judge when you look like you're going to piss yourself by just looking at her."

"I'm just thinking about how I will fuck her when all of you people are ruining my Sunday."

"Gross." She stands, shaking her head. "I'm going to find my man."

"Don't you dare shag in my house," I warn and she just laughs, waving me off.

It's my turn to stand up, the urge to close the distance between me and Nicole is like a fucking need.

I really should've had her for my own this weekend.

And every other weekend.

Upon seeing me, Conrad slips his hand from his mother's and runs to me with the preciseness of a monkey on crack. His entire focus is on his legs, completely and utterly fascinated that the things actually work.

He trips and falls, but he giggles as if the whole ordeal is a comedy show, then he continues running.

I crouch and open my arms and he crashes straight between them. "Daddy!"

"Hey there, buddy." My fingers ruffle his light hair and he giggles like a ball of sunshine.

I never thought I would become a father, not when my own was a scum who only fathered his dick. But the moment Conrad was born and the midwife placed him in my arms, I knew I would die for him. No questions asked.

When Nicole and I first got married, I admit to wanting children only to stake a claim on my wife, but that's changed since I became a father.

And I have the woman standing in front of me to thank for that.

She's the one who taught me that not all fathers are the same. That just because mine was the worst, doesn't mean I'll be like him.

Holding Conrad with one hand, I stand up and grab Nicole by the waist with the other, pulling her against me. "How are you feeling?"

"A little hungry."

"Hold on a second while I beat Levi for not grilling the meat fast enough."

She laughs and the sound is so contagious that I smile back.

"I miss you, Peaches."

A light gleams in her eyes. "I'm right here, Dan."

"I still miss you. I guess I'm traumatized from all the time I spent without you."

She gets on her tiptoes and brushes her full lips against my cheek, then whispers in my ear, "I'm going nowhere. I'll always be by your side."

"Even with all the babies I keep putting inside you?"

My friends call me "Levi on drugs" for loving to knock up my wife without waiting in between, but fuck them. Her opinion is the only one that matters.

"Especially because of that." She strokes Conrad's hair, then palms my cheek. "Thank you for giving me a family, Dan."

"Thank you for being mine, Peaches."

Her lips meet mine and I kiss her at the sound of our son's giggles.

THE END

Next up is the standalone book that features Kingsley Shaw, titled *Empire of Lust*.

Curious about Nathaniel and Knox who were mentioned in this book? You can read their story in *Empire of Desire and Empire of Sin*.

For more stories about Daniel's friends from England, you can read their books in *Royal Elite Series*.

WHAT'S NEXT?

Thank you so much for reading *Empire of Hate*! If you liked it, please leave a review.
Your support means the world to me.

If you're thirsty for more discussions with other readers of the series, you can join the Facebook group, *Rina Kent's Spoilers Room.*

Next up is a pure enemies-to-lovers book, *Empire of Lust*, that will feature Kingsley Shaw who was a supporting character in *Empire of Hate.*

ALSO BY RINA KENT

For more books by the author and a reading order, please visit:
www.rinakent.com/books

ABOUT THE AUTHOR

Rina Kent is a *USA Today*, international, and #1 Amazon bestselling author of everything enemies to lovers romance.

She's known to write unapologetic anti-heroes and villains because she often fell in love with men no one roots for. Her books are sprinkled with a touch of darkness, a pinch of angst, and an unhealthy dose of intensity.

She spends her private days in London laughing like an evil mastermind about adding mayhem to her expanding universe. When she's not writing, Rina travels, hikes, and spoils cats in a pure Cat Lady fashion.

Find Rina Below:

Website: www.rinakent.com
Neswsletter: www.subscribepage.com/rinakent
BookBub: www.bookbub.com/profile/rina-kent
Amazon: www.amazon.com/Rina-Kent/e/B07MM54G22
Goodreads: www.goodreads.com/author/show/18697906.Rina_Kent
Instagram: www.instagram.com/author_rina
Facebook: www.facebook.com/rinaakent
Reader Group: www.facebook.com/groups/rinakent.club
Pinterest: www.pinterest.co.uk/AuthorRina/boards
Tiktok: www.tiktok.com/@rina.kent
Twitter: twitter.com/AuthorRina

Printed in Great Britain
by Amazon